CW00525174

C. M.J.O'Sullivan 2021.

SLICES OF DEATH.
By M.J.O'Sullivan

Chapter 1.

Burnham looked askance at the limpid sky as he surveyed the desk before him. "Chris, I don't know but I'm sure I left my pen somewhere."

"You did Sir. Right by the Thesaurus."

Memory flickered by like a fleeting Sparrow as he looked up from the Computer. "Oh yes of course . There was

Iّ

 Icatter

that word reiteration. It gained common usage by the computer languages , that's right."

"Any way Sir you were saying Ralston has come up with a new staff procedure."

"Yes, apparently he's very keen on top down management . Apparently he wants to stop agenda-led enquiries. It seems we waste too much time following our own little hobby horses when investigating criminal cases. He wants us to follow the bench marks he's put down . It's all down on the notes he's given us. "

Chris looked at the staff hand-outs he received that morning with a credulity that bordered on civility. "So I see Sir."

"Now I know what you may think of them and I know what I think of them. Any way we've been doing this long enough to know what we're doing.

All I'm saying is just pay them lip service , go through the motions and for the rest just use your common sense. You've been here long enough to know what's been going on. If Ralston should ask you at any time , just give him the standard reply . Address your remarks so as to give the impression that you used his recommendations and leave it at that. Am I clear?"

"Yes Sir."

"That goes for the rest of the men too. If they decide to change the procedure , I'm sure we'll just pretend we're disappointed but above all don't let the mask slip for God's sake."

Just as he finished this speech the phone went. It was Adrian from the control room. "Hello Parker ,what's up?"

"There's been a call from Cullompton farm by Thirton Common Sir. A Mister Gordon Williams was found behind his lorry with a wound to the back of his head, quite dead. His wife found him Sir. They thought he might have fallen or something."

4

"Okay I'll send my men over there as soon as I can ." He put the phone down. "I want you and Woods down at Cullompton farm . A Mr Gordon Williams has been found dead."

"Yes Sir .Right away."

Beresford was standing by his car when Justin Woods reached him. "Yes Sir?"

"Farmer in Cullompton . Apparently some accident."

"Foreign workers?"

"I don't know."

The traffic through Thirton was approaching it's anticlimax as it approached the third quarter of the afternoon. They had to negotiate Thirton Way which was the relief road put in to bypass Thirton High street

in the early nineties. Vestigial amounts of traffic remained in Thirton Common and then just before they approached Kessington there were some morehold ups. Cullompton farm lay just off the approach to Sevenoaks. Any casual observer would observe it's outbuilding and barn as they approached the M25.

The buildings looked idyllic and promising as Beresford navigated the direct track that served as one of its connections to the outside world.

The farm at Cullompton was a smart with brand new tractors and equipment . When he parked his car in the courtyard of the farm house a somewhat shocked Iris Williams came out to greet him. She led him to the Crime scene. This was past the outbuildings just on the south east border of the property.

Iris Williams was well composed although she felt a turmoil of emotions inside. The truck was twenty ton capacity used for carrying goods. Beresford thought it was fit for cattle fodder and small goods. Lying at the rear of the lorry was a man in his early forties , short dark hair, dressed in a shirt jacket and jeans. His heads was visibly caved in by something. Looking at the truck he could see the hoist mechanism fully extended ready to pick up a container or bin. .

"Did your husband have any enemies Mrs Williams?"

"No not enemies as such." She said.

"What did he have then?"

"Ian Beasley a farmer. That's Branbourne farm past the Colington Woods near Sevenoaks. When you said enemy , I mean a competitor really."

"I think I've heard of him. So what was the bone of contention?"

"He wants to buy us out. Needs more land he says."

"And Mr Williams wanted to stay?"

"Of course , I've got two daughters and a son. Neither of them wanted to farm particularly. We'll have to decide what to do. Probably carry on for the next two years."

"You think Mr Beasley might have something to do with this? I don't think so."

"No I see did Gordon have any enemies other than Mr Beasley though?"

"Well we deal in cattle farm management .My husband used a man called Lambert Hodge . He deals with the labour and the bills. He could fill you in the bigger details."

"I see and where might that be?"

"He'll be in the milking parlour further up on your left you'll see some buildings."

"Thank you Mrs Williams."

Beresford found his way in to the milking parlour and found it initially empty except for a man placing the pails along the wall. "Excuse me can I speak to Mr Hodge please?"

"I'm Lukasz Bukowski . I'm the general foreman can I help?"

"Most certainly . As you are aware Mr Bukowski your boss has been found dead. I'm going to have to ask who was there at the time of his death." Behind him Beresford could hear the uniform branch cordoning off the area.

"Well I was in the abattoir . I had Biernat ,Anatol, and Adem there at the time. Orman and Mastyle were working on the other side. We were just finishing off the herd. "

"They were all there?"

"Of course the abattoir is a full time concern. We're processing the carcasses now."

"I see what about here in the milking parlour?"

"We have about four full time in the milking section. We have another five handling the herd outside. In another warehouse further along we have five women packaging the meat products. "

"Talk me through this so I'm clear tell me how a typical working day would start."

"The process is fairly simple. Andrew Weathers and Radek Zelinski were generally the first and the rest would follow in a quarter of an hour afterwards

at their contracted time of six o'clock here in the milking parlour. Mat Smith , Teddy Coombes and Mehmet Turget would arrive at half past six to set things up for the outside cattle the others would arrive at the contracted time around seven o'clock. About six of these would help in routine farm duties ploughing ,repairing fences and cattle maintenance . At about eight o'clock Biernat, Wojak, Anatol and Keith Andrews would arrive at half past eight . At about nine o'clock Lambert Hodge would arrive at his office . He would then deal with any problems arising out of his office."

He broke away briefly when he saw Mosely arrive in his car. Dressed in whites Beresford found the wind was suitably cold on what was supposed to be a cold afternoon. He followed Mosely to the crime scene now cordoned off with tape and guarded by a few Police officers.

"What's it like Chris?" He asked companionably.

"Grisly. Can't make it out. If I didn't know better I'd say he was standing at the back of the truck and the hoist came over and hit him."

"Stranger things have happened ."

By now Mrs Williams had departed . Her restrained composure no longer there to distract him. Mosely examined the corpse. "I would say that death took place in the last three hours. "

"Anything else ?"

"Funnily enough without a post mortem I'd say your description of events was spot on Chris. There's no sign of struggle which seems to suggest the machine acted on its own . Someone could have thrown the switch inside the cab while he was standing at the back. The blow I can see on the back of the head would have been enough to kill him. "

"So accidental death then?"

"No , good Lord no. We have to inspect that vehicle inside and out."

"It's a simple roll on roll off mechanism . There could be modifications to it .No I'll have to have a post mortem and have another look. " He signalled for the body to be taken away. "I expect Lambert Hodge would have the cards from the Tachograph available."

"I'll get uniform to send them to you soonest."

"Right , just as you say."

Through the cumulative statements from Lukas Bukowski, and the workers Beresford arrived at a composite picture of what actually happened on the day Gordon Williams
was killed.

Lukasz Bukowski arrived at half past five Radek Zelinski
alerted him to the condition of the cows. Accordingly they iso-
lated the cow concerned and left messages for the vet to come
assist.

At six o'clock Mat Smith alerted them of the fact that that
a field near the gate was scheduled for ploughing. Lukasz made
a note for Hodge. At about eight o'clock Andrew Stevens and
Keith Meadows reported in sick. Lukasz phoned up the temporary agency for more staff.

Beresford found himself outside the office with Lambert Hodge . Lambert Hodge was confident , well educated ,
and well turned out. "So when did you see Mr Williams, Mr
Hodge?"

"Well I got in this morning , I looked at the milk figures .
The yield was satisfying . One cow was awaiting a visit from
the vet. I had a conference with Gordon at about half past nine.
The talk lasted about a   of an hour. He was talking about
the offer Beasley was making . It was attractive and he was
tempted . He went over the figures with me. He said the figures
looked good . He told me and everyone else's job was safe. At
the end he reminded me some cattle feed needed picking up.
Also some supplies for the Abattoir. Though he said he would
see to it."

"The truck , where is it now?"

"Where Mr Williams left it."

"What did you do after that Mister Hodge?"

"I spent the rest of the day looking at matters for the farm.

This included supplies . There were two deliveries today. Fencing at ten o'clock and diesel at eleven. Look here are the receipts for both. "Beresford looked at the receipts for both, the timed delivery on the docket . It all seemed in order.

"I had to look at the absenteeism record for Keith Meadows and Adam Stevens. They had been taking a few days off each month. A written warning most probably . Gordon ploughed the field by the access road at eleven o'clock .At half past twelve he went to see Ian Beasley and returned at half past two."

"At three o'clock we received a call from Mrs Williams." Beresford said.

"By the way Mr Hodge could I have Tachographs from the lorry while I'm Here?"

"Certainly." He handed over a plastic wallet with tachographs.

As they finished the interview Woods carefully taking down everything that was said , Lambert bid them good day. As they walked away Woods said.

"I thought life on a farm was supposed to be tranquil and peaceful. I'm glad I work in the city."

"Not what it seems eh?" Beresford observed.

Branbourne farm was a little way further up past Colington woods on the approach to Sevenoaks . Ian Beasley was the owner. Beasley was a man of few opinions but prompt action. He was known in the county for his straight talking and dealing. He owned a herd of cattle and a dairy herd. He was big enough not to go under in various struggles with the milk marketing board and other conflagrations of organised government.

Beresford came up the long field track that led to the whitewashed farm house and outlying outhouses. To some extent it bore some resemblance to Cullompton farm. When he got out of the car in the courtyard a tanned man about fifty years old greeted him.

"Yes gentlemen I saw you coming up the road. It's not every day of the year I share the pleasure of such company. Can I help you?"

"You're Mr Beasley is that so?"

"Yes."

"I'm detective inspector Beresford. This my assistant Detective constable Woods. Can we talk for a few minutes ?"

"Yes of course if you just follow me into my office."

They followed him to what looked like a new prefab portacabin with filing cabinets and computers. He led them deeper into his own office. The feel of the country farm was very palpable. They sat on chairs surrounding a very large desk.

"How can I help you gentlemen?"

"I'm afraid I have some bad news Sir. A neighbour of yours was found dead this afternoon. Mr Gordon Williams I'm told you met him . Could you tell me what it was about?" Beasley rubbed his chin thoughtfully for a moment"My God , is that right? I only saw him this morning. Let me think" He paused and said ."Of course . You see I need more land to grow. Well on the

one hand, there's the land by Cullompton . I did have it valued with Mr Mathews of Kessington farm for one and a half million. However it fell through . I think it was some misunderstanding between the children Harry and Amanda. I talked to Gordon about his farm. I outlined the whole deal. He certainly seemed to look at my proposals."

"I see, what about your life here Mr Beasley ? How would it affect you?"

"Well my wife was a former debutante in London. She came from old money . Her father was a chairman of a large manufacturing company. The inheritance was divided between three brothers and herself. Naturally she came last in the pecking order. Her mother grabbed a large slice of the pie and left for Austria. I'm afraid my daughters have had a rough ride , Hilary, Theresa , and May. They've got me on the one hand a rusty old agrarian and Cruella de Ville for a mother. I suppose my son Terry will take over. He seems to psyche into the chemistry of the place."

"I see, where were you in the afternoon about four o'clock Mister Beasley?"

"I had to go up to London to see to some details about a cattle sale. It had all been arranged beforehand. I'll give you the phone numbers here. Collins and Fremder , Conduit street just off the bottom of Bond street. "

"Thanks."

Kessington Farm lay right next to Cullompton Farm. It was essentially a small holding and it lay alongside with the small river Witham in between. When Beresford drew up in the courtyard to Kessington Farm the contrast between the two farms was only too stark. The outbuildings had fallen into dis-repair. broken tractors wheel rims littered the landscape.

Beresford got out of the car and Woods whispered . "Ah here are the Wurzels."

"Keep it quiet Woods . We need these people to throw some light on a few things."

"Yes Sir."

As Beresford crossed the courtyard he saw a woman cross-ing toward dressed in a smock obviously having finished some chore or other. "Mrs Mathews?"

She turned intently "Yes can I help you?"

"I'm D.I. Beresford this DC Woods we're here because there's been a disturbing turn of events this afternoon in the neighbouring farm."

"Yes , officer well then you'd better come in . I'm sorry to hear this . "

They went into the farm house . No smart décor , no designer furniture. Instead there was the dresser against one wall in the parlour . The dining table and a settee that had seen better years. Out of the corner of his eye he could see the Aga in the kitchen as they went past. It seemed comforting somehow that the stereo typical farm house existed somewhere in the universe.

"So how can I help you ?"

"Well I'm afraid Mr Williams was found murdered in the neighbouring property. Could you tell us of any suspicious characters down by the river bordering your properties?"

" Murdered? That's only just next door. I must go and see Iris make sure she's okay. Well the local authority control that. Roderick Benson would know more about that."

"We will be questioning him in due course. Could you tell me what sort of relationship you had with Mr Williams?"

"Quite pleasant really . Mr Williams was a good farmer , our children they even went to school together . We had a nice little community here."

"Had?"

"Oh nothing unpleasant . We have a nice community . Children grow up, grow apart. You know the usual."

"I see . Could you tell me more about the operation you run here?"

"My husband gave up trying to run the farm at a profit quiet a long time ago. He gets money from the EEC for set aside . Other than that he works in the local supermarket. "

"What about your children?"

"Well my pride and joy is Catherine. She's going to college next year to study music. Amanda is a trial but she's a sweet girl. I think she's getting wise to the boys , more bragging than substance. Juliet is my youngest , she's the baby , she's going to Kessington Primary. "

"What's it being like living here? "

"I've grown up the daughter of a banker . Gregory hasn't been particularly prosperous , but I've come to accept it all. Then my dad died shortly after Juliet was born. Catherine found music a sort of way through.

I've got a friend called Nancy who doesn't live far away . She usually drops in for a chat. She's divorced . Between us and the kids we've managed to grow vegetables , and run a dairy. Amanda's a bit like her dad she likes to organise. Harry the boy was a problem but he likes to mend broken tractors. I'm hoping when we can make some money . We did have Ian Beasley come round and make us a proposition but Gregory saw him off. If it wasn't for the kids I don't know what I'd do."

They found the warden's office to the river Witham down by the access road. It was a portacabin attached to a gate that gave access to the river. Beresford waited as he rang the bell. Eventually a bearded gentleman in a green uniform with the legend of Thirton Council emblazoned on it answered the door. "Hello, can I help you at all?"

"Yes I'm Beresford and this DC Woods . Can you help us with our enquiries?"

"Yes, I suppose so."

"There's been an unfortunate incident up at Cullompton farm. I wonder If you could help me at all."

"Of course in any way I can."

"Have you had any anglers at all ? "

He looked at the list . "Yes they were Mr Jones and Teddy Wilson they came in the morning they left about two o'clock. Then I had Stuart Linley and Tristan Thomas. They came separately but they usually chat. They do fly fishing."

"Are they still here?"

"They left about an hour ago. "

"Have you got their addresses?"

"Yes Stuart Linley lives at 2 Lyle cottages on Staples Road. That's part of Kessington Green . Then there's Tristan Thomas he lives in Flat 5 Marble Close Colington High Street. "

"Thank you for your time Mr Benson."

About two hours earlier Stuart Linley walked down the bank by the river Witham . Down by the banks the foxglove the teasel which grew profusely was draped on the stones and water course as the river followed idly by. Over to one side he could see a Bearded Tit. The Brambling Blue Tit held a temporary thrill for him. There was break in the hedge further down he could see a Gull. funny though they were quite common they always seemed to herald the freedom of the seaside when he saw one .

His thoughts of late had dissipated mainly because his mates found better jobs. They'd moved on. Here this afternoon he found Tristan Thomas "Good afternoon Stuart how are you?"

"Bored. I came down here I thought I might catch something. "

They settled into silence .Stuart felt it wouldn't be long before Tristan would settle in to his usual preoccupation with literature. Then Tristan spoke. "The art of fishing is quite an old one. It took a leap forward after the civil war. Isaak Walton wrote the "Compleat Angler" in 1653. He fished in the Wye Valley in Derbyshire. In the eighteenth century a culmination of techniques led to a more sophisticated approach. "

"I know , I think you've told me before."

"I repeat myself. I'm sorry."

"It's easy to get lost here." The silence continued .

"Do you read much Stu?"

"Teenage horror books. Horrid histories, not much else. "

"I've been rereading an old favourite of mine , John Steinbeck . It's called "Of Mice and Men." It tells of two people George Miller and Lennie a giant of a man with learning difficulties. They work for a farmer who is jealous of the attention his wife pays to other men. Lennie doesn't know his own strength and accidently kills the farmer's wife. George shoots him to put him out of his misery. You see the main theme of the book is development. George aspires to independence as a farmer. Lennie aspires to be with George. Steinbeck's characters are powerless due to economic and social circumstances. Although I'm uncomfortable with euthanasia."

"Yes I would expect you would be."

"Have you done any drawing drawings recently?"

"I've done a few up by the marshes. I saw a Chaffinch and a Fire crest."

"The colours and the effect you achieve is remarkable. I could have a word with some friends of mine in Colington Village. They dabble in the market maybe I could sell a few."

"That would be fine I guess."

Then Stuart waited for the second phase of conversation to start that was primarily to do with Tristan's late girlfriend

Mary. Of course Stuart realised that Tristan was a man tinged with sadness. Though in a way he found that

there was sense of longing he wasn't totally unfamiliar with.

"Well we'll see eh?" Then he felt a pull on his line. "Ah , I think I've got one. " He reeled in the fish . It was a small trout. Tristan unhooked it and eased it back into the catch net. "Yes I was in a relationship with Mary. I know I've told you a hundred times. We lived in Italy for a while. She was a financial Euro bond dealer. She was thirty when she was diagnosed with Motor Neurone disease. We got a wheel chair and a special motor car. We rented a special flat in Italy. She wanted to see all the great sites before you know.." He gestured uncomfortably.

"I know I'm sorry."

"It was a peaceful ending. Almost happy. We went to Bologna we'd been to see the cathedral . We had a meal that night .She tried to eat what she could .I relaxed with a glass of wine and looked at the sunset from our hotel .

I'd dozed off for a few seconds , I got up about half an hour later .There was Mary in her specially adapted wheelchair, she was quite dead of course."

Up above in the field they hear a distant cry like a shrike and take little notice. Stuart reels in his tackle satisfied with the days takings. Tristan is already walking down to the warden Roderick Benson . They both showed their passes as they go out.

Dora Linley was a single parent mother. She divorced Derek after three short unhappy years. In truth being married to a jet setting lawyer with a degree from Cambridge should have been a meal ticket . Unfortunately Derek turned out to be a serial philanderer and an alcoholic . Dora blamed herself mainly for using rose tinted sun glasses always looking on the brighter side of life. Her father was an evangelical preacher , her mother was a school teacher. To say she had sheltered upbringing was hardly adequate.

Derek totally fooled her. After the marriage when the stage coach became a pumpkin the only rat she could see was Derek. He was usually flat out drunk and canoodling with every secretary between Gray's Inn road and the Old Bailey. Dora signed off from the marriage . The settlement wasn't generous , half the proceeds of the house. It was enough to buy a cottage near Cullompton Meadow with a nice view of the country side and the A21.

Stuart was born and the school he went to was Kessington Primary. After that Thirton Comprehensive. She got a job in the Doctor's surgery in a medical

practice in Kessington . Of course she didn't notice anything wrong with Stuart at first. He was solitary he didn't mix much . Some boys were like that. When he got to his teens he wasn't eager to get a job and he hung about the house. That was when the rows started.

Underneath it all she knew he'd get a job sooner or later. She settled down a bit when Stuart started at the local supermarket . She told him if he worked he could study and get a better job , it might lead to better things.

Dora had few interests herself . She must have met Davinia Peters who was a frequent visitor at the practice and also collected prescriptions for Major Kindersley on occasions. Dora had developed an interest in flower arranging. On occasions Davina would let her arrange flowers for the service.

Little by little Davina let her in to her life and told her about her grandparents. In spite of herself she began to like Davinia , even though she didn't have a life outside the church. This led Dora to have interests outside work. This meant she started attending evening classes in Psychology. She learnt about Freud, Jung, and Psycho analytic theory. She felt Psycho analysis was too genital orientated . She met Maria Campbell a nursery worker from Kessington . She'd thought she'd broaden her horizons get a broader view of her clients. Like Dora she drew a blank on Freud . It all felt Patriarchal . One evening they had drinks at a local pub.

Maria made the first move . She suggested they go on a camping trip together. It was the Lake District . They took the car and went up the M6 . On the second night when the moon was full and the star sign was Aquarius

and a line of stars were ascendant on the prow, Maria crept into her tent and initiated a relationship . She didn't know how she would break the news to Stuart. Slowly she hoped he would take it in his stride. Maria told her not to worry . She had a son and he was good about these things.

Beresford paused mid thought as he walked across the farmyard . He accounted for the movements of the staff. Lukasz Bukowski and Radek Zelinski opened the milking parlour at half past five . Every one accounted for. Mat Smith and Mehmet Turget were in charge of the herd. They were to the left of the farm yard and away from the crops . They turned up about eight . Though they were due to start ploughing and crop duties later on in the month. Everything was quiet on that front. On close inspection he found that the Abattoir was a mixture of entrepreneurship and common sense management. They took in herds , slaughtered them and packaged them with a company they subcontracted who in turn distributed them to supermarkets across the country . It took about eight of Williams men and thirty of Stoughton packaging to package the meat. Biernat Wojeck and Anatol Wojeck did that . Now as far as he could see Gordon Williams had parked up his truck on the north end of the farm. No one else should have been there. Woods came back to him and said he'd checked out Beasley's alibi. He'd been at Collins and Fremder at Conduit street all afternoon. Furthermore Woods had a word with Turget and Smith. They'd been in the abattoir all afternoon. They were up at the gate to the entrance of the abattoir because a snacks van usually pulled up there at three o'clock. They hadn't seen anything. First he would ask Lambert Hodge a few questions just to get an overall picture of things.

Lambert was just coming out of his office by the barn when Beresford came up to him. "I wonder if I could ask you a favour Mister Hodge if you're not too busy."

"What about him , he looks a bit lost." Lambert said pointing to Woods who was trailing in his wake.

"Oh take no notice, city boy . No seriously he takes notes in case I forget anything."

"Okay you better come in to my office. "

They both sat down opposite Hodge. Hodge was obviously discomfited by Beresford's remarks but tried not to show it. "So Mr Hodge when did you start in the farming business. "

"I graduated from Chichester Agricultural college in 1990 .My father was a quantity surveyor from Brighton and was disappointed at my profession. "

"What was your first job?"

"My first job was Cold Waltham in Sussex . It was crop farming and had been taken over by contract farmers. My first challenge was to manage the farm using a minimal amount of sprays. This was difficult to manage . The damage done by insects was colossal . Never the less I managed to optimize the use of crop spraying by about thirty per cent. The next farm was a dairy herd. It was always an iffy commodity , but the occurrence of TB made it more so. Again with the use of vaccination and Badger culling courtesy of Defra we managed to eradicate the occurrence of TB over a five year period. With this I went to my next job. This farm was near Hastings. Cold Ridge Farm near the river Rother . The farmer was a man called Martin Jacques who fancied himself a farmer. Though he didn't know much about Agriculture."

"Basically I told him how it was. We had suitable arable pasture he could probably make more money out of market gardening . We set up a system of poly tunnels tomatoes, cabbages, lettuce , raspberries. I advised against a dairy herd as the milk market was unpredictable. About a year later Jacques returned from the continent with a new wife. She had other ideas. She had other ways, her name was Yvette Goddard . She suggested they bought Beef cattle. This turned out to be a success . Unfortunately the fracas surrounding the BSE meant we had to destroy the cattle.

This left me in the job market again. When Gordon Williams offered me a job as a farm manager it seemed like manna from heaven. As well as managing the farm he occupied I got to live in the Gate House leading into the farm. Then I met Angela Haynes , happily married for three years now. "

"Okay Mr Hodge do you have any concerns about the farm as a whole?"

"Well Lukasz Bukowski . He's a good foreman . I have to keep him on his toes sometimes . Gordon used to muck in sometimes . Though he had complete confidence in me."

"Well thank you very much for your time. I have however one last thing to ask . Could we have the feed from the cctv for today. I notice you have one in the yard. "

"Yes of course . How stupid of me . It completely slipped my mind . You'llhave to come into the main house. Gordon ran it from the main office."

They both followed Lambert in to the main building . Gordon's office was divorced from the rest of the house by an alcove and a corridor. In the office itself there were a few filing cabinets.

Hodge sat down by the screen and operated a few buttons . It was the day's scenes on the screen. Hodge had to initiate a procedure , three cameras one on the court yard , one in the dining room and one on the Abattoir entrance. Hodge took the camera up to three o'clock . There on the screen Beresford could see the grainy image of Williams talking to Hodge. It seemed a fairly innocent conversation.

Then Lambert went back to his office and Williams went out turned right up towards the lorry where he was eventually found. A few times Mrs Williams came out and swept the yard and put away a few agricultural implements away and then went back in again. Then she went out again in the direction that Gordon had gone and came back in great distress. Then he sees himself turning up in a Police Car.

"So let me get this straight . There was no one in the field to tend the cows .They were over the other side. The crops had already been seen to that morning. No one was up this side of the farm all afternoon. "

"Well no. I checked when you came in with Lukasz and the rest they were all down here."

"Okay Mr Hodge thanks for your time. I think SOCO are still up there. I'll let you know if I find anything."

As they came away from the farm house Woods said, "Does that Hodge remind you of anyone?"

"No. Should he?"

" A King with-out a crown. An Emperor without an Empire."

"No I'm not sure you're right there. Though anything's possible."

They reached the crime scene . Valance Kempton forensic officer approached them as they came close. "I think you better see this Chris. I thought it looked significant. "

He took them past the truck . The body had been taken away by now. Valance pointed down to the track . "I found these foot prints . They've been made recently. They lead to the hedge Here." He pointed the hedge that

abutted the field . "You might notice there's a break here. It leads down to the river . It should be cordoned off but the fence work isn't the best. The foot prints go down to the back. Who ever saw Gordon last must have come from here."

"Thanks Valance I'll make some enquiries ." Beresford knew it was going to be a long day. Woods came up racing behind him as they made their way towards the car. "Where are you going now Sir?"

"Lyle Cottage in Staples Road. You better put it in the GPS . That way we know we know where we're going. Benson put Stuart Lynley's address in his book. I copied it down." As they drove out of Cullompton farm . The GPS indicated a left hand turn about a mile down the road on the way to Colington woods . Staples road ran out the back of Colington Green more or less as an afterthought. The cottage was nice enough with the exposed beams but thankfully no thatched roof. They walked up to the cottage and knocked on the door. A woman of about forty answered the door wearing a somewhat flustered look. "Hello, can I help you?"

"Police,yes, can I speak to Stuart please?"

"I'm sorry, is he in any trouble?"

"I hope not . We hear he was fishing in the Witham river this afternoon. We've just got a few questions."

"I see ,you better come in."

Beresford found Stuart in his bedroom listening to records and thumbing through a book. "So Stuart would you mind coming down to the station to answer a few questions? "

"Of course not." He put the phone down and followed Beresford out to the car followed by his anxious mother.

"It's okay Mrs Linley . We shouldn't be more than half an hour, I promise."

"Yes alright ." She said .

As they drove to the station Stuart said, "Would you mind telling me what this is about?"

"Yes briefly. We have foot prints leading from the body of Gordon Williams farm going down to the river bank. I was told you were down there. If we could match the prints we found we'll know for sure."

"I can save you the trouble. It was me I gave Mr Williams a picture I made of a Blue Tit. I saw one in the hedge and took a photo . I showed it to Gordon. I saw him there some time when he'd finished ploughing. He paid me twenty quid."

"I see in that case we'll both go to the station and examine Gordon's belongings Stuart. In any case we won't be long."

"Okay" Stuart said nervously. They drove him to the station. Outside Woods rubbed his hands and said.

"I say we sweat it out of the little monster. " Beresford held up his hand .

"First things, first . If I find a painting amongst Gordon's things . We'll ask him a couple of questions and that will be that."

"Seriously?"

"Seriously."

Five minutes later Beresford was going through Williams belongings. Going through his brief case he saw a folded paper the size of A3 . He opened opened it and saw the image of a bird with a beak and plumage. The sensitivity of the brush strokes and the mastery of the overall effect was magnificent. Beresford heaved a sigh of relief and brought it with him to the interrogation room.

"Is this the painting you gave Mr Williams Stuart?"

"Yes, I showed some from my portfolio . He chose that one."

"Personally I would have said that was worth at least three hundred. You have a steady hand. Any way enough of this . Why I asked you up hereamongst other things did you see or hear anything unusual when you were up there?"

"Why are you asking me these questions?"

"Shortly after you left him. Gordon was murdered. You are our number one suspect. However I have a certain feeling about this . I don't think you had

any motive to kill Mr Williams. If you could throw any light on the matter . If you saw anyone or anything it could help our enquiries."

"I was down on the fishing bank with Tristan Thomas. He was fishing with me at the time . He will vouch for me . I didn't see anything . About three o'clock I heard a curious sound like a bird or thrush that was it ."

"Do you remember Mr Thomas's address?"

"Flat five Marble Close Colington High Street."

"Right well thanks Stuart. You can go home now. Thanks for your help."

After he left Woods said. "What were you doing? He's our suspect. You let him go."

"Of course I let him go. Number one , this could just be an industrial accident . Number two he had no motive .

Number three he told us the truth . He drew that picture of a bird . If you looked at the detail of the brushwork and the care that's gone into it you can see he's gifted . Now any one of these factors on their own wouldn't discount

him. If you put them altogether I'd say he was an innocent bystander."

"But what about the CCTV? You saw there was no one who could have got past the camera. No one in the farm could have got near him."

"Nobody approaching the farm from the outhouses no. The river Witham runs the length of that farm . Someone could have sneaked downfrom the entrance to the abattoir. They might have left some foot prints. I think we should investigate that first thing in the morning."

"Yes Sir."

Jud Fareham and Paddy Stern sat at the local pub in Colington Green. They were experienced financiers in Land speculation. "The way I see it , it's a dead cert. " Jud said.

"How do you figure that ?" Paddy Stern said.

"Well you have to look at Van Gogh in perspective. Although towards the end of his life his artistic skills were at a premium , his mental health was going

to rack and ruin. It's like in Italy they had a custom of blinding a canary so it sings more sweetly."

"Well it's grisly comparison but I take your point."

"Living in Nueuen and Antwerp he drew weavers and their cottages. His painting in these times were in sombre dark times. From 1888 to 1890 his paintings held more colour more warmth and yet his mental health hit zero."

"Look Jud I know but there's something you haven't mentioned all day. Eschlager in Dusseldorf remember? You said you'd sign off the deal last Wednesday. He phoned me up this morning. He was in a rage. I think it's politics you have to give him some sort of option. "

"Like Van Gogh the man can suffer. I brought three options from Russia at a knockdown price . Now they're coming up trumps . Putin is in trouble with

the Ukraine. He wants money , I got lucky."

"Eschlager will only hold out for so long . He'll be lost in the wind soon."

"Very well I give up. Ah, there comes Tristan ." He saw Tristan coming into the bar wearing a worried look . "What's the matter Tristan?"

"Oh nothing much I was fishing this afternoon. Stuart's drawn a picture of a Blue Tit. He gave it to that Gordon Williams fellow. "

"Oh God I heard about that. He's being murdered. "

"We were only a few hundred yards away . We didn't hear a thing." Tristan said.

"Sounds fishy. I expect the bill know what they're doing."

"You'd think so wouldn't you? I phoned him up . They seem satisfied with the explanation he gave them." He paused. "I take it you are talking about the Eschlager Chappy?" Tristan said looking up at Jud.

"Yes I'm hunting for Van Gogh paintings . They all cost a small fortune. I just find him fascinating. "

"It's a dark preoccupation certainly. "

"I've come to that conclusion ." Jud said. "I'm going out with Julie tonight . I'm going to talk to Eschlager tomorrow if he hasn't gone off the boil."

"You play your clients like you play your poker Jud. It's a work of art all on its own." Tristan enthused.

"Julie's a smart one too. She does Euro bond dealing. I can't say she's bad at it either. She finds the pre occupation with art rather odd."

Paddy interrupted . " I start the day with a play on the markets. Nine times out of ten I get it right. It's spotting a trend. I like the impressionists myself . Also I like the Victorian landscape painter John Stringer. He was largely unknown and forgotten . He made a number of portraits of leading ladies such as the wife of the Duke of Northumberland. Then there was Lady Annabel Lynton Greeves wife of a former cabinet minister to Disraeli."

"Hang on a minute . If you go down Staples road there's a turning there off Hanger's Dyke. The old pile there. It' s still standing that was something I forgot."

"Lord Stretford Myles husband to Lady Arnold Greeves right on the money Tristan." Jud decided to ignore that remark as the afternoon wore on.

Davinia Peters looked out on the green area behind the vestry of All Saints Kessington Common. Jenna Brighton sat passively on a bench looking at the same view. "Aelred of Rievaulx was an interesting character . He was born in Northumbria in 1110. Educated in Durham spent several years in the court of King David. I assume this is a reference to the crusaders and their occupation of Jerusalem. Then he became Abbott of Rievaulx in 1143."

"Why is he interesting ?" Jenna asked.

"Why should someone born in Northumbria end up in France?"

"Odd I grant you . Ambition is a funny thing."

"My own fascination is for the former Lord of Kessington Roger Armstrong. He used to be a local landowner . His property extended from Colington Green all the way to Thirton High street. Of course nowadays a lot of the land had been broken up ,roads had been put down and houses built . He gave pride of place to All Saints Church. I always make sure his grave is well tended. "The Lord Armstrong " The local pub kept its name despite the various attempts to modernise it."

"So you say Davinia . Working in the city I feel so lost sometimes."

"Lost Jenna? You seem to be the most together person I know."

"Oh God here she comes. I've got to dash. I'll see you soon Davinia."

"Don't forget Vespers on Sunday .It's a must."

"Sure thing."

As she turned Davinia would see a familiar figure come into view. "Hello Pat." Pat was the wife of the bank manager in Thirton. She was the embodiment of the middle class Thirton in form and style. However this measured off by the Stirling work she gave to the community.

"Hello yourself I see Jenna taking the air so I decided to come over."

"It always surprises me that you're drawn to the place." Davinia was glad of Pat's company mainly because she was an ally in providing pastoral care in the community. One of the charges was Major Kindersley . Kindersley had served in Northern Ireland , Cyprus and Aden before that.

"I was talking to the Major today . Very brash sort of chap . Deep inside himself there's a hollowness he can't reach."

"Yes I expect it's some sort of PTSD."

"Yet somehow it makes him more human don't you think?"

"You see a lot more in the Major than most . Yes Pat you're a saint to put up with him."

The year before Davinia had found there was some

marsh land out by Kessington. She was reading of Aebbe the daughter of some royalty actually came to the area in 1035. She was instrumental in promoting Christianity in the Northumbrian Coast. Her name was Aebbe of Coldringham. The religious monastery she established lasted for forty years. Further research revealed a Hilda of the Marshes in 763 by what was now Kessington Green. To look into it further she went to the British Museum. She looked over the back of the Church to Kessington and thought for a minute.

"I see the Reverend Wallis will be back from his Sabbatical at the end of this week. Do you think he'll have some new ideas up his sleeve ?"

"I expect so ." said Davinia." Odds on, he won't be going into raptureswhen he hears that I want to dig up the baptismal font to see the remains of St Hilda."

Davinia had found some old maps of Kessington it was part of the Thirton Hundreds. Roughly she could see that the area where All Saint's church was situated was called the crossing point in to Kessington Marsh. Thus providing the original term of Halsen brigge a term forgotten in the tenth century. There was a marsh area between Halsen brigge and Kessington up to the Sixteenth century when engineering works drained the land for agriculture. The text that in the British museum read that Halsbridge (Anglicised version) was the site of the burial of St Hilda. Davina calculated that the Narthex of the church hadn't been built yet. The main altar and knave dated back to Saxon Times. Studying the composition of the land around the entrance to the Church Davinia calculated that Hilda's burial place would be where the

Baptism font lay. This was mainly because the sand and gravel composition was greater than that of the surrounding soil where the church stood. All this notwithstanding she knew she was in for a fight.

The day was overcast as Maria walked into her cottage in Staples Road . It was funny how love changed things. The clouded looks , the lonely days on one's own. The endless repetition of routine . Dora was usually got lunch in the evening . It was part of a ritual . However she thought she'd do something different this time. She carefully laid out the ingredients when Stuart walked in. "Hello Stuart. Had a good day?"

"No, not really, I have to go to my room. I'm upset."

"What's the matter?" She came forward and touched his shoulder.

"I was fishing down the river. I'd seen Gordon Williams he bought one of my paintings. I found out afterwards he'd being found dead. The Police interviewed me. They didn't think I was to blame. The only thing was I couldn't help them. I felt useless."

Maria held him close. Her fears of holding an adolescent boy close in an intimate embrace were temporarily forgotten. "Don't worry Stuart . Just so horrible occurrence. You were entirely innocent . Perhaps if you lie down you might feel better."

"Thanks Maria you're very kind. I think I feel tired anyway. "

He went upstairs and Maria watched him go. She knew something of Gordon Williams the local wunderkind . He took over the farm from his father and started up his own abattoir and turned round the fortunes of the farm over-night. So who would want to kill him? She put the finishing touches to the Lasagne she was making as Dora walked in. "Hello what's cooking?"

"Lasagne. I thought you might like a change ."

"Of course , anything at all. I'm glad you decided to do something . I've had a bit of a day"

"Dora I think you ought to know something."

"Yes what?" She looked slightly alarmed.

"Stuart he just came in. He looked a bit upset . He'd been fishing out by the river with that Tristan fella. I suppose. He met Gordon Williams the farmer.

Unfortunately afterwards Williams was found dead . Stuart's been down to the station for a statement. They don't know what happened."

Dora's face looked strained, Maria could guess what was coming next.   "Yes I know. I was here when they came here. I was under the impression it was only routine."

"Routine? God I'd be more upset than that!"

"It's nothing to worry about Maria. I'll go up and talk to him I'm sure it'll sort itself out."

Dora was careful not to intrude into his space . She knocked on his door and came in. "Stuart are you awake?"

She saw his form on the bed . "Yes Mum it's okay."

"Well did you see anything. Did anybody hurt you?" She bent down to the bedside and stroked his hair.

"No of course not . I sold him a painting . I had no idea what happened either."

"Where were you when it happened? "

"Fishing with Tristan. Tristan seemed in a reflective mood. The whole thing seemed a mystery to me."

Dora bent down and held him close. "Oh Stuart you mustn't worry . It was awful but it's over now. Maria's got Lasagne ready . Do you feel you could manage some?"

Stuart relaxed and found his mother's concern touching. "I suppose so. I'll be down in a minute. It's been a shock that's all."

Back in Colington Green when they finished dinner

Jud Fareham said. "Paddy is quite serious about this deal with Walter Eschlager . Virtually accused

me of neglect."

"It is of importance . Brokering is your livelihood ergo, you are supposed to be committed." Tristan said.

"Mmm, I suppose Eschlager is just a haggler. I got the right bottom line and he went for it. It's not that difficult. Putin's in for a long run. Love or hate him."

"Nicely put Jud . Couldn't have put it better myself."

"Anyway you were in the Limelight today. Your protégé was in the Police Station helping the local plod with their enquiries. I'm surprise you're so calm about it."

"My Protégé ? Yes ,Stuart . It was a shock the Inspector spoke to me . We neither   of us heard anything . It was quite awful in a way. "

"Look I've got to go Tristan. Busy day tomorrow so everyone tells me. Ivan Vykovsky from Kiev will be barking at my heels."

"Of course I imagine Pat will be looking at the view from the window and trying to make an oil painting out of it."

"Or someone else's ." With that Jud left him as the shades of evening came in. As he heard the door close Tristan thought over the day's events. He enjoyed the conversation with Stuart . It brought sombre reflection to a long day. The atmosphere in Tristan's flat cleared as he cast his mind back to former times.

"Some hopes linger don't they?" A familiar voice said. Yes Tristan thought a familiar voice. As he remembered it he was looking at a scene of St Mark's Square Venice. They'd booked a room overlooking the plaza. They didn't know if they'd get another one.

" Hopes linger on you'll get better Mary."

"You could say that Tristan . It's best not to think about the future just yet."

"No I suppose not." He said in a subdued voice.

"Shadows grow long in Venice . They have the masked ball. Originally a tribute to the God Saturn. It's all very romantic ." She said in an ashen voice.

"I expect it was a time for settling old scores."

"In the time of the Borgias no doubt." In order to distract her from the line of conversation . Tristan tried to change the subject ."Mr Montgomery forgot his lineament this morning."

"Probably because of that hangover he got from the God almighty bender he'd been on the night before."

"Yes he was knocking back the Cinzano a bit."

"The old colonial types are funny I suppose . God's greatest gift to be an English man and all that."

"They come with the package holiday. The important diplomat , the diabetic septuagenarian, fifteen tablets for everything. The amateur historian correcting the guide and the loud conversation."

"And Colonel Mustard in the library."

"I thought Mrs Tilden was going to streak down the plaza naked last night she was so full on."

"Thank God for the unbuttoned middle class divorcee from Broadstairs."

"They add to the mystery of the place."

"Yes you can marvel at the chapel dedicated to Cardinal Zen. You can see the Bridge of Sighs . All however stand amazed at Mr Stanbridge from Cleethorpes and the full extent of his rheumatoid arthritis."

"We count ourselves lucky I suppose."

"Do you miss,,,." He stopped himself in time.

"Yes I miss everything Tristan. I miss not going to the toilet by myself. I miss being able to sit down without Miss bloody Thornton asking me if I liked a hot water bottle."

"The days go past you see it before you."

"Well yes I am patient. We've got a week or two here. Then we go back for more tests. It's like a life sentence already."

"Some hopes linger don't they?" She said, and that was it. Venice gone like a flash in the pan like a fleeting song of happiness before the storm.

He thought briefly back to the afternoon with Stuart. Mary died from her illness. He could have taken her to Switzerland but she felt too scared . In the end it didn't matter.

He had his practice up in London doing accounts for a catering firm . It brought in the money . Not on par with Jud Fareham or Paddy Stern . Yet they didn't seem to care . He'd been living like a shell , hollowed out for the last four years. Even the events of the afternoon hadn't reached him. One day he'd forget Venice. It would only be a memory. It offered temporary warmth and that was enough. They hired special Gondolas for the disabled in Venice. Mary managed to see most of the sights and bore the presence of the other holiday with fortitude. Eventually he would go out again. That's why he talked to Stuart in many ways he was lost like himself. Looking across from his window across Colington Green he comforted himself. If it all went tomorrow he still had Venice. The thought went fleetingly as the wind.

Beresford turned up at the Hospital for the Post Mortem of Gordon Williams. Mosely was his usual reserved self. "This shouldn't take long. However if you have anything to add let me know. "

Beresford demurred. If he had anything to add Mosely would scold him fiercely. The body of Gordon Williams was wheeled forth and Mosely duly made the opening actions of any Post Mortem. He made Y shaped cut from the shoulder peeling away the flesh at the sternum. "Evidence shows no markings across chest and stomach. Male white Caucasian about mid-forties "

"I am now going to make an incision from the stomach up to the neck."

He did so. At this point took out the stomach heart and lungs for examination ."I am extracting vital organs in order to rule out any other cause of death including lungs heart and stomach." He paused" the heart looks a bit odd, I'll have to look at the tox screen when it comes through." Then using an electric saw he delicately cut a line round the head and tapped the skull as the cranium came off. He stated "There's evidence of real damage to the cranium and the Meningeal layers and the cortex to the brain. A blunt instrument of about five inches wide. I would say that was the cause of death."

"So how would he fall after this blow?"

Mosely looked at him ." . Assuming he lay where we found him . I would say the blow came from behind . He would be standing with his back to the truck."

"Would you say an industrial accident ?"

"Possibly but we have to exclude every other explanation."

Beresford thought for a moment. " There doesn't seem to be much point in standing behind a truck to be hit like that ...."

"Unless what?"

"Unless there was a second person pulling the lever."

"That's where you come in Inspector. I'm only the pathologist."

Delaney my assistant has been looking at the make of the truck. It's a ford model latest on the market. He was quite impressed with it . He'll be submitting his report later on today." He paused "I'll be submitting the toxicology report tomorrow."

"thanks Doctor I'll wait for the report."

"Apart from the apparent lack of motive the apparent lack of method was quite odd as well." Whether Delaney was going to make out a report on the truck Beresford decided to see the vehicle for himself. He drove back up to Cullompton farm to see Lambert Hodge'

Hodge was in his office Beresford parked his car alongside. He knocked on the door and he could see Hodge sitting at his desk. Hodge came up to the door .Woods was with Beresford in case he wanted to make a statement.

"Good morning Inspector . I didn't expect to see you so soon."

"Yes I wonder if you could let me have a look at the truck again. I just wanted to look at its features . Do you think you could walk me through them?"

"Of course ." Hodge obliged.

They walked to where the tractor was parked. "I have to switch the Isolator off first." He bent down and turned off a small switch behind the engine.

Then he got up and sat in the driver's seat and switched on the engine. Beresford climbed up with him. "This shows the oil level and the various levels of lubricants in the engine. " He pointed to a screen and using certain controls changed the display. "It'll tell you if anything is really wrong. It usually comes up with a warning about the back axle. That usually goes off after a minute."

"I see. Could I look around the truck for a minute ? I want to check something."

Beresford walked round the back of the vehicle and saw the hook which could be raised or lowered about twenty feet long. Hodge had followed him round . "That hook attaches a bin we want onto the back of the lorry.

It's a quick way of carrying crop feed or supplies around the farm or taking goods to market."

"I see could you do me a favour? I want you to put the truck in gear and put the brake on. "

"What for?"

"I'm working on a theory here . I want to see what happens."

Hodge put the brake on and left the machine in reverse gear. He got out and stood to one side as Beresford inspected the engine. After a minute the machine slipped the brake slightly . He pulled a lever at the back of the lorry. As if on cue the hook came crashing down. "Good God!" Hodge jumped forward and stopped the machine.

"How often do these Machines get serviced Mr Hodge?"

"Well they get serviced every six months. We inspect them every day for any serious fault." He stopped short only to outline the serious dysfunction of the procedure.

"I pulled a lever at the back of the truck . I'm still not sure what happened. I think I'd like to go up the site of the accident and inspect it again if I may."

"Of course."

In the North of the farm they stood at the site of the accident. Beresford recognised the place because the hedge was only a few feet away. "This is where we found Mr Williams . Could you tell me what these wheels are here?"

"We keep equipment for the tractors ploughs and sprays."

"Can you open it?"

"Yes I've got a control here." He produced a small box that operated the release on the shed door behind them. Slowly the door opened . Behind the door stood a threshing machine . It stood ready to be hooked up to a tractor. Beresford approached it slowly.

"Yes I suppose so. It looks as though Mr Williams was standing behind the lorry and was knocked down and killed by the hook . "

"I'll have to have forensics to check the truck and equipment. I believe one of the team are checking the specifications of the truck at the moment. If it all checks out this may be covered by your insurance, but I think you're heading for a loss Mr Hodge."

"I suppose we are. I'll have to tell Iris."

"Don't say anything until we're sure."

Beresford turned. "Anyway thank you for your time ."

He pointed to Woods. " I'm phoning forensics. " He phoned the path lab so they could check the machine for any signs of blood and the mechanical state of the hoist and the other functions of the machine.

Delaney from forensics cast a tired eye over the machinery. It had been twenty four hours since Beresford was last on the farm with Hodge. "What can you tell me Ron?"

"Well I've been looking over the latest specifications for this number. It's specifically your basic truck souped up a bit. Built by Ford one of the latest off the assembly line. This business with hook is not uncommon with a lot of machines. A hook on a hoist operated by a PTO mechanism . It seems our Mr Williams was in the habit of leaving the PTO on all the time. This explains the delay in the hoist mechanism. What happens is if you depress the lever here outside for the hoist to come down ? Nothing happens for a full ten minutes. Then all of a sudden it comes down with a juddering crash. My guess is our man switched on the PTO depressed the lever and nothing happened. Then the lever comes down very

quickly.

" I see. "

"So it looks like a tragic accident I'm afraid. Best to check with Lambert Hodge . If they keep a manual or defect book. "

"This makes insurance null and void."

"No the policy will probably cover accidents. Though obviously not as much as if it was negligence on the part of the manufacturer."

"I still have to get the tox screen back from Mosely." However at the moment it still looks open and shut to me."

"Right Inspector see you later."

Gregory Mathews had a legacy to deal with . That is to say he should have had a legacy to deal with. His family had held the farm for four generations. It's stock had plummeted and its out-put diminished. He married Marcia under the impression he could somehow square the circle. Then 1998 came along and the foot and mouth epidemic . That more or less caved in any ambition he had. He took a job in the Supermarket.

Mary however carried on employing labour so they could sell produce at the farmer's market and get enough to break even. He paid the bills and helped the place to tick over. It seemed an odd arrangement but it worked . Catherine was going to go to college and everything was looking good.

Amanda was more concerned about her looks but also about the farm as well as Harry.

It seemed a promising combination. Of course unless it paid more money it was all doomed. He realised by now of course he was suffering from depression. Sooner or later he would either leave the job or sell the farm.

The stasis annoyed him.

Thinking back on the last three hundred years he remembered Nathan Mathews. He started up the farm from a small holding and managed to buy out three neighbouring farms. This was in 1850 , Of course with the sudden reliance on food imports at the time meant it was a bad investment. However he used the modern machinery at his disposal in 1870 he managed to replace a lot of manual labour. He also had a lucrative contract with the Crown supplying the British army with beef. With this good fortune he built the grand farm house, now all but in ruins at the far end of the field. During the first World War William Mathews joined up. He never came back but a nephew Stephen Green Mathews took over. Stephen Green Mathews married Grace Cates. A sturdy woman from Buckinghamshire . They had two daughters and a son called Justin. Justin took over the farm in 1945 coming back from the Second World War. By now fortunes had changed . They sold off Cullompton farm to Dennis Williams . Justin seemed to experience strange symptoms recovering from the war. He was never quite the same . Gregory's father James would say he got up early and went to bed late but Justin was never right. They'd built another farm house nearer the A21 . It seemed important to keep up the old farm house . Justin had been living there since the War.

One thing that was buried in his mind was how James would sometimes go in to a room upstairs and come out . This followed the death of his sister Martha at the age of Six. James his father took over the from Justin who was committed to mental hospital in 1978 . Whether they didn't believe in Primogeniture or they didn't care about farming , Ian, Fred, Mary and Theresa left the farm as soon as they possibly could.

He took his responsibilities seriously his mother Clair was a bastion of common sense and guided him in making decisions . That was until her death in 1988. After that he married Mary. Beef cattle was still the going concern it was more important than dairy or crops. That was until 1998 and the foot and mouth epidemic. Gregory wanted to cut his losses and sell out. However Mary persuaded him to stay. One of the things he allowed himself to do was to enter the room upstairs . He saw a photograph of a young girl about six years old. The whole room was an altar to her existence . Her school books her clothes , nothing had been touched for thirty years. He found out and to some extent knew that the room was dedicated to Martha.

The whole incident was never explained. Justin died in Warlingham in 1988. The murderer was never found . However Grace Amelia Green Mathews vowed never to change anything in the room. To their credit Catherine Harry and Amanda never queried the reason why .It seemed that Martha's ghost hung in the air watching over everyone.

For some reason Gregory knew that working in the supermarket was avoiding reality. It was avoiding growing crops, avoiding making the farm a going concern . Although Mary and the family made it a going concern now,

It was just enough to pay the bills. The overheads and the changes were a nightmare. He was waiting for the children to leave so he could sell up and buy a small flat . However Amanda had other ideas. Stoically he accepted the future in front of him. He noticed the changes when Gordon took over in 2000. He saw how Gordon built the abattoir and packaging plant at the back of the farm. The fact that Gordon hadn't missed a trick was not lost on Gregory. It would only be a matter of time before he would sell out to Beasley, or Williams it didn't matter. It seemed odd that Williams should have died in such an awkward manner.

It was early Thursday morning when Catherine had got up early. Gregory had already gone off to work when Catherine started practicing her violin Scales . It was nice in the barn where she practiced because the sound carried. After she finished she tiptoed back into the kitchen. Mary was there carefully tending to Judith who was about to start a bowl of cereal. "You going to school

today Cat?"

"Yes , I've got a few essays to come in soon. I should be okay."

"Well did the teacher say your maths was progressing?"

"Good enough for a good grade. I should get in to college. Hopefully this time next year. I should make it to Bath college. "

"Yes, I'm sure it will work out. I'm worried about Harry . I'm not sure where his head is most of the time. Like his dad I'm afraid."

Catherine briefly breakfasted on cereal while Mary gainfully tried to make Judith eat the contents of the bowl and not spread it on the floor.

Suddenly Amanda appeared her hair blaze of glory as she exploded into the kitchen like a firework. "Hi , what's for breakfast?"

"Sugar Frosties, toast, baked beans. "

"I'll have the Frosties then. God what's happening ? If I don't get my essays in today I'm toast. "

"You should have done it last week Mandy, you know what Fraser's like."

"Yep, I knew God. I can't wait to leave '"

"And what will you do then Mandy? "Mary weighed in . "You have to have some options."

"Why this farm of course. Dad doesn't know what we've got here."

Gregory Mathews sat in his office and ruminated briefly. The job as manager of the local supermarket was a useful stop gap to breach his earnings on the farm. Of course Mary viewed it as useful hobby horse to sow vegetables and crops over the meagre patch of land they

cultivated. Harry was a wonder as well. He got some Gloucester Old Spots and bred them and had them slaughtered and with his van went to factories selling burgers and kebabs. It was certainly innovative.

However the running bills of the farm still had to be paid. If the expenditure of the place didn't improve the place would haveto be sold. Obviously Harry was waiting to take over the farm andtake it in a different direction. That was good. If however Harrydecided he was too big for the farm , then he'd probably leave. Amanda seeing Harry's acumen seemed minded to follow suit. They'd started buying dairy cattle. She'd made discreet noises about setting up a yoghurt processing plant and increasing the dairy herd. In all fairness Gregory gave it consideration. It was still in the basic stages. He'd given his agreement. The builder had come in to set up the milking parlour. Gregory had seen the plans. It all looked feasible and had said so to Mary. Mary he suspected would be involved as well . Mary had a friend called Nancy , together they'd done well in establishing a roadside business in selling vegetables at the farm gate. Nancy was quite willing to lend a hand inpicking the cauliflowers , carrots and turnips. Apart from the nominal wage she helped Mary in the kitchen. She had been an all-round help on the farm even mucking out the pigs for Harry.

The fact was that as the farm was concerned Gregory had a full scale mutiny on his hands. To this end he kept his peace.

He knew at one point that Harry would assume responsibility along with Amanda. His own crisis of management in 1998 was just a blip in the ocean. He thought about his ownfather James Mathews. The debts piled up and the selling off of the farm. He looked forward to Harry taking over.

Harry looked over the beets and the cauliflowers he loaded that morning for the farmer's market , with a little more backing he could go places. It was a small .job to what they were capable of . He was going to have to talk with his dad about it. Of course there were burdens, Catherine was going to University. By the time she'd be leaving she'd be either a teacher or playing in an orchestra. On the other hand if they invested more in selling Pork and Beef and vegetables they would have enough money to give her a career anyway. Ultimately if he wanted to expand more he knew his father would give him the money. The obstacle was Cathy's education. Which meant he could only expand on the visible results of the farm from the sales so far. That meant another Nissen hut among the poly tunnels but not very much growth. It seemed like living in the stone age with Jethro Tull the pioneer of the seed drill. Expansion if possible was going to be slow . As he finished another row of car

rots he saw the shape of his father's Land Rover turning upat the end of the field.

"How's it going Harry?"

"We sold all our cabbages and beets at the market I did four trays of sausages and beets at the market. We're showing a healthy profit."

"Good the Supermarkets should be coming up with more orders soon."

"The only thing is we can't hope to catch up with demand if we don't invest . We want to keep up."

"You can contract out that way you keep the brand name."

"Yes Dad but we lose impetus. If we maximise output we get bigger."

Gregory drew a face. "The market looks tricky
I felt the same way as you back in 1998 then along
came foot and mouth, it nearly wiped us out last time."
Harry felt powerless in the face of such reasoning.
The shadows of yesterday hung over the farm. Every night he
saw the passage upstairs in the East Wing vaguely he heard the
snippets of tales about her. He knew
Justin Mathews was damaged after the war. He couldn't
put his fingeron it but he knew his father was in some
way harmed by what happened in the past . In his child
hood days he managed to sneak into the room occasionally . It
held photographs of a small girlwith brown hair.

There was a wardrobe full of clothes and a diary. It
seemed melancholy. Somehow to keep those belongings placed
there like a shrine. Eventually Harry would have to break away.
He had potential however to do better.

He looked at plans to become a tenant farmer. He heard of a
scheme around Heathrow Airport . Maybe, he thought to himself.

Andrew Williams was a lawyer but had been in the UN
Peace Keeping force some time ago. His brother was also a lawyer with the UN. They were both struck by the death of their
father. However Gordon made the

decision to keep the farm and make a go of it. Andrew was
different and now lived in Brussels content to protect big business and their interests.

One thing had struck Andrew , he wasn't surprised at

Gordon throwing in thetowel. Of course he was married

to Iris . She was a bright woman and they were an ideal match. And yet there was a pause.Up until 2000 Gordon had been in the thick of negotiations on the borders of any conflict . In Bosnia , Herzegovina, Sarajevo he made countless interventions . Usually trying to extri cate refugees out of impossible situations. Completely married to the job they went everywhere, The Gulf States, Malaysia Singapore . Usually they pitted them selves against hopeless odds. One obstacle they faced was human rights abuses brought about by American nationals. That is people who were United States citizens. These people did not come under the jurisdic tion of the European Court of Human Rights.One of the biggest problems they faced was prosecuting multi nationalCompanies. These companies set up factories inThird World countries employing people paying sub standard wages , working long hours in dangerous con ditions using chemicals . Frequently they found them selves tackling officials who had no interest whatsoever in alleviating the conditions of these workers.One such official was Joseph Chin who worked for the Marian Cor poration.In Indonesia. The workers in the factory Marian were responsible for worked twelve hour shifts. Many of them were female , many of them had miscar ried pregnancies because of the long hours they worked and the burns on their arms due to the chemicals they worked with. Chin had a comfortable job in the Marian corporation as managing director of the factory. It was not subject to the human rights laws prescribed by First World countries and who supplied to companies that ap plied these rules only on an approved basis. One worker Amir Siregar had approached Gordon with recordings and evidence of abuse in the factory that Gordon was going to put to the Hague . Although the factory was in Indonesia , it was placed in a free zone not accountable to any government. Never the less Gordon felt with his connections to the Hague and certain forces of the government in Malaysia he could bring pressure to bear.

Of course when Andrew heard the news about his brother's death a hundred and one things ran through his mind. Among them was a friend Caroline Broadley. He imagined she joined another quango and disap peared into another part of the Diaspora. Relaxing in his flat late in the night Andrew wandered who or what had taken over Gordon. Did he pursue those people in Indo nesia ? Knowing the pressure of running a farm probably not. Farming was a full time job . He relaxed in his office in the Hague . A lot of wrongs of the nineties had been addressed. Milosevich had died in Prison.

 Milosevich had diedin Prison , others were con victed .However the Gulf War had provided a minefield of legislation. Human rights abuses by American forces were largely unaddressed. Added to this was the surge of refugees from Syria .

The camp in Calais seemed to be largely symptomatic of the reality of the Third World countries to deal with the lack of food and climate change. In Bosnia and Ma laysia he'd been only relatively influential in what he could do. There in the Hague the grey lines were far from clear . Gordon had written to him a number of times about activities there , as he liked to keep his hand in. Andrew had to look at his life in perspective. The differ ence from drawing boundaries settling trade disputes and settling human rights abuses ,to marking out a year's growth on a farm , such as how meat, dairy produce , cattle and crops was tremendous, along with dealing with workers. It was like a Gamekeeper turned Poacher. Gordon still felt passionate about human rights abuses. However he still had to run a farm and a factory and keep a tight profit at the end of the year. Sometimes he would wistfully write a letter to An drew about a new director of Unesco about regulations in agriculture. Andrew sensed something but he didn't know what.

It was 1995 Andrew Williams woke up in his flat in Jalan Pattimore . At £30 a day it was a bargain . Being there under UN auspices meant he had to attendto busi ness. His first appointment was at the central Police Sta tion in Denpasar.   That was Jalan Gunung Yang in Denpa sar. His appointment was to see a Lieutenant Ahmed Asang. This was in response to human rights abuses being conducted in the Pangembam area in Negara. It was a warm summer's day when Andrewarrived at the central building . He addressed the man behind the desk and showed him his credentials. Andrew was asked who he wanted to see. It was a warm summer's day when Andrew arrived at the Central Police building . He ad dressed the man behind the desk and showed him his credentials .Andrew was asked who he wanted to see. Andrew mentioned Ahmed Asang . The officer immedi ately straightened up and said that officer Asang's office was on the third floor pointing to the lift.

Asang's office had air conditioning and had a good aerial view of the road. Ahmed Asang was seated at his desk . He was about five foot five . He seemed to exude a commanding presence."I see you are a man of punc tuality Mr Williams. How long have youbeen in our country?"

"About a day or so."

"And how can I help you?"

"I've come to talk about human rights abuses in Pangembam in Negara."

"And what company would that be?"

"Marian Conglomerates . Apparently workers are suffering from radio active burns . It is very alarming."

"Andrew Williams you must understand that most major compani have signed undertakings not to trade

with firms that undertake unnecessary risks in the pro
cess of assembling or producing goods for export."

"It's only a code of conduct. There's nothing
binding with legal penalties . The abuses will continue."

Asang made a brief not of the address and noted
down some particulars "You must appreciate Mr Wil
liams we are only a small country, there is only so much
we can do. However I will look into this matter. I will no
tify you if I get any results.

"Thank you Mr Asang . I've left you my email
address . If you could let me know soonest."

Asang bade him good day. He left the building. He
went down to the Coffee shop down the road. Then he
arranged to meet Asmara Rivat . She worked as a jour
nalist for a newspaper in Denpasar. She'd being to school
in Denpasar and met Andrew originally in the Hague.
"How did it go Andrew?"

"The usual he made polite noises and left it at that."

"I told you it's global politics here. If we don't
produce the cheapest possible price we don't make any
money. I could have told you we're fighting a losing
battle."

"The usual he made polite noises and left it at that."

"Why not? Anything for a good night out."

He left and returned to Jalan Pattimore to his
hotel . To his dismay he found that his flat had been
turned over. Straight away he went back to the Police

headquarters. He stood in front of the desk Sergeant. "I demand to See Farel Djatta immediately. "

Mr Djatta was in charge of internal security and would have probably authorised the search. This time the desk Sergeant volunteered the information that Officer Djatta 's office was on the fifth floor. Only this time the Sergeant gave Andrew an escort to show him up there. Of course Andrew was quite aware the situation could turn ugly. When they got to the fifth floor the officer escorted him to the door at the end of the corridor . He said a few words to the receptionist who ushered them into Djatta's office. Djatta was a much older individual . He looked up from his desk . "Ah Mr Williams . I've been expecting you. I see you seem upset what is the trouble?"

"My rooms have being searched . I must object most strongly."

"Relax Mr Williams we are all civilised men here. You must understand we have enemies everywhere. One can never be too careful."

"Of course Mr Djatta if you give me your assrances this will never happen again."

"Mr Williams I suggest you come outside with me to get some air. We must discuss this in a more civilised manner."

They went down in the lift and Djatta walked him to a nearby shopping centre.

"You can see the wealth that tourism brings us . All is relative. It could all be gone tomorrow. You must under stand Mr Williams we are under great pressure. "

"Yes Mr Djatta . However I would be grateful if you did not search my room again."

As they traversed the concourse of the leisure centre he felt a pair of eyes boring into him from the other side of the square. He turned and saw the familiar figure of Carol Broadley staring in absolute dis belief. Sensing his disquiet Djatta cut short his inter view with Andrew. Andrew then retired to his flat. Later that night he relaxed in the nearby hotel bar with As mara Rivat. "Went The day well?" She said.

Andrew stared meaningfully into his glass. "I hope so. " He said dismally.Of course the tide of events grad ually wore Andrew down . A rift had developed with his brother. Andrew knew it was about many things , Asmara wanted to marry and have a luxurious lifestyle. This meant that Andrew had to entertain a not very so phisticated change of clientele. the years went past. The bigger money meant a luxurious house outside Denpasar. Asmara had three children. Pretty soon her at tention wandered to bigger fish until she divorced An drew and married a steel magnate from Guatemala.An drew rarely saw the children but heard that Asmara was quite happy,on their visits to him. Of course the change of clientele meant that Andrew was helping the people he'd been prosecuting. A fact not lost on Gordon. In recent years Andrew moved to the Hague and just helped small businesses. Returning to the present An drew recollected he had to make the journey from the Hague to England. He collected his bags from his flat and took the plane from Schiphol Airport that evening and had arranged to stay at a hotel in London. It was a fifty minute journey by train to get ThirtonSouth from Victoria . It took another fifteen minutes to get a bus from the station to Cullompton farm. Iris Williams ru minated over the past years before they took on the farm. The camp took on refugees from China and Korea.Gordon as Lawyer for the UN in Indonesia . These thoughts were running through her head when she met Andrew in the farm house they exchanged the usual courtesies. However Iris's manner was terse and unnatural . "I'm sorry Iris was it something I said? I'm sorry , I'm missing something here."

"Well yes Andrew there are questions that need answering . You knewGordon and I were working there. You knew we were concerned about the situation re garding the export processing zones. All in all I'm sur prised you even came here."

"I really am at a loss here could you just tell me what's

wrong?" It must seem strange to you to think that I

should resurrect Indonesia after all these years but I'm

afraid I have to say it is relevant however"
"Relevant ? In what way?"

"It was 1995 , Indonesia , remember? Alright?
Amir Siregar was working in the export processing zones
in Panembang. They were working with dangerous
chemicals in making electronic goods. He made films of
it unbeknown to Marian Productions a multi-national
company. Gordon had arranged to meet him in Tang
naan village in Bali. The meeting would be in the village.
At that time of year they would be holding cockfights.

Cock fights are sacred to Indonesians. They have
certain leading families who would place bets on these
cockfights . The bets are fairly big sums of money . The
money however is not important . The bet is important.
The family will lose the money or might gain more. The
fact is that through the year they will get the money
back. The families are the static quantity in village life
and are respected as such. The whole cockfighting cere
mony is basically religious. It's a celebration of what the
community has in common with each other."

"So why did Amir Siregar agree to meet there?"

"He was related to Bachtior Naing Dan . Naing Dan
been the old family in the village going back hundreds of
years. Amir agreed to go there because he was protected

by tribal loyalties rather than people who worked for the government."

Andrew nodded his head slowly ."But you must realise there is a certain amount of traidcraft in these proceedings . I mean Gordon didn't turn up in some obscure village for no reason."

"Of course the cockfighting was a tourist trap. Lots of tourists turned up for the tribal cockfight, they were highlights of the show . It was serious business. Cockerels would be armed with talons if they were felt too seriously handicapped in any conflict. Gordon and I were just harmless tourists."

"You'd been working in Kuala Lumpur for ten months Iris. That would've been hard to swallow."

"Meaning?"

"Meaning Amira Gintra head of security was a worthy adversary. If I smelt a rat she would too."

"She had her hand full with the local bandits. bandit There was enough local crime to keep her busy."

"We were going to meet Amir at Daud Pho's restaurant or should I say Cafe. It was a pretty rough and ready affair. The main cockfight was going to take place in the square. It was a fight between the Nainggolan's and the Nainbolans. Of course it was only a ceremonial fight . Money changed hands but would change back again in the course of the year. "

"So what went wrong?"

"Well I suppose you have two or three levels of punters. You have the local village punter. Every year he or she will bet for his clan regular as clockwork. Then you have the casual punter. He'd bet occasionally. Then you

have the habitual punter. He lays a bet all the time and is usually skint. Amir Siregar was the casual punter. He'd place it now again. We had set the meeting up . He was going to give us films and information of the Negara In dustrial Park ."

"Even if he did it was an export processing zone. No one would touch them. They would do what they want."

"This was big I met Amir three days before the handover. It was a small handover. It was a small shack outside of the village. He was schizoid I think he was speeding or something. This really didn't make him a reliable witness . However what he was saying rang true."

"What was that?"

"Well he spoke of burns on people's arms. Only when he spoke it was about chemical burns . It sounded really serious."

"Did he elaborate?"

"He said he'd provide more information at the hand over . He hada friend called Hasia Labin . This is what raised alarm bells. I'd seen Hasin Labin in the village. He was a habitual gambler . He turned up drunk most times and would lose his money. It struck me the whole thing was precarious. However when I spoke to Amir about it he demurred. He said Labin was reliable."

"Okay. So what happened?"

"Me and Gordon agreed to meet him there. Well the day came. The big cockfight was in progress in the main square. Labin turned up and said he was sorry. Amir couldn't make it. Naturally me and Gordon were alarmed . Something had happened, we were sure of it."

"Then what did you do?"

"We went to the Hospital in Densapar they told us a dead body had been found by the Nquah Ru bypass. That fitted the description of Amir Siregar. Well we went to the morgue and there he was on the slab. We'd seen dead bodies before . Now we were sure ."

"So you never got to the bottom of it."

"That's not the point and you know it Andrew Gordon had his heart set on nailing the Marian corporation. Amir was the result of a lot of hard work. When he died Gordon felt like giving up. If your father hadn't died he would have become a solicitor in the city."

"Doing Probono work I suppose."

"Yes or something."

"Well we can't really do anything about it now can can we?"

"That's just the thing . Carol is coming here in a few days time. She wants answers."

"Well pardon me but all I know is what you told me. I met you in Denpasar a week before. Believe me I thought you were tilting at Windmills even then."

"Yes , but you knew Andrew."

"I knew something. I was on holiday. I was going to Saigon after a well deserved break. At least I picked a battle I could win."

"Well if she comes I'll do my best to answer her questions. I did what I could the authorities shut up completely. No one would say what the last hours of Amir Siregar were like. I only know that night Hasin Balin stood in Daud Pho's restaurant he was drunk and smiling . I'll never forget that grin."

Mathew felt the silence fill the vacuum . "What have the Police said about Gordon's death?"

"The Police haven't said anything about it until next week. They suspected that poor boy Stuart Linley. I wish my boy was like that. Anyway they let him go."

"So they're still looking for some one ."

"Yes it's all a bit frightening."

"Carol will be here soon you can talk about old times."

"She knew Amir Siregar quite well."

"I see."

"Yes and she saw you talking to Farel Djatta hours before we were due to meet Amir in Tenge naan."

"Look Iris it's not what you think . I had some business there with an insurance company that's all. As a matter of fact I'd been to see the Police Official Ahmed Asang about Panembang. He told me he would look into it.I came back to my hotel and found it had been searched. I went back to the Police station and remonstrated in the strongest possible terms with FarelDjatta. He took me for a walk to the nearest shopping centre. I saw Carol there. I tried to explain to her but she wouldn't listen."

"It was an unfortunate coincidence."

"Yes it was an unfortunate coincidence."

"Well let's hope so."

Mosely bent over the bench as Beresford came in to the lab . "Yes Albert what have you got?"

"The tox screening came back . It showed a certain amount of Sodium Chlorate in the blood. Looking at the heart attack induced by the chemical . The thing is a weed killer, you have a farm where such things are used or tightly controlled I'd say it was a case of poisoning. I wouldn't say it was accidental either. We analysed the Taco graphs nothing there either really."

"I'm sorry Bert walk me through it I'm getting confused . Give me a scenario. I'm getting uncertain."

"Oh I see yes well. Let's say for arguments sake he has a snack. We'll saythe food is somehow laced with So dium Chlorate . It's not unreasonableassumption . You're man finishes his driving . He eats the snack beforewind ing up at the end of the day. Accidentally he leaves the brake on while leaving it in gear. This triggers the auto matic PTO to come into play. He feels a pain in his chest standing behind the truck and falls on his knees, accidentally pulls the lever the hook comes down hit ting him on the head. "

"All of which is possible."

"Yes."

"I don't really buy this. How many coincidences can you have?"

"More than three you start to wonder."

"Possibly I'd say he was poisoned beforehand and dumped there to make it look like an accident."

"Concievably . The left ventricle to the heart was in really bad shape. He wasn't in a position to walk anywhere. The question is how long was he standing at the back of the truck?"

"I'll have a word with Mrs Williams she might know something . She was the last person to see him alive."

He drove up to Cullompton Farm. Irene was in the process of arranging the kitchen when Beresford knocked on the door. "Good morning Mrs Williams I wonder if you could help me with a few questions?"

"Of course how can I help?"

"Well we think your husband may have had something to eat before the accident . Did you give him a snack or anything?"

"A few sandwiches and an apple pie."

"Can I have a look at your apple pies?"

"Yes of course . "She went to the kitchen and pulled out a few apple pies she'd bought from the supermarket. Beresford could tell everything was still supermarket fresh.

"Well, could I take these away?" He said thoughtful fully.

"What's the matter Inspector ?"

"What sort of insecticide or weed killer do you use on the farm Mrs Williams?"

"Roundup. Glysophate. Normally it does the job I don't keep it anywhere near food."

"Are there any batches of Sodium Chlorate you keeplying round?"

"Concievably . I think we were doing strawberries some years back. There might be some by the old farm by the fence."

"Up by the fence?"

"Yes there where a couple of sacks there."

"I see thanks very much for your help Mrs Williams."

Beresford went up to the fence and the shed . Looking at where the truck was situated he saw the position of the sacks stacked up against the side. There were small oil drums there . He thought for a moment . If Gordon got off the truck , goes over by the sacks and oil drum which is lightly sprinkled with Sodium Chlor ate . He puts his sandwiches and apple pie down there. He eats the snack. Feels ill goes over to the truck . He falls down and hits the lever. Then the hook comes down and hits him. Mosely was quite specific, it wasn't accidental poisoning. It was murder. Though he felt not with the pies he had in his evidence bag. His instinct was to play it by ear. If Mrs Williams poisoned her husband then there was friction in the family. That would mani fest itself soon enough. Most likely the pies he took from Mrs Williams would prove free of any poison. A further phone call to Mosely clarified matters. He examined the ground where Williams had fallen. Williams had vomited up a considerable amount of food. The amount of Sodium chlorate thus lost made it hard to determine whether it was contamination or deliberate poisoning.

He goes back to Mrs Williams ."I'm sorry to bother you Mrs Williams . It seems like murder . I'm afraid I can't rule it out. I may have a word with Lambert Hodge. If that doesn't alter things then that's what I come up with. . I'm sorry for your loss but that's what I've come up with."

"Oh this is an awful business . I'm sure the insurance company will pay up or something."

"I'll get back to you as soon as I can."He left the building and walked further down the yard to the Port a cabin where Lambert Hodge worked. When he got there Hodge was bent over his desk looking at pie charts and production yields.

"Good morning Mr Hodge do you think you can spare a moment?"

"I expect so officer how can I help?"

"Could you tell me what operating controls or manuals yopu have as regards the tractor?"

"Yes I have somwhere. Just a minute . " He went over to the filinf cabinet and pulled out a big yellow instyruction manual. It was a FordD351 Model . "It came on the market last year."

"Do you have inspection sheets that show faults on the machine?"

Lambert looked a bit vague. "Well it was Gordon who drove it. Yes, however , he usually made a sheet out every morning?"

"Can I have a look?"

"Here you are." He produced a small book with a list of faults on it.

"Our mechanic came every month .He's usually

quite good. Gordon would have shown him what needed doing."

Beresford looked at the book . Quite clearly two weeks previously he marked down the hand brake had been faulty.

"I'll keep this if I may." Beresford said.

"Of course anything else?"

"No it was your standard twenty ton truck no frills. Except for a small device at the back that could operate the hoist."

"I see well thanks for your time Mr Hodge. It all seems to meet my requirements for the time being." Iris Williams braced herself as she saw Beresford drive off. It seemed Ironic that after all the work that was done on the farm , something like this should happen. Money was an issue of course, but that wasn't the main thing. She needed Gordon here. She had Beatrice and Stanley . Beatrice would be taking her exams soon and Stephen would be going to his first year at agricultural college. It seemed a far cry from a settled family life.

Andrew displeased her, and she let him know it. Of course as he said the past was just a coincidence. How ever she was there , she knew it couldn't be It rankled still , Andrew had become a settled Brussels bureaucrat. It wouldn't surprise her if he resigned from the Euro pean court of Justice and became another fat cat lawyer.

As she set the oven for dinner that evening she

saw another car pull up outside the courtyard. She saw the familiar figure of a woman in her forties with tawny brown hair. It was of course Carol Broadley.

"Hello Iris." She said coming out of the car. She was wearing a pale blue trouser suit , she came over and embraced her. "My condolences this must be awful for you."

"It's not being easy Carol. It's being a while how've you been?"

"Oh you know Syria, Iraq, Egypt , Israel one crisis after another. It never stops."

"I can imagine."

"What out here here amongst the turnips and the carrots? It's hard to see that."

"It's not all pastoral calm Carol. I've got two teenagers to deal with.That can be warfare sometimes ."

"Yes well that at least escaped me."

"What about you ?"

"Has Andrew been?"

"Yes he seems to like his position in the Hague for the most part."

"Did you go over old times?"

"Yes we did .He was as lucid about it now as he was then."

"You were in Tange naan village to meet Amir Siregar . You turn up there , he turns up in Denpasar with Farel Djatta. It's too much , I was in two minds whether to come here or not."

" I can't believe you moved in the same circles and not cleared this up."

"I've been avoiding him. It's not hard . He's mainly in Brussels . I move in the Middle East . I investigated that Export Processing zone myself. It turned they were manufacturing a new type of radar equipment using an isotope they weren't being too careful with the raw materials. This was affecting their profit margin so they closed down that particular factory."

"So will you have any searching questions for Andrew?"

"Enough to make him fairly uncomfortable . I have enough information on his deals in the past to know why he just stays in the Hague these days. He's no saint. I'm not about to launch a major enquiry but I'm not about to give him a free pass either."

"When Gordon came here he was pretty sick with what happened. Mainly because he suspected Andrew had sold him out . He turned all his energies on to this place. He built an abattoir out the back and a meat processing plant. This was because of the foot and mouth epidemic in 1998. There aren't many plants that stood up to the requirements of the new acts passed afterwards. He made a lot of money out of it. He does well out of the dairy , crops and cattle. The meat however is the mainstay."

"Mmmm, as a vegetarian , I can't say I approve .However I must say you're a Hundred per cent committed. How do you think he died?"

"It all sounds like a murder. Apparently he was eating a snack and he left it on a drum by the shed. He left the tractor in front of the shed.He picks up the snack . By now it's soaked in Sodium Chlorate. He has aheart at tack falls down behind the truck. The amount could have been contamination or poisoning. He's decided to keep the case open because there are so many suspicious circumstances surrounding the case."

"What about insurance?"

"We'll get something. Not much."

"Who would do something like that? I mean it's vicious."

"To think if he was out in Syria he might still be here."

"You'd think so wouldn't you? I can only think someone got to him talking by the hedge. There's a gap there. The thought he could have eaten something

and then fell ill. I still can't take it all in."

"It's not Thirton is it Iris? Then I suppose. Good grief!"

Davinia read through the history again as she wasn't exactly sure . Hilda of the Marshes was originally Abbess of Thirton Abbey . She held her position for thirty years. Then she decided in order to truly devote her life to God she should go and live in the Marshes and become ascetic. People claimed she healed them and had a number of miracles to her credit. An itinerant beggar chanced upon her one day and struck her dead, stealing what little food she had.

Her body was buried on reclaimed Marshland in AD749.

At the time Kent was thought to be the centre of Christianity in England. Looking at the old Marsh and its border with the Church grounds and the old plans, Davinia composed herself for the storm to come when she met the met the Vicar.

It was a fine Spring day as she came into the rectory. The Reverend Wallis was suntanned and in fine health. "Did you enjoy your holiday Alex?"

"Davinia ? Hello yes as you can see I took some sun. It was quite magic as you can see."

"I see well the Parish hasn't been static . Things have moved on. We have things to discuss."

"Yes I see. Well no time like the present. What have you got for me?" He smiled beatifically.

"Well I've been researching the local Saint. Hilda of the Marshes. It's interesting, she was Abbess of Thirton Abbey in 763 and decided to become a hermit."

"Go on."

"Well she was murdered by a thief in 769 and her body was buried in reclaimed land from the Marsh. Records show that would be where the baptism font is now."

By now he had rapidly regained his composure. " I see and what do you intend to do about it?"

"Well I wandered if we may relocate the font somewhere. By the entrance would be good."

"I absolutely forbid it. Such a thing is monstrous. We barely get enough Parishioners through these doors as it is. You're talking at least five thousand pounds."

"We would make it back by making a shrine to St Hilda over her grave.

We're sure to get tourists anxious to see the local saint."

Somewhat pacified by the prospect of money the Reverend Derek Wallis reconsidered his position . "It would take time to make up the revenue.

Are you sure it was where you say? Where did you check?"

"I went to the British Museum at first and then I checked the records in the rectory. It's all there."

"I'll put it to the ArchBishop . If we get the money you're on. However it's going to be like a burden round our necks. You'll be in the dog house Davinia."

"Yes Vicar." Davinia retired quietly delighted.

CHAPTER 2

Thirton Police station represented a reasonably accurate facsimile of modern British Policing at it's finest, at it's worst a badly disorganised dysfunctional

Police Station. At this moment in time as in most processes in life it was straddling the crossroads between the two. At the head of this organisation of well intentioned souls stood the chief constable Ernest Ralston. Personal friends with the Mayor and Barney Paignton of Ace Casinos and other establishments that surrounded the borough. Also personal friends with

the Police Commissioner of London.

The head of the homicide division was Harry Burnham . Burnham of course

Kept his light firmly under a bushel . Although the head of a squad of detectives he was weary of the ambitions of Ernest Ralston and where they

could lead. Graham Cather was head of Traffic . Jean Mason was head of domestic and social abuse. Dennis Humphries was head of commercial and financial fraud. Vincent Marks was the desk Sergeant. Genene Caldwell was head of the forensic service and her staff got called out all the time. Stephen Waites was in charge of the evidence room and of keeping evidence locked up.

Barbara Harris was of incoming calls and dealing with emergencies. Her staff included Virginia Wilson and Marian Fulford . They worked in rotation supplemented by other members of staff.

Jean Mason was perplexed because a case of what had been domestic abuse mutated to murder. Jean Simmons a housewife who had made repeated calls about her husband and had him banned from coming within a mile of the premises on a restraining order had been found strangled in her garden of her house in Tilson Park Road.

Tilson Park Road ran parallel to Mosely Road that ran out of Thirton High street until it came to Baynes Field Road . This went through to Mosely Green.

Joan Simmons's house was a tasteful semi- detached house. All in all it could be said to be a tasteful part of Thirton. It's houses were going into millions of pounds in some parts. Alec Simmons was a quantity surveyor who although running a successful business had an unfortunate predilection for alcohol and violence. At the moment Beresford was standing in the garden in Mrs Simmons's house as they were taking the body out in a stretcher .Ernest

Ralston, obviously feeling claustrophobically inhibited by the confines of his office was holding forth to Beresford.

"Obviously there's no need to be obsessive about this case Beresford.

It's a clear case of abuse. I've already put in an alert out on Mr Simmons the sooner he's put behind bars the better. "

"Yes Sir."

"As soon as you finish here you can come back to the station, I'm sure there's plenty of other cases for you to sort out. "

"Yes Sir." As he finished Burnham appeared behind him.

"Hello, Harry I was just telling Chris , no need to bother over long with this case . The sooner you get all this sorted out the better. See you back at the station."

"Yes Sir." Harry guardedly replied as Ralston disappeared into his Hyundai and headed back to his office.

Burnham looked at Beresford . "Everything okay?"

"Improving Sir."

"What have we got?"

"She was found about four o'clock in the morning . Well it's white Caucasian female about thirty four , five foot six in height . They hadn't been

that long married .Death was caused by strangulation . Certificates I've seen suggest she's been to University. There's a copy of the degree certificate and other paraphernalia . I'm aware that Mrs Simmons had some differences with her husband. He'd been banned from the premises."

"But what?"

"I'm not sure I've been looking round . There's no sign of breaking and entering . If it had been the husband she wouldn't have let him in. Whoever it was , it was someone she trusted."

"Yes, I felt that way too. What do you want to do?"

"I want to look amongst her things, have a word with the neighbours. There must be someone she knew who could shed more light on this. "

"I'll tell Ernie something came up and let you get on with it . I'll have a word with Jean Mason, see if she can shed any light on the matter."

"Here she comes now Sir. " As he turned Burnham saw a woman about five feet ten in height with long dark hair and a fierce determined look on her face.

"Well gentlemen what have you got for me?"

Burnham looked back at the crime scene . "As you can see not very much Jean. Would Mrs Simmons have let her husband back in after he'd been banned?"

"No , of course not. She changed the locks . She's been fooled by him a number of times."

"So that makes it look far from obvious . Whoever did this was known to Mrs Simmons and more importantly trusted by her. Chris I want you to interview Mr Simmons under caution but we will not be arresting him as of yet."

"Yes Sir."

"What do you make of Mr Simmons Jean?"

"I would say he's not a bad chap . Obviously a handful when he's had a drink taken."

"Capable of this?" He gestured at the scene.

"Ah there you have me. Yes I suppose if he was driven into a corner. He's

successful , he's relatively well off, but I don't see why not."

"Well it's in her case file I've sent to your office , but as you ask there was an Alice Fairfield . Alice is a financial accountant in the city. They knew each other from university . Alice lived in Mosely Road . She regularly dropped in from time to time . Let's see . " She looked up her diary ."Yes Flat 5 Mosely Road just outside Thirton. " Beresford took it down.

"Right thanks Jean. That's a good place to start."

Flat 5 Mosely Road was a respectable two bedroom flat situated amongst respectable apartments . It overlooked a spacious front lawn and parking spaces for five or six cars . Beresford knocked on the door and a woman in her mid-thirties answered . She was wearing a blouse and a black skirt. She had short blond hair brushed back but evinced an air of efficiency.

"How can I help you?" She asked as she opened the door.

"Hello , I'm DI Beresford and this is my assistant DC Woods." He said pointing to Justin behind him. "I'm afraid I've got some bad news . Can we come in?"

"Yes of course." She appeared flustered by the imminent disclosure of bad news. When they got inside Beresford noted the wallpaper and furnishings were tastefully done. Light pastel colours predominated .Pale cream wallpaper with a recuring motif of Daffodils and picturesque farmhouses. Perhaps a little chic maybe. The furniture was brown with a sideboard and fitted cupboards and a splendid oak table centre stage.

A television and hi-fi were off to one side. The overall impression was impressive yet understated. "Well as I said how can I help you gentlemen?"

" I'm afraid your friend Mrs Joan Simmons has been murdered. We thought you could tell us about her circumstances."

Alice didn't lose her composure for one second . "I see would you like to sit down and tell me more?"

"Yes." He said still standing. "We found her in the garden. She was found by the next door neighbour. It appears she was strangled ."

"I see."

"Can you tell me anything about her friends ?"

"Well I would say it was her husband Alex . He was a completely useless idiot. However , I don't have any grounds to say that other than I don't like the man."

"Did she have any friends you can think of?"

"She had a friend called Ann Cameron . She lived a few streets away in Aviemore Road. That runs from Mosely Road through to Baynes Field Road."

"Yes I know where it is. Could you tell me what number?"

"Number 57 I think . She's lived there for quite a while."

"Alright Miss Fairfield I think I will sit down as it happens ." He and Woods sat down on the sofa facing Alice who was sitting in the armchair . "How well did you know Mrs Simmons?"

"Well I'm really quite shocked . I can't think why. I mean I know how this must sound . Joan was always disaster prone in so many ways. She got a good first in Economics. She could easily gone into business like me. When she met that brute of a husband I was mortified. Ture enough it all ended badly . However as bad as I found Alec . I never though him capable of murder."

"No quite."

"We would go out on a girl's night out now and then. There's a pub by Coal Street called the "Railway Signal".

"Opposite East Thirton Station?"

"Yes , that's the one . You know you've got the pub down Stour Street where all the restaurants and shops you can go to. We've been there a couple of times as well."

Beresford was picturing this in his mind's eye.Thirton had a high street pedestrianised and traffic went through Thirton Way, the relief road. However Stour Street was a bad mixture of road and pedestrian precinct. Extended pavements with traffic running through the middle. At night the venue was populated by restaurants and pubs. He'd dined out a couple of times with his

Wife and found it quite tasteful . He could see the attraction . "And when you dined out did she ever talk about friends and neighbours or people she knew?"

"Your best bet is to talk to Annie. I was working full time , have done for five years . Joan was adrift as a housewife , she navigated foreign waters to me. We went out occasionally . I was more fixated on my job . I'm aware

she had developed an interest in archaeology with her friend Averill Green and Anne Cameron . Anne would tell you more about that. As far as history goes I'm lost after 1066. It means nothing to me. I'm forgetting myself . I've

got Anne's address here . Let's see 57 Aviemore Road. It connects this road to Tilson Park Road and then to Baynesfield Road. " Woods took it down quickly.

"I see well thanks for your time Miss Fairfield , if we have any more enquiries we'll let you know."

As they left Justin said "She was a bit of alright then wasn't she?"

"You like them older do you Justin?"

"I wouldn't say no."

"You surprise me , I had you down as a ladies man at the disco . I didn't think you like career women. "

"It's something I never focused on. I like women. I never focused on a particular type Sir."

"You young men never settle down eh?"

"No Sir."

Aviemore Road was a road with old Victorian houses adjoining Mosely Road. They had three or four storeys leading up to the junction with Tilson Park Road. At this point there was a massive United Reformed Church . It's spire towered over the surroundings like a monolith. Further down the road near some shops was the modest semi detached house that was number 57. The front end showed signs of neglect. Beresford knocked on the door and rang the bell. After a brief pause the door opened . There stood a lady into her mid-fifties with short black . She wore the scholarly air of a professor. She wore

Corduroy trousers and a brown jumper. It was obvious she was in the middle of gardening.

"Hello, can I help you gentlemen?"

"Yes, I'm inspector Beresford , I'm afraid I have some bad news for you Miss Cameron, can we come in?"

"Of course."

They came in. On this occasion there was a subtle difference to the last house they went to . The hall seemed neat and tidy but there wall paper had obviously been put up there many years ago. This was the case in the front room and the back room. Beresford could obviously see the walls were lined with books. When they got to the sitting room they were faced with a functional three piece suite. Everything was tidy and functional but no money was spent on furnishings. "Please sit down." She said. They sat down " Now what do you have to say Mr Beresford . I assume you are a Police Officer."

"I'm afraid we found Mrs Simmons's body this morning. I'm afraid she's been murdered."

The shock seemed to affect Ann Cameron straight away. "Good God how awful."

"I'm afraid so. Is there anything you can tell us?"

"Joan and I were members of the Albion Psychic Society. The President of the group- was a man called Arnold Bream . You know I suppose he's a good man in his way . You may have a picture in your minds of a group of people sitting round a table with a moving glass receiving messages from the dead.

Well what Arnold wanted to do was investigate separate individual hauntings as he had a number to look into. There was an old lady called Celia Pheeney in Addley Road in Kessington . She said that her husband died two years ago and she felt her presence there. It was troublesome , jars moved doors slammed , that sort of thing. Well Arnold turned up . He gave Mrs Pheeney a long interview. He asked her about Harold , their relationship. Apparently Harold was not a good husband . He used to be abusive and drunken frequently. He would fly into rages. He developed cancer of the Prostate and treatment was unsuccessful. He died after a short illness.

Well after a long period of questions and answers Arnold held a séance. He acted as a medium and his voice started to change. Mrs Pheeney asked a few questions . The spirit answered in short terse sentences . Afterward Mr Arnold

told her not to worry . He said Arnold was okay but he needed to move on. In fact that was the only thing holding him back. He recommended that Mrs Pheeney go on holiday. Well she did , a few weeks later she came back the haunting stopped. I believe it was just a bit of amateur psychiatry.

About three weeks later we had another haunting . This time it was a retired soldier, his name was Ian Pettifer. Well Arnold again had a long talk with him. It turned out he was a second World War veteran. He had a chum called Harry Hollis. . They both survived Dunkirk and were in the invasion force of D Day. When they were demobbed in 1945 . Mr Pettifer joined the civil service . Hollis however joined the council as a labourer. About 1949 Harry was run over by a car in Thirton . It was a hit and run , but the driver was never found . Arnold began asking Mr Pettifer a lot of questions then. Mr Pettifer had a recurring dream of Harry pointing a finger at him . Arnold did have a séance then but his spirit guide wasn't any use. Afterwards Arnold contacted a psychiatrist friend of his Henry Baynes > He worked at Thirton General Hospital .He seemed to think that Mr Pettifer was suffering from a case of PTSD . A month later Mr Pettifer killed himself , in the garage was va very old Ford Prefect . The right bumper was badly dented and had been dented in an accident a long time ago."

Beresford listened patiently, "I see Miss Cameron . How does this help us with our enquiries?"

"Not in any obvious way. But I began to see Mr Bream as some sort of therapist masquerading as a clairvoyant . Usually it's the other way round. Well me and Joan had enough really . We both stopped going . We were lulled into thinking that Mr Bream was a messianic figure."

"Why?"

"Nothing really it was silly. It's just that there's an excavation going on in the Green Weald Site. It's being sponsored by the British Museum . You know there are a lot of businesses round there. Fishbourne Music , Maidline Productions. A shopping centre a mile long at the end of the round about on the A20 on the Green Weald Site. Andrew Blandford is the head of the site . I can't go into too much detail but apparently they've been excavating for a few years . It was an Anglo Saxon village . There was evidence of Ancient Druid settlement there and an altar. That would have been earlier about two hundred Bc . It provoked some interest . I think some yobbos broke in there and sacrificed a goat. Well Arnold goes along and meets this Martin Grimshaw.

Some sort of Goth type . Well apparently he spooked one of the workers , Paddy Coombes . Arnold falls for this hook line and sinker . He feels the place is infested with spirits and wants to seal the place up.. Well Jean and I had had enough at this stage. Arnold lost it basically . Underneath it all I think he was trying to placate this Coombes bloke. I believe that Arnold was in cahoots with Andrew Blandford who runs the site. They were trying to work a little magic on their own on Coombes.

Anyway that's all I know. I haven't seen Joan for a few weeks . It's terrible news . I don't think it's got anything to do with Arnold however. He seems to

overpowering sometimes . I'm not sure anymore . Was there anything you wanted Mr Beresford?"

"No Miss Cameron you've been quite helpful , Come on Justin off we go. "

"Yes Sir."

Outside Woods said, "What do you think?"

"I'm not sure I think we ought to go and see Mr Bream."

Not far from East Thirton station ran Vent Street. This was the heart of Thirton . Parallel to that ran Thirton High Street, a part that wasn't pedestrianised. The continuation of Vent street was Fallows Road that

Led down to Baynes Field Road and then past that to Parish Moor Road that led to London. Parallel to that lay Calmington Road. It was here in a three storey house worked Arnold Bream.

It was an impressive house and big enough Beresford felt to hold a meeting. He knocked on the door in the hope of finding someone. Presently the door was opened by a man in his mid-thirties. "Hello, can I help you?"

"Yes, I'm DI Beresford and this DC Woods my colleague. We're here because of some disturbing developments and we believe you can help us with

our enquiries. "

"In any way I can I suppose . Please come in." He showed them into the front room. It seemed to resemble a doctor's waiting room with benches lining the walls. "How can I help you Inspector?"

"It's a bit awkward actually . It's bad news I'm afraid , I know you run a Psychic group here. One of your colleagues has been found strangled .A Mrs Simmons. Do you know her?"

Suddenly Mr Bream went white. "Good Lord how awful . Yes I did know her. Her and Miss Cameron used to attend our meetings . Who was responsible do you think?"

"Well at the moment we should be meeting the ex-husband and interviewing him. I'm pursuing other avenues of enquiry . How well did you

Know Mrs Simmons?"

"Well she was an intelligent woman . I believe she could have had a good career once she decided to go back to work."

"You felt she was a frustrated housewife?"

"In the career sense yes."

"Did she have any enemies?"

"Not as far as I know. Why do you ask?"

"Well Miss Cameron pointed to the strains with in your group. She felt you were a good psychic , though more interested in people's personal problems than the actual phenomena itself. However when it came to the Green Weald Site and Paddy Coombes you reached a dead end. Recommending shutting the site down was capitulation if you like. "

"It's difficult to draw the line somewhere. Since Anne and Mrs Simmons left I've had to re-evaluate my position. I fear they may well have been right.

I think Mr Coombes was acting out some trauma in his past. This came out in the excavation . I put this to Mr Blandford head of the excavation team . Of course he didn't agree. Obviously it's a site of great archaeological importance, I suppose it's hard to rewrite one's past with one's future."

"Was Mr Simmons in Psychic trouble that you were aware of?"

"Obviously it was a difficult marriage. I think there were obstacles there. She made an unwise choice. A young woman, economic pressures . Life isn't easy. Coming to the Psychic group was a way of expressing an interest getting away from more pressing concerns. I helped as best I could. She had a knack of talking to people and getting to know them. She was useful to me. I'll miss her. As to who could have done this I must confess I'm at a loss."

"Miss Cameron seemed to think you developed a charisma or a Messianic air about you. In fact she thought you were a cult figure."

"That was probably gilding the lily slightly . Anne was a sage figure in the group always ready to cast a dystopian shroud on something. I lead the group,

no apologies about that . I'm conducting a social experiment here. That is of course as well as trying to help people. I investigate Psychic phenomena. I started as a redcoat in Butlins entertaining people. Then I noticed I could help people. So I decided I could help people. So I decided to do this. It's a knack I can't quite explain it."

"What about Psychic phenomena ?"

"Well it's real. I can tell you that. People get comfort but there's so much more than that. I'm always learning."

"It all looks interesting Mr Bream. I'm disturbed about the events surrounding the demise of Mrs Simmons though. Can you tell me where you were last night?"

"I was attending a séance last night in Addley Road. It runs from Aviemore Road to Thomson Road. Number 43 actually. It was Mrs Emilia Asquith. I was there until nine. Also present were John Alcott, Louisa Parsons and Felicity Crooke. We left at approximately nine o'clock."

"If I go there will Mrs Asquith be able to tell me you were there?"

"Yes she's about seventy but she has all her faculties about her."

"We thanks for your time Mr Bream. Let me know if you know anything more about Mrs Simmons."

"Yes of course."

As they left Justin Woods stood by the car as Beresford looked at the house. "A right David Koresh if ever I saw one." Woods observed.

"I beg your pardon?"

"He is a Messianic figure. I'm not fooled by the talk. "

"That's why I have to make enquiries. See if he's legit."

"Yes Sir." Woods said and got in.

The Green weald Site in the Albion Valley had been excavated because it was a site of historic interest. The site had been an industrial site originally.

Fishbourne Inks and Mail Finn Productions had there factories there.

Beresford read through his notes as Woods braced the afternoon traffic of shoppers trying to get to the business Park and eventually gain entry to the site. When he got out of the car Beresford carefully looked through his notes again and approached the Portacabin bearing the logo "Green Weald Site. Authorised Personnel only." He opened the door to find a flustered secretary thumbing through some notes. "Oh hello, can I help you?"

"Yes , I'm DI Beresford and this DC Woods . Could we speak to Mr Beresford please?"

"I'll just see if he's ready." She quickly got up and opened the door of a very small room and came out again."

"He'll see you now." She indicated the door .

"Of course." Beresford lead the way into the small room. Andrew was a tall man about six foot two, slim for his height but had a body kept in good condition. He had a lean face one might associate with a scholar with a keen mind.

"Yes gentlemen what can I do for you ?" He gestured to the chair for them to sit down.

"We're here to talk about death of Mrs Joan Simmons."

"Never heard of her."

"No . She had some dealings with Arnold Bream of the Albion Psychic society. "

"Arnold." Andrew nodded his head sagely.

"Yes , I've seen some of his work. Bit of a rogue if you ask me. How can I help?"

"Could you tell me a little about the site and what you're

doing here?"

"Yes, I think we have an Anglo Saxon village. I've found a cairn and a burial mound for the chieftain and several bits of bronze armour and shields . In the left part of the excavation near the motorway I found what looked like a burial site of a Saxon Queen. The river Witham runs through the Albion Valley. The banks of the river have been moved a bit but there are signs of amphibian dwellings there. The water table is only twenty feet deep. There is evidence of a pagan altar and Pagan sacrifices took place. This was obviously before the Roam invasion , so part of the site probably dates back to a Pre Christian era before Alfred the great.

My staff includes Pat Shaw a student from Bristol. Paddy Coombes and Helen Mansfield from London. Pat Shaw had digs locally and met some chap called Martin Grimshaw . It turned out he was a Goth and had keen interest in the dig. Helen immediately gave him the cold shoulder. However for all his Goth clothes and wearing crucifixes she could tell he was a harmless anorak. "

"I see Mr Blandford could you tell me more about your meeting with the Psychic society?"

Blandford drew a breath . "Well basically I wanted to generate some local interest. I asked Mr Bream to come down and hold a séance at the site. I knew Arnold and it seemed like a harmless wheeze at the time. Of course we had a good attendance. Martin Grimshaw and about twenty Goths turned up. _Plus quite a few members of the public. Basically there was Celia Pheeney. Joan Simmons, and some of my staff, Paddy Coombes and Pat Shaw.

Well the séance got going with an audience of about thirty Arnold does a passable speaking in tongues. Now I don't know if Paddy dropped some bad acid or Crystal Meth o0r if he was just plain frightened, but he acted up a storm.

He claimed he was possessed by a spirit . Well naturally

Arnold sensing a prop acts up. He claims there was a spirit of an evil ,Saxon Chieftain in the burial site and we should close it up. There's a stir amongst the crowd I can tell you.

However Ann gets up absolutely disgusted after a few minutes as well as Joan. A few members of the audience looked quite pale shortly afterwards. "

"What about Paddy?"

"He's getting over it slowly. I should have made allowance for Paddy he's a good worker."

"Did it promote interest in your site?"

"Well Mister Grimshaw was impressed . After the séance he kept his distance."

"Was there anyone there who would have constituted a threat to Mrs Simmons do you think? An altercation or argument?"

"No , I can honestly say I didn't see anything of that nature.

"Do you think I could interview Paddy at any time?"

"Yes, he's in the trench digging. Now I'll get him if you like."

"Please."

"As Blandford left the office Beresford turned to Woods. "Well what do you think?"

"I think holding a séance in a site of historical interest is a dodgy thing. They want as much privacy as possible to guarantee their integrity of their findings. "

"That's right Justin . You would have thought that wouldn't you?" I think Mr Blandford wants his shot on time team. "

Presently Blandford returned with Paddy Coombes who was the same height as Blandford . He had dark short hair and a beard. "Hello gentlemen Can I help you?" He sat down as Blandford made his excuses and left.

"If you could answer some basic questions Mr Blandford I would be very grateful. "

"Basically what can you tell me about Saxon Society?"

"Well the Saxons occupied the Ilse of Thanet under an agreement with the British King Vortigern. This was about the fourth century . The Saxons had no Kings but Ealdemen. A military stronghold or Gaue was their characteristic settlement. The Germanic gods were Woden , Frigg, goddesses were Eostre and Hretha. All pretty straight forward really."

"Okay so when Mr Blandford agreed to have a séance take place here did this upset you?"

Coombes seemed agitated . "Yes, I'm not a religious person, but I think sometimes you should leave well enough alone. I mean we're digging human remains and artefacts. I prefer hard science to a paranormal freak show. The presence of the Goths and the audience turned it into a carnival."

"Quite understandable could you tell me if you had any previous acquaintance with members of the audience?"

"No , I'd never seen them before."

"No , I see and that of course would include Joan Simmons?"

"Joan Simmons no, I've never heard of her."

"Are you sure? Not a chance encounter perhaps?"

"Outside the dig I live in Lewisham in digs. I don't socialise here so no."

"I see well thank you for your time Mr Coombes."

As they left the site Woods turned to Beresford . "What was all that about?

All you had to do was ask him if he knew Mr Simmons. Why the preamble?"

Two things he displayed signs of distress at the séance. That means he could have drug problems or dependency problems.

Both these things would have hindered his ability to give a coherent explanation. "

"So?"

"So , I asked him questions about the dig that would have required extensive knowledge of his subject. Also to see if he was corporae mensanae. That's to see if he was able to give a co-ordinated response. "

"And?"

"And he was quite convincing. Just someone who was highly strung . So when he told me he didn't know Mrs Simmons I believed him."

"Blimey talk about round the houses."

"Yes, Woods indeed." He paused, "I'm still interested in this Martin Grimshaw. I think we should go to the local pub and investigate later."

Iris Williams sat in the front room. Thankfully Lambert Hodge had stepped up to the plate as far as running the farm was concerned. Andrew had lodgings in the town knowing full well the antipathy that his sister in law held him in. Beatrice was taking it quite well considering the circumstances.

Obviously the shock had not seeped through yet. Through Iris rationalised that Beatrice had an ability to focus on things   that Iris had never been able to grasp. In that way she was like her father . Beatrice was good at science subjects. She had done well at college . Her path to University looked untroubled. Of course the farm virtually ran itself. The meat processing plant, the dairy produce and the cattle seemed to run on auto pilot. Lambert was an absolute soldier maintaining the farm with Lukasz. Iris had another priority of course that was Stanley.

Stanley her son was not academically successful as Beatrice. This of course was not a set-back. Stanley was good at mechanics and good at repairing tractors and equipment round the farm. He had a lot in common with Harry on the Kessington Farm. Of course with any luck he should have enough good grades to get in to agricultural college and help manage the farm with Lambert.

She knew that Gordon had plans to sell the farm to Beasley in the summer. Now that had been put on hold . Lambert told her he wouldn't mind if the plan went through. In truth Iris felt she didn't want to go down this route becauseit meant uprooting Stanley and Beatrice. Winter seemed far way.

It was a freezing cold day in Freedom Square in Kharkov . Whilst Jud Fareham snuggled down in an Astrakhan coat smoking a Cuban cigar. He felt not untypically conspicuous as he waited for his associate to turn up. Vlad Vykovsky was a product of his generation. The nouveau riche that very nearly didn't make it. The collaboration of Putin's government and Yukanovich meant an immediate disaffection with population. Vykovsky's instinct was to withhold investment. Thankfully the Orange revolution saw a rise in his fortunes in electronics with extensive use of the internet. He formed a company in derelict buildings in Kharkov that made flat screen televisions and other components making them a viable competitor to Korea.

As Jud finished his coffee the remains of the Pirogi was left on his plate He saw a figure opposite him ."Good evening Vlad Glad you could make it."

Vlad looked over at him questioningly. "What is it you say in your country there are two certainties death and taxes?
"

"Something like that. What's on your mind Vlad? The exchange rate is going down . That's going down . That's good news for you and your boys that means raw materials are cheaper."

"Mr McAwber would have been proud of you. You seem to forget that we've had five centuries of Peter the Great, Catherine the Great and Ivan the terrible. All in their own way pessimists of a sort. Pessimism lurks deep in the Ukrainian soul. "

"But you're a dreamer Vlad, is that not so? Only a dreamer could build a factory deep in the outback of the Ukrainian wilderness and hope to make a go of it."

"Have you agreed terms with Mr Eschlager yet Mr Fareham? I have a fleet of lorries and a thousand workers waiting for your orders. I know you're waiting for the right moment. "

"Ah as you say the right moment Vlad. I'm meeting Walter in DusseldorfIn a few days' time. By the time you get a phone call o0n Tuesday morning the

deal should be signed and sealed. "

"Good, I'm looking forward to doing business."

"Well I suppose it's a good omen. After all these are interesting times. "

"Interesting times yes. The Vietnamese have built the biggest Buddhist Temple in Europe here in Kharkov . Gorky Park has a large number of attractions. We could even do a dissipated rerun of Doctor Zhivago."

"I beg your pardon?"

"Forgive me . I do not underestimate your country's ability for nostalgia."

"Well if there's nothing more Vlad it's been interesting . I'll be ringing for a couple of days. As I say the news should be good . Do you have any plans for the future?"

"Only expansion to Siberia , I'm not sure."

"Well then Do Svidaniya my friend."

"Good bye."

Jud walked off into the dense urban landscape of Kharkov. It's interesting architecture a momentary blur to him . Vlad Vykovsky comforted himself with the feeling that in a few weeks new markets could be opening up in Germany. France and Holland and England . That he was undercutting the market was not a consideration that after all was the pitfall of competition. Martin Grimshaw sat in his usual spot in the Green Dragon as Maria Krantz sat next to him. "Well Marty what's new?"

"Nothing if Mr Beresford of his majesty's constabulary is at this momentchecking my alibi regarding the demise of Mrs Joan Simmons. It looks like I'm in the clear."

"Were you ever in the clear Martin? You call yourself the Grand Wizardof the inner circle . I should imagine Mr Beresford has you figured for some pretty powerful amphetamines and drug use."

"He may have Maria , but you know in your Lower Saxony Heart that I'm as innocent as a new born babe. "

Maria shifted uncomfortably , she did not always take kindly to being reminded of her German heritage. "A new born babe with a liking for Burton Ale and pies may be."

"The Saxons worshipped Frigg " Thoresden and Odin. They had a fairly Liberal regime even though they believed in slavery. The Druids believed in a sort of void and human sacrifice. They believed in a sort of Pantheism investing the groves and woodlands with god like deities. I'm not so hot on sacrifice but I believe the woods and trees are vital to us."

"The only thing you believe in at the moment is too much Woodland ale you've been drinking."

"I'm worried Maria. I've been talking to Arnold Bream . He said the last time he saw Joan was a week ago . She seemed happy , not depressed in the

least. Arnold is a clairvoyant."

"You mean he's a fraud?"

"That doesn't mean he's a Charlatan."

"No I'm saying I believe him though when he suggests there was something wrong with Joan , I could sense he knew there was something wrong with her."

"What do you think happened?"

"Well at first I suppose it was that husband .I talked to Joan briefly

after the séance . She told me about Alec, a high flyer. A very typical pattern emerges. A go-getter, typical of his ilk, fast cars, fast lifestyle, fast women. The last commodity being the last straw for her."

"She was drawn to Psychic research because her friend Ann Cameron lived only a few streets away, and they met in a supermarket in Thirton. You see if her husband didn't kill her then it could be someone attending the séance. Someone at the Green Weald Site saw her and thought her an obvious target."

Suddenly Maria looked concerned. "That was one of us. No, that can't be right. Rita, Charlene, Agatha, I'd stake my life on them. Same as Bob, Charlie, and Vince they're Teddy Bears. "

"Yeah , they're good for a beer up or getting stoned . However physical exertion is not their strong suit. Still the mystery remains."

"I've got to consult the crystal. I'm sure I can find a way through this."

"This is a time for clear thinking . I'm afraid I'm going to sound like my friend Arnold . You're going to have to keep your wits about you in the next few weeks . I'm not sure about everything but I've got a few ideas. Your spirits can't harm us , but they might not help us Maria be careful."

Jud Fareham freshly arrived in Dusseldorf Airport . He quickly found a cab to take him to Heineman's restaurant in Koenig's Allee. Once there he caught a corner table and ordered some Schnitzel and fried eggs along with some Neirsteiner . The Lieder by Richard Strauss Op 27 was gently floating in the background as the suburban traffic flowed by.

He picked up his mobile and dialled Eschlager . He lived on the North end of the city. Eschlager picked up the contact immediately. "Herr Fareham

good news I hope."

"Of course Walter, what else? I have arranged a good price . I can arrange a delivery on Tuesday. "

"Was it the price we agreed?"

""200 Euros a piece retailing at 300 Euros. A 62" smart tv. Competitive you could clear stocks easily."

"And the other products?"

"Computers at 200 Euros obviously Ukrainian with the best trade names . Everything is ready to go."

"Where can I meet you?"

"The usual , here in Heineman's Koenig's Allee."!

"Sehr Guht. Auf Weidersehen."

"Yep, cheerio." Jud said folding his mobile . The Vier Op 26 continued . The dulcet tones of Fischer Dieskau somehow blunting the edge of reality, while the good citizens of Dusseldorf walking through the streets pursued their livelihood. Walter as good as his word emerged about half an hour later. He appeared flustered and yet relieved. "I'm sorry I couldn't go with you

to Kharkov. Relations have not being the best. "

"Don't mention it Walter. I spoke to Vykovsky . He was more than glad to close your agreement . The shipment will be ready by Tuesday . Delivery is only a formality."

"I think it will give us an edge in Essen, Spain ,France and the UK. We can use the Ukraine for other things as well. Economic conditions are so depressedthere we can capitalise on this for a while."

"Of course Walter it's only a matter of time before we switch markets and start all over again. "

"This is the country of Beethoven, Goethe, Wagner. Yet we the Barbarians at our gates. So many Gastarbeiter we have become strangers in our own land. I'm not nostalgic for Hitler but we still have something to offer the World. I thought the New Economy would kill us. "

"Yes Walter you are shrewd . You praise your country but you don't trust it an inch. You bring in foreign goods and undercut wages. "

"Never mind we get the goods and start distributing Herr Vykovsky will be a rich man. I speculate to accumulate , you get your commission. "

"Of course Walter that's my price. " A thought that kept him going until he got to the UK.

Iris waited in the Chapel Crematorium in Kessington Cemetery. Stanley and Beattie were with her. Beatrice was very emotional when she got back from University. This to some extent surprised Iris , because in her experience she had always found Beatrice a cold fish. However after a chat on Thursday night she found Beatrice had come together especially after a chat with Stanley

her brother. Andrew of course arrived just after the hearse was coming into the cemetery. Lambert Hodge and his wife Anne plus Lukasz and his wife Jean were in attendance plus the workers from the farm. There was also Mr and Mrs Mathews as well as Catherine, Amanda and Harry and Gregory. Carol Broadly had arrived about an hour ago. Whatever the animosity she had towards Andrew she managed to sublimate . Over to one side of course hardly noticeable were DI Beresford and DC Woods.

The reverend Wallis stepped in as Pastor on this occasion. "It comes in every once in a while in the back waters of a community like Thirton that a leading light , some one with an insight come amongst us. " He said starting off the eulogy. "Gordon Williams was such a man. Out of the ashes of the foot and mouth epidemic Gordon Williams managed to salvage Culompton Farm . Building an Abattoir with the latest technology and monopolising his position in the meat trade. He rebuilt Culompton Farm to its former glory rarely seen since the seventeenth century. It's not often in our lives we ever

have the privilege of genius amongst us. However Gordon Williams was such a man."

Iris concentrated during these moments on something else. "Of course Gordon was all these things . " She thought."He was my husband , a rather fallible and sensible man. I just got to keep my composure .Let this moment pass. I've got to keep it for Beatrice's sake." She thought.

After the last ritual of the ceremony had been read out and the congregation were moved out on to the lobby while the music played. Jupiter " by Holst, A request by her husband funnily enough. He never

wanted people left feeling sad.

Carol approached her as the workers , Lambert and Lukasz wandered away. "How are you feeling Iris?"

"Fine , I've got Lambert looking after the farm. You can see that."

"You won't be selling up?"

"No of course not. Not until Stanley and Beatrice have finished their education. "

"Beasley offered you a good price ."

"I know but Stanley needs a future. I'm sure about Beatrice.

But Stanley needs something. "

Carol cast a look over the congregation . "I could have a word with Andrew but I can't be bothered I mean what's past is past . I'll be leaving next Monday. I may spend some time in London . I'll be seeing you before you go. Are you sure you're alright?"

"I'll be fine thanks."

"Good , I don't know if I'm leaving Gordon behind or taking the farm with me."

"A bit of both. Speak to the insurance company. They must come up with some sort of insurance package for something like this."

"No Inspector Beresford said there are still some suspicious circumstances. They're keeping the file open for now."

"I suppose it's for the best." Carol said as she made her departure.

Beatrice stood for a while in the Church as the mourners dispersed. She had got to know Kessington as her home and was happy to see Amanda and Harry again. Sibling rivalry was not enough to disguise her joy at seeing Stanley . However the fog of knowing she would never see her father again lay over everything.

She remembered some movies her father had made of Serbia and Croatia during the previous war torn years. A BBC reporter was standing to one side and she saw a very much younger version of her father trying to describe what happened in Srebrenica. "What's happened here is a tragedy of unparalleled proportions . Thousands of Muslim men have died . Thousands of Muslim women have been raped. We have stood witness to a massacre and have done nothing." The indignation was palpable on his face. The International Court of Human Rights later prosecuted Ratko Mladic but the damage had been done. A tracking shot that was taken coming away from the town of Srebrenica caught some of the gaunt faces of women who had managed to escape the massacre. A line came to her unbidden. "Out of the suffering strongest souls , the most massive characters are seamed with scars. Martyrs have put on their coronation robes glittering with fire and through their lives have first seen the gates of heaven." Who was that? Khalil Gibran that was it.

To his credit her father gave no hint of the scars he bore in his time with The International Court of Human Rights. She remembered something Amanda said a few months before University came up. She said "You never

really remember what people have said when they pass on. You only think you do. They seem to fade away almost unwillingly. Amanda was a bit of a feather

brain. She remembered the occasion was the funeral of an Uncle of Amanda's in Essex. She was down for a while but she soon cheered up that was Amanda.

Memory came again in a tight loop in her brain. It was a home movie from a video recorder . It showed a young Beatrice about five in a fluffy pink jumper

and Gordon only thirty five picking her up and putting her on a Shetland Pony.

It was after the reception and the guests had departed and she sat in the kitchen and she started to read a novel or at least distance herself for a while. Her mother came in. "How are you darling?"

"Coping I expect . Mum could you tell me I know I shouldn't ask. What really happened?"

"What a question but relevant I suppose." She paused. "Well here it is. your father was bringing supplies on that truck of his. He finished driving.

He stopped the lorry . He had some sandwiches with him. I think he put the sandwiches on an oil drum were there was some old weed killer. He ate a few sandwiches and felt woozy . Well he went over to the lorry and pulled down the lever . The result was the hook came down and hit him on the head. By this time he was suffering from a heart attack brought on by the weed killer."

"I see or don't see . He's done this before . How did he manage to poison himself?"

"That I don't know. Inspector Beresford is looking into it."

"How is Stanley?"

"Like his father . A chip off the old block as far as I can see. Have you spoken to him ?"

"Yes, it's as you say the same old Stanley. Still ,underneath I think he's shaking."

"We all are Beatty. We all are." She said. One of the things she would do before she went back to university would be to have a long talk with Lambert. It wouldn't bring her father back but it would make her easier in her mind.

The Green Dragon was a pub of changing times. It started life as the Farmers arms . It serviced a population of shift workers who were gainfully employed in the Kessington valley . After the advent of the seventies this gave way to the service industries. This featured retail shops , selling household items such as furniture, DIY, tools and equipment. This meant the Farmer's Arms saw a dip in clientele. With the arrival of computer games and Virtual reality an inventive owner changed the name to the Green Dragon. This encourage a new clientele of Goths and Teenagers.

This of course was not entirely welcome to the local populace. Of course since the participation of the Psychic Society interest in in the Green Dragon had increased. The local populace were in quiet rebellion. Tremors would no doubt later be felt later on. However after the séance there were no reports of break ins to the site or any mysterious rituals being performed. Martin

Grimshaw a former employee of British Telecom and an engineer had become a customer of the pub. At worst this meant going to festivals and parties when they came his way. This also attracted some drug use and a self-destructive life style.

Grimshaw however was discriminating. He only played the outlaw. He was careful in his alcohol consumption and discriminating in his friends. He had a genuine interest in the occult and the paranormal. He had amounted some capital and had his sights on setting up a tattoo parlour. When he went to the séance at the Green Weald site with some of his friends from the Green Dragon he realised it could be awkward . In this respect he was only thinking of his friends rather than himself. This was because they had interests invested in the exchange of illegal highs that might come to light if the Police raided them. Of course in thinking of this he was also thinking of his chances of setting up a shop by the Albion Valley Railway Station.

Some of the younger kids looked up to him as an authority figure. He felt they were middle class kids halfway between University and business. Therefore he didn't take them entirely seriously. Yet the success of his enterprise depended on the empathy he had with his customers. He noticed how one member of the archaeology team had freaked out at the séance. He laughed to himself because he had seen many people like Coombes who had flipped on Ecstasy. Conceivably Coombes was a similar casualty. Even so the site and it's history interested him. He had talked to Blandford on occasion and found him quite helpful when talking of the site and what it held.

Of course his one interest was the Pagan site. Obviously very little was known about it. What little he did know left a vacuum for a whole realm of fantasy . Realistically though one Pagan site was not an excuse for a party or a concert to raise Pagan spirits.

As they sat back in the office Thirton Police station , Beresford waited for Woods to put in his paperwork and said "I'm sorry Justin , we've got one more port of call to make. "

"Which is where Sir?"

"Well as gathering evidence I noticed that one name kept cropping up did you notice?"

"No I was taking down notes . It must have slipped my mind."

"Martin Grimshaw self-styled leader of the Goths. I think the best place where we might locate him is the Green Dragon. So here we go."

This of course was not entirely welcome to customers when Beresford arrived . Of course since the participation of the Albion Psychic society some of the clientele had gone up-market. It seemed peaceful enough when Beresford arrived . The evening was beginning to go into full swing.

"Right what are you having?"

"Lemonade Sir."

"Same as me. Now the question is which one is Martin Grimshaw?"

Justin surveyed the crowd with a shrewd eye , "No Sir , I

can't help you there."

"Okay let me see." " As he waited to attract the attention of the barmaid he looked upon the young fresh faces of Albion Valley's youth generation. Amongst them he could see an older crowd but not by much. Over to one side by the door sitting down with long black hair and older than the others by a good twenty years sat a man taking an interest in a girl a few years his junior.

"At a guess I'd say that's him by the door Justin. " He caught the attention of the barmaid who duly served him up the drinks he ordered. "Okay come with me I'll do the talking . You can leave your phone and your notes ."

"Okay Sir."

He sat opposite the man with the leather jacket and introduced himself .

"Good evening Mr Grimshaw . You don't mind if I introduce myself to you?"

"Of course please yourself . Why, are you the old Bill?"

"Police? Yes of course . I'm DI Beresford and this DC Woods . Would you mind answering a few questions?"

"Fire away Inspector. Anything I can do to help?"

"Right, Mr Grimshaw , you're getting on a bit , isn't this a bit jejune for you?"

"If you mean am I a superannuated teenager. I will confess , I'm trying to have another go at life."

"Alright let me ask the question another way. What path in life led you to be here? Why aren't you a married man?"

"I started out as a British Telecom Engineer. I found the pub here focused on the music I liked. I could have a good time . I take an interest in Medieval Culture and beliefs and take an interest in the supernatural . I've never settled down . Couldn't say why I'd been employed by British Telecom for ten years then they made a lot of people redundant. Bang went my prospects. I had a job as a sign painter. After a couple of years they went bust as well. I'm clean. I don't take drugs.

"Which leads me to another question. What interest did you have in the Green Weald Site?"

"I knew Arnold Bream leader of the Albion Psychic Society. He's an interesting character, I wanted to see how the séance played out."

"How do you make it as a Goth?"

"Some of them look up to me as an authority figure. They're middle class kids halfway between chic and respectable. I don't take them entirely seriously. I have some capital saved up. I'm thinking of opening up a tattoo shop by the Albion valley station. If it falls through it looks like it's back to the old grind."

"Which would be?"

"Sign painting or cabling at a pinch."

"Could you tell me your experiences at the séance?"

"At the Green Weald Site? Yeah, I noticed how one of the archaeology team freaked out at the séance. I've seen many people like him also freaked out. Maybe it was a bad vibe or an illegal high. Conceivably Coombes was a

similar casualty. The site and its history interested me."

"Did you notice anything strange there?"

"Yes and no. There were some of these guys there." He gestured to some people standing nearby. Beresford recognised this as a sign of group solidarity.

"That's as strange as anyone could wish for.

"That's not what I was asking. I mean new faces. People

you hadn't seen before."

"No not really . The usual suspects . I'd seen the crowd from the Psychic Society before. Ann Cameron , Joan Simmons, . No one else springs to mind."

"It's Joan Simmons we're interested in. She was stabbed to death last night. We think there maybe a connection."

Grimshaw paused . "Really ? How awful . I really only knew her name and a few words from Bream. That was all."

" So Mr Grimshaw thanks for your help. If you hear of anything you'll let us know."

"Of course. I'm sorry to hear of this . I suppose Arnold was upset."

"Yes or at least surprised . Goodbye Mr Grimshaw."

Beresford and Woods got up and left as Grimshaw resumed his conversation with the young lady next to him. "Did you get all that?"

"Yes Sir."

"It was interesting."

"I honestly didn't notice Sir."

"Yes, not because of what he said, but what he didn't say."

"I see Sir." He said as they walked out of the pub.

Martin Grimshaw lived in a little run down flat on the Weald Road about a mile away from the Green Weald Site. It was still in the industrial area of the Albion Valley, but in the residential sector . It had been a busy day , he had been to see Andrew Blandford . He asked him if he could walk round the site. He promised not to disturb anything. Maria Krantz was with him.

Blandford was defensive at first anxious in case anything got in the way of his research. After a moment he could see the hunger in Martin's eyes and gave his consent. Together they went to the various pits that had been unearthed.

Of course there were a few Broaches that showed some sort of advanced Bronze Age culture. Various pits showed evidence of Amphibian dwellings.

There were some tanning pits for dyeing . Most interestingly there were some pits that showed some that were burial pits that had magical seals. Maria tried to feel in her own way what significance they could have. However she felt she was unsuccessful. Martin reminded her that the significance would have been more obvious if the River Witham would have been more obvious when the river Witham was a navigable river. She argued the burial pits had a greater significance , the marauding bands of thieves had avoided them. This argued some importance to the druids.

The morning ended unsatisfactorily . However they both agreed the Green Weald Site merited another investigation. Later that night they retired with a bottle of Chablis and an early night.

A few nights later a shower of rain came to Weald Road and a visitor came to call. A knock came to the door . Martin got up and answered it."Oh it's you."

"Yes , I thought I'd come."

"When I heard of the death of Joan I'd no idea you'd come as well."

"It's been a long time Martin."

"It certainly has. Thirty years ago . It seems time plays tricks on us."

"Aren't you going to invite me in?"

"Of course , please." The visitor came in as he shut the door."

"I was just enjoying a glass of Chablis . Would you like

some?"

"I don't see why not."

They both sat around the table . "It was a cold evening when you left, rather like this one . The harbour lights were out in Portsmouth. I remember walking

along the sea front . It rained occasionally . It was a melancholy night you never explained why you left. "

"I didn't have to."

"Really? I suppose not . Then again you were always independent. "

"Did you want me to stay? You know I would have . We argued. I'd had enough. Martin you're an incurable sentimentalist. You hang on to things long after their significance has vanished. "

"As far as I remember , you always had a bad time engaging with people ."

"Is that what you mean with James?"

"You brought that up not me. I didn't blame you"

"I had no other choice he needed me."

"James came along for the ride like we all did. James got hooked on heroin. He became dependent. He couldn't handle it. You threw him a lifebelt and you ditched me. I'm not complaining God knows. Did you honestly think you could save him."

"I thought so. I thought we could start again . I went to Southampton. I got some new digs . It was all going well. He was going to kick heroin. We were going to have a new start. It was all so simple."

"What happened?" Martin asked fatalistically.

"After the third month he fell back. The methadone

wasn't working like it should. He tried Marijuana , he tried alcohol, he tried downers, he tried uppers. Nothing was any good. In May I found him in a roadside café he hadn't been home for three days. I could tell by his glazed eyes what he'd done."

"What did you do?"

"I took him back to his flat . I cleaned him up. I made sure he was comfortable and left him. I finally gave up to. About a fortnight later I was sitting in a café by the sea front . My friend Trish told me they found him in his flat. He od'd by accident."

"Yeah. I heard something of the sort. James Holroyd late of this parish esteemed member of the community."

"I remember the harbour nights. I mean the long nights we had together, I never forgot them. We could have had something together if we tried."

"Why did you leave?"

"I explained or at least I thought I did."

"It always seemed we lived our lives in parallel lines"

"Quantum theory is always a good substitute for good old fashioned romance. That's what I like about you Martin. You're a surrealist at heart."

"Of course." He explained reluctantly.

The morning light crept reluctantly along the branches outside the flat in Weald Road. The Crepuscular light thus afforded by the first light of dawn showed very little in the windows of the living room that gave on to the view of the road. The usual chorus of errant crows welcomed the primal dawn scene again yielding little relief to the suburban landscape thus evident outside.

The occasional shift worker came down the road to catch the morning Train, thus making their daily pilgrimage to the

Albion Valley Railway Station.

An electric milk van silently stopped and at a few addresses dropped off milk, Yoghurt, and may be a couple of loaves of bread.

As the light grew in the street, although not visible to the casual passer- by, the light grew on Martin Grimshaw's front room. The candle by the big chair had burned down . Martin himself sat in the chair . His own sightless eyes stared out in to the street. His jacket and his shirt had been torn open, and his entrails lay in front of him. His face no, longer capable of any emotion stared sightlessly into eternity as if to seek explanation for such an indignity.

Beresford made a discreet entrance to to Weal Road number 43 . He could see the ambulance outside. He could also see the Pathologist hadn't arrived yet. Bernard Thomas was like a drowning sailor surrounded by a sea of misfortunes . "I'm sorry Chris , I was looking for some one on speed dial. You're the only one I could think of. I know Archie Foulsham . He's a proper Albion Valley Criminal. I know all the good honest villains around here. I don't know what all this is about."

Beresford looked at Bernard somewhat non-plussed . Balefully Thomas pointed to the corpse on the chair. "This is the late Martin Grimshaw or what's left of him. Can you make anything of this?"

Beresford looked down at the corpse. Grimshaw looked blissfully unaware of his demise or anything else for that matter. His stomach and rib cage had been torn open , and his lungs had been splayed out , his intestines forming a puddle round the floor beneath him.

"Without consulting someone , I can't really say. I think." He paused " I think it has something to do with a Viking Ritual."

"What sort of thing?" Bernard asked anxiously raising his

voice.

"The way the lungs are splayed out. It was a typical thing Vikings did to their slain enemies. They're doing a dig near here. The site director is Andrew Blandford . I'll ask him to come over and give a hand."

"I'm sorry. I should have thought of it. "

Beresford looked up his mobile phone and rang the number Blandford had given him. It came up with a message . It was interrupted by Blandford himself. "Hello, can I help?"

"Morning , Mister Blandford. I'm afraid I've bad news for you. I'm DI Beresford from Thirton CID. I'm afraid Mr Grimshaw has been murdered. The circumstances are such that I think you may be of some use. Do you think
You could help out?"

"Well I'm in the middle of processing some documents. Will it be long do you think?"

"Hopefully not."

"Where would that be?"

"Number 43 Weald Road. It's not far from you in the Albion Valley."

"Hmm. I've got it that's Martin Grimshaw's place?"

"Yes."

"I'll be right over. ." As he hung up another car drew up. It was Mosely

"Hello people " He said as he came into the house."Well Inspector can you direct me to the victim?"

Wordlessly Beresford pointed to the armchair facing the front window. Thomas stood to one side, eyeing both people suspiciously. "My.my this one was angry. I can see that." Beresford went outside to meet Blandford , while Mosely inspected the corpse. About five minutes later Blandford drove up in a Cherokee Chief.

Beresford told him the protocols first of all. "First you have to put on a white suit and overshows and gloves and a mask. I'd rather you saw the vic yourself . You can probably throw some light on what is there. "

Blandford entered the house thus attired while Mosely was examining the corpse. "Crikey what mess."

"Exactly . but what observations do you have Mr Blandford?"

"Yes, this is reference to Einorr and Halfdun. A Blood Eagle in a ritual method of execution , Halfdun was ritually executed with sword and cut the ribs all from the backbone and drew the lungs out and gave them to Odin

for the victory he had won. Oh dear it's Martin. " He said , his composure momentarily slipping.

Mosely gave a chill little laugh. "You do realise Doctor Blandford that with so much information you've made yourself a prime suspect?"

"Of course Dr Mosely . Though I was in Peckham last night enjoying a good Beaujolais with a good friend of mine. ." He said barely recovering his composure.

"That's alright Doctor Blandford . You came here at my request. I'm grateful for your help. "

"Though whether it was an enthusiast or devotee of Viking practice I doubt somehow. There is a good case to say it was a literary invention. "

"Then" Mosely said "That would mean the author of these crimes has a good education. "

"Unusual I know but yes I would say that."

"That rules out half of Albion Valley suspects at one stroke." Thomas said slowly.

"Well it looks like more work for me I'm afraid." Beresford said.

"Grimshaw had links with the Albion Psychic Society . They did have a séance at the Great Weald Site. I've had one unresolved crime there already. A Miss Joan Simmons.

"Simmons of course." Mosely said. "I finished the autopsy yesterday. Death by strangulation. Probably a nylon cord or a skipping rope." He paused for a minute . "If this is the same person, I see a worrying sign the anger is building up. " Beresford drove Dr Blandford back to the site while Mosely inspected the corpse.

Henry Stein was from old money. That is to say his grandfather made a lot of money out of manufacturing and selling furniture. From there he sold the products to the financially emancipated working class after the second World War. Along with the Cooperative Society and their hire purchase offers he was able to sell perfectly respectable armchairs , three piece suites , sofas, sideboards , chest of drawers and Wardrobes and chairs at a price they could afford.

Of course the end of the second World War afforded even a second bonanza. These of course were the labour saving devices called washing machines, electric kettles ,and vacuum cleaners that helped make life

easier. The disposable income of the average household went up as the service industries grew. The company of Stein and Co were as most manufacturing companies suffering a manufacturing malaise. Henry Stein who saw his company grow from a back street in Bethnal Green to a major holdings company on the stock exchange had one son. That was Steven who had himself grown to middle age and was in the process of winding the company down. As people graduated from council houses to mortgaged properties and bought their furniture from chain stores throughout the country. Most of the labour had gone to third world countries . Stephen had reluctantly taken their business abroad. Stephen had a spacious fifteen room house in Kessington Common with electric gates . Henry his son was a prodigy immensely talented , Harry however had no time for business. His main talent was getting into trouble with the Police . A few drug busts ensured he changed his dependency habits . He only occasionally drank alcohol. However he had taken up a passionate interest in alternate religions . He had a house in Weald Road. He called it the "Sanctuary" on the far side away from Martin Grimshaw's flat. It was stuck on a hill with a prime view of the Albion Valley.

Any time of the day or night there would be a lost soul soaking up the charity provided. Henry was a sociable character.

As far as Bernard Thomas could make out Henry was sincere in his interest in Druidism and had been to Stone Henge a couple of times for the Solstice. Andrew Blandford knew him by reputation but never seriously considered him a threat to the site.

Martin Grimshaw had been a regular visitor this much Beresford discovered by talking to his girlfriend Maria Krantz in the "Green Dragon" as it was slowly filling up. "Who else did he know there?"

"Well it's hard to say . First I must emphasise that Martin was serious and dedicated in his interest . There were others at Stein's house who were quite interested , they formed a fringe group. There was Gerald Moore he was a Brummie, he came down looking for a job . As far as I can tell he had a degree in History from Nottingham University . However he's between jobs at the

moment. I would say that was Martin's best friend . Gerald

specialised in early history of England such as King Alfred and Ethelred ."

"Was there anyone else?"

"Mary Green. She came from Lewisham . She has a degree in English Literature . She had a teaching job in Deptford then she gave that up. She had a conviction for soft drugs, again nothing serious."

As he sat there he noticed the pub filled up . Maria slowly grew silent and then made her excuses and left. As he got through his second pint he noticed the pub filling up. He recognised Graham Moore sitting at a table

by the window.

He sauntered over. "Can I talk to you Mr Moore ? "

Moore looked up distrustfully. "What about?"

"About Weald Road you know the movement and things?"

"You mean Henry Stein? " He shrugged his shoulders non committedly.

"Of course. I suppose but a in a bit less conspicuous place may be."

"I've got a car outside a white Renault . It's down by the telephone box. I'll go first . I'll meet you down there."

"Okay."

Beresford finished his pint and walked out to his car. He waited for five minutes thinking Moore wasn't going to show. Then he heard a tapping at the window. Moore was standing outside, he let him in.

"What do you want to know?" Beresford could smell marijuana on his breath but decided to let it pass.

"Could you tell me more about Henry Stein? I mean he's

rich but so what? What's he doing? I mean do they just have a good time? Is there something going on?"

"It's only fun and games as far as I know. That's to say the Druid Religion is quite serious but Stein isn't doing anything illegal."

"Explain it to me. Walk me through it. "

"Well Stein organises his house like a Druid council of Elders. There's Amergin and Bohmaid who's a woman. They organise the council."

"Was he on good terms with his father?"

"You better ask him that . They run a small community up there people come and go. Sooner or later they steal something and Harry gives them their marching orders."

"So Henry runs a tight ship?"

"In a way yes. He has good management skills . Any one with a pronounced antisocial tendencies gets shown the door in no uncertain terms. "

"Out of the people you knew was there anyone who knew Martin well?"

"Maria knew him well. That's all I knew really. "

"Any girlfriends you remember ?"

"Before Maria I think there was Helen Edwards. He dipped his hands into many things. He did have a go at being a commercial artist. He gave that up when Helen Left him. "

"These people in the group what are their real names?"

"Amergin is Geoffrey Duncan. Bohmaid is Angela Payne. Duncan is an accountant in the city with a Pharmaceutical Company. Angela is a consultant with a firm of brokers in the London Wall. Then there's Meg Ruth and Taliesin they're in charge of the livestock and keeping the grounds clean. Meg Ruth is Bridget Downs . She was a parking Warden and Taliesin was a park keeper

in Wandsworth. Both have good manual skills . Then there's Rebeo Nemedean was a catering assistant at Thirton Hospital. She's a good cook and Dormoli

helps out in the kitchen. His real name is Ian Stevens. He's a qualified Chef he works in a department store in Thirton.

Well, they run the day to day affairs . They get the usual head bangers and flake jobs. They usually sort the wheat from the chaff after a couple of days."

"What's the philosophy of the place?"

"Basically we are all connected by the force of life and inspiration. The Druids call this force Awen and say it's the divine spirit that flows through all things . "

"What sort of deities are we talking here?"

"Well you have Lugh Lamb fadu son of Cam of Cuchulainn known as the Master of Craft. Dogba the Good he's good because of the diversity of his skills. Nianha Argut Lanh also known as Silver Hand because he lost his hand in battle. There's Marrigu , Bobel and Nemhain. The last one is who decides who gets in to the next world. There's Bridget a triple goddess of fire, poetry and the forge. Dion is the God of healing he crafted a magical well that could resurrect any one thrown into it."

"Do they offer sacrifices and homage to their Gods?"

"Only livestock usually nothing really serious."

"Okay Gerry thanks for your help."

"What's this about?"

"It's about Martin . I want to know what happened . Can you tell me anything?"

"Only he was knocking around with Maria Krantz. I'm

not to judge. I think the house is a rich man's folly. Only rich people rise to the top. I mean I'm as spiritual as the next person but I think Harry was born with a silver spoon in his mouth. They're rich people but I didn't get involved. "

"Well thanks for your help Gary. "He took two twenty pound notes from his wallet.

"No really it's fine . If you catch who ever killed Martin, it's fine by me." Beresford put his money back in his wallet.

When he got back in the station next morning he gave Burnham his findings. "What do you think Sir?"

"Well we could run checks on the main personnel. We could send some one in undercover."

"I'll tell Dunkley, see what he says."

Vincent Appleby was a shop keeper in Stalbridge . He ran a shop that sold objet d'art and curios. This sort of shop made its' money out of second hand furniture. This of course reached it's peak in the 1990's. This was because home owners who showed antiques of any value had reached their three score years and ten and passed on. However Mr Appleby was a rare bird among shop keepers because he was aware of social media. He marketed curios and antiques on the internet. He specialised in Broaches and Necklaces. Of course this had run its' course and he was running on empty. His last resort was

Bibliography . Old Atlases and family bibles could just about keep him busy. Stalbridge was pretty much commuter belt territory. He knew pretty much who the regular traders were. They came and they went . It was a surprise when one particular afternoon he found a gentleman with a sunny complexion wearing a Panama hat and a dark blue shirt. "Good afternoon how can I help you?"

"Strange, that's exactly what I was thinking, how can I help you?" Jud Fareham said giving him his best smile.

"I'm sorry I don't understand what do you want?"

"Well Mr Appleby I'm Mr Fareham . I deal in objet d'art and things. I came here looking for a bargain. I'm afraid you're too quick for me. I can see I'm wasting my time. "

"No, please tell me what you want."

"Well I have something here to offer. I have two paintings of dubious authenticity. It was given to me by a dying stockbroker . He was down to his last thousands . This was all he had to bargain with. Like you I'm a business man . I thought I'll buy them . It'll pay for the funeral I suppose. I didn't think twice of it."

Fareham looked at the rickety cupboards and hallstand that populated the front of the shop amongst the faded photographs and books. Appleby's eyes seemed to light up with that most of fleeting of all qualities, hope.

"Yes, go on."

He produced a portfolio. "Well he left these two canvases. They seemed distinctive in a way I couldn't put a finger on. I paid fifty thousand for these two." It was a picture of the congregation leaving the church at Scheveningen by Van Gogh . Fareham nodded , he could see the old man's eyes light up.

"Anything else?" He attempted a smile.

Fareham nodded , he showed him a cubist painting by Picasso . "Le Pigeon aux petit pois." Appleby smiled sensing his disadvantage . "But my dear friend I'm sorry to inform you that you were hopelessly duped. These paintings are forgeries. They have to be. I'll tell you what they don't seem to be in bad condition . I'll take them off your hands for ten thousand. "

Fareham checked himself. "That's preposterous! I can't afford that. I put my life savings into this. I have nothing left.

I thought you were wise to the trade . You must know these paintings are worth more than that."

"If you need money Mr.....?"

"Fareham , Jud Fareham."

"Mr Fareham I advise you to take my offer. Indeed it will probably be the only offer you'll get."

"Very well Mr Appleby ?" Fareham said putting every ounce of conviction in to his portrayal of outrage innocence . "Let me have your cheque . If I must,

I must."

Appleby relaxed and went to the back of the shop to get his cheque book. Fareham put his Portfolio on the counter. Appleby stood behind the counter and said "How do you spell your name Mr Fareham?" Fareham spelt out the name he gave him and his address. "Thank you . Well it's been pleasant doing business with you Mr Fareham . If I have any problems I'll get in touch."

Fareham came out of the shop and walked down Stalbridge High Street. He reached his SUV as Paddy Stern was reclining in the driver's seat reading his copy of the daily Telegraph. He got in and gave a chuckle . "He swallowed it can you believe it?"

"How much?"

"Ten thousand for an afternoon's work."

"Well cash the cheque and make ourselves scarce."

"We only use the account once."

"Of course."

"You know Jud , I don't know why you bother. You clinched the deal with Eschlager. I checked the office . They said it was worth four million. You had at least five percent of that. You're set up for life."

"It's the Adrenalin. I can't live without it Paddy."

"I was telling him I was a down and out businessman on his last buck and he bought it."

"We've done this a couple of times now . If the fraud squad know their onions they'll know the characteristics of the artist they'll track you down yet."

"I know being an adrenalin junkie has it's downsides . What can I do?"

As they drove out of Stalbridge Mr Appleby was looking at the painting.

"A view of the sea at Scheveningen " It was a good painting . Good enough to be genuine . This was stolen from the Van Gogh Museum in 2000. If this painting was genuine he'd be surprised. No doubt Mr Fareham would be back.

CHAPTER 3.

Ralston was sitting in his chair when Burnham entered the office. "Burnham I want results. I thought I made it perfectly clear that Mrs Simmons was an open and shut case. Instead I find not only has he not being interviewed but another horrific murder has been committed in the Albion Valley . Am I going to sleep? Am I fucking dreaming?

Burnham faced him placidly . As a ploy it usually worked even if the blood pressure seemed to rise. "We are interviewing witnesses Sir. It was Tuesday the second attack took place. He was in the Farley Arms in Baynesfield Road.

There are witnesses to say he was there between seven and closing time."

"Had he seen her since her last encounter?"

"No apparently there's a Christian Corner Stone Centre in Alderton Road he's been attending recently. "

"This can't go well with the drinking."

"He admits he has lapses now and then , but he doesn't go near his wife."

"Did you have other suspects?"

"We have other people who knew Mrs Simmons."

"Who were they?"

"There was Anne Cameron who lives in Aviemore Road. They both went to the Albion Psychic Society together. It's head is a Mister Arnold Bream. He lives in Calmington Road, that runs parallel to Parish Moor Road.

"And what did you find?"

"Apparently Joan had developed an interest in Psychic research . Arnold talked to her on many occasions. Arnold Bream according to Mrs Cameron was Psychic in name only. She think he's a fraud."

"I see did you find out anything else?"

"Yes, there was a séance at the Green Weald Site near the round about."

"I know it."

"Well it went well. A lot of people attended including one Martin Grimshaw a Goth. He'd worked as an engineer for British Telecom. I suspect there was some casual drug use but not very much else. At any rate a couple of days

after being interviewed his remains were found horribly mutilated in his flat."

"Do you think it was the same person?"

"Mosely will give the details on Mrs Simmons this morning Sir. Grimshaw will follow this afternoon. I reserve judgement until after I hear from him."

"I see though it's unlikely it was the same person. I've been premature Harry forgive me. I suppose you know of course the killer is getting angrier."

"Yes Sir."

"Have you got any leads?"

"Beresford is developing a possible link at the moment Sir. Gerald Moore. He gave us an insight into this Druid Society headed by Henry Stein." He paused . "I want results Harry is that clear?" Burnham affirmed his response.

Stein called his sect the "Sanctum". It was based loosely

on Druidism. Sanctum was meant to represent somewhere that was holy and of course somewhere that was also sanctuary. Of course there was a charitable aspect to the proceedings . They did run a soup kitchen at Albion Railway Station at Christmas and Easter. They even provided a Christmas meal to the Parish

homeless on Christmas Day.

To be initiated into the group required one reference . On this occasion Beresford had required the services of one Helen Fielding who worked in theGreen Dragon to talk to Mary Green. She told her of a man called Shawn Larkin. Larkin was in fact Justin Woods . However they had met on one previous occasion. Helen had convinced Mary that Shawn had finished college and was working at a department store in Thirton called Atkinson's. For this they arranged for Woods to have a "Job" in the store itself. Woods would have to work normal hours as a delivery driver for the store. His main purpose was to look at the inner workings of the "Sanctum." It was Thursday morning that Woods turned up at the station and asked about the assignment he was going to do. Beresford squared up to him .

"Right Mary Green will meet you tomorrow at the Green Dragon . You'll have just started your job at Atkins department store. I take it you're already familiar with the records."

"Yes Sir."

"Good Mary will introduce you to the group on Saturday . You'll meet Amergin he's the second as command . You'll be given a name then you'll be assigned quarters. Your grade will be either Bard or Ovate. The highest order is Druid. While you're in there you'll have to check out the people . Who are they? What sort of finance do they receive . Is there any coercion?

The usual way with these sects are they recruit , they indoc-
trinate . What sort of shade of illegality do they descend to?"

"They sound pretty tame to me."

"Someone killed Martin Grimshaw. The Sanctum is
looking good for this. You'll have to establish what relationship
they had with Grimshaw."

Just as he finished Mosely made an appearance." Well
gentlemen you seem to be engrossed in your dealings . I hope
you don't mind if I take up some of your time."

"Of course Mr Mosely tell me what you've found ."

"Well Mrs Joan Simmons . I've found yes she's been strangled . I'd say it was a different killer. This one came along by
chance. " As I've said probably between eight and ten on the
evening before. The body was found about

four o'clock in the morning. So death would have been between
ten and twelve."

"And Grimshaw?"

"There by hangs a tale. He was already dead before he was
mutilated. Stomach and lungs show traces of cyanide poisoning. Actually the mode of killing is very similar to Gordon
Williams."

"In what way?"

"Well the victim is subdued and killed before the
body is mutilated."

"So there could be a connection ?" Beresford looked
worried.

"Yes , I think you'll have to do some more digging to
the bottom of this."

"Thanks Doctor."

As Mosely left the room Beresford turned to Woods. "We still have to pursue this avenue Justin , have you got your story straight?"

"Yes, I finished a course in Computer Maintenance at the South Bank University. I'm between jobs and driving a van in Atkins department store

mean while."

"Perfect."

The following Friday night in the Green Dragon Woods was introduced to Mary Green by Helen Fielding . Helen was a friend of Martin's and dressed in a long black robe. Mary however was dressed in a long green dress and had long red hair.

"I've been working in London previously . I've finished a year's course in computer maintenance . I'm working doing deliveries in Thirton at the moment. Soon I'll move on to other things . What can you tell me about other Druidism?"

"The point of the ritual in Druidism to leave the World behind you a sacred place for entering and giving thanks for existence."

"How did it start?"

"Well it started in earnest in the nineteenth century. The revival that is. Edward Williams adopted the name of Lolo Morgan weg and claimed that he was reviving Druidism descended from the Iron age. He performed rites in Primrose Hill. After him came William Price he was more political. He supported the Chartist Movement."

"Well it sounds like something I'm interested in. I feel the World has lost it's focus. Druidism is more geared to nature."

"We're from all walks of life. If you come along tomorrow you can meet some of the other people. We can talk then."

It was stuffy in the anteroom of 81 Weald Road. 81 Weald

Road was the headquarters of the Sanctuary used by Henry Stein . I was seven o'clock in the evening and Justin along with five other people were eagerly waiting

the speech to be given by Henry Stein to his followers . Stein was dressed in white robes as were other staff members of Sanctuary House. He noted that Green was dressed in a similar fashion.

Stein came up to the lectern and addressed the congregation. "Good evening new members. First let me address the nature of our group here, our hopes and aims . Afterwards we'll perform a simple ceremony and say a few prayers.

Now as the World progresses outside into increasing automation and confusion we see amongst us the results of Chaos. The alienation, the drugs, the despair.

Druidism does I believe offer the individual an answer to these forces. I believe that with the spread of Christianity in the first ten centuries after Christ there was a lot lost in the Druid tradition that became obscured. Much of what was handed down to us is vague and not specific. To this end I believe that the beliefs of the Indigenous tribes of North America give us a good guide as to what they may have been. I believe Pantheism featured very heavily in the beliefs of the original Druids. There are Gods in the valleys , the dales,the streams , and we venerate nature and keep a balance in all things.

I will introduce my staff to you. There is Bridget. " He pointed to Mary Green , "She interviews all new Ovates such as yourselves. There is Amergin and Bohmaid , they both run the administration. Meg Ruth and Taliesin are in charge of livestock. Rebeo Nemedean does the catering and Dormoli." Woods recognised him from the department store.

"Druid groups are largely known as groves . Large organisation are known as orders. Each Druid organisation conducts its rituals in a unique way. Druidic

rituals are seen as a stance or experience and perception of nature. Ceremonies usually take place outside . Rituals reflect the season and the time of year. So now we will go out to the garden.

They went outside and stood in a circle and their movements described an imaginary circle round themselves . Justin and the other Ovates followed the movements in this regard . Then drawing the circle in the air to the North, to the South, East and West , they marked out the place in which the ceremony would take place. The members were handed vials of liquid which were poured on to the ground but which Justin could see was nothing but Lavender Water.

Food and Cake were also passed round. After this there followed a period of meditation . Stein asked them to visualise a form of energy . The main aim of this was to see various members as victims of war or epidemics or of War. After they retired back to the hall they had a small lunch. Then there followed a prayer by St Bridget . it was Morganwg's Gor Sedd prayer . After this the ceremony ended . Justin was given his name from the sect. There were five other people with him. Two men and a woman. Quickly over dinner he got to know them. There was Steve Harris. He was an electrician , he worked in the

Albion Valley in an industrial unit for an engineering firm. There was Monica Thomas , she was a secretary, she worked at an employment agency in Thirton.

There was Shirley Keyes she worked as a nursing assistant in Sevenoaks. There was Henry Smith he was a delivery driver from Butts a mail order firm in Kessington. There was Charlotte Finsbury she was a courier for a travel firm in London.

After a brief introduction they each gave their reasons

for being there. Invariably Justin found out it was the same thing boredom. Boredom with their jobs and unfulfilling lives. Would Stein step into the void and exploit them?

In a little ceremony Justin apart from having the alias of Shawn Larkin now had the Druid name of Cenarius. Steven had the name of Nefarius. Monica was given the name of Isolde. Shirley was given the name of Sativola. Charlotte was given the name of Nora and Henry Smith was given the name of Arlan.

This thought Justin was the perfect setting for indoctrination. If you give someone a name , give them a uniform , they adopt a different identity. Once they adopt that identity they become pliable. He could already see

the effect on members. They felt empowered they felt unique. Having being called Justin from birth it felt awkward enough. Cenarius was probably a boost. They were expected to keep their jobs but were given a room and would be given board and lodging for a suitable remittance. Bridget or Mary explained it to him afterwards. "Harry felt that the mistake most other religions make

is to take over the assets of members. This the leaves them open to charges of being a cult and manipulating people."

"And Henry doesn't do this?"

"He was trying to find a way through I suppose. We all play a part here." Yes thought Justin trying to keep his scepticism from being too obvious.

Atkins department was based in Thirton High Street. It had been established there for a long time . Of course with the increasing financial pressures of business they had to narrow their range of products to mainly clothes. The traditional department store had all but gone. Atkins was no exception. It had taken the store an incredible amount of money to achieve a new refit. This involved speculation about job losses.

In the shake up they managed to keep their furniture department as well as an extensive electrical and electronic section. Stephen Carter was manager of the Furniture Section. There were three sub departments to this, Kitchen, Bedroom and Household furniture. The main emphasis was still on clothes.

Janet Diamond was in charge of household furniture. Susan Charles was in charge of kitchens and Beatrice Hammond was in charge of bedroom furniture. That meant if a query came up Justin would have to report to either Beatrice Hammond or Janet Diamond. It should have been Danny Kelly who handled this but he was usually busy chasing orders himself.

Shawn quickly got to know the other drivers Tony Cartwright was youngish chap like himself in many ways. He just set himself up in the Albion valley with a wife. He was looking about for something with more money, though he thought he'd do this for now. Brian Lester had been in the job for years . He'd been there since Atkins was a fully fledged department store. He lived in a council house on the other side of Thirton. In him Justin could see a stick in the mud like his immediate superior Beresford. Though if any delivery hit a snag he could phone up Brian who could get him out of a fix. Another driver was Arthur Massey . Massey was like Lester to some degree . He'd only to come to the job a few years previously. Justin made a note to see if he had any previous form. Barry Kelsey was a Jamaican who like Massey had previous work experience. Though he was far more easy going in nature. For some reason Justin felt he was a legitimate character. Saleem Patel rounded off

this group of workers. He had plenty of experience in the garment industries and was beaming with enthusiasm.

The only person who knew Justin's real identity was Peter Norman the general manager . Of course he knew this was for other purposes outside the store itself. He still expected to be kept informed if there was

any pilfering going on. Justin rationalised that he could only do one job at a time. He decided that he couldn't blown his cover. During the week he formed an overview of the inhabitants of Thirton. They were by and large

middle class . They had second homes outside the city and lived in quite spacious houses . He didn't envy them . He did find the atmosphere oppressive if he had a difficult day.

Justin Spent a fitful night in the Sanctuary. He was given one from with a toilet and ensuite bathroom. He had a microwave and an electric kettle . Everything else was provided downstairs in the refectory. He also had

a plasma tv. He got up early and found Rebeo in the refectory laying out the tables. "I've got to go early. It's the start of the shift , they expect me to start at seven o'clock. "

"Is there anything else you would like?"

"Coffee and toast would be fine."

"Alright and a poached egg with that perhaps?"

"Yes fine."

"Dormio works there too. He might start later." This registered with Justin when he entered the house on Friday. "He works in the canteen."

"Ah yes I think I saw him."

After a quick breakfast for which Rebeo did a nice poached egg he quickly bid goodbye and headed out for the road. When he got to the car park behind

Thirton East Station it was a short walk down Coal Street to Thirton Square and Atkins department store. Once there he located the office where Danny Kelly sat. "Okay Danny here I am. Anything new?"

"Okay Shawn we've got Terry going with you today. He's a new boy. He's about eighteen . You should be okay. You've got five settees , two fridges one plasma TV and two armchairs. "

"Have you got the dockets?"

"Here you are. The van was loaded last night so you're ready to go. " Justin looked over and saw a young man of about eighteen with the Polo neck sweater and jeans. Mentally he was registering if the bloke had enough heft to carry a sofa up three flights of stairs . He resigned himself to carrying the heaviest articles. He approached Terry. "Okay? I'm looking at a docket'

The first road we'll come to is somewhere past Kessington judging by the post code I'd say it's somewhere near Seven Oaks. "

"Okay off we go."

When they got in the van Justin studied the route . What he'd have to would be to go down Thirton Relief Road , then join the Kessington and turn before Culompton farm and drive three miles to Kessington High street. He then would cross Kessington Valley Road , Grey Beam Road which would take him to Brierly Road . It was more or less straight forward . Justin had a HGV2 licence from when he joined the army and so he roughly knew how to handle the width and dimensions of the lorry.

As he was driving down Thirton relief road he asked Terry. "How long have you lived in Thirton Terry?"

"My Mum lived in Lewisham with my dad , but she had to come out because he was violent."

"Why did you move to Thirton?"

"We live in Plains Road just at the bottom of Dawson's Hill Park ." This rang a bell with Justin. Dawson's Hill was at the centre of Thirton he'd been there a couple of times.

"I know it . The Park is nice . The flats must be a bit rough though.

"It's alright if you mind your own business. "

"Do you keep out of trouble?"

"Mostly."

"The first address we're going to say Flat 13. 37 Brierly Road . So that means we have to go up two flights of stairs. Are you up for that?"

"I'm up for anything . I've taken stuff upstairs before."

"Good." The first three deliveries were quite onerous . They arrived at Flat 13 number37 Brierly Road . The Sofa was thankfully on the light side but proved quite awkward on the narrow stairs. The little old lady prevailed on them to take the old one away . Justin made a mental note of this . They would eventually turn up at the local tip and their firm's account was automatically debited.

The next two deliveries were up to two flights of stairs. One involved a fridge . Thankfully they employed the service of a lift. They collected another sofa on the way out. By lunch time they had divested themselves

of three sofas , two plasma tv's two washing machines and a fridge. The last few items Danny had omitted to mention. They only had two sofas to go.

This meant going down through Kessington Valley Road making a delivery on Weald Road and another near the Albion Valley Station. On delivery Two Plasma TV's had to go to Meyer Park Road that ran through Felstead Woods. It was quite a rich area . The income level in such an area was conspicuously higher which was made evident by the proliferation of expensive cars Lamborghinis and Lexus's , BMW's all recent registration.

Topologically Justin had built a map of the area along architectural linesloosely based on income. The area that was south of Kessington Valley Roadwas council house territory . This was all built Post War. Around Kessington

Valley Road towards Weald Road the buildings became more diverse with private residential dwellings . Kayleigh Hurst was due East of this and was rich stockbroker belt. This more or less permeated through to Pennington

Rise that led to Greenwich.

When they got back to the department store he met Daniel. It was half past three. Bearing in mind the workload Justin was careful to take an unofficial break so they could recuperate. This was about an hour."Well

done Shawn . Now you've got the dockets here for tomorrows delivery . Best thing is if you load up now and you can be away tomorrow, and that's it okay?"

Justin nodded dumbly , knowing that this was far more tiring than any Police work he'd done . Together with Terry they loaded up with more Settees furniture and electrical goods for the next day. When they finished

Shawn was a bit too tired to go straight home. He had a cup of coffee with Terry in the refectory. "So how do you like it here Terry?"

"It's hard but you get out and about."

"Anything strike you as odd around here?"

"Yeah it does as it happens that house in Weald Road, the weird one? The Sanctuary?"

"Yes, I live there . I thought I'd try something different."

"Yes well as you might know you have that fellow Jacob Evans he lives there an all. I think his name there is different , Dormio?"

"Yes, I've been meaning to talk to him haven't had a chance yet."

"Well every Wednesday one van drops off a crate of wood carvings there. It's come from the airport from India I think. They sell them on their open days. Even so it's a little strange."

"You're right it's a bit strange. Look I've got to go see you tomorrow."

"Yeah sure thing Shawn."

As he left the store facts kept going round in his head . Wooden Elephants ? He looked at the gift shop when he got back to the Sanctum. Stein designated certain open days during the week as a guarantee of income.

It was all probably quite innocent.   Amergin using his own name Geoffrey Duncan worked in the city. The

name of the firm he worked for was Saunders Squire and Havelock . A reputable firm of city stockbrokers who dealt with Europe and markets overseas. They were based in Gracechurch Street in London. Although his outward appearance was respectable , he made appearances at Druid festivals

when the occasion demanded it. Amongst other things he kept an eye on Henry Stein's stocks and shares . Recently because of climate change he did invest in renewables to some degree. However the main area of his portfolio was in the Third World Countries and China ensuring that his investors got a good return for their investment.

Of course he was very much aware that this was very much against his philosophy as a Druid. There in lay the rub . He became a Druid in order to relax the pressure on him as a stock-broker . To some extent being a stockbroker relaxed the pressure on him as a Druid. There was some ethical investment he undertook such as environmentally green third world development. Of course the realism of the city was to make money regardless.So for the most part he could only take a realistic view of any company portfolio.

In so far as the ceremonies and the rituals of the Druid culture provided a release , Amergin was obsessive about the role and nature of each individual in the Druid ceremony. To him it was important what part each person played in the ceremony. To him it was important what part each person played in the ceremony . They would have to pay homage to the four elements , Earth , Air,

Wind and Fire. To pay homage to the god of the rivers, the valleys , the Stream.

In business he had to pay attention to profit. To approve the building of another home garden centre outside Thirton for example. This is where customers would buy decking and garden furniture made out of rain forests in Brazil. He would have to give approval to building an export processing zone in a Third World Country. The loan would be enough to build the factory and supply it with workers. The dividend would pay back the loan many times over.

This cycle of events had an effect on Geoffrey . He began to feel rough most nights. Stein was quite happy to preside over this state of affairs and see new recruits.   The metaphorical acorn of the Sanctuary was going to take some time to turn into an Oaktree. The contradiction was that Geoffrey did feel he was doing something useful.

He'd seen Martin Grimshaw on occasions inside the house. He dismissed him as a layabout at first . Bohmaid or

Angela Payne said he was quite intelligent and easy to talk to. He seemed knowledgeable about Saxon and roman Britain. Though he could tell the strain of living in two different worlds was beginning to tell on Bohmaid. He could tell though that like him she developed a synergy from the two different systems. In his obsession for ritual he was missing something . Grimshaw had been brutally murdered in this very street. He looked amongst the celebrants in each ceremony. Was there evil there ? He knew some of the long term members of Staff were solid citizens, but who else? He could only pray to the elements to help him. Was this retribution from the Third World? Only time would tell.

Rebeo Nemedean was in charge of the catering. Her real name was Elisabeth Sanders. Elisabeth had been in an abusive relationship was with her husband . She found a woman's shelter in Thirton and heard about the Sanctum. Stein and Bridget had encouraged her to join and learn new skills. Under Stein's new tutelage she started a herb garden . among her herbs she introduced Arnica, Borage, Gingko, Bifolia , Milk Thistle, Skull Cap,

Turmeric and Valerian.

The dishes she prepared were vegetarian as well as some meat dishes . She noticed comings and goings of other members of the group. Her closest confidant Bridget or Mary which her real name . She told Bridget about her husband Jack. She said after a year her husband became violent and began to drink heavily . He would inspect what she brought home from the supermarket and question her if he thought she spent too much. He would stop her going out and keep her prisoner. She recognised that his behaviour was following a manic depressive pattern . One day he went out to work and left the front door open. She took all her belongings and made a run for it. Bridget told her that she heard the story many times from other women in an abusive relationship. She also knew that Rebeo had been in an abusive relationship.

She also knew that Rebeo was in to self-harm when she was confronted with the scars on her arms. She told her eventually the feelings would go away.   She gave her ointments and creams and dressings to use when she cut herself.

Bridget also noticed the movements of other people in the Sanctuary. Taliesin the Park Keeper during the day and in charge of the few cows they had. Though Rebeo took on some of the duties herself. There would be a delivery from the Atkins department store to be delivered to the stables. Taliesin told her not to worry about it and the delivery would disappear the next day . Out of curiosity Rebeo had a look one day and found the box contained packages of small wooden elephants and Buddhas . After that the whole thing went out of her mind. Bohmaid was the chief accountant . She asked

and noticed she had quite a few anti-depressants. She told Bohmaid that Holy Basil was good for depression but not take it if she was pregnant.Bohmaid seemed quite pleased at this and took some of the leave away with her in powder form.

Amergin approached her later and asked if she could arrange for plants to be used in a pre-package formula. If they could get regular suppliers

and then make them available for people who would be staying there. Cautiously Rebeo said she could do this. She said however these medications came with health warnings. Amergin seemed satisfied at this . Meg Ruth

confronted her after a month She knew what it was like to be in an abusive relationship and that she had been in one herself. She told her that if she felt she was in a trap in the Sanctuary. Meg said she could get her a job as a

parking Warden and get her digs in Thirton if that was what

she wanted. Rebeo laughed and said she would think about her offer , if things changed, So far they had been fair with her. She had no complaints this far.

Bohmaid or Angela Payne was a consultant with Bowes and Aitken of London. This situated in Moorgate just by the London Wall. She was a consultant with a firm of brokers. In her capacity as advisor it meant she had to go up to North to advise on the financial situation of factories in Bolton, Leeds, Salford and Leicester. Her last port of call was in Salford. It was a ball bearing factory. It had by some economic miracle survived the eighties . It had a total of forty employees . They had been pared down from an original staff of two hundred. automation had taken care of the rest . The aftermath of the financial crash had left them sorely depleted and demand had fallen off.

On an impulse Angela had talked to the manager of the factory Richard Price. He was tall steadfast character with a no nonsense air about him.

"I don't give a shit tell me how many." He said fiercely.

"I have to see the factory first. What production figures are."

"I need every person here. I tell you that . One cut will finish us." He sighed "But I will do my best."

"Of course . Look I want to see around the factory. If I get a feel for it , I'll tell you my findings afterwards."

She saw the delivery of the sheets of metal. They were delivered into the machine shed . From here they were smelted down into various sizes of ball bearings. They came out in five conveyor belts. They were then packed and sorted into various stores waiting to be sorted for delivery.

The woman in charge of the despatch was Mavis Dunnock . She completely sorted out these deliveries for various customers and arranged them for the next day. She had two women Alice Smith and Denise Waring to help her. Angela cast a steely eye on this procedure.

In the break time she had a word with Mavis. "How long have you workedhere Mavis?"

"Thirty years give or take . I've got two sons , both left home . Arthur worked on the railway , but he got made redundant. He's just got over cancer."

"Do you like your job?"

"It pays the bills. It pays the rent. I'm used to it."

"Good , well I'm looking at everyone. I'll let you know what I find   "Good enough." She said matter of factly. Angela decided on a few cuts here and there. The production side could do with one person less. The input side could also do with one person less. However Mavis was surplus to requirements. They could put her somewhere else in the office perhaps, but another manager would do her job just as well as his own production with out breaking a sweat.

It was then she felt the strain. It seemed an awful weight . Praying to the forces of Earth ,Air , Fire and Water and to be so materially linked to the result like this was a strain. She made her report to Price. He looked flustered and huffed a bit . "She won't like this. " He said.

"You can employ her somewhere else."

"Is that going to happen do you think? Stuck here in Salford ?"

"I suppose not." She said sheepishly."

"It's just your job, it's your livelihood. We used to live and breathe manufacturing . In all likelihood she'll get a job filling shelves in a supermarket or join one of those cleaning firms. It's not the end of the world. "

"So you'll see it through ?"

"I'll have to." He shifted towards the head in the manager's office. "Mr Humphries said you had the last word and that's that,"

"It's just a job Mr Price. I don't like doing it anymore than you do. We're up against international capital. We have to do what we can. "

It was five days later she made her recommendations that she was coming out of the factory after a discussion with Mr Humphries a rather portly gentleman with gruff manners , she saw Mavis standing there. She was wearing a green jacket and a yellow scarf .Her eyes were reflecting a light showing she was in a temper. "You are a fine one being a woman, I thought you would have shown more solidarity."

"I'm sorry Mavis , it's just a job. There was nothing I could do."

"Well it's goodbye to my alcoholic husband in a few months time. I suppose it was only a matter of time? How do you sleep at night?"

"If it's any consolation I will say it was a hard decision to take."

"No doubt Miss Payne , no doubt." She turned and walked away. Angela got in her car and drove away . When she got back to the firm She asked Mr Anthony Bowes about the report. "Oh fine Angela . It was stiff medicine . I trust your instincts. You probably saved them five thousand quid in wages and gain twenty in profit. It can work well."

"Yes but I worry about the human cost. People need work it's an essential part of their lives."

"We're not social engineers. Plus there's probably something else they can do." Bowes had rehearsed the argument before. She smiled but inside she felt the dissonance. That night when she came back to the Sanctuary she dressed in the robes of Bohmaid and mentally composed herself to be calm for the ceremony ahead. It was an effort but the release she felt seemed worth it somehow. It was when the ceremony had ended that Stein addressed them together. "Good evening Brethren I wish to speak tonight of the great holy man of the Oglala Sioux Black Elk. On coming to New York in 1886 he said

"I did not see anything to help my people. I could see the Waischus(Whiteman) did not care for each other the way our people did before the nation's hoop was broken . They would take everything from each other if they could . So there were some who more of everything than they could use, while crowds of people had nothing at all. A people's dream died there. It was a beautiful dream . The nation's hoop is broken the dream is scattered."

It was almost too much for her . She knew Henry didn't mean it but he was really laying it on. She fought for consonance and slowly it came.

"Finally the last quote from Black Elk which most accurately reflects our philosophy . "We should understand all things are the work of the Great Spirit.

We should know the Great Spirit is with us in all things, the trees, the grasses, the rivers, the mountains , and the four legged and winged peoples and even more important we should understand all this deeply in our hearts, then we will fear and love the Great Spirit and then we will be and love as the spirit intends. "

Angela fell asleep that night and dreamt of Mavis Dunnock wandering lost in an industrial landscape . On waking in a cold sweat she looked out on the lawn

at the back of the Sanctuary . She breathed in deeply as the night air calmed her down.

It was Saturday when Justin started in earnest living in the Sanctuary. He had the weekend off from work and didn't anticipate any more jobs. He'd already phoned Beresford and told him there was nothing he could see so far. Beresford told him that another three weeks and they'd pull the plug. There were cases mounting up.

Justin had met Taliesin once or twice over meals . He was a fairly rough and tumble character , but he worked hard and Justin felt he knew where he was coming from . The others with the exception of Dormoli were out of

his league altogether. City types and academic types . Taliesin he discovered had a strict regime regarding the Garden. Apparently he discovered Amergin had a brain wave . Rebeo who was in charge of catering had stores of Herbs. She used them to spice the food on occasions. However Amergin decided they should have more herbs thart could provide benefits to those who needed it. He decided there should be a patch of ground given over to a

Green House at the end of the Garden. They would need trenches to provide footings for the building. Amergin hired a skip and JCB the previous day. It was Justin's job to make sure that no vehicle or person strayed into their area of work while the job was in progress. Taliesin drove the JCB and expertly dug out a long narrow trench, emptying the soil into the skip as he did so. By about lunch time they had dug a trench five feet deep twenty feet long and five feet wide. They already filled three skips provided and Taliesin decided they'd done

enough for the afternoon.

Over a fish curry that Rebeo had knocked together they looked at the chart that Taliesin had been given . "Amergin feels these plants would sell well.

Of course underlying the warnings of what the side effects could be."

Justin looked at the list , "It says here Anise, Borage, Burdock, Butter Bar, and Catnip."

"Amongst others."

"It seems fairly safe. How does he intend to sell it?"

"Well at first leave it on sale here . We grow Camomile, that makes tea, we already sell it to the local café."

"It doesn't seem to me that Stein needs the money" Justin said.

"No Amergin needs the to show he's doing something. It keeps me busy, I can't complain. Those skips cost four hundred pound a time."

As they went to the garden this time to do more excavating Justin cast his mind over the previous week. Amergin and Bohmaid were admin and had jobs

in the city. He could almost see the pressure coming off them as they took part inj the ceremonies and relaxed physically into the environment. Personally he preferred a pint, but well it was healthy anyway. Looking at the institute it all seemed sincere and well meaning . Rebeo would be better off in a health centre as a dietician. It seemed quite frankly some airheads idea of heaven.

He didn't know but he was sure that Dormoli had health issues. Meg Ruth was also in charge of gardening. She probably helped Amergin what herbs they should grow.

She arranged the flower shop in the Sanctuary itself. Justin was aware that they had three open days a week with visitors allowed to dine in the restaurant

and buy flowers or herbs. He could see she was quite artistic and had adorned some of the corridors with pictures of sea scapes reminiscent of early Victorian painters. It was Saturday and it was open day and she was playing hostess to the visitors so they could buy something to show for their visit. There were postcards , mugs, tea bags and various kinds of cake on sale.

Mary Green also known as Bridget worked in the office and she did the admin work for Stein. This involved scheduling deliveries , checking finances and chasing up orders. Because he was working Justin had to pay a hundred pound a week board and lodging . Obviously Rebeo and Taliesin were paid a nominal wage and their keep was deducted from that. Justin thought back to the curios that Meg Ruth had told him about. He saw the little Elephants on sale in the shop. They were exquisitely carved and they cost fifteen pounds each. If Taliesin was involved in something he would follow up later on. The only mystery that remained was Stein himself .

Locked away in his office for hours on end. He wasn't very communicative.

He had to admit this sanctuary was run efficiently . It might not make money but it wasn't losing it in any discernible fashion.

Stein sat in his office and contemplated the coming weeks. A dark shadow had descended in Weald Road. The murder of Martin Grimshaw left it's mark. He felt disappointed because he hoped to recruit Martin . He would have made a worthy disciple. Amergin and Bohmaid had kept accounts and shown that their incomings and out goings were keeping up well. Amergin was of course excited because of the development of the Green House. Stein reflected that it all looked a bit like mission creep . Still it probably won't last long. Amergin had these enthusiastic bouts . He didn't want to lose him.

Stein hadn't seen his father for a while yet. He'd grown

weak with arthritis and probably regretting the fact that Henry hadn't taken over the running of the company by now. His mother died when he was young and he'd being sent of to Boarding School. This was part of the reason for his aloofness now.

Like Amergin and Bohmaid he felt the pressure building up on him. He'd asked Bohmaid if he could have small ceremony at the bottom of the garden.

He knew which part he wanted . It was the grove just near the river Witham. He wanted to appease the river god. The offering could be a book or a plant He knew Amergin and Bohmaid were averse to blood sacrifice. He chose a copy of Lyall Watson's supernature.

He decided it would be a Friday night and concentrated hard on what he would do that day. One of the tasks he appointed himself was tracing the ley lines that led to the Great Weald Site. He decided that the Great Weald Site hadn't b een chosen by accident but because it was a site of magical power.

To this end he discovered that there were a number of Coffin paths that actually led to the Great Weald Site. There was another that led from the Albion Valley station. A coffin path was a path chosen by country folk to take the dead body of a loved one to the church withy out passing houses fields or crops or cattle. Superstition had it that if the coffin passed three sites. Superstition had it that if the coffin passed these sites someone would die or

the crops would refuse to grow.

The path from the Albion Valley station was passing mainly through fields and back alleys of houses. As these were Post War buildings Stein reasoned that they must have originally been coffin paths. When he looked at the old maps and the lay out of the region , it showed how the lines of power radiatedfrom the area. He had briefly acquainted Andrew Bland-ford with this information who in turn gave him a ;look to say he'd seen it all now.

Despite it all Henry had a good feeling about the place. He would dispelthe grey cloud that hung over the Sanctuary . He called on the powers that be.He didn't hear the doubt, he didn't hear the silence, he just heard the wind in the trees. One by one the negatives would cancel themselves out. Civilisation would fall in on itself and they would be one with nature.

CHAPTER 4.

He felt he was sinking in aw marsh as if he couldn't help himself. Every time he looked for something to grasp on to he found himself slipping further away. The young Christopher Beresford found himself in his bedroom in Lewisham overlooking Lewisham Way. His brother Michael lay in a bed over the other side of the room, wasting away from Leukaemia.

Michael so bright, so vital was now staring up at his younger brother. His face was gaunt and his features were distorted by the Chemotherapy that wasn't working. Christopher had a helpless feeling that was entirely new to him. His dreams of this time consisted of drowning in a marsh. Michael lived for approximately three months after the initial diagnosis. Afterwards it affected his mother so much she left him with his father who brough him up on his own.

The feeling of helplessness gradually left him. Christopher developed coping strategies and managed to hold the house together .His fatheran engineer at a local factory managed to hold the house together but

developed a drinking habit. Gradually the sinking feeling left and Christopher'sdreams stopped.

Waking up in the semi-detached house in Mosely Green Thirton, he looked at the new day. Not exactly deliverance. He'd been in the force ten years now. Thirton was a step up. He visited his father every month in Lewisham. Retired now Leslie would always serve up a cup of coffee and talk about old times though they rarely mentioned Michael.

To a great extent Christopher had left his old life behind him. Of course Justin had the bit between his teeth in the investigation. Rather than raid the place right now they had to make sure there was no connection between

the Sanctuary and Martin Grimshaw. It looked all but certain that there wasn't. He had one last interview with Mr Simpson the husband of the victim.

"Mister Simpson ." He said relaxing in an armchair in a house in Pennington Road. It ran parallel to Thirton High Street. "I'm sorry to have to do this. Could you run through the details of the night of the twenty fifth when your wife died?"

"I was in the Pennington Arms in Aviemore Road. I left at about ten o'clock. I walked from there to here . I just collapsed on the bed. There was nothing else for me to do."

"I see could you tell me more about your marriage ?"

"Well I'm a venial character. That is I commit sins of laziness, sloppiness, inconsiderateness. I take other people for granted, I don't consider their feelings. I'm a quantity surveyor, I do a job, I get loads of money. I don't

consider other people's feelings.

In all of this I inhabit a social sphere . I talk to women who are reasonably intelligent . Joan was such a person, we got married . Unfortunately the constraints of married life were beyond me. I left her simple as that. I came back a few times and tried to make a go of it. She had had enough . I'm sorry it's over, I really am . I'm sorry she's dead I hope they catch ewho ever is responsible. There it is what more can I say?"

"You were under a restraining order is that right?"

"Yes of some sort. What of it?"

"Were you ever violent towards your wife?"

"On one occasion . I'd had few . Believe me I mucked up. I

know it. None of it was her fault. I own up completely. That's all it was. "

"And nothing since? No phone calls , threatening letters , anything at all like that?"

"No absolutely not."

Beresford looked round the house . It had all the ingredients of Bachelordom, rooms in a semi state of disarray. Though the furniture was expensive and he could see that Mister Simmons for all his devil may care manner was a man of substance . The book case behind him held manuals on building regulations and pie charts .The stereo was state of the art . Simmons was a busy man who occasionally liked to socialise. To see him as

someone who would stalk his wife and kill her didn't seem a reasonable assumption here.

"Thank you for your time Mr Simmons." Christopher gave a nod to DC Barren and they both bid him good day.

Chris Beresford studied the file on Joan Simmons again. He was convinced they were missing something here. He looked up Facebook and studied the page on Alice Fairfield . It seemed the usual trivia , a successful woman in her field , she was in contact with several women like herself that she was in day to day contact with. That seemed normal enough . Then he noticed she was in contact with a Peter Stanbury. It was short and polite but not offensive. It read simply "Sorry we didn't meet. Was it something I said? Let me know soonest."

A number of things struck him odd about this. If they were having an affair why put the message on Facebook? Why not have a private contact email?"

Beresford looked up the details of Peter Stanbury. He noticed he lived in Barking. He could make enquiries there.

On a hunch he phoned up Barking Police Station. He knew a friend of his Alan Owens . He worked in CID like himself , he'd been a mate at Lewisham Station where he started but kept in touch. "DI Owens can I help?" said a

gruff voice on the phone.

"It's Chris Beresford here Alan. I'm on a promise do you think you can do something for me?"

"Depends Chris , I'll do what I can . What is it?"

"Well I've got a suspicious death here. One of the people seems to have a connection with a Peter Stanbury who lives in Barking. Can you dig up something your end   . Anything I mean anything?"

"Give me five minutes. I'll be back soonest."

Chris brewed his coffee and looked over the paper and was left wandering about the Facebook page. As far as he could tell Alice Fairfield was a fairly competent woman with good communication skills. If that was the case why avoid this Peter Stanbury?

After a few more minutes of this quandary the phone rang. "Chris I've got something . I don't know what you're looking for but here it is. A Peter Stanbury reported a fraud on the internet. He was asked to hand over five hundred thousand pound because he was told that his account was not safe. He did so only to find out the company had a bogus address at Carlton Business Park . The Premises had been derelict for years.

"And no clue as to the whereabouts of the firm?"

"No one as far as I can tell. Any way what sort of lead have you got there?"

"I'm not sure Alan. I'll let you know when I've got more."

"Fair enough . Cheers Chris ."

On a further hunch Beresford looked up thev firm that Simmons worked for Brown and Simcox estate agents and valuers . He looked up the website. It all seemed very posh. He phoned their offices and asked to talk to Marylin Adams the contracts manager. "Hello, can I help you?" She asked.

"Hello , I'm DI Beresford from Thirton CID. I'm investigating the death of Mrs Simmons . I wonder if you could help me?"

"I'm aware of this . Mr Simmons is on holiday at the moment. How canI help you?"

"Could you give me a list of Jobs you've done over the last five years?"

"Well Inspector if it helps catch who ever killed poor Joan, I'll do all I can . I'll tell the IT boys to email it to you as soon as possible."

"Thanks That's Thirt homicidesquad@gmail.com"

"Got that . Let me know how you get on."

"And keep this to yourself Mrs Adams . This investigation is at a sensitive stage right now."

"Of course." She said in a more reserved tone. "Bye now."

It was about half an hour later he received a comprehensive email of names and addresses of companies in and around Barking. He phoned up the Clerk of Works at Barking town hall. "Clerk of works Barking can I help
you?"

"Yes this DI Beresford from Thirton Police Station. Can you help me?"

"If I can."

"I want to know who the original owner at Unit 37 Carlton Industrial Park was." The clerk hummed a bit, it was obviously a slow day for him.

"Unit 37 had some extensive renovations three years ago."

"What was the name of the building company?"

"Let me see , Towson and Howard . They're here in Barking shall I give you the phone number?"

"No it's alright."

He consulted his list . As it was in alphabetic order he found it down the bottom . Towson and Howard had done some work with Brown and Simcox . Tenuous , but there was a connection . As it was difficult to get any sort of connection on Facebook Beresford decided to use Fairfield's phone company. On request they provided night months of calls that Alice had made . It was a list of five hundred different numbers. Crossing out eight to nine hundred numbers he was left with four hundred numbers. He the names of twenty different people all men. On a chance he picked out the name of a person who lived in Parsons Green London. He phoned up Parsons Green Police Station and spoke to DI Grayson.

"How can I help you Mr Beresford?"

"I want to know if you have any recollection of a Richard Balfour in the last two years?"

"As regards what exactly ? Complaints robbery or missing property?"

"Robbery or fraud anything like that?"

"I'll check give me five minutes," Beresford took his hand set with him so he made another cup of coffee . The cup of coffee as usual tasted foul. However this was mitigated by the taste of the chocolate biscuit. Eventually the voice came back on the phone." DI Beresford are you there?"

"Yes ."

"June 17th , 2015 Richard Balfour of 37 Kinsey Street reported a theft of Forty seven thousand pounds. He was a victim of internet fraud. The address was Unit 25 Wildfell Mansions Parsons Green. Is there something you know?"

"I'll let you know eventually. That's all I'm afraid . Hear from you soon Inspector." This time the tone was not so formal.

Beresford was pretty sure he was on to something. He decided to phone up the Angelsey Bank and look at Fairfield's bank account. When they submitted accounts on the computer he found she had almost five hundred

thousand pounds . As a city analyst this was not unusual . However with the extent of Fairfield's investment he had to make further enquiries.

He went down to the staff canteen . He saw an available body there.

"DC Barren?"

The red haired northerner turned round somewhat surprised and said

"Yes Sir?"

"I've got a job for you . It involves going on Facebook and talking to women. Do you think you're up for it?"

With mock severity he answered "If I have to Sir."

"Good tonight I want you to contact Alice Fairfiel   d on Facebook and arrange a romantic meeting. I assume you know how to do these things."

"And the catch is?"

"The catch is that it's work Charlie. I want you on your guard. Make up some story of how much money you've got. In a few weeks' time they'll try and scam you. When they do let me know. Then we'll make our move."

"Yes Sir."

Beatrice Williams came down in the morning it was the

third day back from uni . Iris looked at her speculatively as she picked through her muesli. "How are you Bee?"

"Oh you know the usual. Doug that guy I used to go out with."

Iris this morning struggled for a moment to locate a memory. Douglas Winterton. He was a good looking chap studying to be a mechanic. Yes Beatrice only felt a certain amount of compatibility . "From Lewisham wasn't he?"

"That's the one. Well he's studying in Dagenham. Moved up there full time. Anne and Gloria are doing secretarial jobs . I had a drink with them last night. They've got money , they're happy but they want to leave. I don't know their job preferences . They got GCE's but it's all a bit bleak at the moment."

"So you're going back?"

"Oh definitely. Doug notwithstanding . I think I'd like a job in computing . Once I get the degree I'll be set up."

"I wish I could say the same about your brother, He mucks about the farm if he gets good grades he should go to agricultural college. He's just so wild."

"Don't worry Mum he's finding his feet."

"I hope so. " Iris cleared the plates after Beatrice went out. Mentally she counted the days Beatrice had left. Beatrice headed for the manager's office.

When she got there she found Lambert Hodge hunched over a computer "Well Mr Hodge I expect you can give me an account of what actually happened last week. "

Lambert stood up . "Yes of course . Miss Williams look I've got the book here for repairs. All the books here have repairs owing.'"

"I see what happens there?"

"If the machines have a defect the operator has to write it down. Once they decide the mechanic who comes usually on a Tuesday but will come with in an hour's notice."

"Can you show me?"

"Certainly this is a book for the D325 tractor. It is used for ploughingand sowing crops . We also use it for towing goods to and fro from the farm and to the town if necessary. It has a road licence."

"Can I see it?"

"Yes of course." They went out to a space by the barn where he demonstrated the tractor and showed her the controls.

"Can you take it round the farm?"

"Yes of course." Lambert drove round the farm past the dairy herd and round to the abattoir . He turned round and came back . Beatrice got off.

Lambert followed her. "As you can see the controls are working nothing wrong with it."

"Yes, what about the truck my father was driving?"

"Well look at the defect book. He gave it to me every Friday for an update. He was hopeless. When I got the book there were three or four defects on it that needed seeing to. I persuaded him to let me to keep the defect book so I could knock it into shape."

Beatrice looked through the book. The pages were scribbled with defects. "There's notes there for two or three repairs .Why the difference?"

"It was a piece of electronic wizardry . We had to call Guy Balin a computer whizz kid . He'd come out and sort it out eventually."

Beatrice slowly began to understand what happened. She

knew her father Gordon was notoriously absent minded about some things . Slowly the picture

before her was making sense.

"Look Lambert you knew that machine was in a bad state of repair. As manager you had a certain amount of responsibility for my father's safety."

"I did certainly .However he was sometimes a headstrong character. The new truck was his toy. He was the proprietor he over ruled me. Lord knows . I told him each time he handed me the damn book that it wasn't

good enough. He had a duty of care to himself . I've cleared up the batch of weed killer that was by the garage door.The Police took some away as a sample. I'll make sure this never happens again. Beatrice if you're not happy I'll resign. I'll get another job.I'm upset as you are."

Beatrice gave way instantly ."No of course not I see your point of view. It's a terrible accident .My mother would never hear of it anyway. I can see the other machines are safe. It was a terrible accident, thanks for talking to me Lambert."

"Thank you Beatrice. Now if you must excuse me I've got some jobs to do."

"Of course."

Though of course Beatrice while easy in her mind about Lambert, felt uneasy all the same . Her dad was absent minded , whimsical at times but the accident

seemed to contrived somehow. She resolved to leave the issue for the time being. She had study and a new life ahead of her. Grief such as it was hasd to be gotten over. It was new experience , there would be others.

It was a Saturday evening and Justin had a chance to relax in the Sanctum. By chance or design some of the Ovates were there.

A bearded man came up to him. "Hi, I'm Nefarius or should I say Steve Clark. I'm an electrician . This sort of thing is strictly off my beat. Strange to tell I find the ceremony relaxing at the end of the day. I think I could make a go of it here. "

"Hello I'm Shawn Larkin. Like you I'm experimenting . My thing is computer repair . I'm thinking of setting up my own business when I get my own capital. As you say it breaks the monotony . At the monotony I'm delivering to the great and good in Thirton . Usually hulking three piece suites up three flights of stairs . It's great for the stamina though. "

"I bet. I'm installing wiring at a garage in the Albion Valley at the moment.

The mechanic should be savvy enough to do it himself but he seems more comfortable with me. After that I've got a house up in Kessington Common. After that it looks like back to the city. "

"The culture shock isn't too much for you?"

"No not really . The people are a bit strange . Then again , I suppose we're a bit strange too."

Justin paused for a minute . "In what we would you say that?"

"Amergin , I mean he's a bit of odd bird isn't he? Comes over like he's the Head Domo sometimes . I get it, but what's the game here? We do a little bit of work round the house , contribute some of our wages and he comes out with rules and regulations."

"I get the objection, but the way I see it , I suppose we come here to inject some order in to our lives. " Justin said trying not to look to inquisitive.

"What I'm getting at is I work in the city. I can spot a city type a mile off. They hold themselves differently. They have poise and confidence and control.Confidence you could call it that and more. Amergin's a dealer you can tell. He doesn't need any of this and yet he's here."

"What do you make of the other one? "

"Bohmaid? The same thing, she has an absolute presence and yet behind it there's almost a desperation. I suppose it's the strain of a high pressure job. The place is a release from every-day life and yet it's still strange somehow."

Suddenly a man of about twenty came and sat next to them. Justin Immediately recognised Arlan or Henry Smith. "I don't think you'll get far analysing these types . Above our pay grade too cerebral."

"Hi I'm Steve . I was talking to Shawn . I think this place is release from everyday life and yet it's still strange somehow."

"The whole of Kessington is strange , if you ask me .Built after the war we got all the drop outs from London. It's graceful here I don't mind it. I suppose I like the mystic aspect because I want to get away from myself."

"Well it's nothing like getting away from myself here." A young woman entered among them wearing a Sari. "My name is Satiola or should I sayShirley Baynes. I work in an old people's home in Seven Oaks . I've spent

a day in the Kitchen here. I must say it's an experience with Rebeo who is different. "

"Different ? In a nice way? " Steve said.

"Yes of course. She uses some herbs and spices I haven't seen before."

"Was there anything you saw today ?" Steve Harris said.

"No , not really . You work in the Kitchen the routine

is usually the same Everywhere. You get the morning meal , then the lunch , and the dinner. Sometimes she'd go out to get some vegetables or something . I'd say she's well organised, she knows her stuff."

"The place has it's good points. It's well organised . Then we do the ritual and then it's like you're anaesthetised . " This was Steve again.

Henry gave him a look." I think I know what you mean . That's the point though . You're anaesthetised you get away from yourself."

"My, my boys aren't we being metaphysical here?" She turned to Justin "What do you think Shawn?"

"I think it's a good lark. You can escape . The point is at the end of the day how much do you want? "

"What do you mean?"

"Well you've got the religion you've got the house . Do you take it with you or take it somewhere else? Or do you just stay here? "

"I think we have to stay here and see how much it can give us for the time being. " Steve said . "You've put your finger on it though. How much do you take with you? Eventually you develop and move on."

As the conversation developed Justin saw another Ovate standing to one side . Her name if he remembered rightly was Charlotte . He'd checked her out. She was a travel courier from London

Checking back in his memory he could tell she'd be the cerebral type. Reserved unwilling to come out of her shell . Basically experiencing the hot release that Steve was talking about earlier would not fall in to her list of requirements. It was funny how Steve got all the character types right. Could be a shakedown artist. He remembered he checked his record it was clean.

Eventually the conversation headed back to what was on telly that night. They all seemed eager to see a documentary on BBC 4. Though they might Head back to their rooms and things might change. The important thing was though that Justin noticed nothing out of the ordinary had emerged. That in itself was significant.

It looked as though after another week he'd be heading back to the station with nothing to show for it. The details about the Elephants could be cleared up after he'd gone. He'd seen Bohmaid Amergin and Stein that evening they'd given their evening address. The ceremony would come tomorrow in his mind's eye he could see the place had a function in normal society. Satiola for instance looked happy in a non-judgemental environment . She'd obviously experienced some traumas in her life. Likewise Henry Smith . He wanted to lose himself in a community. Justin thought about this for a moment. To lose oneself in a community . Justin thought about this for a moment . To lose oneself in a community and become anonymous .Could there be a reason for that? A reason perhaps more ominous than apparently would be the case? He could always check the records at the station. He could always check the records at the station. Tomorrow they'd finish the foundations. Monday more

work. Than Taliesin could decide his own fate.

Burnham had something on his mind this morning, Having narrowly avoided a melt down with the Chief Constable Ernie Ralston he decided there must be

something on the agenda. The fact was that the murder of Gordon Williams disturbed him. It disturbed for a reason he wasn't quite sure of.

To quieten his mental turmoil the only way out of this mental conflict was to go and see Gregory Mathews . Their acquaintance went back to the eighties when Burnham found himself in the court yard of Kessington Farm. Despite the chaos and the apparent disorganisation , he'd heard that Harry was doing a fine job of turning the farm round. So much so in fact that Gregory would have to give up his day job and manage the farm with him.

Well that may be so that wasn't what he'd come to talk about . When he got out of his car the first sight he saw was Mary with bin full of Carrots ready for packaging and her friend Nora and girl Friday probably. "Hello Inspector surprised to see you here, anything I can help you with?"

"Yes as matter of fact I was wandering if I could have a chat with Gregory. It's been a while since I'd seen him last. I do hope it's not inconvenient ."

"Of course not . He's up in his study . He'd normally be at work. I believe he's looking at some figures."

"Good I'll go up if I may. " He gestured to the farm house.

"Of course, if he makes a fuss tell him I said so."

"Oh if I'm not welcome I'll be off soon enough."

"Nonsense . Have a cup of tea when you come down."

"Of course . Well see you then."

Burnham went through the house . A humble farm house it was to all intent, but Burnham it held a lot of history of Thirton inside those walls. Ascending the narrow stair case he knew the study entrance was a sturdy oak door that stood on the left of the corridor in front of him. He knocked on the door and a gruff voice said "Come in."

He opened the door . He found Gregory sitting behind a

desk going through some files on a computer. Looking round the room he saw various manuals

on management and procedure plus journals on livestock and feed .

"I'm sorry if I'm disturbing you right now Gregory something's come up It's been bothering me."

"Well Harry you're in what the Americans call the catbird seat in Thirton Police Station. Envy you I do not. Anything I can do to help?"

Burnham sat down ."As you know Gregory the history of your family goes back a long way here. I keep going back to something that happened before

my time. I knew George Cunningham , he was an inspector before at the time in 1968. Martha Mathews was found strangled . I'm sorry to bring this up. George told me it was strange .Justin never got over it apparently."

Gregory's happy demeanour evaporated and he became quite sober.

"Yes I'm afraid Uncle Justin had to go into a nursing home . Nobody ever said Why, I just put two and two together. It traumatised my early years .James my father took it awfully hard. I still can't clear the room now."

"Do you know what happened exactly? "

"Delicate question Harry, but yes I've got a rough picture . You see Martha used to go and play with Jeannie Smith on Tuesdays it was a regular thing.

The family lived in Kessington . Every Tuesday of course Martha met Jeannie at Kessington Primary School. They became great friends .At any rate Justin was never right after the War you see. It was shell shock . The slightest sound would set him off . First I knew about it was Jeannie and Martha were having an argument and Justin was stacking hay in the corner shed. Well James my father managed the farm to help Justin out. The truth was that Justin couldn't manage .

Justin had finished the hay and Martha and Jeannie were still arguing. It was a devil of a job to get the tractor going. Well he primed up the tractor when it gave an enormous bang. There was smoke everywhere. Well Justin flew into a panic.

He was hiding under the sink in the kitchen. Only there was Martha lying face down in the yard. She'd been struck by something . Jeannie was crying beside herself. We couldn't get any sense out of Jeannie . Every one thought it was Justin. We assumed in a moment of panic he'd strangled Martha. At the inquest it was considered death by misadventure. However your Inspector

Cunningham made it quite clear that poor Justin should be packed off to Kessington Asylum poste haste. Poor Justin, he never came out of there. He died in 1982. He was seventy."

" I see did you keep in touch with the Smith family?"

"Well we gave Evelyn Smith twelve thousand pounds as a good will gesture . Evelyn took the money and we never heard from her again. I'm still not clear what happened. I'm sure Justin wouldn't hurt a fly.

That however doesn't explain what happened."

"Did you ever see Jeannie Smith again?"

"Well in the Seventies you see the people they disappear. I mean it's like a time warp if you see anybody from back then."

"But you think you saw her when?"

"It seems odd when I think back . I went to a festival in Plumpton I think it was . A rock music festival . She was there I recognised her. She was wearing a Denim and dyed her hair pink. She spoke a few words , she seemed apologetic but not really forthcoming."

"Odd and no animosity or anything. "

"No it was as if what had happened in the past was a dream."

"You've kept that room as it was all these years . Is there anything you remember about Martha ? Her characteristics any peculiarities?"

Again Gregory seemed to sober up fairly quickly. "Well of course she was my sister. There were deep psychological moments we shared in our childhood

. She had her favourite dolls and she was starting to read. The thing was she never liked Jeannie that much. Though why they played together that much was a mystery really. " He paused. "I asked James why they played together. He was evasive on the subject. He felt that Martha should know all types of people. It did her good to see others less well off than herself." This was all he said. He kept his grief hidden most of the time."

"He never doubted that Justin was guilty? "

"No. Not really. Justin was being kept safe and that was all he cared about."

"You see how the impact on my present case presents itself. I'm struck that there could be a malcontent wandering the farms. Someone we know quite well, but only manifest their true colours at certain times. "

"Well 1968 and 2017 i9s a bit of a stretch don't you think?"

"You're right Gregory I don't know what I was thinking. These things get buried we never know what we come up with."

With that he left Gregory to his figure work .He decided his next port of call would be Evelyn Smith . She would be in Kessington. Blyth Meadow Road was set off from Kessington

High Street by about four or five roads of Council houses. Each looking more nondescript than the last. Burnham discovered that Evelyn lived at number 87 Blyth Meadow Road .On venturing on to the road he found two vans parked adjacent to theproperty.

On enquiring at a Post Office he was reliably informed that Evelyn still lived there. So, unabashed by the two swarthy plumbers who were unpacking their vans he walked past them number 57. "Is it Evelyn you want mate?" One of them asked.

"Yes, is she in?"

"Yeah, hardy as old socks that one. I reckon she'll never die." He said with a hint of admiration.

"Thanks ." Burnham advanced on the door and listened for approaching footsteps. Instead he got a shout, "Just push it!"

So saying he pushed and the door opened. The hall before him was moderately decorated recently done in a Lavender Cream style with wood work in a pale blue glossy finish. "I'm in the back kitchen Jerry don't hang about!"

Burnham advanced to the kitchen closing the front door as he progressed . When he got to the kitchen he saw a woman about eighty sitting at a table peeling carrots and assembling the ingredients for a stew.

"Well who are you stranger?" So said fiercely.

Burnham produced his credentials. "Hello Mrs Smith . I'm DetectiveChief Inspector Burnham. I was just wandering if you could help me with something."

"Harry Burnham? Last time I saw you, you were a copper . What the hell do you want?"

"I'm sorry Mrs Smith you saw me before?"

"Yes of course, my Terry . My worthless God forsaken husband. Scoundrel and professional ratbag."

Memory or waves of it went through his mind .Terence Smith? Ah yes a car thief in 1983 it was odd to find a forty year old guy trying to steal a ford Cortina. As far as he recalled looking at it , it had been parked in the forecourt of a garage in Lewisham before it was reported missing.

"They caught him in the Kessington Royal Hotel. Stupid bugger never changed the number plates or anything." Burnham felt his memory returning.

He remembered turning up at the Royal Kessington Hotel. He found a red faced culprit embarrassed to be found in the saloon bar and taking him to Thirton Police Station.

"Ah your memory does you proud Mrs Smith. Actually it was another matter I came to see you about. It was your daughter Jean Smith."

"Oh you'd be a long time looking for her. She got to her teens and scarpered just like her brother before her."

"Is there anything you remember about her? I mean did you keep any mementos?"

"Well yes." She got up shuffling for the dresser that was over by the wall. She pulled out a drawer. "I've got some photographs here. It was taken when she was 19, pretty little thing wasn't she?"

Burnham looked at the black and white photograph . It showed a young woman with long dark hair. She wore a cardigan. He couldn't tell what colour it was. She wore a skirt . Her appearance was attractive but her face had an absence of something, of what he couldn't quite say.

"Do you think I could borrow this for a while?"

"If you must . Let me have it back when you've finished. It's all I've got left. Would you like a cup of tea?"

"If I may."

They sat down as she managed to fill up an electric kettle and watch it boil. "You know what annoyed me was she went off without any warning. She was her father's favourite. I mean he was a worthless sod, but his one soft spot was Jeannie. He always treated her well."

The kettle boiled and Harry helped her with the cups and saucers. As they sat down he asked . "Do you have any clue as to why he left?"

"None what so ever . That incident up in Kessington Farm didn't help. I mean I know I got that money, but the scoundrel Terry took most of it and blew it.

God, I never had any luck with men."

Burnham finished the tea and said as he left. "It's been nice meeting you Mrs Smith. If you think of anything to establish Jeannie's where about let me know."

"It's been a long time Inspector . I don't know if I'll ever hear from you again. Good bye ." She said with a trace of sadness.

When he got back to the station the first thing he did was to phone up Mosely." Mosely can you help?"

"Yes Harry you've got my full attention. How can I help?"

"It's an old case dating back to 1968. It concerns Martha Mathews aged six. Show me what the autopsy showed?"

"That far back eh? As far as I can remember the practicing pathologist was Anthony Stringer Lyons. Double barrelled name. That's all I remember off hand. Give me ten minutes , I'll email a report through okay?"

"Thanks a lot Dave."

"Don't worry I'll put it on my tally sheet."

"No doubt."

The tally sheet he remembered was drinks at the Christmas do. Half an hour later a full report was emailed. Burnham read through the details

"White Caucasian girl age six years . Cause of death was blunt force trauma."

So it was a blow to the head. That's how attention centred on Justin Mathews. Yet he still felt uncomfortable about it. He looked at the photograph of Jeannie Smith and wondered what did she know? He photocopied the picture and sent the original back to Mrs Smith.

Jud Fareham sat back over a brandy as he reflected on the day's takings. He was in the throes of pioneering a merger with Monroe and Cavett / Beirsley. Surveyors. Beirsley were basically skint but had some assets worth looking at. Monroe was a shark of the first order and was out to extract his pound of flesh . Jud was brought in to turn a disorderly rout into a civilised proceeding . The trouble was that Anthony Beirsley was in his dotage and not disposed overly much to care what happened to his company. The balance of power lay with Edith Beirsley who was fending off Monroe with the Lion tamer's chair and a whip. After one afternoon of heated negotiations Jud had finally agreed on a price for the sale of the assets agreeable to all.

Paddy caught him in his ruminations in the "Traveller's Rest." "How are things Jud? I heard you made a killing last week."

"For a while now hectic. I've put the Lion and the Lamb to bed. I've other problems."

"Meaning?"

"Meaning Ivor Monroe and Mrs Beirsley who else?"

"Well I'm afraid I've got some bad news ."

"What would that be?" Jud looked over to where Paddy was sitting . Suddenly a presence loomed over them. It was a tall gentleman with a striped shirt and a Paisley tie and wearing a pale cream jacket. "Excuse

me Mr Farrell but I believe we have a mutual friend in common. I've already introduced myself to your colleague Mr Stern."

"I see and you are?" Jud said sensing mischief of some sort.

"How remiss of me of course. I should have introduced myself at first. My name is Aaron Mallin. That's neither here nor there really. I speculate in art like your selves . Our mutual friend is Mr Appleby from Stalbridge. He brought to my attention the painting you sold him for ten thousand pounds."

"He seemed quite happy with it." Jud said defensively.

"Quite so Mr Fareham , quite so. However the painting is a forgery. Quite a good forgery by the way. I hope you appreciate that my friend Mr Appleby could get you into quite serious trouble if he wanted to."

"I don't understand what you're getting at Mr Mallin. What do you want?"

"Quite right Mr Fareham . Well with out beating about the bush my colleagues and I want to carry out a robbery . It will be from a Gallery in Nice. The picture I wish to acquire is the "Judgement of Paris " by Cezanne.

It's a most exquisite work and I would be delighted to add it to my collection."

Jud laughed briefly . "And how do you propose to do that Mr Mallin?"

"Well of course you are going to assist me Mr Fareham. You will bring me a reproduction of "The Judgement of Paris" so that we can replace the painting"

"Where is the gallery Mr Mallin?"

"It's the gallery Ferrero in the Place du Charles Felix in Nice. You might know it."

"From what I know of Galleries in that area it is well guarded . How are you going to get access to it?"

"I have a friend , shall we say who is an art restorer. He owes me a favour or two. I can swap the painting while it is in his care."

"All well and good Mr Mallin now why should I help you?"

"Because Mr Fareham if you don't I will approach the Police with the painting you sold Mr Appleby and the receipt . I will tell them that you deceived an old man and demand recompense."

"Why should that concern me?"

"Because you're a financial dealer Mr Fareham . Any sign of dishonesty and your reputation would be ruined."

"What's in it for me? I don't like threats . I must say I don't like you much."

"Well I know a private collector willing to pay thirty million pounds for this Painting. I could give you ten per cent. "

"Three million? Well it's an inducement Mr Mallin."

"Are you agreeable?"

"Yes as far as it goes."

Mr Mallin. "Very well Mr Mallin it is as you wish. How do you propose to do this?"

"It will take me two months to get the materials together."

"I'll leave my contact details here Mr Fareham. As soon as you are ready please let me know ." Jud ran a practised eye over the business card and saw it was a London phone number.

"Okay as soon as we have the materials ready I will let you know."

"Very good Mr Fareham. I will see you soon." Mallin walked out of the pub not looking back. Paddy looked at Jud unswervingly . "What have you done now Jud?"

"Look Paddy it's just business. I'll give the boy a break. It won't get back to him . He's just doing us a favour."

"By favour, I don't think crime is a favour."

"Look Paddy the boy's a genius , even you can see that. Be reasonable we're just giving him an outlet for his talents."

Paddy relented ."Alright Jud. Just this once, but if that Mallin character comes back for more tell him to get lost. Either that or use someone else. Stanley's a good boy, he doesn't deserve this."

"I have something in mind don't worry."

Paddy shook his head witheringly . Jus considered how he was going to sell this to Tristan.

Jud was on the phone to an art gallery friend of his in Taunton. "It's complicated James. You know that friend of yours Ambrose Benton?"

"Who you mean the millionaire philanthropist? Daft as a bunch of lights."

"Well okay I know he's doing something about young talent. It's a competition or something. Reproducing works of art. We're holding a festival this year. Why what's the deal?"

"I've got a promising young painter I want to enter him for the competition."

"Well the entries have to be in for the beginning of June."

"How much is the prize money?"

"About ten grand."

"Good send me a form. Where will the venue take place?"

"At my gallery in Trenton Street. It will be in the first week of June.

Good for business and tourists of course."

"Excellent give my lover to Vera."

"Of course Jud. See you in a couple of weeks' time."

Dora looked at Maria speculatively for a moment . "Well he said he was going with some friend to Exeter. It would be two weeks,he was going to a nice hotel . On the face of it I shouldn't worry. I suppose all the expenses are paid, and they are older but..." She tailedoff.

"But what for God's sake? "

"They are older men. They're more experienced , they know moreabout the World . However it would be more natural if he went outwith people his own age. After all Tristan and Paddy are quite nicepeople. Why do they take such an interest in Stanley?"

"You don't think they're taking advantage of him do you?"

"I can't say the thought hasn't crossed my mind. Well for one thing they're being quite honest about their professional life. They have girlfriends they appear quite normal. On balance I should put the thought out of my mind."

"You mean if he was going out with some crazy teenagers to a music festival and got out of his head on drugs you'd feel better . Actually Dora I know how you feel. Teenagers are strange you have to feel your way."

" I suppose so it's just I don't want him to become damaged by this."

"You can't help being a mother, so far so natural. Let

him go out in the World and become shaped by this. Let him use his own radar. Sometimes it works."

The front door opened and Stanley walked in. "Hello people , what's for dinner Mum I'm starving."

"The usual Pasta and dessert . If not there's probably something in the fridge."

"Your mother and I were talking about your trip to Exeter Stan. I think it's a good idea. The only thing is why?"

"Why?"

"Yes you know three adult professional males and their lady friends why you?"

"They want me to do some painting for them. I think Paddy wants me to knock up a few pictures I can sell to the locals. It's in preparation for a contest.

There's a painting contest in Taunton. They want me to enter for it. If I win I get ten thousand pounds."

"Wow that's quite a lot . So it's a working holiday?"

"Effectively that's it.Though I'll have time to relax as well."

"I suppose it's okay. Though always question their motives Stan. There's no such thing as a free lunch. If it gets tough plan your escape route."

"I'm not indebted to them in any way. I know the one I can count on is Tristam. He needs some one to talk to. He Keeps on about his exwife . The one thing we have in common is fishing."

"Listen to Maria though Stan . Question them if you have the slightest doubts.Come back will you?"

"Yes Mum." He said as she put his pasta in the micro wave.

Davinia looked up from her cards . She liked to play a small game of Patience in the afternoon. It was passing mild. She arranged the flowers for the service in the morning . She'd been to see a few parishioners about complaints in the morning. Usually it was because they were lonely. A comforting word over a cup of tea and a chat about the weather usually was enough to put the World to rights. She still remembered the thrill she felt when they got the letter back from Kent Laboratories . The radio carbon dating revealed that the remains they found were at least one and a half thousand years old. The Reverend Wallis was still sceptical when the Bishop gave them permission to put the shrine there.

So thinking she looked up from her cards as a shadow loomed in the door way. "Oh hello Vicar I didn't see you there. Is there anything I can do?"

"It's not good enough Davinia. The workmen have been here all day long. To say it's causing a major head ache is to make an understatement."

"Did they find anything else?"

"Apart from the bones no. I think it was just a burial site."

He looked temporarily stumped for a reply at any rate we will hold a service for Saint Hilda. We can start the leaflets and literature as soon as we get the notification from the Archbishop."

"Isn't this better? It will bring in the revenue."

"You don't understand Davinia . What about our parishioners ? What do they feel? What if they want to go to Church and pray without gaping tourists?"

"We'll if we're making money we'll still be here. Otherwise who knows?"

Justin turned up for the beginning of the shift at Atkins department store. He was relieved to see Terry his assistant was there even if it was there even if it was with a hangover. Danny Kelly was standing on the loading dock with the delivery dockets in his hand." Brand new day to day lads. I want you on the dot with we've got a lot on."

Brian Lester had already loaded up and was just going over the list with.Eddy his assistant . Barry Kelsey kissed the air in a mocking way as if to say he'd seen it all now. "This is a diabolical liberty . Arthur he gets the easi est shift while the rest of us are working our asses off. Arthur will do two drops off Kessington Valley Road while the rest of us are hauling ass up Albion Valley,or Kayleigh Hurst or some where ras else."

"Now Barry you know that's not true. We have this argument every time. I give each of you an equal share and you know it.There wouldn't be any point other wise."

As they went to their lorries to do the deliveries

Terry said. "I shouldn't say this but Barry has a point. Arthur does get the easier drops. I think he's getting on a bit."

"Nothing else to it then?"

"Well you know I suppose Danny is scared of losing Arthur."

They were working through their deliveries on that day when Justin came to the street called Calendar Street. It was on the outskirts of Thirton. It was a Bungalow and there was no response. A neighbour came by to say she would take delivery. He phoned up Brian Lester. "What's the name of the client Shawn?"

"Cleo Wainwright."

"She's the World's worst. We've had the trouble with her before. Deliver the furniture to the neighbour's address. Get a clear signature and ask them to print their names as well."

"Okay thanks Brian." He cursed himself for not thinking of that himself. As they drove along Justin asked Terry what the fuss was surrounding Arthur.

"Well." Terry said relishing the narrative. "It starts off Arthur gets three Sofas for or near Kessington Valley Road. Then he has fridges televisions and Furniture for the rest of the trip. Never fails to set Barry off. "

"Always?"

"Always. He's got a charmed life. Out of every shift he must work only two hours. It works every time."

"Hmmm there must be a reason." He said to himself.

That night when he got home he phoned Beresford up "There's something fishy about one of the drivers. Ar thur Massey . He only works two hours out of any given shift. Could we have someone tail him. See if there's something going on?"

Beresford checked his Calendar. He had his hands full checking on Alice Fairfield. "Okay I've got a car I can use tomorrow. Can you give me the reg?"

"Yes. A three five six, O for Oliver, P for Patrick , S for Stephen."

"Right I'll send someone tomorrow. What's his normal route?"

"Kessington Valley Road first then the smaller roads afterwards. His actual address is Thirteen Arlingt on road Thirton."

"I'll have someone on his tail tomorrow."

"dead as a doornail. Apart from the rituals it really is a peaceful sanctuary I've come up with nothing."

"Right. We'll look into this." It was the following day Arthur Massey and his assistant . Peter Philpott were finishing their deliveries to Kessington Valley and it's environs. Then Arthur made a detour and headed for Heathrow Airport where he took a consignment. It was three crates that came from India. DC Canning reported that the goods were placed on the back of the van with a forklift. Then Arthur took them to the store .

Danny took them to the back of the store.

When Justin got back from work Beresford phoned him up. "You were right something is going on . Massey went to Heathrow to pick up some consignment and delivered it to Atkins Department store. I've had a word with Burnham. We're pulling you out of there. Tomor row is your last day. The next day we're raiding Atkins Department Store and the Sanctuary."

"Yes Sir." Justin said with something approaching relief. When he got up next morning he faced Rebeo with something approaching reluctance. "It's being really great being with you Rebeo . You're a good cook but something's come up. I have to go yonder and leave this happy abode."

"I'm sorry to hear that has my own ideal Ovate found the cause wanting?" she said channelling a lowly Zen disciple .

"My Aunt in Durham has been taken ill. I have to leave. I may not be back for a while ."

"You're leaving Cenarius? The Sanctuary is always here if you want to come back."

"That's good of you to say that. There haven't been many places I've been made this welcome."

"Well I will tell Amergin.He will be dissappointed Bridget had hopes for you. You seemed to be intuitive in your approach."

"Well you know what they say you can't choose your relatives."

Rebeo fixed him with a stare . "Seriously Shawn make the right choice. This may not be for you but something will."

"Good bye for now." He said lightly.

The day went slowly he decided he would approach Peter Norman when he came back from his shift . It seemed the right thing to do.He found the return ad dress he'd been to the day before, Calendar Street, They had actually to take the furniture and deliver it to the next door neighbour, Cleo Wainwright. Mrs Wain wright was about forty who had straight forward way of talking. Although Shawn didn't take an instant dislike to her, he felt he could get there eventually.

When he got to the store Danny gave him the dockets to load up for the next day. "I've got to see Mr Norman Danny, I'm sorry it's urgent."

"If you disturb him and it's not urgent you better be prepared for one hell of an argument Shawn."

"Of course , I'll be down in a jiffy."

He went up the stairs to the manager's office. He found Norman's office tucked behind the refectory up at the top of the building. His Secretary Maxine had the tenacity of a bull dog. When Justin turned up she was instantly on the offensive . "You're Mister Larkin aren't you? How can I help?"

177

"I've got to see Mr Norman if I may?"

"I'll see if he's free ." Justin relaxed. She picked up the phone and exchanged a few words. She seemed rather surprised when she came back.

"Mister Norman said please go through."

"Thanks." Justin went through. Norman a rather sparse looking man was surrounded by Charts and tables. He surveyed Justin through his glasses.

"Yes , DC Woods can I help?"

"They're pulling me out today. Sorry it's been such short notice."

"Good please let me know of any irregularities you spotted whilst you were here of course." He stopped for a moment and picked up a folder.

"Is there anything I should know?"

"No pilfering. I'll let you know more in due course."

"Thanks. Well then you better go . I'll phone through to Danny telling him you've been called away."

"Thanks ." Justin felt that Norman was a strange man even if he was a store manager.

Beresford reflected somewhat meaningfully. You could be a saint or a politician and conviction could leave you suddenly a Damascene conversion could be turned into ashes. Unfortunately that never happens when you're a Police Officer. So when he contacted the inland revenue about the financial status of Alice Fairfield he was told the sh are e inherited four hundred thousand

pounds from her father who was a banker . The sale of her father's house contribute a further three hundred thousand to her income. This of course explained the money in the bank. However Beresford had an instinct that something wasn't right. Saint Thomas Aquinas never had this problem.

Alice Fairfield sat at the bar as she reflected over her gin and tonic. There can't be many women waiting for a man to turn up at a date. She remembered the face of the man on Facebook. A nice man about thirty he seemed amicable.

He seemed quite friendly really , he sounded nice on the phone . Too much on his plate maybe. She was about to pay her bill and walk out of the restaurant when someone approached the table. "Good Evening Alice I'm

sorry I'm late, how are you?" There he was a virtual Adonis , a nice young man in a blue serge suit.

"Hello Charlie, kind of here and there as they say."

"Oh yes ." He said recalling an ad logo."I was held up by work.Lots of Gremlins . Sometimes I think my whole life revolves round computer viruses. Can I get you anything to drink?"

"Well, I was thinking I could go straight on for a meal."

"Yes , of course. " They found a table eventually . Over the Shrimp Cocktails. She found out he worked in IT with a firm in East London. She found out the stock of IT engineers had dwindled over the last few years. They were literally ten a penny. The computer industry dealt the same way with programmers. Of course that didn't mean to say he wasn't good looking intelligent and all round nice person. However there were aspects to consider. At the end of the evening she asked him over to her place for a night cap and he accepted and the inevitable followed. About four in the morning she woke up to an empty bed. She picked up her phone dialled a number . A gruff voice answered on the other end. "I think we've got something." She said.

"Good let me know how you get on."

Justin Woods and four other Police Officers assembled outside Atkins Department Store. Their job was to raid the store. Another group of officers were detailed to raid the Sanctuary in Weald Road. Justin would lead the raid on the department store.

Two vans pulled up outside the department store delivery bay. Justin got out . Danny Kelly somewhat surprised said "Hello Shawn surprised to see you here. How can I help?"

"It's a Police Raid Danny. We've come to look at your supplies and inspect your deliveries." Danny's expression hardly changed.

"Oh, okay they are in the warehouse . You can see for yourselves."

"You could save me sometime. I know Arthur Massey went to Heathrow yesterday to pick up supplies. Where are they kept?"

With something approaching resignation Danny led him and a troop of Police Officers into the Warehouse past the serried ranks of televisions and fridges to the furniture side. There amidst the wardrobes and cupboards and settees sat four boxes labelled "Fragile."

"These are what I expect you are looking for." Justin nodded to the men with crowbars who then took the crates apart. There in the straw wrapping lay beautifully modelled individually carved Elephants , Buddhas, and images of Kali . With a wantonness approaching vandalism Justin took a hammer and smashed a Buddha open only to find a bag of white powder . "Right ,

we'll take this lot back to the station. That includes you I'm afraid you and I'm afraid Mister Massey." Kelley was going to say something. " We're also raiding

other premises right at this minute."

Beresford pulled up outside the premises of the Sanctuary . He knocked on the door of the house. It was answered by Rebeo Nemedean. "Hello, can I help you?"

"Yes I'm DI Beresford . I have a warrant to search your premises ." A very ruffled and upset Henry Stein confronted him.

"What is the meaning of this Inspector? I must protest in the most strident terms."

"We are searching your premises for drugs Mr Stein. We have reason to believe there are narcotics being held here. I will be interviewing members of staff in due course. So if you will allow us to proceed I'm have a job to do."

"Very well."

As Beresford walked through the Kitchen he found one of the two officers going through the supplies and food stuffs. There was spilled grains on thev floor. There he found a chap he knew as Taliesin.

"Taliesin or Jacob Evans?" The man was under Police Guard and handcuffed.

PC Presser said "I found three cases of Buddhas and other images in the garage. They've started breaking them down and distributing them into packets. "Who was in with you Jacob? If you tell us now it will go easy with you."

"Dormoli of course. There's no point in not telling you. "

"You can tell me the rest down in the station. Okay Dave take him away"

As he came back through the hall he found Stein in his robes still protesting quite vehemently to PC Daniel Carver." This is a disgrace , I'm going to write a letter to my MP."

"Mr Stein we've discovered a large quantity of class a drugs in your garage. We also discovered Taliesin and Dormoli have been involved in distributing these drugs. If you could come down to the station and answer questions I would be most obliged."

Somewhat chastened Stein calmed down. "Of course officer I'll do as you say."

About four hours later in the office with Woods and Beresford , Burnham looked round the office. "So what was the upshot of today's proceedings?"

"Well we've had had two upset eminent members of the borough of Thirton here today. Mr Henry Stein and Mr Peter Norman. Both unaware of the full extent of the drugs ring in their neighbourhood . It was Taliesin who

masterminded it all. Together with Danny Kelly they picked up deliveries for Atkins Department Store . All of this was bough and paid for by Taliesin. The invoices were delivered to Kelly's office who would redirect them to Taliesin. After delivering the Heroin to various dealers in the Albion Valley and Lewisham , they would automatically divvy up giving Kelly about thirty percent."

"Was Stein or Morgan involved?"

"We're almost certain they weren't. Amergin who normally kept an eye on development was blindsided by Taliesin who got him interested in developing homeopathic remedies. He thought the deliveries were part of the retail side."

"What about the institute ? What about the cult aspect of it?"

"We're certain all that is pretty innocent sir. " Woods said ."Which is a pity . I quite liked Taliesin. He was a crook , but he was a hardworking guy."

"So what about the murder?"

"Blown I'm afraid, this was blind alley sir." Beresford said apologetically.

"Never mind it's being a good haul . We've got some drugs off the street .Though I expect Justin won't be able to shop at

Atkins department store again.

"Oh I don't know Sir. Peter Norman let me keep the store card."

"I didn't hear that DC Woods."

"Yes Sir."

CHAPTER 5.

Barren sat back when he heard a call come on his mobile . "Hello is this Kevin Barren?"

"Speaking how can I help you?"

"Hello, I'm sorry Mister Barren but I'm afraid your account is insecure . We've had a questionable transaction on your account. You'll have to transfer it because it is no longer safe. We're I.C. Accounts Limited ."

Without hesitation Barren replied ." I see what do you want me to do?"

He paused, "About the account that is."

"Well if you could transfer your assets to the bank account number I'm about to give . Then we could wrap up this business."

"I'm afraid I 've got a building society account , they won't transfer that amount over. The most they'll give me would be two hundred and fifty pounds."

"That's okay if you let us contact you and you can get the money from the bank and we'll transfer it for you. "

" I see well I work in 124 Kingsland Road Hackney. The name of the firm is IT installations. I should have the money ready. At about 4o'clock."

"Alright Mr Barren see you there."

He hung up the phone. "Who was that?" Beresford asked .

"It was I.C. Accounts Limited. I've arranged to meet at

124 Kingsland Road at I. C. Installations. "

"Right get your skates on . I'll phone through to Hackney Police Station. They'll be waiting for you. "

Barren took some bundles of phoney cash with him to complete the picture. Journeying from Thirton through Blackheath proved quick and easy and was the other side of the Blackwall Tunnel in less than half an hour. Through Bromley High street he arrived at Kingsland Road in quarter of an hour to spare. When he got to I. C. installations the manager Malcolm Ritter

welcomed him. "You're Mister Barren? I've got some chums upstairs . They've been waiting for you."

"Good we've got to get this set up as quick as possible." When he got upstairs there were two gentlemen wearing leather jackets . They stood up as he approached. "DC Barren? " Barren nodded.

The man who spoke was tall with a beard wore a grey shirt and jeans. "Hello ,I'm Dick Clarke this is my partner DC Fennel. " Fennel was the same height and build and wore a brown shirt and black jeans. "Any way we're waiting for your Perp right?"

"Yes he'll be expecting me to hand over Seven thousand pounds. "

"You've got the bundles?"

"Yes." He showed them.

"So I'm going to look like I'm an employee . I'll do some filing here. Fennel will do the same. As soon as you hand over the money we've got him. Any resistance we'll steam in. Got it?"

"Yes Dick." Barren felt a faint resentment about his operation being taken over but he hid it.

Barren sat at his desk in the pretence of work as did

the other two. The other employees carried on with their work and pretended not to notice. At four o'clock a man dressed in a black suit came to the door of the firm and pressed the buzzer. Malcolm got up and with a look from Barren carried on down to reception.

Ritter showed the gentleman in. He said he was IC account Services . Ritter showed him to Barren's desk.

"Are you Mister Barren ?"

"Yes how can I help you?"

"You wish to transfer some money to our account Mr Barren. I'm here to help you do that."

"Very well." Barren opened his brief case and took out three bundles of what to all appearances were fifty pound notes. "Here it is . You can count it if you like."

"No. It looks ok to me." He quickly took the cash." As I'm in a hurry I've got some scales here. I can weigh the cash if there's any discrepancy my accountant will text you okay?"

"Certainly."

"Right now here's the first bundle. Yes about three ounces. Now the next. That's about two thousand three hundred and fifty is that correct ? The last bundle is two thousand yes?" As he said this he was ticking off

the weight on his scales. "Now if you just sign here , I'll give you a receipt and I'll be on my way."

Barren signed the receipt and the man gave him a carbon copy of the chit.

"Well thank you Mr Barren good bye."

"Good day." Barren said slowly.

As he turned towards the door DC Clarke intervened. "Just a minute Mr.........?"

"Mr Jackson." He said casually.

"Mr Jackson you're from IC account services and you look after people's accounts is that right?"

"Yes I'm busy though."

"Mr Jackson I'm afraid there has been a misunderstanding. You'll have to come to the Police Station you'll have to come with us."

The composure of Jackson didn't change. It seemed as though he felt a heavy resignation seemed to come over him. At the Police Station Jackson told them the address of the company. Barren looked it up . It was forty Jenner Road Hackney. It proved to be a derelict building previously worked on by Brown and Simcox three years previously.Cheney approached Jackson in the   interrogation room. "Good news Mr Jackson forty Jenner Road is a derelict building , that was your firm's address. The news is good because it was previously developed by

Brown and Simcox."

"There must be some understanding. "

"On the contrary we understand only too well Mr Jackson. Now why don't you tell us all about it?"

Eventually after careful questioning the link between Mr Simmons and Alison Fairfield was established, and they were picked up at their separate addresses.

Beresford faced Simmons over the interrogation room the next morning.
"Okay, I get it. I'm running a scam and you got me I own up. I still didn't murder my wife."

"It will do for starters though. You and Alison Fairfield have amounted to quite a tidy portfolio . If you tell us now everything , we'll make sure the Judge knows you've been co-operative. "

" I've nothing to be co-operative about . Alison and I

didn't need the money. We were doing it for kicks."

"You'll be charged with obtaining money under false pretences. You and Alison will be serving four to five years each. If there's anything you know about your wife's death tell me now."

Simmons looked like a broken man for the first time simply shook his head and said "No."

Four hours later Woods walked through to the next interview ,just as Beresford switched on the machine in the interrogation room. "We are now interrogating one Alison Fairfield of 47 Mosely Road Flat 4. Present, are DC Woods, DI Beresford and Mr Andrew Barclay Miss Fairfield's solicitor. The time now is 8.42 precisely . The date is the 18th of July 2017.

Miss Fairfield it's only fair to warn you that what you say will be taken down and used in a court of law. You have the right to remain silent. If however you withhold information this will be held against you in a court of law is that clear?"

"Yes." She replied. Beresford felt she was keeping her composure quiet well. Alison was wearing a blouse and blue trousers. The effect was smart casual to quite good effect .

"Now Miss Fairfield I want to go over again the events of early afternoon and early last week. It was then you paid a social visit to one Mr Barren . you were seeing him with a view to a relationship is that right?"

"I did. However it wasn't right for both of us , so I didn't return his calls."

"I see. Now yesterday Mr Barren received a call to say that his account had been compromised . I believe we have the individual who turned up claiming to be from his bank to take the money. I believe his name was Mr Jackson . We later ascertained that his name was Mr Arnold Roberts. Looking up the phone records we see there were extensive calls between you and Mr Roberts and Mr Simmons. Can you explain?"

"I thought it was all perfectly innocent at first. It was a victimless crime. I didn't think we'd get found out."

"You mean Mrs Simmons ? She was the one wasn't she?"

"What are you talking about? Poor Jean . She wouldn't hurt a fly. No we just wanted a bit of money."

"But you have to what amounts to a personal fortune."

"I needed the adrenalin . The thrill of it when they fall for the sting. Dealing in the stock exchange is never enough."

"So if I've got this right , you own up to the scam but not the murder?"

"Nothing to do with me. It's true I knew Jack through work. I knew Joan as a school friend . I was appalled to hear of her death .Jack and I had something in common . I could have been responsible for ending their marriage. However I never had any plans to replace her. What Jack and I had was a simple partnership. We wanted to see if we could work the system."

"By conning people out of their money?"

"People who could afford it."

After the interview when Alison was taken back to her cell, Woods approached Beresford. "What do you think?"

"For what it's worth I believe her. She's ruined her career, she'll get another job . She's got nothing to lose by lying. Plus Mosely couldn't find any DNA trace of Mr Simmons or Fairfield at the crime scene."

"What do you think she'll get?"

"We're only prosecuting cases we know about. That'll be about five years each. Time off for good behaviour they should be out in two."

"Hard lines."

"She's got loads of money she'll be fine."

It was late on Saturday night Beresford sat back in the

Green Dragon relishing the luxury of a pint counting the minutes before he had to give up and go home. As he looked over the welter of young people relishing their last pint of the week he spotted the leather jacket he'd seen some time previously . It was the person he'd seen before Gerald Moore immediately nodded   recognition and indicated with his head that he wanted to see him outside.Beresford drank up and followed him out . When he got to the Vauxhall Corsa he found Gerald standing by the kerb. They both got in. "Well any luck Mister?"

"Yes and no Gerry. We found some illegal drugs and Taliesin was using the Sanctuary as a base for selling drugs. As far as we can tell there was no link to Grimshaw."

"I see."

"Yes and that's a case in point Gerry. Were you a friend of Martin's, how long do you go back?"

"Well I 've got a history degree from Nottingham . I took a job teaching in London . I met Martin at a pub in Islington . I thought he was a reasonably sussed out sort of guy. That was twenty five years ago."

"What can you tell me about him? "

"Well he first decided amongst other things to do some voluntary service overseas I suppose. This was after he left British Telecom . He was in his thirties then. He was living in Thirton at the time. I didn't think anything of it at the time. I mean Yugoslavia , Dubrovnik it was a tourist destination. Then it all broke loose."

"Grimshaw was there? "

"Oh yes absolutely . When he came back he looked pretty shook up. Any ambition he had to be a journalist was pretty much in tatters."

"Was there any one else you knew from that era? "

"Only Marian Krantz . Marian and Martin had been

friends going way back . She might know some of her friends back then. I could never keep up."

"Okay anyone else?"

"Um no not really. Martin was interested in Goth music bands. He was interested in Medieval literature. In time he could have joined the sanctuary.I've told you as much as I can really. I'm sorry nothing has helped so far."

"Don't worry Gerry you've told me loads. " Gerry nodded and left the car. Beresford noted he didn't go back to the pub.

Two days later Beresford found himself at the doors of the Sanctuary once again. This time he found a humble and re-pentant Henry Stein badly trying to hide his resentment.

" I must say Inspector it is with the utmost reservations I grant you an audience this afternoon. I might even request a lawyer to be present. "

"Be my guest Mr Stein. I'm sorry to inconvenience you again. I thought you might not mind helping me out."

"Very well Inspector how can I help?"

Beresford leapt at this chasm of opportunity. "As you know Mr Stein Martin Grimshaw was murdered here in Weald Road. It was a grievously horrible crime. Things were done to the body. You're a spiritual man it must have troubled you deeply. Even now after the investigation that is over you must have thought about this horrible act. What ideas have you had Mr Stein?"

"What possible benefit would a man from the mater-ial world gain from a spiritual leader such as me Inspector? You deal with the living . To me sometimes it's the dead who make more sense."

"To be frank Mr Stein it's material men such as myself that sometimes don't see the truth right in front of our eyes. We don't learn to use our senses." While he said this he cast a look at Woods as if to say "just shut up and keep it quiet. "

"So you think my awareness is a matter of merit. Very well Inspector. What you say is true . I say true only in the sense that it may have some limited bearing on your investigation. Evil is power. It's an energy like any other. These are energies that have to be channelled like any other.

To this end I looked up some old maps of Kessington . Indeed there was a church on the site of the Green Weald Site. It was knocked down in 1930. Of course you might not know Churches were built on Pagan sites of worship.

At any rate the locals would have to take the bodies of their loved ones to the church for burial. They would use coffin paths . These paths would avoid fields of crops and rivers. There was a coffin path from the Albion Valley Railway station to where the Green Wealds Site is now. Of course since industrialisation fields have been covered with factories building estates and houses. Curiously enough the Coffin Path remains as a series of alley ways. As I say it's a path of energy."

"What was your conclusion from this?"

"That whoever killed Martin Grimshaw knew of these Coffin Paths . They were drawn to the site. They can go back and forth unseen."

"Okay. Well I'll be frank with you Mr Stein I was fishing. I haven't come up with very much. I will tell you this though you've given me something to think about. Thanks for your time."

Outside as they got in to the car Woods looked Beresford. "What was the point of that discussion?"

"Well we can look round Weald Road for alley ways that might have any significant meaning to our investigation. "

"That would include the service alleys that the dustmen use to collect the rubbish and alleys leading there on?"

"Almost certainly."

"That would lead us where?"

"Well I expect we'd be able to trace this Coffin Path that Mr Stein talks about because I have a feeling it almost certainly went through Weald Road."

"So it would lead us to Evil ?"

"No not in the sense he was talking about. However if we're talking about it we're talking about the Pagan mind if you could call it that.

Somebody wishing to perpetrate an atrocity of this nature would think along these lines. They would have their routes mapped out. It's worth a try. " Woods reluctantly nodded in agreement.

Davinia Peters was sitting in her house . In truth she was seeking reconciliation. The Reverend Willis had told her that the laboratory findings although definitive were not the last word on the subject. There would have

to be a group of Bishops drawn together before a they could officially declare the site official. They would have to consult official documents before they could come to any decision.

Davinia dismissed this as red tape. However the Reverend Willis would have none of it. He demanded that Davinia desist in her efforts to hold a dinner in the event of having the Church rededicated to Hilda of the marshes.. He lay down very firm rules and guidelines. Davinia felt crushed yet she still felt strong enough to carry on with the flower arranging.

Amongst the Parishioners that she knew was the house of Mr and Mrs Hanbury. Mrs Hanbury was a great philanthropist . She devoted several days a week to the women's aid shelter in Thirton High street. Mrs Hanbury owned a huge mansion in Felstead Woods. Her eldest son Graham was an oil executive in an oil company in America. He came over , he was taciturn laconic and sometimes positively rude. Mrs Hanbury would in-vent jobs for Davinia to do around the house. Most of all she would invite her round for tea and to have a chat.

Davinia knew for a fact that Lydia Mrs Hanbury's daughter was working as a doctor in a London Hospital and rarely came home for visits. She knew that Amelia or Mrs Hanbury as she was always careful of calling her thought about her all the time.

Davina knew there was a gulf between Mr Hanbury and his wife. He would go out to his golf club in the morning and rarely come back before tea. Sometimes he would be away for weeks at a time. He ran a publishing firm in the city . He would be called away on a book launch or some merger. Davina had seen sham marriages before they didn't surprise her. She looked at Amelia and felt she had been made a victim of her own marriage.

Tristan sat back in the Excelsior Hotel in Exeter as Stuart went through his materials again. "I must say I'm not sorry I brought you into this Stuart. I mean it's strictly legal. It should be okay "

"Relax Tristan I've got my materials here. I'm sure we can sort this out."

"Okay what do you need?"

"Well I'm looking at anything literally. At the beginning of his career Cezanne used unprimed canvas. Cezanne applied print inn thick blocky patches that would form cracks on the rough surface on the unfinished canvas. Especially as can be seen in the face and clothing of the Judgement of Paris. In this way he bestowed life on his subjects.

The paints that Cezanne used were a base group such as in the Bay of Estaque. An electron scope detected ultramarine and Prussian Blue. Chemicals were detected in the paper as well as the paint such as Sulphur and Potassium. In the green he used they detected arsenic. White comprised a mixture of lead carbonate and Barium Sulphate. Now with a bit of reverse engineering we could do that."

"How do you mean?"

" I mean by adding these elements into the painting so as to give it more authenticity."

"Your first result will have to look convincing ."

"I'm sure it will. "

"Do you know what the judgement of Paris was?"

"No. not exactly. Something to do with the Trojan War?"

"Spot on. In Greek mythology Zeus was holding a banquet in celebration of the marriage of Peleus and Thetis who were parents of Achilles.

Eros god of discord was not invited because she would have been a disturbing element in the proceedings. She turned up anyway with a Golden apple from the garden of the Hesperides . It had the inscription "to the fairest one."

Three goddesses claimed the apple, Athena, Hera, and Aphrodite. They asked Zeus to judge which of them was fairest . Zeus passed this task on to Paris. Previously Paris had to decide who would have a bull , Ares or a Shepherd. Paris decided on the God.

Paris therefore had to decide who was the most beautiful. Aphrodite bribed him with the World's most beautiful women. Hera offered him the leadership of Europe . Athena offered him wisdom and skill in War. Aphrodite offered him the World's most beautiful consort Helen of Sparta wife of the Greek King Menelaus."

"So he chose Helen?"

"Correct."

"I think I know how to approach this. It's fairly

straight forward. I've had about a month to get it right."

"If you're not sure pull out. It's not too late."

"Don't worry Tristan . Jud and Paddy are down in the bar. I expect they'll be around looking for results. It'll take time stuff like this always does. When will I have the copy to look at?"

"Tomorrow we'll be meeting Aaron Mallin ."

" Right I'll need to look at it constantly for at least three weeks."

"No need to rush . Personally I think it's folly."

Down in the lobby Jud and Paddy were ordering another round of drinks . "Paddy I'd like you to meet my great friend and raconteur Oscar Steinauer . Scourge of the moderate and undecided and no stranger to the roulette tables of Paris. "

"Hello I'm sure. " Paddy said nonchalantly "What brings you to this part of Cornwall Herr Steinauer? Is it the good weather or just the company?"

"Well Mr Stern I'm a connoisseur of art and the crafts. I suppose my friend Jud embellishes my reputation . I am a man of moderate means. Do you drive

Mr Stern?"

"Yes I have a Renault it does me. Yourself ? "

"Oh Mercedes of course. Only the best . As I was saying I'm thinking of going to St Ives . I believe there is an artist's colony there. Is that not so?"

"Yes I think so."

"I like the hills here they are so dramatic and the coast line. It reminds me of Lorna Doone and other romances. In my country we have Goethe and Wagner. Here you have Elgar and Shakespeare. It is so different."

"Careful Oscar you're letting the side down old boy."

"Oh I am patriotic but I am universal man when it comes to art."

"Which reminds me Jud when is Aaron coming?" Quickly Jud's eyes opened up like two guided missiles. "Oh I'm sorry."

"Arran you say?" Steinauer said, in a flash Paddy could see he misunderstood it to be the Island instead of the biblical character.

"Oh my that reminds me . The Hebrides I must go there some time." Steinauer finished.

"Yes you must ." Paddy finished for him, fending off Jud's glare for an instant.

The next day Stuart and Tristan along with Paddy , Jud and Steinauer who followed in another car took the road to Taunton.

"Who do we hope to find there Tristan?"

"Our sponsor apparently. It's a Mister Ambrose Benton. It's friend of Jud Fareham's. I believe they met at one of these conventions in Frankfurt. At any rate it appears that Jud has caught his ear. Mr Benton decided last year to host this competition for young painters who can reproduce a good masterpiece. It appears a Mister Stangrove owns a gallery and is very much up on the idea."

The journey only took an hour before they reached the suburbs of Taunton. They located a National Car Park near the town centre. With a knack that argued lots of practice Jud located a five star restaurant with in five minutes. After a meal that lasted an hour Jud briefed Stuart on the procedure.

"Ambrose Benton has offices here to look after his interests. He finds it easier than London. Lower rates , cheaper labour that sort of thing. He's an industrialist. Above all he wants to give back something to the community that's made him rich. Have you got that Portfolio with you?"

"Of course. Well when we see Mr Benton that's the first thing he'll want to see . If he thinks you're good enough then we're in. "

"Okay so I start painting for the competition then what?"

"Then if you win you go home Ten grand richer."

"Yes Mr Fareham. So what do you get out of it?"

"I have mutual concerns with Mr Benton that will profit from the exchange. I do charity work as well."

About half an hour later Stuart found himself face to face with an elderly gentleman of about seventy. He had a thick American accent that hinted at Brooklyn. He scrutinised Stuart for a minute. "Is this your boy

Jud?" Jud nodded laconically ."Okay let's see what you got."

Stuart lay out a group of drawings and paintings he'd done over the Summer. There were several paintings of Birds and landscapes. The colours of the plumage were dramatically depicted. One painting of a house in Colington Green called Clayborne house was featured in stark contrast to a cloud filled sky giving it a sinister context.   Slowly Benton surveyed the work. "Well I got to admit Jud you got me hooked. This man here is remarkable

I would say he should make a good contribution to the contest. Well thanks young man it's been a privilege. I look forward to seeing your work in a month's time."

Relief briefly crossed Jud's face. As they left Jud ushered them to a café nearby . As they sat round drinking coffee Stuart saw a man of rather pale complexion. "Hello ,Mr Fareham did it all go well?"

"Yes Mr Mallin it went fine. This thing is virtually in the bag. Why do you worry? "

"We'll be going to St Ives in about ten minutes everything is sorted out there. When we've finished I'll let you know."

"Be sure you do Mr Fareham I can't afford for anything to go wrong."

"Of course not ." Fareham said in an uncharacteristically timid manner.

True to his word the short journey to St Ives proved uneventful. Once there Stuart found an artist's studio and all the materials he had requested wrapped in polythene to one side. A chill feeling at the back of his ,mind told him it was all too good to be true. However the thrill of actually attempting to paint a portrait of Cezanne was totally absorbing him.

Sunday came again when to his surprise Beresford had the day off. Jean had taken the afternoon off to attend a tutorial at college . Mary who was ten could fend for herself . At least for a while anyway . Beresford studied the map he'd got of the Albion valley it quite clearly showed a path way leading from Albion Station to Circus Road that was about a mile away. He felt somehow when he asked Henry Stein about what he knew of the area

it rang a bell. The best way to follow this through was to find a path. The murderer was obviously someone who followed the occult. The least he could do was follow the lead.

The path was initially lying between two sets of houses . After about a mile he had to cross a road and follow the path on the other end. After another mile of fences and lock up garages going past service roads and abandoned cars he found Circus Road. Looking across the road he could see the path way carried on in an even manner. He could see that one side of the fence was a wire fence with pallets and stacked metal drums of chemicals .

He could see forklifts moving about. He carried on regardless. He would have asked Woods to do this for him. However he felt that Woods was not empathetic . That is to say he had no intuitive feel for the job. This could be the ritual disparagement of managers to their staff on his part. At any rate Beresford felt better doing this himself.

A person who could do this would pass by unnoticed . A person of no account , low self-esteem . All this comprised a criminal profile . A person who could read and write up ancient texts. As he walked by, he could see after miles of fencing that he'd come across the river Witham close by. This struck him as odd because he remembered Stein saying that the Coffin Paths avoided fields crops and rivers. Because they would be blighted by the passage of the corpse. The river would bear no fish the field no crops. He looked at the banks carefully and noticed they were covered in concrete. More probably the road nearby would only have being built by having the river diverted. Through the hedgerows and the other side he could see the lights of the Sanctuary House. Then all of a sudden he could see Weald Road. It was something of a shock. Grimshaw's House was further up the road. Inwardly he flinched. Being in the footsteps of a killer was contagious he thought.

Across the way he could see a path entrance. He followed this , it comprised of part of a service road that was part of Weald Road and led to the back of the houses. Repairmen refuse workers probably came through here every day . Then the path led downhill to more houses past the back of more factories. As he progressed he heard the sounds of traffic. Emerging from a closely fenced alley he found he was looking at the opening of South Weald Site making his original theory correct . A path some one knew. A path someone used regularly . This would mean he would have one more path to investigate.

Davinia sat in the Parish hall with the Reverend

Wallis . She listened patiently as he told her about the Gospels. They had this session once a week.

It was at her request. Nonetheless the Reverend Alec Wallis duly turned up and divesting himself of the tasks of the Parish gave himself wilfully to the task.

"There are three books in the "Imitation of Christ " by Thomas a Kempis. He instructs the reader on inward peace and purity of heart and good conscience. In this way Kempis feels moderating one's longings means a

no man's malice can't harm anyone. We have to attribute everything to God. He advocates that believers should carry the cross willingly, if we carry it grudgingly another cross will come along.

In book three he talks of consolation. He feels that the world promises things that are passing and of little value. When one is furthest away from God is when he is nearest.

In book four Kempis cites the bible and says the followers of Christ unless they renounce everything they cannot be disciples. He advocates followers to make clear the mansions of the heart, shut out the world and it's awful din.

I want to read out a passage from the "Imitation of Christ". Prophets may speak with eloquence but if you are silent they do not stir the heart. They record the message but you make plain what it means. They show us the mysteries but you reveal their hidden sense. They declare your commands but you give power to obey. They point out the road but you give a strength for the journey. They act on our outward senses but you instruct and enlighten the heart. They water the ground but you make it productive. They speak the actual words but it's through you one can understand them."

Do you understand the significance of this Davinia? Here is Kempis is speaking of a soul that comprehends and understands .He's appealing to a level of consciousness not revealed by the listener before. The power to think and act.

Mausse the anthropologist and Social Scientist stated in his book "The category of the human mind" the development of the Western Conception of the Person as self begins with the Romans. The first relative distribution of personhood to individuals comes about with the establishment of rights to individuals. A person had moral obligations and an independent moral identity

and consciousness which are linked to the individual , so we have introspection and inner regulation.

Before this, before civilisation men and women had person hood distributed amongst groups of people they thought as a unit. One identity would be to keep the fire going. Although these lifestyles have many things to

teach us in saving the environment the ability to take the initiative to be different was stifled. Thomas a Kempis accentuates the ability to think and Act. The idea of the soul to have inner reflections we dwell on were intrinsic in this. Kempis tells his readers not to rely on Prophets . In singling the individual he paves the way for the secularisation of the church.

In the coming years Hume would divide the World of Superstition and fear, Holy relics and raise the gospel of science above all else. After Darwin all churches came to depend upon the secularised values to do their everyday

tasks. The time of day told by clocks , disease cured by pills. Formerly they would tell the time by saying prayers depending on the time it took to denote the passing of the day. Disease and it's cures would revolve around prayers.

This is important you realise how as you as a person with a soul with the ability have come into this modern world of Science Davinia."

"But we still have a duty to God. "

" We have a duty to ourselves as well. We treat other

people as persons who can reflect and act the way we do also."

"Yes there is. Above all regard those around you with equal rights your own." Davinia nodded with complicity. For all her devotion Wallis wandered how much she understood . He knew she would have preferred hellfire and brimstone. It was more comforting to be besieged by demons and devils and to be rescued by angels then to take responsibility to manage one's own self. He had to make Davinia see she had sovereignty over her own body. She could control her own actions. She wasn't play to the devil's temptations.

She was good , she was kind, she was devoted. All in all he was lucky. Some day soon he would make her a curate probably.

Another Sunday Beresford sat in the breakfast room while Clair cleared up the dishes. Johnny and Mary had cleaned up the play area . Johnny was watching a video of "Fireman Sam." on the television while Teresa was upstairs doing homework from school. Clair exhaled loudly "Surely you're not telling me you have to go out again Chris?"

Beresford paused strategically . " "Yes it's this case . I can't get to the bottom of it. There's something bugging me about this."

"What about God almighty Mister Burnham himself? Does he give a toss? Last I heard he lives in Tonbridge and just turns up to say nice things to his Chief Constable. "

"No he does a lot more than that. There's something about this I can't quite see. I'm trying to enter the mind of a murderer, it's far from obvious."

"Give it a risk profile, he's a loner, it's definitely a he. He doesn't go to parties, got a badly paid job, doesn't date women or men. He has an immense anger. Lower income bracket."

"Is that what you think?"

"No it's what some crap psychologist would think relying on Empirical data. "

"What do you think?"

"Probably a woman. Otherwise the profile is similar. Follow your nose then. It's not my cup of tea. I'm writing an essay then I'm doing dinner at about half three. Then it's quality time with the guys yeah?"

"Yeah okay."

It was quarter of an hour later Chris found himself outside All Saints Church Kessington. He could see the great and the good filing in for the morning sermon. He looked around the meadows for something resembling a foot path.

It was about twenty feet from the long disused cemetery that stood next to All Saints Church he detected a path. He followed this and noticed it was going in the direction of Kessington Valley. The fields on either side were flowing with crops . As he walked past he noticed he went past some kennels and a stable . It was about a mile further on the path came to an abrupt end

or rather a road interrupted his journey. He noticed the path carried on over the other side. After going over a hill in the direction of Sevenoaks it turned abruptly. He looked at a map and found that the path turned to the left. The map he held was of the "Thirton Hundred " and dated back to the fifteenth century. As he saw the path he found himself coming out opposite William's farm and the entrance to the Abattoir. Over the road from the footpath he found a locked gate that descended down to the river Witham. Looking at the map he found this was the continuation of the path and the river itself lay

in an adjacent course about half a mile to the left. He reasoned with himselfthat the original farmers probably had the river diverted for reasons of irrigation and agriculture. At any rate he climbed over the gate and would

talk to the warden when he reached his booth by the next road.

He found the going easy , he also found he could easily reach Cullompton farm by this route. So far the theory of Stein's was proving accurate. The perpetrator had to be someone with a knowledge of ancient knowledge of Thirton. Someone who had a hatred and anger that was immense. The question was who exactly? The obvious culprit was Stein and his associates

but Woods and his investigation turned up nothing.

It was the next day Beresford reached the house on Parish Moor Road where Celia Asquith lived. It was grandiose by any standards . It had two front gables , the style was unashamedly mock Tudor. The front gates even had rampant Lions standing by the gateway. He noticed that the garden though formerly grand had fallen into a state of disrepair. He climbed the steps. "Is this someone important Sir?" Woods asked.

Beresford nodded "You could say that. I'm asking some questions of Mrs Celia Asquith . You'll have to be patient with me. I'm not sure what I'm looking for. Let me know if you think of anything as you go." Woods nodded.

Beresford rang the bell and waited . Presently he heard the steps approaching the door. When it opened he found himself looking at a woman about the same age as Clair his wife. She wore a check dress and wore ear rings. Smart and well turned out. "Yes, can I help you?"

"Yes my name is DI Beresford. I'd like to talk to Mrs Asquith . Some questions if that's okay?"

"Mrs Asquith wasn't expecting any visitors today, but you can come in . I'll ask her."

"Of course."

As they entered the entrance hall he saw it was quite grand in an old fashioned way. The house itself was kept spic and span and papered with exquisite taste. When the woman appeared from behind a green baize door.

She came forward "Mrs Asquith isn't ready right now. If you follow me she'llbe with you presently."

They followed her through to the front parlour with a Chesterfield sofa and a bookcase full of books and a portrait of a man in his seventies . Beresford could see a little plaque underneath "Henry Richard Asquith." "Oh take no notice of that. That's my husband . He died ten years ago bless him. It's good to meet you Inspector Beresford. I confess I have heard about you . Please do sit down." Mrs Asquith who was sitting on the settee wasted no time with introductions. She gestured to the chair . He obliged and Woods sat down in a chair opposite him.

Beresford studied Mrs Asquith for a moment. She was dressed in a green dress that covered her thin frame. "Thanks for seeing me Mrs Asquith . I'm sorry to see you at such short notice. As you know I've conducted a series

of interviews regarding the death of Mrs Joan Simmons."

"Oh yes poor Joan . Such a dear creature. How can I help?"

"I'm trying to discover more about Thirton . I know it seems silly . I think the more I know about Thirton , the more I seem to get a flavour of what happened. "

"Well I don't know how I could possibly help you Inspector but I'll try."

"Okay could you tell me something of the history of Thirton from your point of view?"

"Where could I start?"

"Davinia Peters?"

"Not quite Inspector. Sarah her mother would be more appropriate. Sarah was born in Thornbury House . Gabriel Thomas Peters her father wouldn't have it any other way. It stands in Elderberry Road , that's an extension of Gatehouse Road that leads down from Terminus Road that goes past Thirton East

Station ." Beresford nodded his understanding.

"Gabriel Thomas Peters was a strict man . His wife Edith Lorraine Peters was the head of the woman's institute . They had a child Sarah. Sarah was married to a Police Detective but had nervous breakdown. Sarah had a child called Davinia . Davinia grew up for the main part with the grandparents ."

She paused. "There were many outstanding personalities in Thirton at the time. Hector Robert Turnbull was Mayor of Thirton from 1975 through to 1989.

During that time he served in a time of expansion for Thirton council for housing or lack of it. He had a wife and five children. They lived in a nice house in Colington Green . It was called the Maples and had iron gates . Hector's children were all daughters. His wife Harriet devoted her life to her family and had more or less turned away from Hector. In his long hours in the office Hector took comfort from his secretary who was Sarah Peters . That was during the eighties when Turnbull left office he could no longer afford the charms of Sarah so he cast her aside. He returned to Hampshire with his wife, his five daughters had all grown up and married. This of course left Sarah in a dilemma approaching retirement herself and one daughter who was twenty.

It was one morning in September in 1991 they had found the body of Sarah Peters at Kessington Common in a thicket. She'd taken an overdose of sleeping tablets. "

"What about Mrs Turnbull? " Beresford turning warning eyes at Woods as if to say don't interrupt.

"To say that life more or less turned round Hector Turnbull in Thirton was an understatement. So the funeral of Sarah Peters was well attended at All Saints Church of course . My husband was an accountant. " She nodded to the portrait . " We used to attend Bridge Parties held at Hector Turnbull's House in Colington Green. Hector's wife came from Cornwall. She was an aloof sort of woman but didn't suffer fools gladly."

"Not even Sarah? "

"No , as far as she was concerned Hector provided the money and she ran her own life. I used to attend the bridge parties there. There was Sandra Goodman whose husband was a finance director of a transport firm. Diana Adams whose husband was a head teacher at a Grammar School in Kessington.

Vincent Coulsdon an electrician and Bertrand Randlesdon an auctioneer and valuer. These formed the nucleus brought together by Harriet and she was definitely Queen of the Castle. Sandra Goodman was an incorrigible gossipand would talk endlessly about the scandalous goings on of Sarah Peters and every week we would come back for more. (Unbeknownst to Harriet of course who had quite a wooden ear.)

Bertrand Randlesdon was a business man but had no patience for gossips and usually played a good hand at Bridge. Diana Adams was the reclusive one of the rest . Her husband was a meek soul . There was a chap called Victor Hurst who was an accountant from Lewisham of all places who'd being to a few bridge meetings . He had definite designs on her. As far as I'm aware it all ended in tears on a Saturday afternoon at a meeting in Thirton ornamental Gardens were they met for the last time. I never saw Victor again.

Through this time Gabriel Thomas Peters lived to the grand old age of a hundred and died in 1987 . By this time Davinia was fifteen . His wife by now 90 was looked after by Davina and died shortly after at the age of 95. Davinia was approaching the age of independence with something of a jolt.

She was initially successful in education . She decided at the time it was 1992 she would volunteer for voluntary service overseas with a group of others. I kept her photograph somewhere . I can't remember where ."

" I felt that Davinia had never been treated fairly. They didn't live that far apart and Davinia would come round to see Sarah regularly. She would come to see me of course, I would mother her in a self-conscious sort of way. Giving her the support she needed and the strength to carry on.

For some reason after she came back from Bosnia , I very rarely saw Davinia. It was as if she was a different person . More outward going doing good works for the Parish and devoting herself to the Church , All Saints in Kessington Common. It all seems rather odd.

The Bridge Club went it's separate ways at the end of the eighties. Sandra Goodman and her husband divorced in 1989. He died of a heart attack in 1991.

I sometimes sit her like I'm doing now and reminisce about old times in Thirton. We would sit the whole gang of us in the Royal Hotel in Thirton High Street. We were the cream of Thirton Society . Hector sitting up at the top of the table with Harriet by his side. Then there would be Diana Goodman and then there would be the borough surveyor Eric Faversham and the council leader Brian Carpenter Sarah would be at the end sitting meekly talking to Fey Underwood , office manager at the planning department. They would pontificate on the great and the good. They would discuss the scandalous goings on in Thirton Area Health Authority. The chief medical examiner and pathologist included. All I've got now is the Psychic society with Albert Bream. It's all such a long time ago. I still go past Thornberry House occasionally but I never go in."

"Well Mrs Asquith that was delightful. I hope I can use it somehow. Though you've told me a lot."

"Would you like some tea. I'll fetch Mildred."

"I'm sorry but we have to go. It's been a very generous use of your time Mrs Asquith thanks a lot."

"My pleasure Inspector. " She got up as they left. As Beresford walked out he could see the relief on Woods's face was quite palpable. He decided he wouldn't ask him any questions.

Averill Green was another name that Albert Bream had

mentioned . She lived in Addley road . Duly following up his interview with Celia Asquith of course he would have to tread carefully . Addley Road was the road that led from Aviemore Road to Thomson Road more or less central to East Thirton. After a while Averill who's house was quite modern compared to that of

Celia Asquith immediately disabused him of any notion of grandstanding. They were sitting on an imitation Louis XIV settee. "You can put your feet up if you like. " She said.

Beresford accompanied by Woods laughed gaily. "Mrs Asquith was telling us of the Bridge Club she ran with Diana Adams and Sandra Goodman . She mentioned how they were friends with Hector Turnbull . How strange it was that Turnbull retired out of Public life in 1988."

"Strange? I should cocoa. Hector was one of the leading lights Thirton Council. This was true. He moved the council offices to property newly acquired by them from the Church of England. A move that was seen at the

time as a stroke of Genius. However the discrepancies began to emerge in Turnbull's accounts that meant he had to leave. Hence his quiet departure to Hampshire in 1988. "

Beresford reminded her that the Bridge Club was still intact. Without prompting Averill mentioned Sarah Peters. She was she thought a perpetually wronged woman. Brought up with a brute of a father she latched on to Turnbull and that proved her undoing. She'd seen her a few days before she died in Kessington in a pitiful little bedsit. It was pathetic.

The odd thing about all of this was Davinia. She was a socialist the bell of the ball. She got the urge to join the VSO. She joined in fact a lot of them joined in 1992 they went off to Bosnia. When she came back she changed entirely . Off to All Saints Church every opportunity, out doing pastoral work for the Vicar. She lives in that house in Elderberry Road . I suppose it's some sort of shell shock.

She felt sorry for Celia Asquith all alone in that house. Good thing she had that Psychic Society to go to. Averill informed Beresford that Celia's husband died in 1996. That was why she joined the Psychic Society. Averill never really got on with the others. She talked to Celia but never really hit it off with the outsiders.

Davinia Peters sat outside her house in Elderberry Road. Thornbury House was where the great and the revered Peters family lived . Sarah was their only daughter . For some reason Sarah never married when she fell pregnant with Davinia. However Edith her grandmother took care of her. It was more accurate that Davinia's care was supervised by a long chain of care workers who had to look after Edith and Gabriel her grandfather. Her grandparents were in their dotage.

For reasons she never really went into, Davina never could recollect her childhood and always remained glib on the subject. She had an annual income and lived on that. She devoted herself to All Saints Church in Kessington . Mainly because the Parishioners there couldn't associate her with any part of Thirton she had a partial anonymity which suited her fine.

Davinia was clear sighted in what she wanted . She did pastoral care in the community . She had a sort of paid job looking after Major Kindersley . This was despite the allowance set up for her in a trust fund by her Grandmother. Major Kindersley was a slight fellow in advanced years. He joined the army in 1953 when he was twenty. He had a good recollection of those years and had albums of photographs to show what campaigns he's been on .

Davinia dusted the place and generally made sure he was okay. She was part of a network of informal carers that All Saints pastoral care mission had organised by Mrs Stevens the Parish Council Chairwoman. It was in this way she also managed she managed to become a bursar for All Saints Church.

The Church committee to decide the small alcove to be devoted to St Hilda was

due in a month's time. Davinia felt a thrill of excitement.

She still felt a thrill of disappointment as to how her mother could linger over Hector Turnbull the former town hall leader. Those years she would draw a veil over and never properly talk about them.

Her teacher in Yoga told her to live in the present not the past. Whatever happened was not important , now was all that mattered . Of course there were other reasons why she was so present time orientated towards but enough of that.

Her day would start early in the morning with getting Major Kindersley up and ready for the morning breakfast. She then would get to All Saints Church , check the flower arrangements dust around the pews . Get the floor polisher out and do the floors . She then would organise the coffee mornings with Jennifer Brighton.

Jennifer would talk interminably . Married with two children she had the knack of doing three things at once which could be annoying if you didn't want to talk.

When the coffee morning was done she would help out with the toddler's class in the annexe . By about two o'clock she would go back to Major Kindersley , help clear up after he had his meals . On Wednesday she would visit the Reverend Wallis who would be taking a bible class. That at the moment was a big problem . Because of his notion of consciousness and the soul seemed to focus on loving and forgiving and not enough on evil. She was sure there was plenty of evil in the World. God said he would come with a sword and a flame. She talked of the Saints in England at the time of the Saxons. She knew there was an excavation in the great weald site . The artefacts there were mainly heathen and had no interests for her.

Beresford had to find Marian Krantz . He located her in

the Green Dragon on a Saturday night. A woman in her mid-forties with a mildly bohemian dress sense excited his curiosity but he kept his presence of mind.

"Miss Krantz , I wonder if you could help me . I want to ask you some more questions about Martin Grimshaw.

It would be an interview in your flat. There'll be another Police Officer present."

"Oh dear I do hope I'm not under suspicion ."

"No of course not. It's just I want to find out more about Martin . I'm not getting the bigger picture here. There's something I'm missing and I'm not sure what it is."

"Well of course officer if you think it will help. When? Tomorrow afternoon if you think it's best. I'm free. My address is flat 4 Victoria Gardens . Gardenia Walk , Albion Valley. Not exactly the Ritz but it does me."

"Thanks very much Miss Krantz . I look forward to seeing you there. "

It was a summer afternoon when Beresford drew up outside the Victoria Gardens . Gardenia Walk was set away from the Industrial quarter of Albion Valley and had a somewhat genteel air. When Maria Krantz opened the door Beresford thought the interior was tastefully decorated with prints of artists. He guessed the print covering the wall was Modigliani. Though he had no idea of what period. Inside the living room he saw a few reproduction prints of Haitian Women by Goya.

The furniture was Chinese lacquered furniture . Beresford had no idea how much it had cost but had an idea that it must have been an immodest amount of money. "I know for a woman of insubstantial means I do accumulate stuff. I was an accountant , still am. As a matter of fact. However I've always been attracted by the bizarre . It's held an attraction for me. Now enough about me.

You and your assistant want to talk about poor Martin , yes?"

Beresford and Woods were sitting comfortably on a settee while Maria surveyed them from her armchair . "Yes I'm afraid so. Now Miss Krantz when did you first meet Martin?"

"It was about nineteen ninety. Martin had just finished his stint on British Telecom and was looking about for work. We met in Thirton at a concert . We seemed to get on quite well. Anyway we had an on off relationship mainly because Martin couldn't settle down.

It seemed odd at the time. I think when his job went , his partner went as well. At any rate he wanted to do something new. I couldn't blame him really. The only thing I was married to my job . I had to put some money on the table. Martin decided to do Voluntary Service Overseas. There were a gang of them from Thirton in ninety two who went over to Serbia. Well I've got a photograph somewhere. Just a minute."

She fished through her belongings and emerged with a photograph album. She opened the album. Briefly Beresford could see pictures of Marian as a young girl and her mother and her father. She turned the pages briefly "God yesterday was so long ago. There's me as a teenager." Briefly Beresford could see a lithe young girl with big blond hair wearing a bikini obviously Marian herself. "Anyway , let's see." She turned a few more pages.

"Ah here it is." Marian turned a page and showed Beresford a picture of a group of people standing outside Thirton East Station . Here he could see off to one side a young Martin Grimshaw with long hair. He was a handsome man with a young Marian Krantz standing by his side. Off to one side he could recognise a young looking Gordon Williams and Iris Williams and a man standing next to Gordon who he could recognise as Andrew his brother. That was if his memory of the funeral was serving him correctly. He saw two young women standing off to one side standing next to one another. "Those two women were inseparable . Davinia Peters and Jeannie Smith."

One woman had blond hair the other had dark hair.

"I see these people went to Sarajevo I take it. Did they have an overland jeep or something? I think I can see one locked away in the corner."

"Yes your right there. Gordon Williams organised it. He worked for the Hague but he organised the journey to encourage money for Bosnia."

"What happened?"

" I believe something did happen as a matter of fact. They were stuck on the road to Bihac in a coach. This was coming from Sarajevo. The coach got stopped by the Serbian militia and all the Croatian women had to get off. Martin was terribly upset . I think he took a job labouring when he got back. At any rate it took him a long time to get over it."

"Do you mind if I take this picture. I could use it . It might mean something , it might mean nothing. I'll let you have it back as soon as I've finished ."

"Of course Inspector be my guest."

As they came out of the house Woods said." Do you think you've got something at last?"

"Yes maybe."

"God , I don't know what you see in her . Mutton dressed as mutton. "

"You do not appreciate the finer things in life Justin."

Anne Cameron relaxed for a moment as she drew up outside her friend's House in Hastings. His name was Thomas Knight . He had PhD in history and had written many academic tomes . Anne regarded him as a friend and companion. She worked as a teacher at Thirton Grammar school and had met Thomas on a rambling holiday on the South Downs. It was shortly after the death of his wife, they had become good friends. It was true to say they corresponded on a monthly basis. He had been intrigued to hear of the fiasco surrounding the séance at the Green Weald Site. Of course he didn't want to be associated with it in any way but basked in the Schadenfreude. Anne had been concerned of late because he had been diagnosed with cancer of the colon.

Though he was receiving treatment and apparently doing quite well.

Knight's house stood on a promontory outside Hastings and looked out on the bay and surrounding areas . She always thought it was his Emperor complex that led him to occupying such a magisterial position on the coast. Catherine his wife had died five years previously , they had one daughter who was married with children but Knight was too proud to ask for help. She knew he had a home help called Monica who came in the mornings.

She parked her car outside the house. It was an ordinary house not out of place in any suburban street. She walked up to the front door so forlorn in this setting and knocked . She could hear the slow footsteps coming up to the door,

meanwhile she turned to look at the panoramic view behind her as she did so.

The door opened and there stood Knight. He had blue Corduroy trouser and his white hair was swept back. He looked in the pink of health. "Hello, Anne it's nice to see you. It's been a bit rough here but see me as you find me."

"Don't I always."

Being as they were old friends there was no need for pleasantries. Anne took her bags and established herself in her usual room overlooking the bay at the back of the house. It was always a pleasure to come down here and see such a view.

When she came down to the kitchen Thomas had a cup of tea ready and a plate of biscuits. "How's it been going Thomas?"

"The diagnosis came through a month ago. They've recommended Chemotherapy and that's what I'm on. I can't complain. I've had a good few years , most of them brilliant. Not being like back in Sussex."

"It never is . You never seem to stop though Thomas, thesis after thesis."

Thomas let out a long sigh. "Yes of course the analysis of the end of Politics."

"Oh that was Daniel Bell as I remember not quite right, neither was Fukuyama as I recall."

"Right again Anne . Yet I feel they weren't entirely off the mark."

In her memory she knew that Thomas was an incorrigible pessimist. The glass was always half empty. If this was the start of the debate she could wait until after the lunch ."You said you had dinner ready?"

"Of course. I'll just mike it up. It won't take more than a few seconds ." Diplomatically Anne sat back and let Thomas make the arrangements. Presently Anne sat back and admired the Lamb cutlets potatoes and Broccoli

that lay before her. She washed it down with a good wine and helped with the washing up afterwards . As they sat in the study afterwards , Bach played in the back ground. Thomas settled down to his main theme.

"So you were saying that Daniel Bell and Francis Fukuyama weren't entirely mistaken. Would you like to outline in more detail?"

"Yes of course. I suppose this is going to sound very hackneyed to you but I fear we're nearing the end of civilisation as we know it."

"Well I suppose given you're disposition you're entitled to be pessimistic . What's you're premise?"

"Spengler stated the World would enter a pre death emergency in the year 2000. He felt there would be a period of 200 years of omnipotence before the final collapse. He wasn't a democrat but he believed the Nazis , Mussolini and Cecil Rhodes were tyrants. He believed that the existence of social entities called cultures had no metaphysical sense. Mankind had no plan. Each culture had its own entity even to the end. These cultures had their own age phases, childhood , youth and old age which becomes civilisation. This characterised in the modern age by technology , imperialism and mass society.

To underline this I quote Schopenhauer that the World as will is a product of blind and malleable will . Using Kant who argues that a conscious subject

cognises an object not as they are but in the way they appear to us under conditions of our sensibility. Hume conducted an assault on this reasoning. Schopenhauer felt that empirical concept of causality presumes knowledge

of causality therefore Hume's concept of causality is disproven."

"So different cultures perceive things differently? Anne asked.

"Yes, that's it basically."

"And you're proof?"

"Well I can think of two different civilisations that collapsed with two different value cultures already. The Roman civilisation began to crumble with the defeat of two legions and five cohorts of infantry at the battle of Teutoburg Forest in 4BC. Then in the third century came the reign of Julian the Apostate. Then in 476 Ad came the last Roman Emperor in Rome, Romulus Augustus.

My other example is the Mayan Civilisation that ended in the ninth century because of the internecine warfare and the environmental degradation and drought caused by their farming methods couldn't support

their society any more.

In the case of Rome , because they recruited soldiers from their slaves they were running out of lands. Also the cavalry tactics of the Goths and the vandals were superior to that of the Romans who were used to fighting in the Desert. In the case of the Mayans their methods probably led to desiccation of the soil, famine and the death of their civilisation. In some ways all of these lead back to our present predicament, pollution and depletion of resources. Spengler was right we're in the "Old age" of our civilisation."

"Really Thomas are you sure? I thought you'd be a bit more progressive than this . You used to quote Hobsbawm at the drop of a hat."

"I suppose my disposition has become more pessimistic Anne." He sighed "But I'm getting tired these days . You turn on the news...." His voice tailed away.

" Well." She added slowly "Take the idea of cultural identification . Each culture identifies an object differently according to our sensibility. Look at Nietzsche. Nietzsche felt that the philosophy of utilitarianism was a product of a bourgeois lifestyle. He felt that the superman or ubermensch was the answer to the death of God. He felt democratic man was unable to dream but

just earn his living and keep warm. One must have the strength of the overman to dream and have some continuity in society."

"What about antisemitism and so forth?

"Nietzsche wasn't antisemitic . He was antichristian because he considered it wasn't forward looking enough"

"That nudges us out of civilisation and bourgeois values?"

"Precisely."

"You know I think we'd both be better off with Hobs-bawm at least he was constant."

She laughed for a moment feeling she'd got him out of his pessimism.

"Okay , I'll have another one if you join me."

CHAPTER 6

Thirton High street being a main juncture for popular commerce had by the late twentieth century become a pedestrian precinct , and the traffic of course ran through Thirton Way. This effect of course led to the bottom half of Thirton High street still being subjected to some traffic such as buses and motorists wandering through out of curiosity . The road leading to Allman's Road leading to Thirton Common and then to Kessington.

Of course after Thirton Common was a significant left turning called Bateman's Road. This road held several council estates . Stanley Williams having left Cullompton Farm that morning had attended Thirton Comprehensive . To this end he was studying for his physics and chemistry A levels in the hope of gaining entry to Chichester College of Agriculture.

Stanley had developed firm friends whilst at School . There were three, Mitch , Will and Terry. Terry and Mitch were now at the present moment eliciting the pleasures and hardships of the present day in Will's parent's council flat in Bateman's Road. "It was gross Stan Three hours of Chem and the teacher flunked me on my test." Will announced.

"You have to do the basics Will. You have to study."

"Mmm, yeah I know . I'll get a job like my dad on the motorway. I'm not worried."

Terry laughed ."Seriously Bill wise up. Road repair? I mean you're going to be doing that for forty years?"

Will took another draw on the spliff he made about three minutes earlier. "It's methodical I'm sure . I can do Chemistry . I like hard work though it's no biggie."

"Good I'm glad that's sorted ." Stan said. "Even if I get this Chemistry I'll end up working on a farm it looks like I'll be on a farm for the rest of my life. That means hard work whether I pass or not."

"Not necessarily you can turn it into a massive orchard . Having a grape harvest that would be fun." Terry opined.

Stanley looked doubtful , "I've seen how my father worked. He was definitely hands on. I'm down with Chemistry and Physics. It's being a shock the last three months. I can work the farm though. It's given me ideas."

"What you mean a cannabis farm?" Will laughed .

"Nah, I mean there's possibilities in farming. I'll meet Bea when she gets back from university. We can discuss things."

The discussion meandered in this fashion in an abstract fashion. It was early evening when Stanley entered Cullomp-ton Farm , his plans not yet crystallised. Though his mother Iris had made it perfectly clear that Beatrice had gone to University to study economics she seemed to have no vocation for farming , therefore the future of the farm would be up to him.

Stanley had gone up to his room after exchanging a few pleasantries with his mother. He looked round the place. To tell the truth he still felt in shock. It felt as though time was still held in place three months previously after the funeral of his father. Gradually of course things were coming back to normal .

His School work was still bearing up . Reluctantly Stanley faced the situation that life would carry on. Will, Terry , and Mitch had been there for him no question.

Jud and Paddy looked out of their studio apartment in St Ives. "I thought the Excelsior Hotel was quite adequate for our means Jud. Stuart and Tristan seemed quite happy about it."

Jud turned round . "It was indeed quite adequate for our means Paddy. Except of course we have Oscar Steinauer with us . You would of course have to ask him more clearly what he did for a living in the restaurant of the bloody hotel."

"I don't see how that affects the situation. "

"Not in itself . However Stuart was making plans on how to work on the canvas in the hotel room leaving drawings and where everyone could see them. That in itself was no big deal . No the tin hat , the icing on the cake was when you nearly made Oscar Steinauer talk about the whole fucking business that he was an art restorer of oil painting to the entire restaurant."

"How would they notice anything ?" Paddy said.

"Because Paddy my dear chum that is how people get caught."

"Well it's nice here. I've been down to the beach a couple of times. How's the office?"

"My office is quite satisfied with the work I've been done this year. If anything needs fixing I can go back at a moment's notice."

"I've taken a few extended months , they owe me anyway. " Paddy resumed.

Downstairs in the studio Stuart was surveying the canvas with Oscar Steiner . "Where is your friend Stuart?"

"Tristan? He had to go back , His work needed him. He only came for moral support. "

"From what I can see you've caught the effect well. The brush work is pretty accurate . I notice you've tested the paints until ,they match the effect Cezanne created. The whole thing is a masterpiece in itself. The only worrying thing is that the paints make the painting look brand new."

"You can lightly bake it. That wears off the sheen to some extent."

"That would be overkill no. I was thinking of Ultra violet rays . That would be more effective."

"When will the painting need to be submitted?"

"By the end of the month. I can put it off until the end of August. I'll see it might not be as long. It will look as though we've restored some of the faded

brushwork the main tableau has a stunning effect . Art experts such as myself might be able to tell the difference. They would have to look behind the canvas and wood to determine the age . Still there would be an element of doubt. If we can get over that initial hurdle then we would be in the ball park."

"Where is the other painting going?" Stuart asked. He pointed to the copy he had been studying assiduously for the past two months. "To some rich man's home in Florida I expect. These rich people have conceived of art as a commodity in itself . It has no soul , it has no life. It is merely an object that accrues money . Whatever artistic merit Van Gogh or Titian may have is irrelevant. To them the accumulation of capital gain is everything. The aim of possession is the acme of meaninglessness in a meaningless world. They are victims of alienation, so estranged from their roots and origins it has ceased to matter anymore."

Beresford looked again at the results he had obtained from the interview he'd held so far on the Williams case. "I'm not sure where this is getting us right now. I've got one more interview before I make my decision. I'm going to interview Iris Williams again she might shed light on this. "

"Sir , I don't mean to put you off the scent but we've been interviewing these old biddies about Thirton in the old days . As far as I'm concerned about as relevant as Aunt Nelly's bunions have to do in forecasting the weather. They've had their day in the sun and now they're out to pasture. What ever happened in the old days doesn't seem to have much bearing on what's happening now. "

"Which is why I'm going to interview Iris Williams now. She's been living with Gordon all this time. She may have been aware of something we've missed . I'm pretty sure it's there somewhere."

Woods hunched his shoulders fatalistically "If you say so Sir." They drove down to Cullompton Farm . On that particular day it was approximately two months after the funeral. He noticed that the lorry that Gordon had been using was parked to one side with a tarpaulin over it. Other than that , things seemed pretty much back to normal. Beresford parked his car in the farm yard by Lambert Hodges's office.

As he came out of his car Iris came out of the house. "Good morning Inspector. To what do I owe this visit? "

"Good morning Mrs Williams . I wanted to come and have a word with you about a few things we've uncovered in our investigations. It won't take long. I know you're busy . It's just a few things I need to clear up."

Iris stood to one side. "Of course Inspector this way."

She ushered him into the farm house . It stood just the same as before. It always seemed to Beresford a shock to re-visit a murder scene. Not because it changed , but because it hadn't changed much. It was as if life hadn't meant that much. The office where Gordon kept his accounts was pretty much the way he kept it. Beresford afforded himself a glimpse as he passed through on the way to the parlour.

As they sat down in the room where Beresford guessed Mrs Williams received her guests he said. "I see nothing much has changed round here

since the accident."

"No . Lambert keeps the accounts . Lukasz manages the farm. The whole thing pretty much runs itself. Lambert submits a report to me every day and I do look round and have a chat with Lukasz .Other than that everything is pretty much as it was."

"Right Mrs Williams as you know I've been conducting interviews in Thirton about your husband and Thirton itself. As you know we had a recent murder

in Albion Valley not so long ago of one Mr Grimshaw. There were certain marked similarities . One they were both pretty horrific . Two they both seemed motiveless. I started looking at possible causes. It came to my attention that both you and Gordon had been lawyers for Amnesty International and worked closely with the Hague before you bought a farm here, is that correct?"

"Yes we did as a matter of fact. Gordon's brother came to the funeral. I was still pretty cross with him about things that had happened. Why do you mention this Inspector?"

"Could you tell what the disagreement was about perhaps?" "

Gordon was working on a case of a man called Patrick Shin. He was a factory manager in Bali in Indonesia. The prosecution rested on the testimony of Amir Siregar who we met in the course of our investigation. We were meant to meet Amir in Bali during the holy festival when they engage in cockfighting. It has religious significance."

Woods coughed to hide the laugh that Beresford knew was coming. "I see Mrs Williams carry on."

"Well we went to the ceremony. Only Amir Siregar didn't turn up. They found his body later it had been found by one of the road traffic junctions outside Bali. A friend of ours Carol Broadley had seen Andrew with the head of Bali Security in Denpasar that same day. The significance wasn't lost on us I can tell you."

"So you think Andrew was in cahoots with Balinese Security?"

"There was the possibility. Though Andrew protested his innocence even at the funeral."

"I see well that doesn't have any bearing on what I was going to ask you."

"What does?"

"I'm sorry Mrs Williams what do you mean?"

"What does have any bearing on Gordon's murder? It's been two months. You must have some clue."

"Yes of course . Well it's come to my attention that both you and your husband visited Sarajevo in 1992 is that correct?"

"Oh yes of course. How stupid of me. Yes we just married in 1991. We both had an interest in current affairs , we joined Amnesty and went to various places where human rights abuses occurred . Sarajevo was a one off, quite a disaster what can I tell you?"

"Who did you go with?"

"There were a group of us from Thirton. Gordon and I were more concerned with individual cases. Of course the Serbian authorities were only concerned with human rights abuses because the UN was there. We took up a few cases in the courts but there was mayhem in the streets."

"What were the other members doing . Martin Grimshaw for example?"

"Oh of course poor Martin . He was a telecom engineer. He was able to do some routine repair work on the telecommunications. There was Jeannie Smith same age as me . She was a nurse I believe she did some work with the Red Cross and Davinia Peters. Honestly I'm in my own world with this place. I see them occasionally in town . I'm so busy , I hardly notice."

"Was there anything in particular about the trips that stand out in your mind?"

"Well yes as you mention it. We decided to take a trip to Bihac. It lay some miles outside Sarajevo. We thought nothing of it. Amnesty was paying. We decided that we'd take the bus to save on petrol. Anyhow as we were approaching Bihac the bus was stopped on the road by Serbian Militia. They took all the Croatian women off the bus. I hate to think what happened to them."

"Anything stand out in your mind about that occasion?"

"Yes both Davinia and Jeannie Smith were extremely upset . Two of the women taken were friends of theirs. Anja and Julia. We never saw them again. Gordon was furious but when faced guns and militia there was little he could do."

"I see , and nothing else stands out in your mind about that occasion?"

"No, I'm sorry Inspector. It's all about the past . Naturally I was upset for the girls . The truth is as a lawyer you learn to distance yourself . It's hard but what can I say?"

"If you hear of anymore developments or if you remember anything of any significance could you keep me informed Mrs Williams. The investigation is still

current. To be honest I'm at the end of my tether here. I just can't think of anything just yet. If I get any further progress I will of course let you know."

"Yes Inspector . Thank you for your time. I will of course let you know if I hear of anything." For an instant as he left , he saw a look of bewilderment on Mrs Williams's face as the demons of the past came to haunt her.

As they drove away Woods asked Beresford "And what did you get from that Sir?"

"Only I'm not sure what happened to Jeannie Smith. I had

a word with Harry Burnham , Chief to you. He said she's disappeared."

"One loose end."

"Among many . This is not proving fruitful D.C. Woods Not at all. Suggestions on a post card to this address etc."

Celia Pheeney lived further down Addley Road. Beresford had an appointment to see her at eight o'clock the previous evening . It was all Woods could do to disguise his contempt at yet another Red Herring. Surprisingly enough Harry Burnham was quite understanding. "I don't think this is a serial killer Chris. We've had no reports of similar attacks in London. These seem quite unique. All in all I'd say you're instincts are giving you good clues. The killer knows his or her prey. On every occasion no struggle was put up." Burnham said in his office.

"But there's being no resolution. I'm beginning to wander."

"Well you're interviewing more people it's a long process. Someone was careful enough to cover up their steps. There's been premeditation on a grand scale. We thought that the obvious culprit was in Sanctuary House. That wasn't a complete failure. We also got Alison Fairfield and Mr Simmons operating a scam. If we keep going we get more I'd say."

Beresford kept this advice in mind when he came to see Mrs Pheeney at ten o'clock that following morning. Number 83 Addley road just down from Mrs Averill Green.   It was a house of similar character built in the Victorian period with certain concerns as to the plumbing and keeping it dry. Though Chris remembered she told him she had the roof done the previous year.

The garden was a short garden . Chris didn't have a long walk to the front door. He rang the bell , Mrs Pheeney answered it. She was a woman of about

seventy. She had a shock of black hair which she kept short .

She dressed in black giving her a somewhat sepulchral air..

"Hello, Mrs Pheeney I've come to ask you a couple of questions . I won't be long. I want to know more about the community here." By this time she ushered him into her small front room. It had a standard flat screen and some though not many dvds. There were photographs on the mantelpiece of family , and husband who had divorced a few years previously she explained.

"Well I don't know how I can help . I must say . What were you interested in specifically?"

"Anything. I gather you were in the Albion Psychic group with Arnold Bream. Is that true?"

"Yes of course. I mean , I don't ever want to see my husband again the cheating scoundrel , but yes I've seen a lot of things happen. I don't pass on gossip , but what I see stays with me alone."

"I see and could you tell what me you've seen ?"

"What I've seen? Well where can I start? You were interested in Mr Arnold weren't you?"

"Well yes of course . Could you tell me anything about him?"

"Well there were a group of us that went to the Psychic group on Thursday evening. There was Anne Cameron, Averill Green, and Joan Simmons. We went to the Great Weald Site for a Séance. That turned out to be a farce. I joined for a good reason, I had an Uncle and a Brother I wanted to get in touch with.

You know I think he helped me. I felt Arnold was good at heart. May be too good really."

"In what way was he too good Mrs Pheeney?"

"Well I'm not sure I should say. Oh what am I saying , it could have been quite innocent I suppose, but I was never able to look at Mr Bream the same way again. Any way all it was just one Sunday in Lent. I'm a strict Anglican if you must know . I'd come from St James Church , that's the one in Tilson Park Road. I was passing by Mrs Simmons's house . Any way I saw Mr Bream and Mrs Simmons have a very earnest conversation on the front door step.

It even seemed intimate. I thought nothing of it really. I knew she was married to Mr Simmons and I don't think they'd broken up yet. To tell you the truth I put it to the back of my mind and thought no more about it. Then about a month later I met a friend of mine Winifred George she's an old friend of mine from the Women's institute. We were having lunch in the Royal Hotel in the High Street. I mean it's a bit pricey you know , but a treat is nice now and again.

Any way there they were as bold as brass in the Hotel foyer like a couple of newly-weds. I didn't know where to put my face . I thought I shouldn't judge

people and let them live their lives if that's how they want to so be it. Mr Arnold Bream in a serge grey suit and looking smart and Mrs Joan Simmons like butter wouldn't melt in her cake-hole. By this time I was hearing about a split between her and her husband. I didn't stop going to the Psychic group after that. Truth was Mr Bream helped me a lot . It wasn't his fault he was led away by that Trollope. Any way you asked me what I know and now I've told you."

"Not at all Mrs Pheeney you've been very helpful." Beresford turned to look at Woods who for once seemed to be a bit more positive. "Thanks for your time, we'll see ourselves out."

As they came out the car Beresford said "What do you think of that?"

"Classic case of the green eyed yellow monster of jealousy. But Mr Bream hadn't mentioned anything."

"No he didn't. I might as well make him our next port of

call. " So saying he picked up his mobile and speed dialled Mr Bream as the morning set itself in a new phase of sunshine.

The phone rang four times and instead of voice mail he got a reply. "Yes can I help?"

"Is that Mr Bream?"

"Yes who's speaking?"

"I'm Inspector Chris Beresford of Thirton CID have you got a few minutes to spare?"

" To spare um, I'm in my house at the moment. I might have to go out in a moment, but I think I can spare you some time Inspector."

"I'll be five minutes see you, bye."

"Bye ." he rang off.

As the commuter traffic had more or less died down , the road to Mr Bream's house on Calmington Road was clear.

Chandra Hussein was ushered into the office of Thirton Homicide to talk to DI Beresford. He'd seen her on previous occasions . Not that she was that impressed with him really. About forty which was old for a Police officer however she noted that her dealings with him had been polite, never made any racist remarks , and was always straight to the point.

"Good morning Chandra , I may call you that . Can I? I expect I could call you DC Hussein."

"No Sir , Chandra is fine. How can I help? "

"Well the fact is in our investigation I've come across something odd. There's a practising Clairvoyant called Arnold Bream. He hires premises at a big house he jointly shares with practitioners of alternative therapies called "Advocate Power Limited." For myself I'm a sceptic and hold no brief about this sort of thing one way or another. At any rate it's come to my knowledge that he was on intimate terms with one of his "Clients". She was later found strangled .

I want you to infiltrate the group . By that I mean of course Arnold Bream and his group and his customers, find out what you can. If you feel any danger you can withdraw. Our man will be watching the house all the time. You only have to make a call and we'll come running."

"They'll be stationed outside?"

"We'll be maintaining surveillance for a week."

"I see what exactly do you hope to find out?"

"Well if he makes an advance to you that would be considered adequate. It would mean he's trying to take advantage of his clients. We'll have to say you have five thousand in the bank. There's a relative you want to get hold of. He'll come up with a couple of readings . If he makes an advance physically entertain him up to a point but get him to ask for money. When you have the money and make the transfer we've got him. "

"What if he tries to rape me or something?"

"Shout blue murder get on the phone , we'll come running. That cuts the whole process short. We've got him then. It's a case of either or."

"What if he does neither?"

"Well give him two weeks and bring him in any way."

Arnold Bream's premises in Calmington Road was previously owned by Charles Wrenworth builder and former pillar of the community. It had been taken over by Advocate Power Limited a small syndicate of people who jointly owned the property. They paid the mortgage from their earnings . Times were hard and they had to compromise their ideals in order to pay the mortgage.

Therefore there were four Reiki Therapists, Three homeopathic therapists, one physiotherapist and two masseurs but also included three tattoo artists.

However Arnold realised as compromises go it wasn't that bad.

Arnold owned three rooms on the ground floor. Joy and Eunice owned the other two rooms. There were three other concerns on the other floors. Arnold had a flat in Pennington Road. He made regular wages from his work but realised that fortune was a coy mistress and tomorrow he could be cast adrift.

In his career as a Clairvoyant he had seen fair amount of sad widows, distraught mothers and fathers. He truly tried to give them comfort. He felt he had a gift and he used it to make a living. If it was all fakery or just giving them the benefit of his subconscious he'd own up.

So far he'd been visited by the Police. If someone asked to communicate with Mrs Simmons all he would say was her spirit wasn't ready yet. That wouldn't be a lie. In his experience find it's hard to find a voice.

The events of the past few months had shaken him. However he felt he had a gift. Voices and Spirits spoke to him. He had been diagnosed as a Schizophrenic when he was young. Medication made him come to terms with it. However after he'd been to a medium a few times, he's been convinced he had a psychic power.

He'd been a psychic at several pubs and psychic fairs. He'd met several sad desperate people . The odd thing was in some respect they were almost as sad and desperate as he was. Though he learnt how to play a crowd albeit unwillingly.

He talked to the Reiki therapists Joy and Eunice. principally they agreed to give him a free consultation in exchange for a reading. Joy he found had an uncle in Bournemouth who died from Pneumonia in 1984. It was after a long illness. He told her uncle had served in the army forces in Malaya during the emergency. Joy sat back amazed and said that was true.

Joy administered some therapy in exchange . It relaxed

him for a while. He knew though that there was an unquiet spirit out there. The only trouble was it belonged to someone who was still living. He sensed it at the séance at the Green Weald Site. He knew that Steve Coombes could sense it too .

It was useless converting these feelings into facts. Voices dreams what were they? Of course he made a living from it. In the face of evil all he could do was bow to the inevitable. All his clients , Averill Green , Cynthia Asquith, for instance were lonely and needed a good chat more than anything. He met Joan   Simmons on more than one occasion and perhaps that was one too many.

Chandra Hussein was a detective constable at Thirton Police Station. She'd being newly posted from Beckton . Hounslow was where her Mum and Dad lived. She was glad to move away from Beckton for a number of reasons . One of them was the friends and relations . Her father was Mohinder and her mother Harshini were still very much thrall of the community and would much rather she married a man of their choosing. Instead she left home at an early age. After working in a supermarket in Leighton Buzzard she signed up to join the Police Force.

Although her parents lived in Hounslow , there was a strong Asian community in Beckton. She spoke Urdu and Hindi so she was an invaluable asset to the force. She felt invigorated at being valued for what she was and not who she was. Of course pressure from the community began to build up. She would receive visits from her mother and father who were proud of course of what she'd done. They all wanted her to marry a nice Asian boy.

She wasn't so sure. She knew some of her old friends had been talked into marriage and it hadn't worked out in every case. She was sure of her ground and Mister Right wasn't anywhere in sight.

So she was glad to come to Thirton . She could live with the odd racist remark . In a way they weren't so bad. There was no expectation behind it. There was no prospective bridegroom, or looming obligation of the

of the family she should take on.

Her progress in CID had been rapid. She'd seen a lot of cases of domestic abuse . These were usually poor single mothers and married couples experiencing economic difficulties and trying to keep the family together.

If the father was violent and abusive she would persuade him to go outside and get the spouse to issue an order banning him from a mile from the premises.

This happened in Thirton as often as it did in Beckton . She'd got to know Thirton quite well, she thought she fitted in quite well. The racial slurs when they came hardly touched her. It was a Thursday night Calmington Road was at the time moderately busy Usually with the sound of commuters return-ing from a busy days work. As she walked down Calmington road Chandra

remembered she parked her Vauxhall Corsa a bit of the way down . Calmington Road was off the main drag so there hadn't been any hustle .

In finding a place to park . The house owned by the Advocate Power syndicate was imposing to some extent. Outside on the board it read like an orthodox business syndicate . Of course Surinder had met quite a few odd customers in her day. She knew her cousin had started a restaurant in Southall and went into partnership with a Vietnamese Chef and started their own business.

The fact was that Surinder was not exactly a non-be-liever in the hereafter. To this end she had a name ready to give Bream in case he would see through her purpose. Ashok lived in a small village, he was her uncle. He died in 2004 from a case of Pneumonia and Pleurisy. She knew him briefly in her teens .

She went to Pakistan in 1996 . It was a brief summer holiday . Mohinder her dad recommended they go. She was barely ten at the time . Ashok had been a sad man she felt. He lived in what amounted to a shack outside a small village and worked in a factory for very little pay. They had a small meal such as Ashok could afford and then Mohinder her father bid him good day. When she heard he died she wasn't surprised.

She came in to the entrance hall to find some ladies standing there. The Psychic group was clearly marked and the ladies were standing by the entrance. Slightly shy Chandra stood by the side.   One of the ladies came up to her and said. "Are you new here? Have you come for a reading? Chandra looked at her closely . She wore an expensive blouse, Chandra could tell it was Marks and Spencer's through and through. The lady though, about seventy seemed nice enough. "My name is Cynthia Asquith the others are all here for the same thing. We've all lost someone. Is that right dear?"

The appeal was not lost on Chandra she seemed genuine and sincere. "Why yes of course. I lost my husband Ashok. He was a hotel manager in Fulham. It seemed the work was getting him down. He died from a heart attack."

"It must have been a shock." Cynthia said quietly.

"Yes. To lose someone like that . I'd heard of Mr Bream through a friend . He's quite good isn't he?"

"I always thought so. We are a group who come to all of the meetings. If you come more regularly you'll get to know all of us. I was married to Freddy Asquith. He knew Hector Turnbull the former Mayor and through him I knew some other people in the town hall, Gabriel Peters and the like."

"I've never heard of them."

"You wouldn't that was back in the eighties."

"I see well you must have seen a lot."

"Only in Thirton I lost Freddy in 2008. Time's a great

healer they say. I suppose I come here to talk to him. Though Averill and Celia Pheeney are so good to me."

"Come on Cynthia let her go. You'll know you'll bore the pants off her if you keep on." Averill Green said giving Chandra a nice smile.

"It's perfectly okay. I'm here just the same as you ladies. It's nice to meet people we have something in common with."

Averill laughed ."In common? We're probably glad they're dead and buried and have given us some peace and quiet for a change."

"Don't say that Averill you'll scare her away." Cynthia said.

Just then the door opened. Arnold Bream stood there. He was dressed in a green shirt, brown tan trousers and was the picture of respectability. Chandra felt slightly guilty, he was her target. Still a killer was on the loose. She could study him at leisure. He ushered them into the room. It was finished like a waiting room. There was an inner sanctum a consulting room. He would give private audiences there. "Well I hope you all know why you're here." He said once they were seated. "We've all lost loved ones. People who were our nearest and dearest .We know in our hearts we still love them. Well tonight ladies and gentlemen, I'll give you a chance to see how much they love you. If you just let me collect a small fee from you. It's ten pounds as I'm sure you know. Then you can come in separately for a consultation. Sandra has prepared tea and cakes afterwards." He said this and of course Sandra was a girl he hired six months ago on minimum wage. She also worked part time for the Reiki therapist as well.

Chandra listened to his talk and then the ladies having paid by cheque or cash a sum of ten pounds they sat down and waited their turn. There were in all fifteen men and women there. Their names had been arranged alphabetically and Chandra came tenth. When it came to her turn the others where standing outside talking to each other. They all seemed to know each other quite well. She reflected it seemed like an excuse for a social club. She entered the room , Arnold was sitting by the table. "Hello how can I help you?"

"Hello, my name is Chandra Hussein. I've had a bereavement. My husband was a hotel manager in Fulham. He died of a heart attack in 2010. I try to get in touch with him from time to time."

" I see well sit down Chandra. I'll see what I can do for you. I have a spirit guide . It's a bit of an off and on process."

Chandra sat down . She was surprised that there was no soft lighting or subdued atmosphere. The room was plainly decorated in every sense of the word. She looked at Arnold as he closed his eyes and gathered his thoughts.

"What was his name Chandra?"

"Ashok."

"Oh dear I don't seem to be getting anything here. Just a minute . This is most extra ordinary . I see a shack in a small village . I see an old man .He's worked hard all his life. His name is Ashok . He said he's very proud of you."

Suddenly a very real fear gripped Chandra. "Yes I suppose he would be."

"He said he's worried about your mother , her health is getting worse."

The guilt that overcame her was fleeting . "Ayesha is asthmatic I suppose."

"She will grt better. He says that's all for now." Ar nold was roused from his reverie. "That wasn't your husband was it Chandra?"

"It was my uncle . I'm impressed. I didn't mean to lie to you."

"Oh it's alright. People always make up some sort of story . It's just a habit . They can't help it. Is there anything else I can help you with?"

"Well I'd like to talk to the others if I may."

"They'll be chatting outside no doubt. It's like a social club out there. I'm providing a social function here. I'd be happy if you come again Chandra , we could use some young blood."

"Of course Arnold. I'll see you out there."

"Yes of course ,bye for now."As she came out to the outer room she found the ladies deep in conversation . "You know Cynthia that Beresford chappy came round to see me again. He was asking a lot of questions." This was from Averill Green. "I know dear that's what they do. Nosey Parkers the lot of them .Still I gave him my eighteen pence worth. He seemed satis fied with that."

"It's curious isn't it? Asking all these questions? I mean we've had our share of characters in Thirton. I mean at the end of the day it's just a market town. What goes on here goes on everywhere."

"Mind what you say there a young lady present." This came from Celia Pheeney . She laughed gently, Chandra could see that Celia took care to wear a silk black dress. She was seventy but took care in dressing up.

"Oh that's quite alright . I expect I'm here for a cup

of tea and a piece of cake like you. It's nice isn't it?"

Celia managed to smile . "Do you miss him? I mean I can tell you're recently bereaved . How do you feel?"

Chandra heaved a sigh. "Sometimes at night I feel lost. I wish he was back. Other times I thank my lucky stars we didn't have any children. The World seems so upside down right now."

"I'm with you there Chandra. Never seen such a shambles." Celia laughed in a pleasant way.

The time passed and presently Arnold emerged "Hello Cynthia you're my stalwart.If everybody goes you'll still be here."

"You're a comedian Arnold. Of course I'm always here it makes my week. Wouldn't be the same with out it."

After he conversed briefy with others he came up to Chandra and said "Time for a chat if that's alright?"

"Yes of course." She said . They moved surreptiti ously to the side of the room while others moved around the table serving tea and coffee and cake .

"So how long have you lived in Thirton?"

"About three months . I did have a job in Beckton. I got a better offer of a job selling perfume in Atkins department store. I don't make much but Thirton is pleasant. "

"I suppose it is , I don't get much myself really . So

I was wondering Chandra if we could meet later on dur
ing the week. How about Saturday could you manage
that?"

She was surprised at the boldness of his approach.
The other ladies were only standing a few feet away. "Well I
    suppose so. Where do you think we
could go?"

"There's a bar it's not posh or anything. It's called
"Shanties" It's in Kessington. I go there when I want to
have a quiet drink."

"I know it." She did know it. It was quite and
respectable. there was ahotel nearby, obviously this was
it.

"Well if we meet there at eight o'clock this Saturday
just for a few drinks."You know maybe go to the
cinema?"

"Of course ." The sooner the better she thought.
It was late in the night Stanley lit up a joint. It was the
weekend and he'd just sat his A levels. He felt he could
let go a bit. Terry Mitch and Will were all in a van to
gether. He knew that Mitch borrowed the van from his
dad.

"Where are we going Mitch?" He asked in a spirit
of enquiry

"Heston Hollow where else? It's coolthere and I
could do with another Joint right now."

"Lighten up Stan. We've got three months before

the results come through."

"I say we make a run for it." Will said between puffs. Stan could have said make a run for what, he knew what Will meant."

This was a few months of freedom . The next few years were going to be a grind. There was no alternative except to make the most of it.As they rounded the hill he could see the decline would lead to Heston Hollow. The evening air seemed to thicken with antici pation as they entered the wooden groves, he could see the lakes to one side as the anglers with their tents and their patient anticipation as they waited for the fish to bite.

"Great let's get out have a walki about." Will said. Stan got out , his mind fuzzy with the magic of the night. The luminescence from the street lightslending a magic to the place. Terry, Mitch and Will moved as one through the woods sensing the air and the ambience passing the joint."Hi Gill." Will said. Stan thought he knew her, but he wasn't sure. In his mind she had fiery blond hair that seemed to glow. He was aware he was stoned, however.

"Hi Jane." This was Mitch. Stan turned round and there was a brown haired girl that Stan seemed to remember from a previous occasion. It was at a night club in Lewisham he couldn't put his finger on it.

Together theyn sat down by the lake while Gill rolled a joint." Look at Stan. I think he's gone you know?"

"I'm fine. Where's the party anyway?"

"There's no party. We're up here by the way."

Gill said , " Jane just came up for the ride."

Jane turned to Stan. "Won't Mummy be anxious to know where you're gone. You look lost."

"I'm okay." Stan said.

"Stan's okay." Will said defensively. "We've been stoned together before . Any way we,ve got to get bacck."

Reluctantly Stan got up with the others and they drove back to Will's flat in Bateman's Road. The evening ended with a few more joints and Stan made his way home.   William Jamieson was Stanley Williams's friend he lived in Bateman's Road .He'd been Stanley's friend throughout most of his school life. Terry Hammond, and Mitch Patterson were passing friends together in the last three years. They had developed a social bond . They had been to parties and raves but had kept their heads enough to get good grades to study for university.

Of course they all came from Middle class homes except for Will. That last Summer Stan had romanticised his time away for some reason . They'd gone to Heston Hol low it was a group of small lakes just south of Colington Green in the direction of Paxton Aerodrome which had been a former RAF base.

Even so Stan was basically a pragmatic sort of person . He kept his feet on the ground. There was room for pleasure , there was room for study and he had to prioritise. The fact of the matter was the death of his father made him prioritise more than he would nor mally. He was almost sure Beatty was going into ac counting. She never really had an affinity for farming. Although like him she was really shocked at what hap pened to her father. He talked to Harry next door. He was amazed that with so little capital Harry managed to get business going when his father wasn't involved. He really had a thing for Amanda at one stage, but she had a thing for Robin Hingis who was as broad as he was long.

He made a promise to himself, if he made it through the summer and he got grades, he would have one blow out night and that would be it for a while. He respected what his father had done round the farm. It seemed establishing an abattoir and contracting a firm to pack age the meat made good business sense. The other pro jects were working well. Ian Beasley the farmer at Bran bourne Farm may well have had a good offer. However in a few years he will probably make enough money to buy Beasley out.

Of course this all depended on his exam results and to some extent didn't. The farm would still be there .

Lambert Hodge was a good manager, best of all he was flexible. In his mind Stan felt they could devote more land to Beef Cattle. That in the end would pay the divi dend. They couldn't grow enough crops to make economic sense. The dairy herd would probably have to go. The marketing strategies of the government just weren't feasible for this size of farm. Failing all else they could grow tomatoes and strawberries use poly tunnels.

He felt secure in his decision . Lambert would have some ideas . He had more experience so his advice would be worth a lot. He drew on his joint as he stood at the back of the farm looking at the dairy workers herding the cows for the evening. He felt a certainty he could do it. He might even employ Will if he had to. He was a good sort and he could rely on him if there were any foulups. Of course Lukasz was a good manager . He'd been superb managing the farm while Mum was working out the paperwork. Of course Beatty was sceptical about Lam bert , but when the chips were down it was Dad's way of doing things that was the problem.

Chandra stood by the bar. Shanties she thought it sported a sort of chic that went out with the fifties. Out side there was a neon sign featuring a Champagne glass and a cocktail stick. She decided it was retro and there fore a safe motif. Safe? Humphry Bogart in a fedora hat and Lauren Bacall looking forlorn in an airfield wouldn't look out of place. Though she supposed that was the idea. She looked round; the idea of some amateur Bogarts were nowhere to be found. She could see a couple of young business men on their second Gin and Tonic or Whisky mac. Two career girls waiting for a hen party to arrive. She thought she dressed smartly. A dark green dress made her suitably delicate looking. As she sipped her Martini she looked round to see if she could find Bream. There he was dressed in a blue jacket and purple shirt and trousers to match.

"Hello, Chandra can I get you another one of those?"

"No, I'm okay right now . So Bream what have you got for me?"

"Got for you? I don't understand."

"Coy as well. You asked me here. I suspect you have somthing to tell me."

"Well it was more in the way of an assignation I supp ose."

"Okay Arnold take me through this step by step I famncy a meal tonight. If you like you can tell some of the cases you've dealt with."

"Hmm. I see well we could do that I suppose. Listen Chandra how long have you been bereaved ? I know I didn't ask you but now is as good a time now is as good a time as any."

"About two or three years, I'm afraid that's all you're going to get."

"Okay I suppose we can take it slowly. I would

suggest any one who has passed away and you think of them will make you feel better if you just enjoy yourself."

"I'm sorry Arnold. You'll have to humour me. Lunch and home I'm afarid, I'm an old fashioned girl."

"Of course."

As the evening they progressed they each had more to drink. Arnold drove her to a restaurant he knew in Thirton. It was an Italian , Chandra had linguini and Tira Misu to follow as did Arnold.

"My father was a bricklayer my mother was a sales assistant . They madea good living by all accounts. We lived in Dulwich . It was a mildly interesting place."

"How did you become a psychic ?"

"At an early age I thought I was ill I heard voices I went to a psychiatrist I took pills . I mean the trouble was it was all very positive. You're supposed to be mentally ill. So you take your medication and lead a passive life. What good is that? " He paused "I started working doing various jobs. Eventually I found I knew things about people without them telling me. So I de cided to see if I was psychic . I went to see a medium and she said I had a gift."

"I started doing pubs and clubs for a few years. I was moderately successful . I mean a lot of the people I talk to just come to say how are you? It's as simple as that. You saw it yourself Cynthia, Averill, and Celia .

Lonely women but centred in their own way."

"So this is how you make your living. How did you end up in that house?"

"Joy the therapist wanted someone t o pay the rent for the ground floor with her as she doesn't make enough . So I said I'd do it. I needed two or three rooms. Here I am."

"How long have you done this Arnold?" She gave him a long sincere look. This would melt him.

"About fourteen years . It pays the bills. Sometimes it's not all jamScones . I've met some head cases in my time . I couldn't say they hurt anybody , but I couldn't say they were harmless. "

"That's a long time .What a strange way to go."

"What about you Chandra working in the perfumery department in Atkins department store? You must have met some different types in the retail trade?"

Here we go she thought. There's going to have to be some truth here." I worked for a Turkish bloke in Dal ston High street. It was a sandwich bar and we just scraped through every week. I worked for a hairdresser in Ilford. I learnt how to style and cut. I worked as a typ ist for an import and export company in Brick Lane. I've met every single type of trader and commodity broker that's being made. I know I didn't talk about him, but I miss my Husband. Though it gets better slowly."

"I'm sure it does.Look Chandra it's being a long
night. I just thought I'd ask you something before we go.
You see as it's hard to make the rent on the premises I
run. I was wandering if you could help me out with a lit
tle loan?"

At last she thought, I thgought we'd get to it. "How
much."

"About five thousand quid."

"Hmm it's a tall order. I mean I'm near enough skint as
as it is."

"Iknow these are desparate times." He gave her that
charming little boy smile.

"I think I can make it . When do you want it?"

"Next week if possible ."

"Okay I'll meet you at "Shanties" next tuesday,
same time?"

"Next week if at all possible."

"Okay I'll meet you Shanties next Tuesday same
time?"

"Okay then."

They left and he paid the bill. She noticed he seemed
to know thevstaff stood outside as Arnold pulled way.
She stood outside a taxi rank as Arnold left. She dialled a
mobile number and lifted her mobile to her ear.

"Okay Justin take me home. I'm about done."

Woods had followed them to the rstaurant and was
parked in a blue Nissan about a hundred yards away.

"Right you are Chandra."

The next day Beresford was sitting in his office check -ing emails when DC Chandra Hussein knocked and walked in "Forgive me Sir, but I thought you might want an update."

"Okay DC Hussein let me have it."

"Well Mr Bream is a charmer. I'll give him that . He does have a gift. Not that I want to get distracted at this venture . There were some well to do old ladies there. He does provide an outlet for their loneliness. He makes them feel connected I suppose."

"okay, I've been checking his bank account. There have been some deposits over the last few months. Fif teen hundred from Mrs Green, two thousand from Mrs Pheeney. They're not huge sums but they tell a tale."

"The course of our dinner date began well enough. He told he was diagnosed schizoid at an early age. He told me he developed psychic powers when he went to see a medium. Then he went to pubs and clubs and used his talents. At any rate as the meal progressed he told me he would have trouble meeting the rent this month and would I help him out? He said he would need five thousand pounds. I agreed to meet him at Shanties . Same place same time."

"I expect him to phone and ask me to come to a meeting at the house as well in order to do a bigger snow job on me."

"And you're on with this?"

"Yes."

"At the restaurant later on.How do you want to play it?"

"I give him the money when we book the room at 'the hotel and then when I give him the check we nab him."

"Okay."

It was four o'clock on the esplanade of the Excelsior Hotel when Jud finally appeared . Jud and Stone where there eagerly .

"Oscar went back last week. He seemed quite satisfied . I can't see any hitch."

"So today's the big day . The painting 's gone back. The experts will look at the work . They'll announce their verdict and then when they're satisfied the client' will give Mallin the check.

"That's right and in half an hour we'll get ours."

"In an account in the Cayman Islands. Jud is waiting any minute now."

A cloud of rain momentarily swept by as the door on the left and the countenance of Jud Farrell dressed in a light grey tan suit and a jaunty pork pie hat graced the foyer of the hotel. His face was grim and he looked serious though the sunglasses didn't give a clue as to how he felt.He approached Paddy and Stuart who were sitting at a table outside the hotel although they were reckoning how soon they should move inside. He sat down momentously . Straight away Paddy felt the at mosphere tighten.

"Tell me Jud what is it?"

"Well I've had a word with James Stangrove .The picture's in the gallery. Everything is looking fine."

"So when does the judging take place?" Stanley said.

"Next week. The prize money is placed in your account next day. I've looked at the competition Stuart , you've got nothing to worry about."

"That means you can go back to Thirton soon. Stu that'll be a relief." Paddy said.

"Oh I've enjoyed myself , but yes I have to go back." After a while the conversation drifted on to other things. Steinauer and Jud started talking about various matters. Eventually Stuart made his excuses and left.

Jud started talking about various matters. Eventually Stuart made his excuses and left. Jud's face concentrated into a frown."I'm afraid it's serious." Jud said slowly . Then his face broadened slightly"The pro ject is nearly finished. We'll have to move things for ward. Mallin is getting jumpy but I said we have to take our time."

"Next week will be it then? " Paddy said.

"Yes we move out of here. Everything's being set up. I've been to the flat Molyneaux is as good as finished. Once Stuart is finished at the exhibition we

can go."

"Nothing of any of this ties Stuart in any way?"

"No , he's just there."

"Good."

In his hotel room Stuart briefly looked over some maga-
zines and thought about the next few weeks. Stuart was relieved to be going back home. His mother was getting worried.
He felt he could put into motion his plans

for going to college and getting a degree in art then he

could find a job. At any rate he really didn't intend to

stay with Jud and Paddy much longer.Jud and Paddy

laughed and ate a big lunch. Stuart excused himself say

ing he would be going back home early the next day. As

he left they did say they may have a few jobs for him in

the summer. He demurred and said he'd think about it.

As he looked at the moon lit the sky that night he felt

exhausted and glad it was all over. Strangely enough

the success of the venture didn't excite him at all.

Chandra checked her makeup one last time. As she

turned to the mirror she made her mind up she would

go out one final time that week. The phone went she

looked at the number she realised it was Arnold Bream.

It was no good she had to answer it.

"Hello how can I help you?"

"Chandra is that you? Thank God. The voice said

not waiting for confirmation.

"Yes it's me Arnold. How can I help you?"

"Yes it's me Arnold. How can I help you?"

" I know I said I wouldn't see you until Tuesday but I need to see you tonight if I can."

"Of course where shall we meet?"

"At my place in Calmigton Road if you could . I wouldn't inconvenience you but something's come up and I need your help."

"Oh alright would seven o'clock be alright?"

"Yes of course. I'll try and make it short."

"I'll see you there Arnold."

"Yes and thanks Chandra. " He put the phone down.Chandra waited for a minute for the silence to take control and put the receiver down herself. She phoned Beresford . She knew he'd be at home. "DI Ber esford can I help you? " a voice said right away. No voice mail good.

"It's me Chandra . Arnold just phoned, he wants to see me tonight."

"Good hopefully we can bag this by the end of the week. Did he say what he wanted ?"

" I'm not sure . It sounded urgent."

"All thge better . How do you feel?"

"I feel nervous, I haven't done this sort of thing before."

"We're not far away. Where will it be?"

"Calmington Road at seven o'clock."

"It will probably be a professional call. Then nothing

merry. Make him set a date for the hotel or something."

"I'll try . If he's innocent that might not be the fairest way to do this."

"He won't need prompting by the sound of it he's got something lined up. Be ready."

"Yes Sir." She ended the call and looked at the clock and realised she had an hour to go. It was a light rain descending when she parked in Calmington Road . Number 47 Calmington Road looked fairly calm when she got there . She went up to the front door and rang the bell. Arnold answered the door he was dressed in a white shirt and tie and trousers. The effect seemed strained . He looked as though he'd been up all night. "Hello , Arnold you look ill is there anything wrong?"

"Come in Chandra." He ushered her into his office she noticed there was was no one there. "I'm sorry I asked to meet you like this. It's just desperate times." He gestured to a chair and she sat down."You see I know I need the money but I have to talk to you about some thing else. " He hesitated it wasn't a pause. "You see Chandra I've noticed at the meeting you had something special. I think you could have a gift. I really mean it. I could help you. " Great she thought he's trying to snow me.

"I see Arnold. Well how would I develop the talent do you think?"

"Well we can try at the next meeting . I know I said

I wanted to meet you on Tuesday, it's Monday tonight. I suggest we wait until next Saturday . We can hold a meeting and you can see how I operate. Afterwards you can meet some one I want you to envisage in your mind's eye what he might have gone through   and try to speak to the spirits that surround him. If nothing hap pens fair enough. However I've got a feeling it'll be fine. "

Cheeky blighter he's setting me up. "Okay anything else?"

"Oh yes I forgot . Well there's the small matter of money. Well if you think you can get your hands on the money I would like it by Sunday if at all possible. First I want you to try your talent and see your potential. "

"Where do you want to see me on Sunday night then?"

"At the Hackridge Hotel on the Mosely road . Do you think you can make it?" At last she thought here we go.

"Yes of course." Later when she got into her car she could see Woods parked nearby and gave him the thumbs up. The session was over. She phoned Beresford. " Okay what did he want?"

"He wants to try me out as a medium on Saturday night. Then we meet at the Hackridge Hotel in Mosely Road. That's when he wants the money."

"That's good enough that's as far as we'll take it."

"Yes Sir. She rang off and drove home."

Davinia waited nervously in the alcove as the Reverend Wallis tidied his vestments. As he did so he hear a car draw up outside the church. A tall figure came out. His magisterial air told Davinia that it was the Archbishop Clarence of the Diocese. He had with him his secretary Graham Parsons. She hated herself for it but she disliked Parsons. He was a small mincing manwith a sycophantic air. The Archbishop turned to her as he came forward and said "Ah Miss Peters you have been very busy. Derek has been quite agitatedof late , how have you been?"

"Very well thank you, your grace. How can I help you?"

"Well you can tell me where Alex is that would be a start." She noticed the Reverend Wallis had disap peared about a few seconds earlier .At this juncture how ever the Reverend Wallis appeared in his vestments and full regalia. "Ah here you are Derek just finished a service, I'm impressed. I think if we meet in the confer ence hall we can sit down and you can get the tea yes Davinia? " He gave a kindly nod. She noticed the arch bishop had that "Born to rule" way of doing things. She nodded her compliance as the meeting got under way.

The meeting hall was adjoining the Church Hall proper . It also housed the nursery and other function roomnursery and other function rooms that were used by various groups such as the Women's Institute and the Parish Council. There was a small kitchenette next to the meeting hall that Davinia used. She found three or

four cups and a tea pot and managed to find some bis
cuits as well as milk and tea. In about five minutes she
had a plate of biscuits and some tea ready . Using a tray
she ventured out to the hall and set the tray down on a
table.

Archbishop Clarence was sitting at the head of the table.
Graham Parsons
sat next to him taking notes. "Ah refreshments . Well
now that Davinia is hereI think we can begin."

"It appears that Davinia has been doing some
digging in the old archives. She has unearthed the re
mains of what appears to all intents and purposes is the
body of St Hilda of the Marshes. " He gave her a benign
nod as she sat down next to them.

"Well now I've been doing some digging myself
Cuthbert was the Archbishop of Canterbury at the time.
Through Pope Gregory the third Cuthbert laid out the
clerical duties of the priest and the way they should
dress. Hilda died in 755 a year after St Boniface. There
was a ceremony about thirty years later she was canon
ised. Alas along with the removal of the monasteries so
much of our history has been forgotten. However I'm
not going to be doctrinaire about this. The service of re
membrance and the dedication of the Chapel of St Hilda
goes ahead. She was not protestant but on occasions
like this we do not stand on ceremony. The name of the
Church will stay All Saints Church , with a side chapel

dedicated to the memory of St Hilda. A small casket with her remains will be stored will be put on view. How do you feel about this Alex?"

The Reverend Wallis managed to maintain his composure and said "As well you know Derek we're good for the money. We expect the Parish Council will make up for the rest of the expenditure. Tell me how do the Parishioners feel?"

"They feel upset a bit agitated. It's caused a certain amount of upheaval."

He tailed off as the Archbishop held up his hand."I know Derek, I know . Progress however is progress we need more people to come into the Church. You yourself were telling me that the funds were depleted last year."

"Exactly your grace . I don't mean to say I'm not grateful for the attention but some of my Parishioners are in turmoil."

"All will be well Derek. Now Miss Peters I take it you're satisfied with this state of affairs?"

"Of course your Grace."

"Good now I'm sorry Derek but I've got a bust schedule. I'll be phoning you shortly and you can tell me how you're getting on is that clear?"

The Reverend Wallis got up sharply and said, "Yes your Grace." As the Archbishop manoeuvred himself to ward the   door with his assistant.

Grace Palmer , a lifelong member of Kessington Parish
Council stood for a moment in the Church Hall. There
along with her was Bridget Carey, Amanda Treadwell,
Catherine Cairns, and Barbara Simmons. Together they
formed the body of the council. Absent were Davinia
Peters and Kenneth Fenton. This of course was due to
pressing matters elsewhere. Davinia was due in five
minutes time. Barry and Kenneth were a gardener and
electrician respectively. They were busy with their re
spective jobs.

Grace Palmer was a daughter of a colonel in the
British Army. She married a managing director of a mer
chant bank. Her martialling abilities informed the man
agement of the Parish council. This extended to the
local school of which she was a governor. Of course her
present concern was the dedication of a Chapel in All
Saints Church to St Hilda. It wasn't true that
Davinia had done it behind her back. Once the tests had
been done , Davinia had informed them. However Grace
felt this was a rather covert attitude and felt she should
have been informed sooner. Eventually she would let
Davinia have her way but not without a fight. "Right La
dies first off I would like to saythat I must express my
surprise at this outrageous decision to rededicate Our
Ladies Chapel to St Hilda of the marshes. I mean what
ever next ? All Saints has always stood for ordinary com

mon sense. It's all very well having these tourists coming in here with their cameras . We have to have a place to worship . What about us?"

Bridget Carey who in her career had been a civil servant and a mediator in disputes in trade negoti ations between various governing bodies was concili atory. "That's all very well Grace but the Bishop has given his consent even with Alex's disapproval . What can you do?"

" I propose we pass a motion of sanction against Davinia Peters until we see the plans for the develop ment of the Chapel and the outlay of the sum involved."

Amanda Treadwell who had no pretension to higher government or an expensive education had been a publican's wife before he died three years pre viously. She wasted no time in beating about the bush. "Your batting an open wicket Grace. You don't stand a chance. For a start if we voted with you Davinia could probably produce plans in a week's notice and you'd be back at square one. Besides the place needs brightening up a bit. We need new blood. The old times are dying out. We can hardly fill the Church as it is."

Barbara Simmons who had been a hair dresser and closed her salon in Kessington the year previously be cause the arthritis in her left hand had flared up. "I hate to say this Grace , because I sympathise with you I really do, but Amanda has got a point. We need new blood. We need money. Eventually the roof and the steeple are going to need some work. Unless we get some money coming in this place is going to be a carpet warehouse in three years' time. It's a hard fact of life but facts are facts. Davinia has come up with a good plan. At that moment they could hear footsteps in the hall.

"Did someone mention my name? " It was Davinia dressed in Jeans and a combat jacket.
Grace turned ."Yes Davinia . I didn't want to start with out you but we have to debate the issue some time. "

"Oh what issue was that?" Approaching the table and sitting next to Amanda.

"I want to veto development of the Chapel until we've seen the plans and the cost of developing the chapel."

"Of course I wouldn't dream of doing anything with out consulting the Vicar or the council. I've just come from the printers . They've givenme the architects plans and of course Barton and Staines the builders have given me the estimate this morning on company headed notepaper." She opened her briefcase she was carrying with her and proceeded to lay them out on the table.

Grace was surprised for a minute . She looked at the proposed sketch of the statue that would grace the chapel. "How did you arrive at the likeness if I may ask?"

"Oh I went up to the British Museum. They found a small portrait drawn by a monk in the fourteenth cen tury . It depicts Saint Hilda of the Marshes with fair hair. The architects Barton and Staines contacted to do a s culpture."

Grace considered the plans."Of course I'll have to think about this before I make decisions." She drew a sigh . "However on the face of what we have here there shouldn't be any reason why we shouldn't go ahead."

"Don't take too long Grace . Alex will want to get a move on with this."

Sensing she'd being outmanoeuvred Grace said "Of course,I only meant I want a look at the plans first. I'll give them to Alex this evening . It seems you've done a good job in this Davinia. All Saints Church will have a fresh face to present the World. " The admission of defeat was by no means pointless but she was going gracefully.

Catherine Cairns who up until this juncture had been quite silent on the subject spoke. "I say we give a vote of thanks to Davinia. Considering she does volun tary work for the Parish and the flower arranging , she has excelled herself . Let's see a show of hands ." Every one raised their hands even Grace Palmer.

"Yes Davinia you've done very well. "The meeting was adjourned as Davina smiled at Grace the knowledge that somehow it wasn't over yet seemed to hang in the air. However Peace for now.

Beatrice had come home from the University. She looked relieved to know that even the tumultuous events of the summer had come and gone she hadn't done badly in her exams. Iris had been keeping a stern eye on Stanley who had been studying hard. The farm she noticed had been doing well under the ministra tions of Lambert Hodge.

She relaxed the morning after she arrived in the kitchen chewing over a fried breakfast she briefly pre pared. Her mother Iris had been out shopping and came back surprised to see her up to early. "How did you find college Beatty?"

"The same . I settled down to study when I got back. I felt guilty at first settling in so calmly after what hap pened . The cut and thrust of academic life being what it is I soon settled in. "

" I said I could say the same for Stan, I mean he's got in him. In some respects though he does have a wild streak."

"Relax Mum, going to Agricultural college is no big ask. If he gets good grades it'll be a shoe in."

She though for a bit. "Have they got anyfurther with the investigation?"

"Not much . The Devil of it all is Gordon asked for that modification himself . It seems he found it difficult levelling up the bin before picking it up. Of course he op erated it and sometimes the air tanks leaked . When they filled up again the hook would come forward like that. Someone could easily have got hurt."

"Most of all Dad of course."

"Exactly."

"I went to see Lambert Hodge before I left. He was most apologetic. He'd shown me the maintenance records for the truck compared to all of the vehicles on the farm. They were a complete mess.What the pity of it was , that it was Dad's own log so to speak . No one else would go near it. "

"And the weed killer that surprised me. It seems the odd sandwiches he took should become tainted like that."

"We don't know everything Mum. I know Beresford is still keeping an open mind on it."

Just as they finished Stanley came in from the farm. "Hello Beatty Mum. How was College? Heard you've been very busy."

"Okay." Beatrice said glibly. "How was school?"

"Good I've done my exams. We should know soon."

"Well get your results and then we'll see." Beatrice said teasingly.

"When I run the farm will you help me?"

"Fat chance. No but seriously I just might . I mean there could be a good opening for the right products.

"Lambert Hodge is doing a good job. You two have
a mind on what you're saying. I understand ambition
but wait until you have work experience then I'll
be prepared for you to try new ideas. " Iris said. She put
away the breakfast things as Stanley and Beatrice cele
brated their year at college and school.

Chandra Hussein turned up at 47 Calmington
Road at seven on Sunday evening. Mrs Averill Green
Cynthia Asquith, Celia Pheeney and Arnold Bream were
there. So were some regulars from Thirton . Chandra had
seen them before Arnold took Chandra's hand as she
came through the door and paid her close attention.

"I'm glad you could come tonight. I made a point of
finding someone you could work on. It won't be in front
of an audience, there's a room on the side. I'm sure you're
receptive . It will only take a few minutes or a quarter of
an hour almost. I hope you don't mind . As I said I'm sure
you have some sort of ability."

"Are you sure Arnold? I'm not used to this crowds
initimidate me. The person you've got who is it any
way?"

"It's Mister Philip Carter. He's a retired mechanic
who used to work in Thirton. Don't worry just let your
mind wander. Your ability should do the rest. If you
don't or can't do it, don't worry there's no audience, no
reason to feel foolish. I'm sure you'll feel fine . "

"Very well. I'm sure I'm not ready for this . If you think I'm good enough I'll have to go."

"I'm sure." He said the all the ladies and some of the gentlemen sat down waiting for the reading to begin.

"Now I'm glad you're here tonight. It's been a busy week. Now it's odd there's been a message I'm getting from a man in a dark jacket. He's standing by the railway siding . I think it's for you madam the one with the yellow jacket. "

Behind her Chandra could see a woman about her own age. She was pretty in a business like sort of way. She had short blond hair . "He said Martha should pull through . April is an early month. Does that mean anything?"

"Yes it does." She said faintly.

"Right , I'm in a bit of a rush tonight. Ah yes I'm getting a message . There's a lady in red coat she's got pruning shears and she's been doing gardening. She says "Autumn will come soon this year. I believe that's for the gentleman in the red shirt in the front is that right? " A fat man in a red shirt and ruddy complexion nodded vigorously.

So the reading went on. CVhandra had to admit she was quietly impressed. He had the audience under his spell and only a few seemed to be at a loss as to what he was telling them. She was dreading her little test run later. She was also sure that medium or not that Arnold was grooming her. Eventually the evening came to a halt. Arnold somewhat exhausted approached her after wards whilst the others were eating tea and cakes .

"Chandra are you ready now? It won't take long."

"Of course." She said. Arnold led her into a little back room. It only had a table and three chairs. As they sat down a second person came in. "This is Mister Philip Carter I told you about. I left him out of the readings because he knew we'd be here. "

"Hello, I understand you're Chandra Hussein, pleasure to meet you, I'm Philip."

"Hello."

"Thanks for coming Philip now I want you to sit by the table." He motioned to the other vacant chair. Philip sat down as he was bidden.

"Now Chandra I want you to empty your mind if you could of all your thoughts and cares. Then I want you to consider Philip. He is as you can see sitting there. Think carefully of his life after a minute or two or longer, try to think of anything that might come to mind that you might be aware of in your mind's eye."

Chandra looked at the man he seemed a hard working chap. She imagined he worked in a garage . Then she tried to imagine his wife. She imagined her as statuesque blond about the same height for no apparent reason. Moving about the house with swift efficient movements.

"Are you getting anything?"

"Yes I can see a blond woman moving round the house. Keeping it clean. Very hardworking. Very attractive."

"Anything else?" Arnold said. Philip seemed restive at this.

Chandra thought for a minute. She imagined them having an anniversary . It was a special one. She imagined it would be August for no apparent reason. Only this time it was a sad occasion .

"Yes their last anniversary was a sad one . It seemed she had bad news." Philip seemed visibly shaken.

"That's enough I can't take any more."

"Of course Mr Carter would you like to tell your wife anything?"

"No, she knows already." He said, Chandra found the gruff exterior of the man crumble under the onslaught. He got up and left. Chandra's vision of the couple vanished though she wasn't sure she saw it herself.

As he left Arnold turned to her. "You did well. Personally I would have liked her to talk to you."

Chandra looked shaken ."I'm not sure I could have taken that."

"You would get used to it. The spirits will never harm you."

"Well I'm sorry I've had quite a night Arnold. Am I meeting you tomorrow?"

"Yes are you alright for the money? I'm sorry to impose. I'll pay you back of course. I feel awful for asking. It's just that you can see for yourself I have a ready audience out there."

"Of course Arnold . The Hackridge Hotel in Mosely Road?"

"Yes about seven o'clock? If you can make it."

"Yes of course." You poor bugger she thought.

Back at the station Chandra appealed to Justin Woods. "It's just that I feel something. I feel we're on the wrong track here. " Chandra said.

"He's grooming you , anyone can see that."

"In what way?"

"Well for instance this Philip Carter the car mechanic . I checked him out. Yeah he does cars but he also does a few stolen ones as well. He has form . I'm not sure how bad Arnold Bream is either. All this smells fishy Chandra, Arnold's something else. It could be a threshold between straight and bent. I know that the Psychic Society is a racket. It may be a small time racket it could be big time. Maybe what we're seeing is the backend of a drugs deal gone wrong. So various people , innocent people end up dead."

"I'm sorry that's just wild assumption." Chandra said.

Beresford intervened "Now Chandra you're telling me this Arnold Bream made an impression on you . How did he do that?"

"Well we went into this room with Philip Carter . He said empty my mind of anything in particular. Then he said in my mind's eye try and conjure a picture of Philip Carter when I saw him."

"Then what happened?"

"Well Carter walks in . He seems an ordinary sort of chap about five foot ten I suppose. I start imagining him in a garage working on his car. Then I imagine his wife. I imagine she's tall like him. She's tall and has lustrous blond hair. Then I imagine them having meals together and how it was a special occasion."

"I told them what I could see and when I mentioned meals, Carter became very emotional and had to leave."

Beresford paused for a second. "You only made a logical assumption based on the appearance of the man. Anyone could have done that. It could have been set up for the next meeting which is tonight. Remember you're the target here. As far as he's concerned you now think you've got psychic powers. You will now lend Bream a lot of money and he will feel you're in his power. It's the logical order of events. The fact is if this pans out everything else will have a logical explanation as well. It could be the murder of Gordon Williams was made to throw us off the scent as a random killing. Mrs Simmons could be linked to a power struggle between Bream and Grimshaw. Also there's the fact that all these murders were connected by old paths that were coffin paths . I

traced one from All Saints Church to the Witham River and the fishing lake run by Roderick Benson that leads to Cullompton Farm. I traced another leading from Albion Valley Railway Station through the Weald Road through again to Kessington Valley Road and the Green Weald Site. I know that Arnold Bream was like a small time conman but he's taking a great deal of trouble to take

this money off you. It's my assumption that he fits the picture. This could be the tip of the iceberg. "

Chandra seemed mollified by this somewhat. "So he's still our man."

"I'm afraid so yes."

"Okay Sir." She resolved to follow through the course of action they discussed.

It was late at night about seven o'clock outside the Hackridge Hotel. The thoroughfare running through to Thirton being Mosely Road was quite tonight preparing itself for the rush next morning.

She waited as Arnold instructed , in the Saloon bar nursing a gin and tonic . She carried five thousand in ready cash on her already for the transfer . If Bream was going to make a move it would be tonight. For all the talk that Beresford and Woods gave her , he still seemed to be a small time con man preying on helpless women. Still his patter and self-assuredness was intimidating .

After a quarter of an hour she saw Bream emerge from the

lobby , he was wearing a brown suit. It didn't seem particularly well made, but he had thatangelic smile he supposed he put on to win her over. "Good evening Chandra have I caught you at an awkward moment, I'm sorry if I have. Modern life is busy these days. , we hardly have time to know we exist. "

"Not it's not awkward I was wondering if you were going to turn up. So now you're here Arnold what next? "She said with a feeling of trepidation.

"Well I've got a room up on the second floor , we can have a little talk and carry out the transaction we talked about yes?"

She checked her make up ."Yes , good. We can do that." She finished her drink as Arnold ordered a lemon juice cordial. When they were ready Arnold led the way to the lift. "Has it been a busy day for you Chandra? Have you had time to think of your powers ? The future can open up for you as a psychic. "

"I was trying to talk to you about that. That man Carter will he come to a meeting do you think?"

"I'm sure he would . I can't see why not?"

"Good."

The hotel room when they got there was nicely furnished with a view out to Mosely road and the old Victorian Houses opposite. Chandra sat down as Arnold gravitated over to the mini bar and poured himself a small whiskey.

"Would you like something?"

"No thanks, I feel so excited I suppose. "

"Which leads me to another question. Do you have the money?"

"Yes of course."

"Can I see it?"

"Yes. Here you are , you can count it if you like." She took the package out of her bag and laid it on the table. Two hundred and fifty twenty pounds notes in bundles of a thousand each.

"Okay . That's very accommodating of you Chandra. I'll just take care of that. " He produced a brief case and deposited the bundles and snapped it shut. He sat down with a whiskey next to Chandra . The chair he was sitting on had wooden arms and he leaned over to talk to her . "Now down to business."

He leant forward to kiss her and as he did so he felt something touch his wrist. He looked down and saw a pair of hand cuffs attaching his wrist to the

arm of the chair . "I'm sorry Arnold, it's being fun but you're nicked."

There was a knock on the door as she said this. "What's that?" He said.

"The squad Arnold, we're bringing you in for questioning. "

Half an hour later Bream found himself in an interrogation room with three other Police men. He managed to contain his astonishment but exchanged wounded glances with DC Hussein in the meantime.

"I demand to have a solicitor present."

"I believe a duty solicitor is coming. We won't start until she arrives."

Bream looked relieved by this . It was about a quarter of an hour later the Solicitor arrived . The Police allowed the Solicitor to interview her client before the procedure begun.

"What happened? " She asked. Her names was Samantha Miles. She was thirty and wore a practiced smile that he imagined she gave to ex-convicts, shoplifters, and car thieves alike.

"I'm a psychic, I have a practice in Thirton . I met a woman who came to some of my meetings. Her name was Chandra Hussein. She told me she lost a husband by the name of Ashoke. Well I gave her a reading. The Ashoke I could see was an old man. However she seemed impressed by this. She came to another meeting. I got to know her better . I told her she seemed a nice person and asked her for a loan of five thousand pounds to help me with this business."

"Did she agree?"

"Yes , any way before the loan I got her to meet a friend of mine, to try out her Psychic abilities. She performed reasonably well. I thought she had possibilities. "

"What happened then? "

"Well we're to meet at the Hackridge Hotel . She came to the room I Booked . She handed me the five thousand . I put it in a brief case. The next thing she handcuffed me."

"Okay. It all sounds straight forward. Now I want to know why are they targeting you?"

"What do you mean?"

"Why the sudden interest?"

"Well" He hesitated . "There was a previous client a Miss Jean Simmons. We had a romantic tryst of sorts. It was after a month , we met in the Hackridge Hotel also. However six weeks later she was found strangled in her garden.

The solicitor looked grave." This is serious . I'm afraid Arnold. We might have to go to court . At worst you might have to stay in jail until the real culprit is caught or they establish your guilt. The judge is likely to go for a high amount for bail or feel you are a flight risk."

Arnold bowed to the inevitable . "Very well. "

It was almost three hours later Beresford sat in the staff canteen mulling over the facts. "We've charged him with obtaining money under false pretences. Apparently there are several other charges pending but it looks

like the little old ladies want to put the boot in. Added to that we've got the suspicious circumstances surrounding Joan Simmons's death. We found his flat. It's in Pennington Road adjacent to Thirton Hight street. It's a modest affair. He has quite a few books on the occult. He even has a book about Coffin Paths. He's taking a course in counselling unsurprisingly, the number of people

he deals with. We've tackled him on the night of the murder of Jean Simmons. He claims he was in his flat watching television , though he can't remember

what was on. So no clear alibi. "

"What about the other murders Sir." Woods said.

"Well Gordon Mathews died on the fourteenth of May in the afternoon about two o'clock. Mr Bream claims he came from Thirton on that Monday morning after doing shopping. He was having his dinner but there's

no witnesses. As for Mister Grimshaw . That's a bit tricky. Grimshaw died on the twenty seventh late on a Sunday evening . Mr Bream claims he had an upset stomach that day. He was out cold the whole night."

"So no alibi for those occasions. "

"We've pulled in James Carter. He admits they tried the same trick on Joan Simmons. It appears that Carter and Bream have a little racket going on between them . We've got enough to hold them for questioning and gather proof for a case. That's about a month. We might have enough for obtaining money under false pretences . I'd say it looks promising."

"I must say the Solicitor didn't look happy when she went away." Woods said.

"Neither am I Justin. It's all we've got so far."

Ambrose Benton collected himself briefly before he

mounted the rostrum in the main hall. This was the community centre he had built precisely so that it would be used as an arts centre for the local community. "I'm so glad to be here tonight to speak to you ladies and gentlemen. It was ten years ago when my friend and mentor in this area told me of this wonderful place how I could help up and coming talent. Naturally I was sceptical , I'm a business man after all. He said that the Nucleus of talent of tomorrow is born today. He was Charlie Richter author of many books on art in America.

I grew up in Brooklyn. I was just a street kid. I soon learnt the easiest way is the hard way. I started as messenger then office boy then manager. Soon I had my own department, then I set up my own company .It was management of retail supplies. Then I branched out and grew bigger. Eventually I was where I am today. However there was something missing in my life. As you know New York was home to the "Factory". Modern art was and still is beyond me however I became aware of the symbolic nature of the advert and it's power this drew me towards Art. It was then in my travels I met Charlie Richter. He told me how I could encourage talent. This is about thirtieth competition I've sponsored. I've done this here and the states. I've seen the many varied talents on display here and I must say I am truly amazed at what I've seen.

Now the judges have made their decision. I have in my hand the results of the competition. I'm no good at handling stuff like this but I'll hand you over Imogen Schrader from the BBC I'm told who will be your compere from now on."

At this point a woman strode up to the Podium wearing a black dress and short blond hair. People recognised her as the presenter for the late night current affairs programme "Politics Now."

"Good evening ladies and gentlemen. It's a great pleasure to be here tonight. After London it's good to see some country side." Brief laughter.

"No but seriously it is good to see some emerging talent in the arts. For too

long the arts has been the poor cousin to the other parts of the entertainment industry. It's so good to have people like Ambrose Benton help us highlight the skills and abilities of the growing talent amongst us.

Now without further ado I will announce the winners of the competition. In third place. "She said looking down at the list before her " Is Elizabeth Carson for her reproduction of the "Lady of Shalott " by Waterhouse. After

a brief applause a young lady of eighteen dressed in a green evening dress approached the rostrum and accepted a cheque for two thousand pounds and a small statue of Minerva. She gave a small speech and stepped down.

"In second place is Denise Thompson for her reproduction The Death of Chatterton by Henry Wallis." Again a tall girl with auburn hair approached the rostrum. She bowed shyly Imogen made a short speech and accepted the prize money of five thousand pounds and a statue of Minerva. When she left Imogen resumed. "Now in first place the prize . winner of the Ambrose Benton award goes to Stuart Lynley!" The applause died down. "For his reproduction of "The judgement of Paris " by Cezanne.

Stuart braced himself as he walked up to the podium. In the audience sitting next to him was his mother and Maria. They were happy and took pictures on their phones as he walked up to the podium. When he got there Imogen asked him. "Now Stuart tell me what were your thoughts on entering this competition?"

"Well I've painted all my life really it's the one medium I can express

myself in. I draw birds and wildlife mainly . I saw this as a bit of a challenge. "

"So that's how you came to approach Cezanne?"

"Yes of course."

"Right well here's a cheque for ten thousand pounds. I must say it's a wonderful reproduction. I think you worked hard for your money. You deserve it." Stuart took his cue and said goodbye and walked off the stage.

"To finish off I will now introduce our guest speaker Charles Richter." The noise was oblivious to Stuart as he resumed his seat. Dora gave him a kiss and Maria touched his hand affectionately. After the ceremony they spent the night in the hotel and drove back to Thirton.

CHAPTER 7

Dora Lynley sat back for a minute and reflected. It had been three weeks now since he managed to get his job back at the local Supermarket. He was on course for taking two "A" levels at the college of education and compiling a portfolio for Art School. All in all things were on track. There was a letter from the trust that Stuart was working for. She seemed reasonably reassured by that. All in all things were on track. Her own job as a Doctor's receptionist was still going strong. Maria was ever patient . Maria was aware of all her sorrows and travails and was happy with her when Stuart finally came back.

The tranquillity was welcome . The long evenings without Stuart were a burden. Though she realised that Stuart would get qualifications and be leaving home someday. Maria had suggested another camping trip . Oddly enough now that Stuart was back , Dora felt quite agreeable to this. They planned to go to the Lake District in two weeks' time. It seemed feasible anyway.

As she came home that Wednesday she noticed that Stuart's things were on the settee . That meant he was back home from work. He should be showering it off and she would be seeing him at any minute.

As she made tea she heard footsteps or the stairs. She turned away from the stove to close the cupboard as Stuart walked into the kitchen. "How was work?" She said.

"Odd thing Mum , nothing's changed since I went away .Something about staff regulations have changed . We have to direct Customer's enquiries to the

Main desk. Apart from that nothing . Gregory Mathews got me my job back. He seemed pleased to see me."

"You were lucky . I don't know why you went off on that wild goose chase. A job is more important. "

"I know Mum , I won't do it again. I'm sorry but I've got plans now. I'm more positive."

"I'm keeping you to it."

After dinner Maria came in . She'd been working all day in the nursery and looked worn out. "Hard day?" . Dora asked.

"Precisely . I hope you've left some tea for me. "

"It's in the oven . If you sit down I'll get it. "

Later Stuart was in his bedroom . Dora knew he was forever drawing but also revising on his other subjects for A level history. She decided she would leave him in peace. Maria sat on the settee watching the television

as Dora came in with a tray. "I suppose you've been doing the plants again. The new management can't quite make its mind up what they want."

"In a nutshell of course. That and the bruised ego of certain members of Staff. " She paused. "Has Stuart told you what he was doing all that time away?

I mean I know he was painting and everything but still I'm curious."

"No not in so many words . It was for a charity, I got a letter the other day Didn't it you see it? It was called "Tomorrows Gateway." . A sort of charitable trust for young artists. I must say I'm impressed. The painting was fabulous wasn't it?"

"Well , I suppose it's an experience that counts. What does he want to do now?"

"He wants to take two A levels and apply for a course at University on the strength of a Portfolio he's compiling."

"Do you think that he's got a chance?"

"Yes most certainly but...."

"But you can't help worrying. I feel the same way about Jake. He's twenty five with his own career as an engineer . I still worry . We can't help it."

"Yes but as you said he's got his own career. Stuart, I'm not sure . I think people take advantage."

"What sexually or just talent wise?"

"Talent wise. I think they misuse him. I mean so long as he's settled down to a job and education I can't really ask for anything more."

"But you still worry. It's in our DNA . He'll be fine."

The evening wore on as the winter winds blew outside. Stuart mulled over the period of history he was going to study ." The early nineteenth century covering the Napoleonic Wars and Europe."

Beresford sat back in the station canteen. He had a feeling that abated as soon as he looked at the charge sheet. Arnold Bream had been in custody in Brixton for two weeks now . He looked over the charges against him. Most of it was circumstantial evidence, nothing was concrete.

This of course made no impression on Chief Constable Ralston what so ever. He felt the success of method over rationality was supreme and would inevitably overcome all objections.

Beresford went over the files once again. Bream had no previous convictions that he could see. The sums of money he cadged off the widows were in reality trifling . He wasn't too greedy , they were enough to keep a business like his above water. The affairs with Jean Simmons and his attempt with Chandra were innocent enough.

However evidence was evidence . There was a book on

Coffin Paths in his flat. There were also books on alternative therapies, Reiki and Yoga. There were books on healing , on Glastonbury Tor and Mysticism. Obviously Bream didn't take his gift for granted . Theoretically if there was a power struggle between him and Martin Grimshaw then ostensibly he had to lay the ground

first. Taking the coffin path from All Saints Church to Cullompton farm he could have given Graham pies laced with Sodium Chlorate or more precisely switched the ones switch the ones he already had. Then waiting for the poison to take effect take the dead body and place it behind the roll on roll off truck and switch it on. Then sensing trouble over Jean Simmons over their

affair , maybe she was going to see Grimshaw more often, he decided to kill her. He could have done that going through the alley way at Pennington Road

leading to Mosely Road. There was a small cul de sac called Hallows Close that led directly to Tilson Park Road. Of course after that he decides to execute the rest of his plan . Starting from the railway station at Albion Valley and using the coffin path again reaches Weald Road where he comes upon Martin and the final act of carnage.

It seemed probable . The man was schizoid , his dysphoria probably led him to these drastic acts. Beresford wouldn't have to look for any signs of this in Bream's belongings. It was in the man obviously . Yet there was still a lingering doubt in the back of his mind. All these murders took planning, careful planning . Bream could organise psychic events manage his affairs but this as well? He bent down and examined the file again.

"Afternoon Sir? Anything new?" Woods came into the office.

"No just going over the evidence again. Of course the old ladies won't say anything for him. We're stuck for any real evidence , no clothes , no DNA. We've been all over his flat. "

"Something will turn up Sir. They always do. It's the careful ones you've got to watch for."

"No doubt."

He looked outside. Rain gently sprinkled the tarmac on the car park outside as clouds gently ebbed in during the afternoon.

Major Kindersley switched off the remote one last time. As he pushed his wheel chair past the book case he wheeled himself into the kitchen. He was able to fix himself a cup of tea and switched on the radio for company.

Davinia would be due in about six o'clock. He had received a phone call from a friend of his . The friend was an old, retired detective from Thirton CID Roy Cummings . Since coming to Thirton thirty years ago he met Roy occasionally on the golf course. Now that he was in a wheel chair he heard that Roy's wife had died. He'd gone to the funeral and paid his last respects. Now it seemed Roy saw it fit to grace Kindersley with his presence. Cummings

had spent some time in Cyprus during the troubles. He spent most of his time in military intelligence . Kindersley knew not to ask too many questions , but he was always glad to see Roy.

For the most part Roy talked about his wife Gladys. Gladys it seemed came from a family of lawyers and solicitors . So from her family's point of view she married beneath her. Kindersley could tell that he never really liked talking about his in-laws. The past could still hurt. Nevertheless when he came to see Kindersley he would recount the days and nights spent with Gladys, recounting the pains of a childless marriage . The stigma his wife received from the neighbourhood . Eventually his wife trained as an optician and established a practice in Thirton. Together they managed to get through the years. Roy took up stamp collecting . Also he collected butterflies. In truth Kindersley thought Roy wasn't his sort of man. However any company was better than no company. Roy also took an interest in Davinia.

"You know Danny." Cummings always used Kindersley's first name . " I used to know Davinia's grandparents quite well. The Peters family was quite important in Thirton you know."

"She rarely talks about them. She's more interested in Church affairs . She dug up the grove of St Hilda . I don't think she got any thanks for it."

"She wouldn't . Not round here. They're all stick in the muds. They've got their Sunday morning service at All Saints and that's all they care about. "

"Quite. I don't know why she bothers . A young girl like that should be off and Married or doing a job or something."

"Well you know , I know something about Davinia very early on she formed a relationship with Jeannie Smith. This was years ago of course. I knew Jeannie from when she was young. There was a case at Kessington Farm. That's where Gregory Mathews lives now. Young Martha Mathews died from a blow to the head. Apparently the grandfather Justin Mathews was working nearby and a tractor he was using backfired . The next thing Mary was lying dead on the ground. They knew Justin suffered from shell shock . They felt that in a panic

Justin must have hit Mary. He got put away in an institution , died a few years

later."

"You were talking about Jeannie Smith."

"Yes Jeannie lived In Kessington. The Mathews family gave a few thousand quid to the family as compensation. Jeannie always seemed odd to me as a little girl."

"So what are you saying? "

"Only that Davinia and Jeannie were friends for a while in

the nineties. I don't know any more."

"But you think Jeannie was different? "

"Well they say that the old man Smith was a weird kind if you get my meaning. Poor Jeannie grew up in a strange family. She seems to have disappeared."

"Well I can honestly say that Davinia seems a rock of common sense. I haven't any complaints."

"Yes Danny but there's a lot of people sniffing round right now. These murders well you never know. " It was about a few minutes later that Roy seemed to forget his concerns and continued to relate tales of his departed

Gladys.

Later that evening Davinia turned up to tidy the place up and give Kindersley his evening tea. After Davina had washed up she went sat besides Kindersley and said "And what can I do for Major Kindersley today? "

"Well this may seem odd but I was reminiscing about Cyprus of all places with a colleague. It was during the troubles in 1964. I was tortured in Kyrenia.

the Greek resistance were giving us trouble. EOTA had started an offensive on the other side of town. Unfortunately on this particular night they were particularly effective. They over ran our headquarters and demanded we continue broadcasting as normal. Tommy Brown was my commanding officer in Nicosia. I had to send a message to him saying we needed supplies urgently.

In doing this I was to give no indication that I was captured. However we had agreed between us a password if we were captured. In 1882 there was the battle of Tel El Kebir in Egypt. The password was "Send the rifles to Tel El Kebir." Now I thought that was rather cumbersome actually. I said it over the radio and Brown caught on immediately . Oddly enough the insurgents didn't catch on."

"And you got away?"

"Oh yes. Captain Brown came over with a regiment and we were freed in no time. That peace in 1964 was an absolute mess though."

Somewhat mystified Davinia tied up a few things in the kitchen and left. leaving Kindersley no wiser to how she felt.

Iris Mathews sat in the sitting room at Cullompton Farm. Surrounded by house bills , she ruminated briefly on the wisdom of having the children home

for Summer . Electricity had gone rocketing up. Still she reflected right now she'd be totally lost without them. Life without Gordon was one long full stop.

Nothing happened after it.

Beatrice and Stanley however were emerging out into the world. She studied went to see some girlfriend locally who went to University like her and compared notes. No boyfriends yet though Iris knew there were some in the past. Stanley was the wild one. Technical like her father he showed great ability round tractors and engines. She could tell he had designs on the farm. Only she didn't want to disrupt Lambert Hodge in his management. Though eventually the delicate balance would probably fall away. On reflection she wandered if Ian Beasley was such a bad option. She knew however why she didn't chose this option. The farm kept her busy. She only had to ask Lukasz if there was something she could do. Though Lambert felt this showed a bad example to the workers.

Stan was sitting in the Diamond Café in Thirton high street with his friend Will Jamieson. "Have you told her yet?" Will asked.

"No of course not she'll be pleased."

"Of course."

"I'm going to Agricultural College. My grades are good

enough. It all seems inevitable somehow .Though I'm looking forward to running a farm."

"You could be a manager like Lambert Hodge. Just go around people's farms."

"No , then you are at the command of the owner. No , I'll call the tunes. I know Lambert won't mind. He's used to taking orders."

"Will he mind though?"

"In a job you do what you can to survive . If not he can go . I'm sure it won't come to that."

"You have to learn the ropes."

"Of course . I don't want to lose Lambert if I don't have to. It's just you know I've got plans. He'll see to that of course."

"It's a long way off , four years. "

"Not that long. We can enjoy tonight , what is it a party round at Mitch's?"

"I think so . I got my results just a pass."

"And you were going to some redbrick university in Reading wasn't it?"

"Yeah, they've accepted provisionally."

"Okay then no fuss. Skin up some gear and off we go."

They left the café and ventured out to Thirton High Street , their minds full of the summer afternoon. Beatrice sat back in her room as she looked over her texts from college she just put a finishing touch to an assignment she had to do over the summer when her mother came in to the room.

"Still working, why don't you go out Beatrice? You've never been this quiet."

"I was just thinking about Stan. "

"Stan, why?"

"He didn't tell you did he? Typical."

"Tell me what?"

"He got two B's and a C. That means he can go to agricultural college. I thought he'd tell you himself. He's so inconsiderate."

"That's Stan . It's not being inconsiderate, it's just the way he is. He's preoccupied sometimes."

"Naturally you're making excuses for him but honestly Mum."

Iris Drew breath. She knew Beatrice had little patience with men. They either accepted her on her terms or not at all. She was delighted Stan had passed and only hoped he would become serious in his study . She

briefly toyed with the idea of doing legal work again. She could set up a practice in Thirton . It would keep her busy. Plus she could always do voluntary work. As the year would go past she knew she would have to start looking for an existing legal practices to break herself in. Looking at Beatrice , she knew she would be following similar challenges soon. For an economist firms set the bar very high . If she got good marks she would be in demand no doubt . She could feel the family breaking up and going their separate ways. It hurt in a way.

"Yes I know . He'll be sensible and get down to study . It's just one of those things He'll get down to it when he has to."

Beatrice sighed. "Can we go shopping today. I'd like to go to Thirton. I want you to come with me. It'll be nice."

"Of course Bee and a great idea."

The International Court of Justice in the Hague resided at the Peace Palace just off Carnegie Plein and Meervedortlaan the main road. The ICC is the first and only permanent court with the official task to prosecute individuals for the international crimes of genocide, crimes against humanity and crimes of aggression. It compliments judicial systems and exercises its jurisdiction only when national courts are unwilling to prosecute. Lacking jurisdiction , it prosecutes crimes committed with in member states or situations referred to them by the United Nations.

Andrew Williams relaxed in his apartment in Westeinde not very far from the Mainsthause Museum. He just finished a meal at one of the restaurants in the Hague. Abstaining from the finer dishes he had Lekkerkerbje with Stamport. A form of battered fish dipped in sauce and a potato confection consisting of various vegetables and sausage. The mix usually brought an invariable torrent of indigestion . Andrew told himself in that case he would die happy.

The firm he was working with was called Brouwer and Van Hoebeck. Daan Brouwer was his point of contact . He made friends with his wife and family , Roose and two little girls .

Daan phoned him up that previous evening. "Het spigt met .Sorry." He instantly translated . "Andrew this is important business . I know you made plans to leave Holland soon but this case has to be finalised. If it goes through the Hague you only have about fifty per cent chance of getting it through."

"Relax Daan It's all in the balance . I'll go to court on Monday and I'll have them eating out of my hand."

Reluctantly Daan let him go a few minutes later. At that moment Andrew reflected on the case in hand . It was a company called Steinberg and Dekker. They had purchased three export processing plants in Indonesia but subscribed to the charter of human rights. In reality there had been a few changes to the plants but in the main things stayed the way they were. Hopefully with a few photographs and a few medical reports by a few medical officers that he'd given a bribe to , he hoped to get Steinberg off the hook. Dieter Steinberg was one very uncontrite capitalist who was rarely pleased with half measures but when Andrew showed his proposed strategy he seemed mollified to some degree.

As Daan Brouwer noticed this was Andrew's last play of the dice. He noticed Jan Djckman the reigning magistrate would probably be glad to see the back of him. Andrew had acted in defence of more than one rogue company that breached human rights. He gained a reputation as a lawyer of note as the apartment in Westeinde would testify. He had no misgivings about going back to London. He could do Corporate Law and was still quite conversant with English business practices but more importantly well versed in trade with Europe.

The firm of Caron and Brooks in Mayfair had advertised a vacancy about five months ago . They were more than a little surprised and delighted to receive his application . He remembered sitting back in their offices in Conduit Street and thinking where his office would be. It was a dingy little side street . They had other offices . The office manager who interviewed him was quite polished in his approach but was over awed by Andrew's CV. He had little trouble in convincing him of his work experience. It was with quiet confidence that he took the next plane back to the Hague.

It was a month later when the reply came back . The acceptance came as no surprise . Daan Brouwer was crestfallen to see him go. Andrew had defended quite a few cases in the Hague quite successfully. He met his long-time associate Carol Broadley who seemed to be somewhat more conciliatory than she was at his brother's funeral. "So you're going then?"

"Yes I feel a return to some sort of normality is required." They were standing in the bar called the Kali a few streets away from Westeinde.

"By that I mean not defending super criminals . I'm impressed. I suppose you've seen the light. "

"Let's just say in my next firm I'll be serving in an advisory capacity."

"Okay I'll let you have that . I take it you're going to be a good boy in future."

"Of course." He said . To himself he thought it won't wash. If she wants to brush it under the carpet well and good I'm happy.

Stanley Williams looked round his flat in Donnington. He was fairly near the approach road to Chichester and fairly confident of getting to Brinsbury College in Pulborough on time for the lecture . He made few friends since he came down to Chichester. The lecturer Dan Hargreaves was a fairly friendly looking guy. Though he knew the course was going to be rigorous enough.

His flat mate Gavin Peters came from Norfolk and was a farm labourer who had a grant to study. He was a few years older than Stanley. Though it didn't take long for Stanley to warm to him. A few jars at the Wheatsheaf arms in Chichester and they were best of friends. Gavin confided in him that he didn't really have good grades in his A levels and didn't really know what to do. At a loss he took a job in neighbouring farm . It seemed the whole job was going upmarket . Fruit pickers would be hard to come by because of a change in Government policy. They would be employing someone who could use robot

machinery for picking fruit. It had become a skilled job. Faced with this the manager thought it would be a good idea to send Gavin on a course to get an agricultural degree. It would be a way of keeping abreast of the changes.

When Stanley told of his own situation he immediately sympathised over the loss of his father but seemed intrigued at the opportunities that awaited him in managing the farm. Some sixth sense prevailed in Stanley telling him not to tell Gavin of the half ounce of black he had in his drawer. It took some classes at college to seek out like minded fellows such as himself. He was standing in West Street just coming out of a café when he spotted a familiar character just walking past. With his heightened sense of smell Stan could smell the joint.

"Hello you Lionel?" He asked.

The man turned round. "Who wants to know?"

"Hi , I'm Stan I'm at Brinsbury college studying agriculture . I've seen you round here can we talk?"

"Well, hello yes I'm Lionel . I'm doing my second year. Though if I may say so Stan I think you might declare you're interest."

As they walked Stan felt he better cut to the chase. "Nothing really. It's just I've got a stash in my room and I thought if you knew local contacts you could help me occasionally. "

"Of course here have some. " He offered the joint over. "It's skunk I'm afraid, but I'm expecting some soon."

"Great." After the initial hellos Lionel told he went to the Wheatsheaf but there wasn't a scene as such. He himself went to the Butter Cross to a pub called the Golden Lion. It served its purpose as a venue. Lionel gave him his mobile number and set up a meeting in two days' time.

It was two days later at about eight o'clock in the beer garden of the Golden Lion surreptitiously smoking a joint at the back Stan found Lionel.

"So what's your story Stan?"

"My Dad has this farm in Thirton. It's a big concern. I got these A level results . It was a shoe-in really. Sad thing is my Dad got killed about three months ago. So it looks like my job after this will be managing the farm."

"Well you've got a job lined up. It's more than most of us have got."

"Tell me about it. I'm keeping this to a minimum." He indicated the joint.

"I've got to study etc. Though a blast now and then is no harm."

"No of course not. My old man made a living out of selling

burgers made of Gloucester Old Spots he raised. All I've got to look forward to is a Pig Farm."

"Don't knock it. You've got a lot of potential."

"I'm not going to. You're right." He paused . "Look some of us are going down to Selsey Bill next Saturday. It's cool down there, come along , the more the merrier."

Stan noticed that apart from Lionel there was Grace who was also studying agriculture . She didn't have much to say and Stan had the distinct impression he was breaking something up. "Yeah, it sounds a good idea.

I'll see you there."

It was about three days later Stan had already finished an assignment given to him by his lecturers and found Gavin still struggling with his assignment . Though by Saturday he seemed to have managed easily enough.

"Got anything on for tonight?" Gavin said.

"Well I said I'd meet a few friends in Selsey Bill . Though if you've got a better idea than let me know."

"Yes of course the freshers ball. This is where you meet your mates."

"Ah yes sorry. I've got a prior engagement but enjoy."

Gavin seemed disappointed that Stan wasn't coming but hid it well enough.

Stan headed out for Selsey Bill at about half past six. It was a short drive from Donnington. The motley collection of cottages shops and offices didn't raise any problems in his mind. He parked his car in the car park by the beach which was virtually empty.

He walked down the beach until he saw a fire and some people drinking. As he approached he could make out figures. Dressed in a Hawaiian shirt Lionel wasn't hard to identify.

"Hi Stan , glad you could make it. What have you got?"

"Some black it's cool. I'll roll a joint."

"Surely, look grab yourself a drink ." Grace was sitting at a table near by with some other girls not taking any notice.

Eventually Lionel came back with a friend. "Stan this Jimmy. So if you like we'll crack open some beers . You can start up some black . I've got some Thai. we should make a night of it."

After a few joints and some beers the party got started. Stan got talking to a girl called Helen. She came from Cambridgeshire. The conversation was disjointed and she wandered off. Stan found himself sitting on the bench and falling asleep . It was an hour later he woke up and found nobody there.

Apparently everybody had gone. He approached the fire. It was still blazing quiet fiercely. He heard a voice. "Are you still here?"

He turned round and saw a figure outlined by the fire. "Yes but I fell asleep that's all."

He could tell by the voice it was a woman. "I think your name is Stan , is that right?"

"Yes."

"Look Stan if you smoke a joint with me , I'll share some wine is that a deal?"

"Sounds okay. What part are you from?"

"Oh around." She said. Stan wandered what the night might hold still.

The night passed into a dismal dawn and fitful rain fell upon the beach. Arnold Perkins was a retired shopkeeper. He had a shop in Sevenoaks and kept going for thirty years. When he retired his wife suggested they go downto live in Bracklesham . However Arnold was a restless soul. This led him to a hobby that he never would have previously considered, that of Beachcombing. Relentlessly he would comb beaches for odd items , sea shells, watches, keepsakes , molluscs. The odd dead cat or dog would occasionally warrant a trip to West Hampnett to deposit the remains with the local authority tip as he felt it was a health hazard. Today Arnold had elected to go to Selsey Bill.

It was a natural progression from Bracklesham . Wittering was too busy. As he rounded a bluff he only found slim pickings ., then he saw a few tables that were probably put there by the local authority for holiday makers. There was also the remains of fire nearby. More remarkably still he saw a figure slumped on the table motionless. He thought nothing of it. He tried to nudge the figure awake ,but the figure fell away from the table on to the sand. Arnold could see there was a huge ugly gash on the neck of what he could see was a young man. He also noticed that the sand around the table was drenched in blood. Arnold phoned the emergency services. He turned the body over and found the lifeless face staring up at him in mute appeal. The beach bearing silent witness to what had happened.

Chichester Police station was situated in the heart of the town near the Butter Cross . This of course suited Detective Inspector Amsworth quite well. Frequently he had to make forays into the hyper markets for something to eat before being called out on urgent cases . His staff DC Wrenworth , DC Baines and DC Haynes were all experienced officers. Charlotte Wrenworth had previously served ten years on the Royal Navy. Terry Baines had been a store detective in Portsmouth . Mary Haynes had been a gym instructor in a girls school in Worthing. Roy Amsworth felt a moment's apprehension when he

received a call on Sunday morning, that a body had been found in Selsey Bill.

"Tell me Terry is SOCO there yet?"

Terry who had just come in and taken the details seemed barely awake.

"No, they're expecting them any minute Sir. "

"Good, I want Mary and Charlie down there Asap. It's going to be a mess."

"Yes Sir." Although murder wasn't wholly unknown in Chichester,

it was usually domestic or drug related and that did not merit coverage. As he climbed into his car he heard his phone go. He answered it as he got into the driver's seat. "Hello, can I help you?"

"To whom am I speaking to?"

"I'm Detective Inspector Amsworth of Chichester CID can I help you?"

"Hello. I'm sorry to bother you . News has just come in from Chichester about the murder. I've picked it up on the computer. I'm DI Beresford from Thirton Constabulary . I've heard it was Stanley Williams is that right?"

"I've just got details myself Beresford . At any rate this is my investigation How can I help you?"

"Stanley Williams was the son of Gordon Williams who was murdered last May.. There could be a connection . I may be able to help you ."

"I may remind you this is on our turf detective. I don't mind an extra pair of hands, but don't get in our way. If you have any information for me it would be helpful."

Sensing disquiet on the phone Amsworth heard him reply. "Very well, Mr Amsworth I'll be down there in a few hours. I'll give you all the help I can."

About half an hour later Amsworth reached Selsey Bill .

DC Haynes and DC Wrenworth were already there . They already had their forensic suits on.

There was a tent around the table where the body was seated. The Pathologist Leslie Graham from their department was already inspecting the body. Amsworth approached him. What can you tell me Leslie?"

"Well there was no sign of a struggle so I suspect a tox report will tell us more later. There's rigor mortis so I'd say time of death was probably ten o'clock last night. "

"Any sign that he knew his attacker?"

"As I say not necessarily. We haven't had anything like this for a while. Have you heard anything? "

"Well , I got a call from Thirton. They say the man's father was murdered three months ago."

"So not anything to do with our patch of course." Leslie relieved.

"We've still got to catch him or her. " Amsworth warned.

"Yes. I'll let you have my report tomorrow at the latest."

As Amsworth came out he was approached by DC Wrenworth. "Okay Wrenworth let me have it. What have you got?"

"Well you've seen the body yourself . It's a young man basically. A student from Chichester college an agricultural student. We'll be going to his college and his address in Donnington to see what we can find."

"What's your feeling Charlie , what do you think?"

"I think it may be random Sir. Someone at the wrong place at the wrong time. "

"I've had a phone call from Thirton . DI Beresford tells me the boy's father was murdered three months ago. "

"Yes Sir that puts a slightly different complexion on

matters, now that you mention it. " Briefly Amsworth took another look at the body. It was a young man about twenty. It seemed such a tragic waste.

When he got back to the office it was about an hour later, he got a report from DC Wrenworth. "I've interviewed Gavin Peters his flat mate. Apparently there was fresher's ball at Chichester college this weekend. He asked Stanley to come with him but Stanley it appears had a prior engagement. "

"Good work Charlie. That leaves out the college then. Let me know if you have anything else?"

About a quarter of an hour later he received another phone call. "Dc Haynes Sir. I've used a few connections at the Butter Cross. A chap called Lionel Faversham a second year student at Chichester College met Stanley on Saturday night. There was a party on the beach apparently. I'm bringing him in for questioning."

"Anyone else?"

"Yes Grace Parish daughter of the local vicar of Emsworth. She tells me that Stan was at the party but fell asleep at the table. They just left him there. They don't know anything else."

"How about CCTV cameras. Have you got anything there?"

"Yes Grace Parish had a car. She was seen heading off from the beach by about twenty past eight. Apparently Lionel was with her. "

"That puts them in the clear. We still have a suspect at large. This is a Holiday spot the locals will want to clear this up soon."

"Yes Sir.'"

"Good work Haynes. When you're all finished up there , report back to my office at sixteen hundred hours."

"Yes Sir."

For Beresford it wasn't good news. It wasn't good news at all. A suspect at large at the end of a holiday season would be bad news for the local trade. It was half an hour later DI Beresford arrived. Amsworth thought he was about forty and obviously good at his job. "Well DI Beresford have you got anything for me?"

"Yes lots. We've been trying to track down a murderer in Thirton. First victim was Mr Gordon Williams, he died in May. He'd been struck by a mechanical hoist from a roll on roll off truck he used on his farms. It seemed innocent enough until we discovered he was poisoned by Sodium Chlorate. He was dead when hit by the beam. Coupled with that there were two other murders apparently unconnected . We thought we had the murderer ,now it looks like we have to think again."

"So you think this is the same chap?"

"Yes , I'm afraid so."

"Well we've interviewed people around this and we've found nothing really. Apparently Stanley went out on a Saturday night to Selsey Bill. There were some people partying on the beach but they left about two hours before we calculate that Stanley died. We have CCTV footage to prove it. "

"No as I've said this was someone else ." With a hint of frustration Amsworth said "Okay you've got one suspect in custody who's obviously innocent if your theory is correct. Have you got any leads?"

"Nothing as yet. This is annoying for you as well for me. I'd like to be present at the post mortem tomorrow. I'd also like to go to the crime scene if I may."

"I'll instruct my officers to give you any assistance ."

Quoting Shakespeare Iris Williams felt dried up and useless inside. She thought when troubles come they come not in single spies but in battalions. Absently looking over the work top she reflected that she cleared it for the third time that morning. Lambert Hodge stood at the door as she sat down at the table. "I'm sorry Iris , I've just heard . When did you find out?"

"They phoned me this morning. I could hardly believe it. "

"How about Beatrice?"

"I phoned her." Immediately she's coming as soon as she can."

"Good though I must say such an adjective hardly merits it's presence on such an occasion."

"No it doesn't . Let me know if you hear anything your end Lambert. This is an awful bloody day and it's not going to get any better."

It was four hours later Beatrice finally arrived at the farm. Her face was flushed and she'd been crying. Briefly they hugged in the kitchen as Beatrice put down her night bag . "What did they say Mum?"

"They said he'd been to a party the night before. They identified two witnesses who'd been with Stanley. They claimed he'd been there at this party on the beach at Selsey Bill . Then they left. The Police have got local CCTV footage showing their cars leaving. "

"So nobody else?"

"Well I suppose along with the death of your father and other people here it's all part of the same thing. Oh God I wish it would stop!"

"It'll be okay Mum. It will be just fine." She said as she hugged her mother closer.

Arnold Bream sat in the cell in Brixton when his solicitor arrived , it was something of a surprise. They ushered him onto the visiting room with-out ceremony. During his stay there hadn't been time to make friends. The usual remarks about the nature of his crime and if here a sex offender were exchanged. He kept his distance as much as possible . He knew one character called Anthony Teasdale . He was from Lancashire and had been caught stealing a car in Fulham and had led the Police on a merry drive. He was young

well-spoken but one could tell that he was hardened to a life of crime. There were other far more dubious characters he kept his distance from. He managed to steer a course through Prison life without coming to grief.

Sitting in front of his Solicitor she told him her name was Clair Gaines .She was efficient looking and in her mid-thirties. "Now Mister Bream I've got some news for you. I'm afraid they've found another person who's been murdered yesterday. This does rather mean that the charges against you have been dropped."

"Including procuring money under false pretences?"

"The ladies in question were reluctant to proceed with the prosecution,

so I'm glad to say yes , including those. How are you fixed financially?"

"Well I'm paying a mortgage on my flat. That's going to be taken off the market I suppose. As for the premises on Calmington Road, Joy my partner tells me they haven't any takers so it looks like business as usual."

"We'll be pursuing the Police for costs incurred because of your incarceration so you needn't worry on that score. You'll be going to the court room tomorrow , but it's just a formality. After the hearing you should be a free man. "

Arnold bowed his head ."Thank God. It's been a nightmare."

"I'm sure it has Mister Bream. Is there anything else I can

do?"

"No thanks. You've been a great help."

Clair Gaines signed to the Warder that the interview was over and Bream was led back to his cell.

Beatrice sat on a sack of cattle feed on the site where her father's truck was standing. They were using a contractor to drive stuff around until they came up with an alternative. She thought. "If I could shield my body from life and see the way forward. In that case I would shield everybody from harm and yet they come to grief." She knew she missed Stanley , although the recent death of her father was just as grievous. It seemed as though grief had worn her down to a smorgasbord of sorrows. She could barely feel any more, just move through the day like a zombie.

Staring wistfully up at the sky she heard a noise coming from the hedge. She turned around and saw Amanda Mathews standing there , her luxurious hair flowing in the breeze. "Hi Mandy , how's things?"

The minute age gap between them should have been a barrier but knowing Amanda from school they got on somehow. "I'm fine thanks. Heard the awful news. I'm so sorry Beatrice. It must be terrible for you . ."

"I'm not sure anymore. I can't feel anything. It's like someone's cut my left arm off. There's nothing left there. I have this awful feeling of disconnectedness. It's just a bit much really."

"How's your Mum taking it?"

"Not much better as a matter of fact. That's part of the reason I'm sitting here . Just to test the atmosphere. I'm trying to inoculate myself somehow. Some hope."

" It must be awful for her as well."

"She's going through shock . She's talking over management with Lambert.

"I'm not sure her heart's in it to be fair. She's just going through the motions."

"Let's go down and have a look at the farm shall we? I've never had a proper look at it."

Beatrice got up and as they walked down to the farm Amanda said, "What's your fondest memory of Stanley?"

Beatrice smiled for a minute . "We were kids. I was ten and he was seven. I said we should go black berry picking down at the hedge at the bottom of the farm. We both picked some and ate them. I was sick however because one of them was off. Stanley laughed, I never forgave him for that. He apologised afterwards."

"I can think of similar episodes with Harry. Boys aren't kind."

"No, but somehow you can't forget them."

"Never, no never ." Amanda agreed.

As they approached the dairy herd , they were approached by Lukasz Bukowitz. "Hello ladies . Can I help you?"

"We were just going to look at the dairy herd if that's okay. I haven't had a good look at them since I've been back."

"Good job then Miss Williams. I've been to see Iris. She's happy with the cows."

"You don't mind if we have a look?"

"No of course not. Our pride and joy." He added. They were into the extensive dairy shed were the milking machines were kept. Amanda said "This is where the milking is done I suppose. How much cattle have you got?"

"About seventy cows."

"What sort of price do you get from Milk Mark? "

"Not a very good one. We claim tax allowance for loss of

earnings. Our main product is the beef herd and the abattoir. Managing it is a full time occupation. "

"If you could divert some of your produce you'd make more money." Amanda offered.

"In what way?"

"You could make Yoghurt out of it. You could set up a shed alongside . It's not too difficult. It's not too difficult cultivating Yoghurt and selling it. You could try the local supermarket. They'd only be happy to try out local brands. "

"Or Farmer's Markets." Beatrice said.

"What you need is someone with marketing ability." Amanda said pointedly.

"Yes they do Amanda. I can see what you're getting at. I'm not sure I can get my head round that right now. Though I definitely seeing my way round this. Look do you want a job? I mean I know things weren't good next door but I'd pay you a wage. I think you've got some good ideas."

Surprised at this turn of events Amanda said. "Oh Beatrice my goodness. I hope you don't think I'm being opportunistic . You've only just had a bereavement , what must you think?"

"Never mind Amanda. Are you interested ? You're the first person I've spoken to in the last forty eight hours. As far as I'm concerned if you want a job I'll tell Lambert to expect you tomorrow morning." Are you in with this?"

"Oh yes of course."

It was in the business court of the Hague that Andrew Williams sat while Jan Dijk man presided over the case of Steinberg and Dekker. The international Criminal court held these hearings in order to clarify issues of

International law. "It's quite clear to me that that circumstance described by the plaintiff case notwithstanding contrary evidence is of an exemplary nature" Dijk man looked for a moment at the prosecuting barrister with a disapproving stare." I have been presented with evidence , and I am indeed satisfied that the plaintiff has taken due care to ensure the utmost care of life and limb has been taken in these processing plants in Indonesia as does not contravene the factory regulations in this court. I therefore find the plaintiff not guilty. The prosecuting Lawyer Jan Hymans seemed to recoil at such a reproof.

Brouwer congratulated Andrew as he left the court. "Good you've done it Andy."

"Well Daan I fear you're being disingenuous here."

"What do you mean?"

"Well I happen to know that Jan Dijk man comes from the Hord rig Area. I also happen to know that Steinberg and Dekker have a sizeable factory built there. If they were to withdraw from there the result would be disastrous."

"My friend Andrew . What can I say? He gave the court verdict . It's out of my hands. "

"Of course Daan . This my last case. I'm leaving on Saturday . I've disturbed enough people for one week. Give my love to your wife. I'm sorry , I won't be seeing you again."

" Oh Andrew this is just business. We will visit you of course."

"I hope so Daan."

Beresford sat facing Burnham over his desk. "Okay Chris what's the state of Play?"

"They've scanned the cameras round Selsey Bill. They can't find anything. It seemed that Stanley Williams was sitting at the table surrounded by these

college guys and having a party. We've had the registration plates of all parties concerned . They all left at eight o'clock .

Their departure is recorded by the CCTV camera in the car park. Apart from the beach comber who found the body we've got absolutely zero."

"What about Mister Bream?"

"He's being released today. I suppose we should be relieved we haven't convicted an innocent man."

"More to the point we haven't got a guilty one."

"I haven't completely given up on that Sir."

"Glad to hear it. Then in that case I want some results. Oh I know you're trying you're damndest . Needless to say Ralston isn't pleased but who is? Keep at it Chris. Cases can be like this sometimes, you think you know your murderer , then it's just not obvious anymore."

"Well I was pursuing a line of enquiry. It's just DC Woods seemed to feel we were on a hiding for nothing. Now I'm not so sure. There's something here Sir, I'm sure of it."

" I know what you mean. Still water runs deep especially round here. If it wasn't Bream it was someone else. Above all try and keep Ralston happy even if it's nicking a cat burglar. Letting Bream go free is not a good sign. I'm sure we can make up lost ground." Beresford seemed to agree and ten minutes later he resumed checking his notes and interviews to see if he missed something.

Jud came into the foyer of the hotel in Brighton after checking his trade figures when Paddy Stern came in. His face was completely white. "I've just had a call from Mallin. The curator at the gallery in Nice had inspected the

Painting the Judgement of Paris. "The noises aren't good they've sent for an expert from Florence."

"I thought Steinauer was on this What's happened?"

"I don't know some things can't be explained. We've got to go. "

Jud set his face resolutely for a minute. "Yes of course there's no time to lose. We'll just make the next plane to Mexico. I can think of something from there."

"What about Passports? They'll pick us up straight away."

"I've got some made some made up when we were in St Ives. One of those artists did it as a side-line."

"Very well what name shall I say when we get there.?"

"I'm Dennis Holden . You're Randolph Myers. The rest is unimportant. They won't be expecting us at the airport. The thing is to leave now. It won't take long for Thirton CID to come sniffing round. "

"What about Stuart?"

"Stuart Lynne? Well I've got all that covered. I can't go in to this now Paddy. He should be okay."

"You're right of course . Well we better get going". It was three hours later they were looking at a luxury class 748 jet taking off from Heathrow. Jud kept checking his phone and talking to Mallin. Apparently a similar flight was taking off from Orly airport.

Arnold was coming out of his flat in Pennington Road . He just got off the phone to his solicitor . The estate agent was in the process of taking the flat off the market after the solicitor advised him he would be in breach of contract if he sold it with-out his clients explicit consent. Arnold knew there was enough money in the kitty to pay for one month's mortgage. His next worry was going to Calmington Road and facing Joy and Eunice.

When he arrived there he found Joy in her studio writing up her notes about her patients. "Hello, Joy how are things?"

Joy looked at him as if seeing a Ghost. "Arnold your back so soon. What's happened?"

"Well apparently they got the wrong man. All I can say is

I'm relieved. I've got to pay this month's rent. I've got the check here. Is everything alright between you and Eunice?"

"Fine yes. Um Eunice did say she thought of letting the place to someone else. She said it was bad publicity . But..." Joy said thoughtfully for a minute

"If you've got the money of course." She took the cheque and put it in her book writing out a receipt for Arnold.

"Good." Arnold said relieved. The three weeks in Brixton had gone by quickly. I hoped other people would be forgiving."

When he got to his rooms he sat by his desk and made some calls. "Hello is that Cynthia Asquith?"

"Yes who is this ? Is that you Arnold ? Did they let you go? I am glad , I know you wouldn't do anything so cruel. How stupid some people are."

He was glad to hear Cynthia's voice . It relieved him to think that people gave him the benefit of the doubt. After four phone calls to Averill Green,

and Celia Pheeney amongst others he felt sure he could start up his psychic society again.

The thing was he knew the killer was out there. The evil was there . Would it come for him? Time spent in her majesty's prison told him that this was unlikely. The killers he met there where cool calculating methodical people. They knew what they were doing.

He reflected despondently on his experiences. If he were a religious or Christian man he would think that God gave him the experience to humble him, to examine his life and change it. However Arnold was a practical man. Psychic abilities aside he was not a man for new beginnings. He had a good base in Thirton , he could probably become more famous back stabbing aside.

He would take the challenges as they came.

He held no grudges against Chandra Hussein. She had job to do. It was as simple as that. The fact that he was innocent was neither here nor there. He would start another evening looking into people's souls. Tell them largely what they already knew . Let their wounds heal and calm their fears and look after his bank account.

Beatrice and Amanda went down to the cowshed and found Lambert Hodge there. "Yes Beatrice what was it you want to ask about?"

"As far as I'm aware we have a configuration plant here to convert raw milk into skimmed milk is that right?"

"Yes it was one of your father's original projects when we came here. He wanted to sell cheese. In the end he thought it a bit of a process compared to everything we 've got. So he abandoned it. The skimmed milk sells better than the raw though ."

"I see this is the shed here isn't it? It's quite big . Nothing going on here is there?"

Lambert looked nervously around the abandoned barn. "No we've had no plans as such."

"Good I've got Celia Adams coming here from Payne's Dairy consultants. She's going to walk us through some changes we can make. I want to introduce a Yoghurt making section. It may lead us to increase our dairy herd. Do you have any worries about capacity? "

Lambert thought for a moment. "You're talking about a local brand with a view to getting the supermarkets interested ? "

"Initially I'm hoping to set up a shop in Thirton selling farm produce with yoghurt as a main item. But yes ultimately a Supermarket would be good."

"Well yes capacity wise this would be good for distribution . We're starting small I take it? "

"Good here she comes now. " Lambert turned round and saw a woman about thirty in a duffle coat and wellingtons with black hair tied back.

"Hello I'm Celia Adams. You are Beatrice Williams is that right ? So sorry to hear about your recent loss. Any way I hear you're interested in Yoghurt manufacturing?"

"That's correct." Beatrice replied.

"Well Yoghurt is made with a variety of ingredients including milk and Proteins , fats sugars flavours and bacterial cultures."

"The milk should be good quality and should be antibiotic free lest they Kill the cultures in the starting process. This includes modifying composition and pasteurising milk at high temperature(90 C) and holding that temperaturefor a long time about five minutes. Then fermented warm temperatures will set temperatures for yoghurt cultures and adding fruit sugar and other ingredients.

The milk is modified before it is made into yoghurt. This is done by reducing content and increasing total solids. The milk is pumped into a large tank which is chilled . The solids in the milk usually increase by about 60% with 1.5% being fat and 14% being run fat. This is done by evaporating some of the water or adding inumbrated milk . Increasing the solid content improves the nutritional value of the yoghurt making it easier to produce. The substance is fermented until it becomes Yoghurt. Fruits and flavourings are added to the Yoghurt before packaging reducing the tendency to evaporate on storage. Having an SNF factor of 12% will increase viscosity and increase resistance to wheying off."

"Thanks Celia.   This is the building we're going to use for our production. Do you think it's enough?"

"You'll need storage tanks and equipment. Of course you'll need logistics and distribution and most of all networks."

"As we're starting small how big should our network be?"

"Well Thirton obviously and any small shops you can persuade. It's important to have a marketing strategy. The right logo and so forth. In my experience you can start off small and end up big. You have enough contacts with the dairy industry. You could channel outlets such as motorway cafes airports and hotels, then eventually it could catch on. In fact anything is useful even farmers markets."

There followed a big discussion about marketing strategies. After she left Lambert took Beatrice to one side. "Are you sure Beatrice? I mean it's a leap in the dark."

"I'm doing this for Mum. By the time the funeral is over I'll have the machines in place and the labour. I'll take a month off from my studies . Then when I leave I'll have a yoghurt producing plant. More importantly I'll have Amanda to look after everything. What do you think?"

"I can see the wisdom in your motive. I expect your doing the right thing. Iris needs taking out of herself. What is she doing anyhow?"

"House work and fretting mostly."

"Well let's hope we can change that. I've got some work to do. Let me have the figures for this project soonest. Bye Amanda, Beatrice." He said as he took off in another direction dealing with some concern to do with live-stock brought up by Lukasz on his mobile.

"You're off your head right? Me oversee the project? Are you daft?" Amanda said.

"Amanda." Beatrice said pleading in her voice. "Mum's on the edge. I'm depending on you to see this through . Will you do this for me? I'll give you a good wage. Honest to God I don't care if it falls through. Make a go of it for me and I'll make worth your while. Will you do it for me please?"

"Well." Amanda paused "Well alright. I'm only doing this for your Mum though. I don't know what Dad is going to think."

"He'll probably want to help out. In which case the more the merrier I'm only thinking of Mum. She needs you. Anything in fact to take her mind off Stan. God knows I miss him. I know she misses him more. If only I can go after her to concentrate on something . The success of the project is vital, will you help?"

"Of course Beatty I'll do everything I can to help."

On reflection coming out of Schiphol airport and arriving at Heathrow airport was a relatively painless business. Andrew Williams sat back . He'd paid a quick visit to London a few weeks previously and sorted out a small two bedroom flat in the Barbican for £ 750,000. It seemed small compact and ideally suited to his needs . Along with the good references from Steinberg and Dekker. He seemed ideally suited to be a Commercial lawyer at Fein and Gerson a commercial Solicitor in Grace Church street. It was an option that came after he turned down Caron and Brooks.

He'd met Emmanuel Gerson a few months previously and sorted out the details at his villa in Switzerland. Emmanuel agreed it was just the job that suited his talents. Gerson was only too aware that if he prevaricated another company would come along and snap Andrew up. Of course Andrew didn't have any money worries . He relaxed in his flat in Barbican and let the evening melt over him.

There were other considerations of course . He heard about poor Stanley. He phoned Iris who wouldn't comment as yet as to when the funeral was going to be. She told him that Beatrice was at home assuming control of operations. At least that was a comfort.

He knew a Steven Burridge. He was a friend from his school days. As far as he knew he had a business in Tonbridge.

He phoned , he said he might come up one day . This would be rehashing times gone past. He remembered that Steven was a demon for playing tricks on people. The second rate public school he went to produce some characters not the least the teachers themselves. However Steven was in a league of his own.

Iris pulled herself up short as Beatrice approached her. "Beatrice, I'm sure you and Amanda have got all of this pretty much under control. Why do you need me there? "

"We've got the machines organised everything is ready to roll. So far I've got a test batch to be lined up today. We've got flavourings and a logo to put on the cartons. I want you there to see how it works so it won't foul up or anything."

"Yes , but that's what we employ Lambert for."

"Please Mum do this for me yes?"

Iris relented and allowed herself to be dragged away to the diary shed. When they got there they found Amanda in white clean overalls and a row of glistening machines ready to go into motion.

"I want you to see how this goes into motion. We have the storage tank. It has a single and double filter. It's composed of a tank body a heat preservation layer a compressor and stirring device. Controlled by the computer."

"It looks big." Iris commented.

"Then we have the filtration stage. The filtered milk enters the heater and reaches 40 degrees centigrade. The warm up is completed."

"Look Beatrice I don't really see why we have to go through all this now."

"Yes you do Mum. Stanley's gone. Nothing is going to re-place him. I'm trying to keep you busy before this whole thing rips you apart."

"Yes Beatrice ." Iris said ashen faced for once acknowledging her environment and everything around her. "You are of course quite right. I'm trying to keep it together. It's not being easy. You'll have to be patient with me. I seem to be losing everything. I don't know where to start. I was thinking of starting up my law practice in Thirton. Though I'm a bit rusty."

"You must do this now Mum for me. Keep committed stay the course."

"Now we have the homogeniser. This determines the quality and the taste of the milk. This is used for the emulsification of the milk. The original rough milk processed into a very fine uniform emulsion. Homogenous milk globules become smaller and fully dispersed in milk and prevent adhesion."

Iris nodded through all this as Beatrice finished. "You said Lambert is going to do a trial run. How much exactly?"

"About three thousand cartons. They're going to motorway cafes, the local supermarkets and local retail outlets. If we get a positive feed back we'll be supplying Bowlson's with their Yoghurt. It's their brand label we're

selling under. I'm doing it this way because it's all we can do to get more staff to operate this lot."

"It would have been better if we could have had our own brand."

"I suppose so. It's baby steps so far Mum. The main thing is the funerals coming up. Afterwards I have to go back to University. I'm leaving Amanda here. She'll be running the show and I'm making no secret of this , she'll be keeping an eye on you. It's been desperately hard and it's going to get harder.The way I feel at the moment I might even pack it in at the end of this year. More than anything I want to get past this. I've done this for you Mum .What do you think?"

"You shouldn't worry Beatrice. I'll manage. I admit these are not good times. I'll miss Stanley, I miss Gordon. I'm still here though , I'm not made of glass. I'll survive . It's good to put yourself out like this. For what it's worth I'll do my best. It should take about six months to get this up and running. I suppose it's what I needed if I'm honest. We'll have to make some plans for distribution . I'm not sure about Bowlson's really. It'll do for the time being."

"Thanks Mum you've made my life a lot easier. I suppose we better go back." Together they returned to the farm house as Lukasz ushered more staff to help with the Yoghurt production.

Beresford waited as the visiting officer busied himself with the coffee from the café outside. He disdained using the office coffee as beneath him. Privately Beresford agreed with him and usually drunk tea. Gavin Beamish was the art fraud officer that had been assigned by the yard to investigate the theft of the

"Judgement of Paris." By Cezanne. It was his job to discover what clues if any Jud Farrell and Paddy Stern had left behind.

As Beamish ambled in Beresford busied himself looking through files to see if there was anything he missed. He sat down "Right now down to business.

Latte with sugar and milk. Sorry but my tummy knows the difference.

Anyway as I was saying Chris. It's Chris isn't it?" Beresford nodded. "Patrick Stern and Judley Fareham lived in Colington Green . They resided in St Ives Cornwall for a while. Whilst they were there with Heinrich Steinauer and Aaron Millin. All four are implicated in the theft. All four have left the country. The CCTV footage hasn't yielded any results I'm afraid. They lived locally did they associate with any one you might know?"

"Not as far as I know. You're talking about the cognoscenti

of finance in Colington Green. It never comes down to our end of the turf here I'm afraid. We deal in domestic abuse vandalism and drug taking and robbery. The World of high finance and art theft is a closed book to me."

Beresford studied the man's countenance . As he thought Beamish had a high opinion of himself. Only too willing to believe that an ordinary copper would hardly be able to aspire to the heights of society like he himself had done. " Of course Chris . I'd hardly expect any different . Hard working detective like yourself , it's a small town . If you pick up anything on your travels let me know though okay?"

"Yes certainly Gavin , I'll put the word around." He said trying not to look shifty .

Gavin got up and left. "He'll probably make some local enquiries in Colington Green with-out telling me." Beresford thought. If that was the risk he'd take it.

Later that afternoon Gavin drove out to Colington Green .He had an excuse he had to go and pick up something for the wife. He found Tristan Thomas's address. It was just off the common , flat 5 Marbles Close Colington High street. He waited as heard footsteps approaching the door.

When it opened he saw the rather pale countenance of Tristan Thomas . "You've had a visitor I take it Tristan."

"How did you know that?"

"Because Mister Gavin Beamish is not to be underestimated. He's resourceful and cunning . What did you tell him?"

"Only that I didn't know where Paddy and Jud where and I don't have any information for him. Anyway come in."

Tristan showed him into the sitting room that shared company with a flat screen telly, a settee and a picture of the Eiffel tower.

"Yes Tristan ." Beresford sat down . "Though we both

know that's not strictly true don't we? Don't we? Don't worry , I won't give you up to the fraud squad. "

"Hold on a minute Inspector. I'm not sure what you're getting at. There's been some misunderstanding here."

"Yes? Well please enlighten me."

"Well at first I thought something was amiss. Jud Fareham introduced me to Charles Stangrove bursar to the Benton Trust. The trust was set up by Ambrose Benton a millionaire philanthropist who dedicated his life to the spread of knowledge and education. He has his headquarters in Taunton. His aim this year was to spread knowledge of art and the Post Impressionists. Stangrove commissioned Fareham to find someone who could reproduce a painting by Cezanne convincingly enough for an exhibition."

"The result of which was what exactly?"

"The result was a copy of the painting by Cezanne of the "Judgement of

Paris." The painting hangs in the gallery in Taunton for all to see. "

"Are you sure it's the same painting?"

"Did you tell Beamish this?"

" He didn't ask me."

"How did you get involved in this?"

"Well I was with Stuart first we went to Exeter and then to St Ives. Jud insisted that we stay hidden while we were there."

"And then?"

"Then Jud introduced us to Charles Stangrove . We also got to know Oscar Steinauer. He was an art expert and he showed us a reproduction of the picture "Judgement of Paris.".
"

" You thought it was a reproduction."

"Well I'm no art expert. That's what he told us."

"He's on our wanted list. He is an expert in restoring paintings he's missing as well. So apart from this you were unaware there was anything untoward?"

"Absolutely."

Tristan let him out feeling relieved he wouldn't have to undergo anymore questioning. Beresford looked up and down the road. If his memory served him well

Staples Road was just outside Colington Green. When he got there he drove about a quarter of a mile down the road until he got to thatched cottage. This was where Dora Lynley lived. He knew that Dora worked until six and that Maria Campbell finished at the garden centre about four which it was by his watch.

He parked the car on the grass verge near the cottage got out and knocked on the door. He listened to the chimes of birds singing and the quietness save for the opening of the door. There stood a woman of about fifty. "Hello , can I help you?"

"Yes are you Maria Campbell?"

"Yes I'm sorry I don't have the privilege of your acquaintance."

Beresford took out his warrant card. "I'm DI Beresford. I wander if I might talk to you Miss Campbell."

"Oh very well come in this is unusual."

She let him in to the sparsely furnished house. The rudiments of country life surrounding them. Beresford seated himself on the settee. She sat on a chair opposite him.

"So Inspector how can I help you?"

"I'll come straight to the point. I was given some old photographs by Marian Krantz. She took a lot of photographs of people in Thirton in the eighties . I believe there was a bus load of women who went to Greenham Common.

He pulled out a ream of photos . "I'm looking at this one in particular ,it features someone not unlike you. Next to you there's a woman. I can't place her but I think she's ...."

"Jeannie Smith. Yes that's true . This a bit of mystery here. What of it?"

"I have another photograph here outside East Thirton Station in 1992 with Jeannie Smith and Davinia Peters."

"You have been busy Inspector. Well yes I had a relationship with Jeannie Smith. It was a troubled time. The eighties and the nineties ."

"I want to know more about your relationship with Jeannie and that trip to Bosnia it could be important. "

"I see well okay. You said were interested so here goes. It was a misty day in 1984 I met Jeannie Smith in a pub near Thirton South Station. She had so much energy so much passion. It was love at first sight. We went to Greenham and stayed there for a few months. It was the most blissful time of my life. Afterwards I took as job in a garden centre in Sevenoaks. Jeannie however studied and got a degree in history. By the time 1992 arrived we were going our separate ways. I thought I'd go to Bosnia it was a local charity thing. That's when Jeannie met Davina Peters. She was younger and prettier. We all went on the bus to Bosnia. Of course the whole thing was organised by Gordon and Iris Williams. " She paused.

"It was hectic in Sarajevo where we were staying . Whist we were there   Davinia and Jeannie met two Croatian girls. One was called Anya the other Julia. Let me think now ah yes it was Anya Lovic and Julia Markovic.

It was a deep and lasting relationship for a while. Myself, I was exhaustedfor the most part . Ten years of Jeannie Smith left me a bit of a shell.

Everything went well until there was a trip to Bihac. I don't know why exactly . The girls Julia and Anya were excited they hadn't been out of Sarajevo for months. Well everything went well we got into with in twenty miles of Bihac. There was a road block . The Serbian militia took all the Croatian girls including Anya and Julia off the bus. Davinia and Jeannie were terribly upset .

Gordon and his wife were hardened Un officials this happened to them before. Martin Grimshaw to his credit was terribly upset. We never saw either girl again. We came back . I met Dora a few years later hence I'm here."

"Have you told me everything?"

"No, not everything. In Greenham Common me and Jeannie had a little game we played. Because of the battle of Glencoe , the two clans the Campbells and the Camerons were bitterly opposed. I suppose because of this

Jeannie got into the habit of calling herself Mrs Cameron. She later changed her name to Ann Cameron."

"Thanks for your help Miss Campbell."

"What about Stuart?"

"As far as I know he's done nothing wrong. "

"I see."

As he got into the car he felt a shadow cast itself cast against the car. It was the presence of Gavin Beamish. " Hello Inspector . It is curious you know. I go to Tristan Thomas's house . I was told by the locals that they knew

Paddy Stern and Jud Fareham. I was told by someone they knew Stuart Lynley as well. Then bless my soul I come to Stuart Lynley's house there you are as well."

"It's easily explained Mr Beamish. Like you I made

some enquiries. I knew there was some connection to Tristan Thomas. In fact Tristan told me about Ambrose Benton a millionaire philanthropist and Charles Stangrove . Apparently Stuart was commissioned to paint a reproduction of the "Judgement of Paris" by Cezanne. He used someone called Oscar Steinauer.To help him. Apparently the reproduction is on view in Taunton on Devon

as we speak."

The look on Gavin's face spoke volumes. The wind had gone out of his sails. "You appear well informed Inspector. Yes I confess we've hit a brick wall. Whilst you were in there with Miss Campbell did she tell you anything about Stuart?"

"No. I was pursuing a separate enquiry. A murder investigation regarding the spate of deaths in Thirton. "

"Best of luck with that. See you later."

Gavin surveyed the car and looked at Beresford. He hunched his shoulders and walked off into the night.

Andrew sat in the café in Tonbridge absently noting the décor , the passing women talking about their passing husbands. As he glanced casually past an old gentleman shuffling past with a cane he heard a voice say, "Ahoy there?" .

He glanced around and saw a tall man crowned with a head of grey hair. Andrew looked more closely and noticed it a familiar face. "Steven? Is that you?"

"Of course Andy old chap. Haven't seen you in yonks."

"Same here." As he approached Andrew could make out the features more clearly. It was Steven Burridge but the face had grown with age.

"I hear you've been abroad with the European Court of Justice. Sounds a bit of a rum do if you ask me."

"Of course . I made a few bob but there was a few nasty bits too, how about you?."

"Oh well I graduated in law. I did a stretch in the courts . I'm a practicing divorce lawyer at the moment. Other than that it's farming issues. Land and that sort of thing not as exciting as you. What made you get in touch anyway? Feeling nostalgic for blighty?"

" Oh you could say that. The old school all that sort of thing. Steve, I'm getting on. I want to settle down."

"Well you came to the right place. Tonbridge is as laid back as you can get. By the by did you hear about old Somers? "

Andrew thought for a moment .He felt he must be talking about a maths teacher. "Chalky Somers? Oh yes he used to smell of mothballs and paint."

"He ended up teaching in Mexico of all places. Apparently his second language was Spanish. Dashed if I thought he was adventurous."

"What about Mister Green the geography teacher ."

"Oh him he retired and went and went down to Brighton. Can't think who his wife is now."

"Long ginger hair. A lot younger than he was."

"That's the one I can't forget Mr Henderson ."

"Oh Mr Henderson. Praise the lord and offer it up to God. Endurance be thy salvation , suffer little children and then he'd belt you in the mouth."

"Curious chap."

"They all were. By the way sorry to hear about your brother. Awful thing to happen . Did they catch the chap? "

"No developments as far as I'm aware . I tell you Steve , I'm just glad to be back . Gordon made me realise how little time we have left." The afternoon eddied back and forth as they exchanged reminiscences.

Andrew finally made up his mind , he was glad he was back. In a few months' time he'd be looking for a place out here. It definitely suited him.

This time Alex Wallis insisted the funeral would take place in All Saints Church. Iris didn't have the strength to resist.

She looked askance at the floral tributes . They meant nothing Beatrice's magic worked. She'd become involved in managing the Yoghurt production. Along with Amanda who was like a live wire and a second daughter. She was amazed to see Mary and Gregory Mathews and Harry himself turn up for the funeral. Of course she felt the overwhelming lead weight of grief inside her when she looked at the coffin inside the chapel. However Steven's life had come to an end. In no way was it her fault. Though a thousand voices and a million dreams told her so.

The strain of the last week checking yoghurt cartons , taking the temperatures from the machines the constant rhythm somehow contributed to a peaceful static harmony with in her. This was as good as it gets. Lambert

had pronounced excellent results in sales. The contact with Bowlson was on and they could make back the money they spent on the equipment and labour with-in a matter of months.

She still missed Stan , she would always miss him. The cheeky grin, the devil may care attitude to his college work . They would never come back. She missed her husband too. They would have to wait until she was whole again to address these ghosts of yesterday.

As she walked to the entrance of the Church she saw a car draw up and a familiar figure get out of the car. "Hello Iris, I thought I'd come . I'm so dreadfully sorry about all of this." To her surprise she realised it was Andrew.

"Of course Andrew. We must get through this somehow. Have you been in the country long?"

"About three days. I had all this planned months ago. I've got a job in London. I might settle down in London. I might settle in the country. Enough about me. How are you?"

"Oh I'm getting through this. I have two daughters still they're my physician' s right now. I'll be okay in a couple of days."

"You're so strong Iris . I'm impressed. We'll talk more later."

"Of course." She said . No point in being antagonistic. She felt the pain ease as she walked into the church. She went through the service automatically.

She could hear the Reverend Wallis say the words "Snatched away in his youth." or something to that effect . She couldn't register it properly but she stood there as they lowered the coffin to be cremated.

Beatrice stood beside her . Strong , wilful and Iris could tell very angry. She was just like her father. After they filed out Beatrice came up to her and said, "Who was that talking to you as you went in?"

"Uncle Andrew . He seems quite settled nowadays. He'll probably be around later. "

They got through the reception Lukasz and Lambert Hodge and his wife made up the numbers . Mercifully Iris didn't have to make any small talk with any long lost relatives. They had been lost long ago. When she got back to the farm house the pang of loneliness hit her. Then she had to check the yoghurt

Thank god.

Beamish felt a relish as he drove into Colington Green . He thought originally he'd been chasing a dead end. However when he checked back to see DI Beresford moving round he knew something was up. It happened occasionally in the Art Squad . You got someone who couldn't pay his bills overdrawn on his bank account . Lord knows it could happen easily enough . However to take a bribe and look the other way , it was a betrayal of the deepest hue. He personally couldn't forgive or forget. He knew Beresford was bent and he was going to prove it. To interview witnesses he interviewed previously about Jud Fareham and Patrick Stern was deeply suspicious. With this in mind he arrived outside Tristan Thomas's flat . It was early evening and it looked like Thomas was in .As he got out of the car he noticed the evening air was crisp and bright . He rang the bell and the intercom came on. "Hello?"

"Mr Thomas? I'm DI Beamish from the art squad. I believe we talked previously could I see you urgently?"

"Yes of course." Thomas seemed perturbed somehow. Beamish could hear the door buzz.

As he let himself in Beamish ascertained the flat was on the second floor. He went up the steps and found Tristan Thomas standing at the door. "Can I come in. I don't want the neighbours to know our business."

"Yes of course." Thomas stood to one side. Inside Beamish could see it was a pleasant maisonette . There were prints upon the walls . A few book cases of books and CDs. Thomas pointed to the sitting room where Beamish sat down on the sofa indicated. "So how can I help you officer?"

"Our previous interview shows that you said you didn't know the where abouts of Jud Farrell and Paddy Stern ."

"That's not quite true. I knew the where abouts up to about a week ago. Then they mysteriously disappeared."

"I see roughly at the same that the theft of the Cezanne picture came out. "

"Yes."

"Could you explain to me once again Mr Thomas exactly the nature of your liaison with Mr Fareham and Mr Stern?"

As far as I was aware we were being sponsored by Mr Stangrove to paint a reproduction of the Judgement of Paris by Cezanne. It was to be put on show as an example of Cezanne's work sponsored by the Ambrose Benton foundation in Taunton. It all seemed straight forward. This was done with the help of Stuart Lynley a very talented chap. "

"And you and Stuart Lynley never suspected anything untoward during your time there?"

"No of course not."

" I will be paying Mr Lynley a visit in the near future. He will be accompanying me to Taunton to look at this picture. I'm just making enquiries to make sure your accounts match up. "

"I see. "

"Of course you both met this Oscar Steinauer character."

"Yes."

"Well Mister Thomas that's all I need for the time being. It looks like you were deceived by a con man. I need Stuart and you to come with me down to Taunton to the exhibition to see for myself."

Beamish walked out of the flat and smiled to himself. If Tristan made a get-away it was a sure sign he was guilty and they were getting somewhere.

It was about a quarter of an hour later he arrived at 45 Staples Road. The cottage looked quaint nesting there amongst the trees. He knocked on the door that was answered by a woman in her late forties. "Can I help you?"

"Good evening my name is Detective Inspector Beamish from the art fraud squad. I believe we've met before. I've come to talk to Stuart if I may."

"I'm Dora Lynley . I believe my partner Maria Campbell has already answered some questions . Is this really necessary?"

"I'm afraid so Mrs Lynley . There are some matters I'm not entirely clear on. I'd like Stuart to clear them up if I may."

"I suppose so . He's in his bedroom ." She didn't offer him anything to drink.

Beamish noted that Dora Lynley although living in the country was a smartly dressed woman . She was obviously a receptionist or some such. He found Stuart's bedroom at the far end of the cottage looking out over the back. He knocked on the door and a voice said ,"Who is it?"

"Alex Beamish from the Art Fraud Squad Stuart." He said and then came in. "I'm not interrupting anything?"

"Of course not." Stuart said Beamish could see he was playing a game on a computer. "You may remember our previous conversation . You said you had no conversation with Fareham or Jud over the previous three months . Now our records show you had quite a large volume of phone calls over the previous four or five months."

"Er yes I'm afraid so. "

"Would you mind telling me what it was about?"

"Well I believe I already said Mr Fareham wanted me to do a reproduction of the Cezanne painting The Judgement of Paris. He told me it was for Charles Stangrove who represented the Ambrose Benton trust. I had Oscar Steinauer an art expert give me guidance on the subject. He seemed quite knowledgeable."

"I understand you used materials and paints that Cezanne would have used is that right?"

"Yes of course."

"What was the address of the gallery ?"

" It was 87 North Street Taunton. It's called the Grimsley Gallery."

"Right Stuart I want you to come with me down to Taunton to look at the painting. You can tell me if it's the same one. Will that be okay?"

"Of course."

As he left the cottage he had the pleasant feeling that if he found a gallery with no painting he would be taking Thomas and Lynley into custody. However art forgery was a complicated business. Sometimes the obvious isn't always clear.

It was about ten o'clock on a Tuesday morning Alex Beamish and two officers were driving down the M4 motorway with Stuart and Tristan with them. After braving the elements of the late October weather they took some Light refreshment in Membury service station and reached Taunton at about twelve o'clock. They left the cars outside the gallery. It took only a few minutes talking to the manager of the gallery who lead them to the Benton Ambrose youth exhibits. These were on the second floor. Stuart and Tristan felt slightly conspicuous as they were flanked by two plain clothes officers.

As they emerged on the second floor they could see the pictures arrayed on the wall before them. "Can you see the canvas you painted Stuart?"

"Yes that one there." Stuart pointed to a canvas three quarters of the way down the gallery. Beamish went over to the wall and inspected it closely. It was in the style of Cezanne alright. He could see the detail the artist had gone to. It was aReproduction you could see that a mile off. The paint was fairly fresh and there was no attempt had been made to age it. He could see that Stuart might feel it was authentic but it couldn't fool an expert like him. "This is the painting you were working on?"

"Yes, I spent three months on it."

"I see."

Later in the car as he left the gallery , Tristan and Stuart were having lunch in a local hostelry. Beamish phoned Grant at headquarters. "Yes it was an attempt at imitation of Cezanne. It wouldn't fool me though. I think Tristan and Stuart had been set up by Fareham and Stern. At any rate they're clear of any charges. They were just used to lay a false trail."

"So it's back to London Alex. " Grant said.

"Yes for now. The forensic boys in St Ives can look for anything we missed but apart from that there's nothing here."

Back in Thirton Burnham sat back in his chair with a look of undisguised relief on his face. "That was a close call Chris .That Beamish chappy was after your job did you know that?"

"I imagined that would be the case. Where he got the idea that Stuart was some kind of forger was beyond me."

It was late Thursday afternoon . Davinia had taken the afternoon off. Major Kindersley was left to the tender mercies of Jean Moyes. A capable woman by all accounts . Though Davina always had that human touch. After she left she had another visitor . Kindersley pressed the button for the door to open. It was Roy Cummings . Kindersley had mixed feelings about Cummings . Undoubtedly he had a Police career. Cummings had mentioned Cyprus , though a quiet whisper amongst his colleagues revealed nothing . Roy guessed he was in the Red Caps which proved a lot.

Still a visitor was a visitor and he didn't have many of those. Cummings sat down and helped himself to the cafetiere and a biscuit. "I see that Davinia isn't here again today. Funny that isn't it? Look here Danny it's not my place to say anything but something's definitely brewing up at CID. I do hope Davina hasn't got herself mixed up in anything?"

"Why do you say that?"

"Oh one or two things old boy."

"You know Roy you said you'd been to Cyprus. What was

your posting Nicosia?"

"How'd you guess? Yes I was with the Red Caps as it goes. It sounds you got yourself out of a bit of trouble."

"Yes I was as a matter of fact in Kyrenia. EOTA nearly cooked my goose, I can tell you."

The rest of the conversation was pretty mundane , regarding the weather and the television , nothing of any consequence. As the evening drew on Kindersley felt his curiosity grow. He didn't let on when Cummings left.

The "Altruist" in London Bridge was not Andrew's favourite pub . However it served as a sort of refuge from the days toils as he was coming home from work. It was a fairly anonymous place and Andrew managed to avoid any acquaintances . It seemed odd he should that he should seek solitude in this way. The pressures of work were not overwhelming. He managed to drink a pint of ale and eat a mince pie.

It was as he was halfway through his meal he was surprised by a woman smartly dressed in a black suit and red shirt . "Hello, do I know you from somewhere?"

"I'm awfully sorry you must be mistaking me for someone else."

" I don't think so. You're Andrew Williams . I was reading the Investors Chronicle . You managed to pull off that court case with Steinberg and Dekker. Quite a remarkable achievement."

Andrew brightened suddenly ."Well it was a case you know . It more or less unfolded as soon as the reports were laid out. The judge couldn't see any objection to the firm opening up a processing plant in Indonesia . What's your name by the way?"

"Madeleine Rutherford I work in sales for Mr Gerson."

"Ah I see now you saw me in passing . I'm surprised you're

interested in a fish like me. "

"It's the small fish that interest me most."

The evening passed quite peacefully . Andrew invited her back to his flat in Middleton Road . She accepted quite agreeably. On this occasion Andrew splashed out for a cab . The evening air in Middleton Road wasn't quite sinister just yet. As Madeleine sat back in her chair Andrew asked if she would like another drink "Of course a night cap.What else?"

Andrew went to the drinks cabinet and poured two drinks and came to sit down beside her . "Oh blast I've left something on in the bedroom. I won't be a moment ."he said.

At that point Madeleine took out some Succinylcholine and put it in his drink. He came back. "This subdued lighting cane be quite deceptive. How do you like your drink?"

"Quite pleasant actually. " She heard a noise coming from the kitchen. He quickly took a sip from his drink.

"That must be the slow cooker I won't be a minute."

As Andrew came from the kitchen he heard Madeleine 's phone go . As he poured her drink he heard her voice rise in a querulous tone.

"What did you say?"

It was Major Kindersley "Davinia I don't know where you are but send the rifles to Tel El Kebir."

"Are you sure?"

"Fairly positive."

"Thanks Major goodbye. " She hung up. Madeleine , or more to the point Davinia Peters sat down with her drink and considered her next course of action.

As he came back Andrew said "I'm sorry that was wrong number or something. They just hung up."

"Happens all the time . If it's not nuisance calls selling you something you don't want. "

"I know it happens all the time. " He picked up the drink he'd left there.

"Now where was I?"

"Holland the number of cases you dealt with."

He took a gulp of the drink and sat down beside her. "Now there where some difficult cases right enough. I did pull off some good deals. Oh God I fee drowsy."

"Oh that reminds me I've got to meet someone. It completely slipped my mind. I hope you'll forgive me. I'm sorry I'll have to go."

"Of course, I'm sorry if it was anything I said."

"No of course not."

Quickly she got up and made for the door. "Well see you again I hope."

"Yes so do I Madeleine . " He said as he looked at her retreating figure going down the corridor.

As Davinia got to the street she saw Anne Cameron pull up in her car. Anne rolled her window down. "What's the matter?"

"We've been rumbled. I think the Police are here somewhere. We've got to make ourselves scarce ."

In a Police Van not far away Beresford looked dismayed for a minute. "She's onto us! Quick move before we lose them."

"They're driving a Blue mini-van coming out of the service entrance. "

"Follow it."

"Yes Sir." The van came out of Middleton Road then turned left on to Goswell Road. Beresford could tell they were headed for Kings Cross.

"What's your plans Ann? We're blown wide open now. "

"I can see a blue light flashing about fifty yards down the road . We get to the car park in Shaftesbury Avenue then there's a car there we can use."

"They could head us off by the time we get there. "

"They won't know where we're going. By the time we pull away from the car park they'll be looking at the other cars."

Anne appeared certain of this gambit. "Okay Anne." Davinia said uncertainly.

In the Ford Focus Woods was driving he could see the mini-van heading for Kings Cross. Careering down to Black-friars bridge the mini-van turned up Farringdon road and then taking a left turn up to Holborn Viaduct. With the Police car behind them they shot past Gray's Inn Road and onto New Oxford Street." Right. I'm ditching the car here. We've got to run for it." Anne said.

Together they both fled into the NCP car park. Quickly Anne produced her credit card as she heard the Police Car pull up, outside. She produced the token from the car park and inserted it into the machine. "Nine bloody quid?"

"Never mind Anne come on!"

Anne inserted her credit card and took out both cards and made for the First floor. "Walk slowly." She said as she heard footsteps behind them.

They walked up to the second floor as Police officers rushed past them. They located their Astra van and exited the car park with two Police cars parked outside looking round anxiously.

Beresford was parked outside the car park. "Who are we looking for Sir?" Barren said.

"Two women one will be in her early fifties."

"Er I think I saw two women on my way up to the second floor Sir."

"They didn't come up to the second floor?"

"No I think they left in a white Astra van."

"It doesn't matter we've got the cameras in the car park. If we get a clear shot we can convict them on that."

An ambulance was sent to Middleton Road where Andrew Williams now more or less paralysed was taken to hospital. Back at the station Beresford reviewed the situation. "Now we know who the two suspects are we can get a search warrant and search their premises."

"Today Sir?" Woods said.

"Yes , we've got good reasons. Hurry I want to know who we're dealing with."

About half an hour later they were standing outside Ann Cameron's house in 47Aviemore Road. Sergeant Green had a battering ram and managed to break the door down. Beresford came in followed by Woods, Barren and Hussein. "Right Hussein you can do the kitchen, Woods do the drawing room. Barren you do the bathroom, I'll do the bedroom. "

As he went upstairs to the bedroom he saw the individual officers go their separate ways. He ventured into the bedroom situated at the back of the house . A moment's glance revealed nothing unusual. Then he went to one of the bedrooms at the front. There on the walls where hundreds of photographs and press cuttings dating back twenty to thirty years. Examining them he could see they were about Sarajevo and the bus hijack. There were several other Press cuttings about Gordon Williams and his brother Andrew. There were others about the dig at the Green Weald Site and Martin Grimshaw. "Right People! Come up here we've got something!"

As Woods came up Beresford said "I want everything here checked and double checked. "

"The rooms downstairs where full of books. I never expected to see this!" Woods said.

"Well we've obviously got out killer. We should have spotted this before."

"I'll see you back in the station . You can search Davinia Peters house as well. I'll have the warrant ready."

"Yes Sir."

Back at the station Beresford surrounded by crime scene photographs and reports addressed his men. "Now the important thing is we have the brains behind all this. Ann Cameron may look innocent but obviously behind that mild exterior is a dangerous criminal. We still don't have all the details. I gather you searched Davinia Peters house as well , did you find anything?"

"No Sir , just your average middle aged woman."

"Just as I thought. Okay you've got your briefing notes. Keep your eye out for anything suspicious." They departed secretly grateful for an early night.

It had been two days that Davinia found herself couped up in a Caravan site in Coombe haven. Anne had been out briefly. "There's not a lot going on here . What have you been doing Davinia?"

"Looking through some newspapers . I was thinking of finding a job."

"Yes good idea. You've got to keep busy after all."

"Why , is there anything wrong?"

"I was just wondering how did the Police get on to us?"

"I don't know. I was talking to Major Kindersley on the phone. He told me there was something up . I didn't know what."

"Why would Kindersley know there was anything up?"

"Again I'm not sure. He has friends in the Police force that's all I know."

"Really?" She let the sceptical tone hang in the air for a bit. After half an hour Davinia forgot all aboutit as she watched the small telly in the caravan. The next day Davinia came back from a brief spate of shopping and found the caravan alight. The fire brigade had been called and Ann's car was missing.As they were putting the fire out a Police Car pulled up. A woman got out.

"Excuse me Madam are you Davinia Peters?"

"Yes." She admitted meekly.

"I'm afraid I'm arresting you for attempted murder anything you do say will be taken down in evidence. You have the right to stay silent but any thing that you have withheld will count against you in a court of law will be held against you." With that she was led away

In Thirton Police Station as they were sitting back having a cup of coffee they had a report from Coombe Haven. There was a caravan park. There was a fire in one of the caravans . One woman was held in custody. Her name was Davinia Peters.

It was about two hours later Beresford arrived at Hastings Police Station. Detective Inspector Harrison seemed somewhat bemused that two detectives should come down from Thirton to his humble shire. "Good to meet you Inspector Beresford, DC Woods. " He nodded his acknowledgement . "It seems we have a tidy little mess here . Would you mind explaining what's up?"

"It's a long running case here Sir? Basically there's been a spate of murders in Thirton . After a long running investigation we came across Miss Peters as a suspect. At the time we almost apprehended her. We lost her in the City. We have definite proof that her and her partner were involved . What we want to do is interview her and subsequently charge her.

She can go before the

Magistrate in the morning and be remanded in bail in Brixton."

"I see. Is the CPS convinced you've got a strong case?"

"Yes, at least they gave us that impression during the last three days. "

"Funny looking at Miss Peters she looks like an ordinary respectable woman. "

"Her last victim is recovering in hospital from a dose Succinylcholine. You're right of course she is respectable. She's not an ordinary criminal. She can't go back to her former life."

"Yes most odd. Still the interrogation room has been set up. You can proceed .Good day Inspector."

When they entered the interrogation room they saw an ashen facedmDavinia Peters dressed in a grey cotton jacket a polo neck shirt and jeans. Her blond hair hung down and she looked dejected. "Right now Miss Peters I'm starting the interview now. It is approximately 4.30 pm. Present are Di Beresford , DC Woods . Also present is Davinia Peters. Miss Peters you have the right to remain silent . However if you do not say something now that might come up later in court it may count against you in your defence. Is that clear?"

"Yes, that's clear." She said.

"So Miss Peters . Can you tell me more about how you found yourself here?"

"It began a long time ago. I was brought up by my grandmother. My mother fell in love with the local bigwig, but he never married her. That was the Mayor Hector Turnbull. My mother never really got over it. My Grandfather and grandmother died in 1988. My mother followed soon after."

"We could cover other details later Davinia. Could you be more explicit and tell us about the events leading up to the last eight months?" Beresford suggested.

"There were women who lived nearby they awoke my interest. They'd been to Greenham Common. One was quite attractive . I never realised I had such love in me . That was Jeannie Smith . We were in a relationship . Jeannie was like a force of nature, like a hurricane. When she moved into my life I was thoroughly moved it was 1992.

It so happened that at the time we both worked as nurses. We wanted to go to Yugoslavia . This was a local bus going to Sarajevo . This man Gordon Williams was running it. Jeannie decided to change her name to Anne Cameron . I think it was something to do with her ex Maria. Anyway we got to Sarajevo and I met this Anya and Anne met this girl Julia. Again it was like everything before that had a mythical fairy tale quality to it. We never knew such love. There was a call for our services in Bihac. So naturally Gordon decides we're all going to Bihac. On the bus ride up there, was a road block.

To our dismay we found it was the Serbian militia . They herded all the Croatian women off the bus which included Anya and Julia. We never saw them again. "

"Eventually we got back safely. We heard about the massacres in Srebrenica and Mostar. United Nation officials eventually found the graves of Julia and Anya. We went back for the funeral. It was then Anne swore revenge on Gordon Williams and all those who were on the bus."

"Didn't it strike you that Anne was odd in any way?"

"Well she spoke about her time in Greenham Common. She found a lost stray lamb that had become entangled in the briars and had broken it's leg. She just went over and broke its neck quite deliberately. She laughed when she talked about it."

"Did this manifest itself in any other occasion?"

"Only when she spoke about Gordon Williams and his brother. "

"Carry on."

"We found out that Andrew Williams was coming back to England. It was announced in the Investors Chronicle when he gave an interview. Anne had seen it on the internet when she googled his name. She finally laid down her plan to take revenge on all who were on that bus."

"How did you murder Gordon Williams?"

"It was easy really. I came upon him by his lorry by the banks of the Witham. It's a fishing reserve . However I got in there using the entrance by the abattoir. "

"What did you do?"

"I brought some apple pies laced with Sodium Chlorate . I saw Gordon standing by his lorry he was going to pick up a load of compost take it to the neighbouring farm. I said I was just passing through it seemed a nice lorry did he use it for his deliveries? He said yes I offered him a pie. He accepted them even though he had pies and snacks. Well eventually he felt groggy. He leant against the lorry and his hand pushed against the lever . Then all of a sudden this great big hoist came crashing down hitting him on the head."

"But he was dead anyway. "

"Yes."

"Where was Anne?"

"She came up behind me keeping a lookout. When she saw Graham's body we just left."

"How did you kill Jean Simmons ?"

"I'm afraid it was a moment of weakness . Joan Simmons went to the Albion Psychic group in Calmington Road . She had fallen for the charms of Mr Bream . However I came to one meeting with Anne . I don't know what they call it. Gaydar I think. Well I sensed it right there with Joan who was a live wire. Her marriage to John was little more than a sham. So I checked her out. Yes she was willing and eager. Unfortunately

Anne picked up the same vibe. I let slip our plans for Andrew Williams and Martin Grimshaw. She suddenly freaked out on me one night. She was going to the Police. I told her Anne was going to sort it out. I drugged her with Succinylcholine and Anne strangled her.

It all seemed ghastly , but we had a mission to carry out. Lord knows in the third world life is cheap enough. If someone falls off a building site they are just left there. If someone in a processing plant falls ill they have to depend on what little support their family gives them."

"So this was your part of your mission?"

"Of course . I don't think we should treat the third world in this way. Life is precious. Martin Grimshaw was just as much to blame as Gordon Williams. He was our next target. I waited until all the fuss had died down

over Joan and I made my move. I saw him in the Green Dragon and then tracked him down to his flat in Weald Road. It was fairly near the Sanctuary run by Stein. We mutilated the body a bit to make it look like the Sanctuary could have been involved. Anne was the main motivator behind this. "

"How did you do it?"

"I tracked him down to his flat in Weald Road as I said . We had a few drinks. I just added some muscle relaxant that paralysed him. Anne came in and gave him a lethal injection. She did the rest."

"It must have taken some strength to finish a body off like that." Beresford added.

"Oh Anne's very strong. She's a lively active person. We cut open chest and used a small hydraulic jack to prise open the rib cage. We removed the lungs

As you saw for yourself."

"So time passed why was that? "

"Because Andrew Williams was taking too long over the details of leaving the Hague and coming over here."

"So what happened ?"

"Anne wanted to make an impression . She was determined that the Williams family wasn't going to get away with this. To bring hope to a poor country and take it away again was unspeakably cruel. We wanted to make Iris suffer too."

"So what did you do?"

"Occasionally on my walks through Kessington I noticed there were a few teenagers smoking drugs. The fish ponds were a lure for the teenagers . That's when I saw Stanley Williams. Summer passed to Autumn Andrew was finally making plans. Anne thought we'd make one last strike before he came over. Through the grapevine I heard that Stanley was going to Chichester College

to study agriculture. A few evenings spent at the favourite pub and the beach parties at Selsey Bill gave me a clue. The crowd he was with where typical students. I noticed he was sitting on one of the benches. They were all smoking but Stanley fell asleep. They decided to move on. The others had left as well just leaving Stanley by himself. Again I sat there in the late evening and with a bottle of wine we toasted the evening. Only his glass was laced with a drug. Anne came along and cut his throat . It was quite painless."

"How did you feel afterwards ?"

"I felt we struck too soon. Andrew Williams would be completely aware of what he was up against. "

"So what happened next?"

"Well Andrew kept his address secret . Though I knew a bit about his drinking habits . Andrew liked nice friendly pubs. One such pub was the Altruist in London Bridge. I mean there were a choice of pubs he could have gone to. There was Dick Turpin's that's near the London Wall. There was Gray's

Inn pub . On a hunch I tried a few pubs round the Monument with no result. I found the Altruist because Andrew put it on his Facebook page. I struck lucky he took me back to his flat in Middleton Street."

"But you didn't follow it through why was that?"

"My old friend Major Kindersley phoned up to tell me something was up. I never underestimate the man so we found ourselves backpedalling to our escape route. We had another getaway car that you no doubt saw on the CCTV from the car park. Prosaically enough we dumped it in the old Kent road . With what money we had we went down to Coombe Haven and hired a caravan for a few months. I managed to get a job in a café nearby. Anne had some savings she was using up."

"What happened then?"

"Well after three days Anne went crazy . I couldn't handle it anymore I left her there and went for a walk. When I came back I found the caravan on fire. The Police arrested me about two hours afterwards. "

Outside the interview room Woods said ."I never thought I'd say this but that woman was scary. I've never seen such callous disregard for human life. What will she get?"

"Thirty years maybe five off for good behaviour." Beresford said. "The thing is where is Anne Cameron?"

CHAPTER 8.

Thomas Knight stood at the entrance to the house slightly bemused."Well Anne I'm surprised to see you here. Usually you ration your visits , but you better come in."

Anne Cameron stood before Knight and briefly glossed over her choices. She was wearing a parka and she hadn't had a shower in two days. She felt rough and somewhat disorientated. On the face of it she didn't blame Thomas for a slight re-verification." Of course Thomas , I'm sorry to impose upon you like this." She felt safe here however because she knew Thomas rarely watched the news. "I've being thinking about your propositions that you've put forward. I must say I'm finding them disturbing , how can you live with such disturbing ideas?"

"You mean Nietzsche . It's only progress . I mean it's optimism really."

Carefully she settled herself in the conservatory in the garden. Thomas sat opposite her curious to see what argument would come next. "Marx and Engels rejected Hegel's religious alienation for social ills and put it down to alienation from economic and political autonomy. Dialectical materialism asserts the primacy of the material world. " Knight stated.

"Gentile opposed Hegel as well . He thought that everything is spirit. Marx had made the dialectic an external process a material process of historical development. To Gentile the dialectic was something of human precepts part of human thinking. Therefore it was a concrete not an abstract object. Gentile thought the dialectic was natural to the state.

This view Gentile thought justified the co-operative

system where the individualised and particular interests of all divergent groups were to be personally incorporated into the state . He believed the public and the private were to be personally incorporated into the state. He believed the public and the private were a priori identified with each other in an active subjective dialectic." She paused for a minute. "Nietzsche eschewed nihilism the individual at least in Schopenhauer's theory stands apart from the world.Nietzsche felt when nihilism was overcome the state only then can a foundation on which to thrive."

Knight thought for a moment. "So the Corporatist System where nobody is an individual can be looked after by the state because he is part of the dialectic."

"In order to get a better appreciation yes."

"This of course neglects any abuses of the state for the greater good."

"Nietzsche also states when nihilism is past the state can thrive. "

"Yes but Nietzsche also states he believed in a slave master relationship. The masters take over society and people follow like sheep."

"It's more honest than Marx's theory . Marx believed that alienation was the cause of all evils in society . Yet mapping an alternative society only resulted in the loss of the individual just the same."

"It resulted in the loss of the individual in states that never experienced a democracy. Soviet society was guilty of awful things so have most capitalist societies in the past. Gentile's fascist societies were guilty of atrocities in the present. "

"Hobsbawm then I suppose."

"Yes Hobsbawm if we must." She smiled. The night clouds moved in as Thomas served dinner and Anne put on some classical music.

Beresford sat in the room adjoining the interview room. Present where Abigail Sheen a psychologist , Justin Woods, and Chandra Hussein. "Chandra

I wanted you to witness the interview with Davinia Peters. I value your contribution. Now I'd like to start by asking Doctor Sheen what she made of Davinia Peters."

Abigail paused for a second ."Well it seems a classic case of psychosis. She seemed absolutely unphased by it all. She reeled of the events as if she was reading a railway time table. On the one hand she seems to be a sensitive woman conscious of not wanting to hurt others . On the other she's ready to kill at the slightest turn in order to satisfy her picture of justice . Her reaction to the suffering she can inflict is completely the reverse of her normal character. I'd say it's a classic case of projection . Projecting harmful features of her own character on to people she will hurt. I'd say it goes back to childhood , probably abuse and neglect."

"What would you recommend?"

"Long term stay in a mental hospital. Prison would be no good."

"You do know that she's active in the local church . Discovered the skeleton of a lost saint and so forth."

"Yes I read that as well. The psychosis is hidden but it's definitely there."

"Chandra what do you think?"

"I'd say she's a frightening person. Though things can turn even ordinary people. I fled my family home when my parents tried to organise an arranged

marriage . The parents of some children have been known to kill their children rather than endure disgrace in their community. Davinia has no cultural constraints so I'd agree with Dr Sheen, something in her childhood made her this way."

Beresford turned to Justin. "What do you think Justin?"

"Well I'd say I was sceptical . I mean she says that like Dr Sheen said there was no reaction there. She could be reading a railway timetable. I'd say she was an observer. I'd say if I saw Anne Cameron I'd have a better idea. I think there was a third party involved. I think she's not telling us something."

"Yes , I rather thought that myself. However Doctor Sheen , Chandra you've both given me food for thought. Thanks for coming along ."

Doctor Sheen picked up her notes . "I will be here to give a full evaluation on the recommendation of the court."

"Yes of course Doctor."

Even so as they picked up their bags and left the room Beresford thought over the interview . When Davinia mentioned Martin Grimshaw he found the picture of Davinia opening Martin Grimshaw 's chest with a hydraulic jack only too convincing. The world had moved on since Justin's view of women were current. Still it did give him some concern.

Beresford relaxed in his office for a minute thinking over what Doctor Sheen had said. Her opinion was expert medical opinion. This was good as far as it went. What worried him was the impression he had. That stayed with him more than anything. As he looked he saw that Chandra had entered the room. She was quickly followed by Justin Woods.

"Hi, both of you. I wanted a quick word just before we go any further. I want to start with you Chandra. You said that people are capable of quite aggressive acts of violence who are normally quite peaceful. Could you tell with specific reference to Davina Peters what you had in mind?"

"Well , I had an Aunt Jamila . She was married to a lawyer. This is not a good example but it's the only one I can think of. Atul her husband wanted to kill a goat for to celebrate the end of Ramadan. This wasn't in Pakistan but in Bradford. He got the goat from a farmer and he cut its throat in the back garden. I was only three or something, I was awfully upset. Jamila explained it was our religious and holy duty to fast and to celebrate the end of Ramadan. Her face was passive and absent of any expression. I had the feeling that at some level she was just as upset but had lost the ability to show her feelings. She just went along with whatever her husband told her. That's what I felt about Davinia. She had little ability to show her feelings."

"Did you feel the same way Justin? She was just going through the motions?"

"To a great extent yes. It all seemed put on. It seemed rehearsed. She didn't show any emotion. "

"Then that's it. Someone else is involved doing the killing. She's just laying the ground for action."

"Who could it be?" asked Chandra.

"Obviously Ann Cameron. Cameron felt Davinia was unimportant enough to leave her behind in Hastings. The thing is anybody else?"

"Ann Cameron if we catch her probably won't make us any the wiser." Woods said.

"What reports have you had so far?"

"She hasn't used her credit card so far. She's relying on cash. We have a look out on petrol stations and airports. " Chandra said.

"Keep looking." Beresford said calling the meeting to an end.

Iris stood in the kitchen , Judith was just finishing her cereal. In a moment she'd be ready for nursery. Iris looked at her for a moment. Judith didn't think past the next moment. As a young three year old she lived in the moment. For Iris this seemed enviable contentment that she could not possess , not at least for the next year or so. Judith finished her food got down from the table and picked up her bag. "Right now Judith off we go."

Together they left the kitchen. Beatrice had already left for university. Judith clambered into her baby seat in the back of the car. After navigating the roads to the nursery where the nursery assistant welcomed her gleefully.

Back in the front room surrounded by her family photos she looked at the manuals for Yoghurt preparation. She thought slowly how to prepare herself ,

incremental step by incremental step.

"Today we have naming of parts. Yesterday
we had cleaning. And Tomorrow morning
we shall have what to do after batching . But
today we have naming of parts. Stanley
on his fifth birthday running on a beach in
Sicily .
And today we have naming of parts.
This is the storage tank and the milk pump.
The tank body is composed of metal and holds a
preservation layer
Controlled by computer and can reach cooling
time shortly.
Small footsteps in the garden and muddy boots
on the floor.
Which in our case we have not got."

Rain fell slightly as she went to the shed where Amanda and her mother now worked.

Beresford found the old cottage on the outskirts of Hastings. He walked up to the cottage and noted the fine view of the sea and the cliffs. Standing at the door he forgot to knock . When he turned he found a bespectacled man confronting him. "Yes what can I do for you? Though I must say I don't often get visitors ."

"Oh Mister Knight I'm sorry . I'm Detective Inspector Beresford. " He turned round and found Woods coming up from behind. " This is my colleague

DC Woods can we have a word?"

"Yes of course though I don't know if I can help you."

"It concerns a Miss Anne Cameron."

"I see you better come in."

He ushered them into the cottages . Inside Beresford could see the walls were lined with books and so were the other rooms. "I'm a professor in History. I stopped teaching at Sussex University some time ago. Follow me into the conservatory. It's the only place you can sit down. "

Beresford found that going through the cottage that the conservatory was tastefully laid out. The view of the cliffs , the land and the sea was stunning and gave him pause for thought. He looked round and found Woods going white at the gills.

"I say your colleague looks a bit ill." Knight said considerately.

"A slight case of vertigo. It'll pass." Beresford turned towards him and said . "Look Justin go inside and sit down and take down notes from there. You should be able to hear from there."

"Yes Sir . " Justin said relieved. As he sat down Knight seemed more accommodating.

"Now how can I help you Detective Inspector? "

"On the news you may have heard about a spate of murders in Thirton where Ann Cameron came from."

"No I rarely listen to the news. How does this affect Ann ?"

"Well I'm sorry to say we have reason to believe she may have been implicated in them. We urgently wish to know her whereabouts."

"Well I'm sorry Inspector . If she's not living in Thirton then I can't help you."

"Could you tell me how you came to know Miss Cameron?"

"I was Professor at Sussex University. That was when my wife Alice was alive. I met Ann as a mature student . We kept in touch from time to time. When my wife died about ten years ago she was a great comfort to me. So we kept up our friendship ever since."

"When was the last time you saw her Mister Knight?"

"About a month ago. We talked about Politics. Little else in fact. She seemed to be gravitating towards fascism . God knows why."

"That was the least you saw of her?"

"Yes , why what has she done?"

"We have reason to believe she has committed a very grave murder. It may seem out of character . If you see her again be careful Mr Knight she is a dangerous person. "

"It's not the Anne I knew but I'll take your word for it. "

Beresford decided that nice though he was Mr Knight was not going to be of any real help in their investigation. "Well thank you for your help Mr Knight

I'll leave my phone number if you can think of anything."

He was a farmer she could see that. She just answered an ad she saw on a shop window in Folkestone. She used a mobile phone she bought for cash . The man had a ford focus. It wasn't extensively in bad repair. It looked like it could run a couple of miles. The farm was on the outskirts of Hythe and took some finding. He seemed to be glad of the cash though.

Anne was glad of the money she saved up. In the back of her mind a siege mentality was developing. She didn't want to give up Davinia. To be honest it wasn't something she noticed over the years but Davinia was slow to pick up. Ann felt the constraints of her situation were increasing and Davinia was a sacrifice. A nice sweet natured woman. The thing is she was going to get caught anyway. Anne had to make her own future now, it was the only way.

She applied for a fruit picking job at a farm in Thanet. There where itinerant Polish labourers there and she got on with them well enough. It was about a week after the events in Hastings. She believed she covered

enough ground to let the trail go cold.

She had a car and a job of sorts. For how long she couldn't say. The farmers name was Mr Cranbridge. For the time being he had seasonal workers picking berries. The manager's name was Charles Stevens. Anne gave her name as Maria Brown. Although she didn't show him any means of identification she was sure she could use some connections amongst the workers to get a passport.

The leader of the workers community was a women called Lena Bukowski. She was young fit and lean the opposite of Anne. She quickly got to know her workers, Julia, Maja, and Sofia.

Sofia was the one to watch. If trouble was coming she was in the middle of it. Sofia was older and kept a weather eye on Ann almost as if she could sense trouble. The first week went well. Occasionally Ann bought a paper. She saw a picture of Davinia being led from court to a waiting prison van. The passing of time didn't trouble Anne eventually she could find some papers and establish a new identity. She noticed Stevens didn't seem to mind the delay. She expected the farm would be expecting some new machinery in a few months. So these workers would be gone. For the time this suited her purpose. She went to the local church and learnt the responses to the mass in Polish. It seemed odd to form a new identity so soon.

Sofia had been deputised to take some cattle feed from the farm to a neighbouring field with a truck. For this purpose she took Anne with her to load and unload feed. It had happened before and was not in any way unusual. Anne had noticed that the blond haired woman had a secretive way with her. One day she followed her into Folkestone and saw her arguing with one of the market stall holders in the seafront then go into a photoshop. When she came out Anne asked, "Can you get a passport?" Maja made signs to the effect that she didn't understand . Ann showed her a passport . Maja nodded slowly . Maja led her to another shop a few doors down owned by a French speaking woman. Inside she saw sophisticated cameras and computers and pointed to a man turning out photo copies of a document. She stopped and looked round and asked her. "Can you forge a passport for me?"

"For a price. Five hundred pounds?"

"Yes, when can it be ready by?"

"Have you got a photo?"

"Yes." She produced a passport photo .

"Okay." Give me three days and it'll be ready. I want half now."

Reluctantly Anne gave her two hundred and fifty pounds. That had been a month ago. The woman was as good as her word. She showed the document to Charlie Stevens who wasn't in any great hurry for the details. Now she was Alison , they'd unloaded their cargo and were coming back on the approach road to a junction. Unfortunately they got hit by a speeding car.

Half an hour later Anne woke up in Folkestone Hospital. She was other wise unscathed . She was approached by a Doctor . "Your friend tells me you are Alison Parish . Is that right?" This was the name she gave Cranbridge.

"Yes , I am. Will Sofia be alright?"

"Oh she's fine . Only a few scratches . It's you I'm concerned about. You were out cold. You'll have to stay here for some days for observation , then you can go."

"Yes Doctor."

The following day they did discharge her, but when she got back to the farm she saw a Police Car . She'd come to work in her own car. As soon as she saw the familiar face of Beresford she quickly got back into her car and drove away.

"Quick Sir we're losing her. "

Together they got in to the Ford Focus and followed the mini cooper that Anne Cameron was driving to the M20. It wasn't a long drive to get there.

"Don't overtake just keep her in your sights." Beresford said. It was as they got to the flyover approaching Strood that Beresford could see she was gradually getting faster.

"I can't live like this." Thought Ann. "I can't live." She faced up to the contradiction she lived with and saw the pillars supporting the fly over coming nearer and nearer. As she drove past the barriers she could see her path clear

to the pillars of the fly over and pressed down on the accelerator. Woods slowed down the car as the pursued vehicle before them crumpled up against the pillar.

Ian Beasley got down from the tractor he was driving. It had been a long day at the office . Gloria had been difficult again. The girls had been away at sixth form college the whole year and next year they'd be taking their exams.

Adele and Carrie were two halves of the same coin. Adele was practical she was taking Science and Chemistry. Carrie was less practical she was taking English , French and history. During the year the usual arguments about

cosmetics , dresses and boy friends were frequent. Gloria was called in as referee.

Not that this impacted on what was happening right now. Beasley was going for an amalgamation with Corporate Food Industries. This meant a better price for his cattle and grain products. This would also afford him a better seat on the board of the company he was with Witham Food industries.

On this board was Terry Cleland, Mark Bracey, James Henry and Marcel Palings. Of course one long standing member he always remembered Grace Fenwell. Grace inherited her farm from her father Julius Fenwell. Together they formed the land interests in buying and selling of Cattle in the local area.

Terry Cleland had being responsible for breaking a deal with Corporate Food Industries . This brokered a deal with Park Pies who sold their pies nationwide who had ties with Motorway Service Stations and Ports and airports throughout the country. Not only that but Marshall Foods which was connected to Corporate Food Empire supplied Poland, Yugoslavia , Italy and Greece. It was a good market with buyers eager for the product.

Today he made an address to the South Eastern branch of the Farmer's Union. It was to do with the thirtieth anniversary of the European Alliance in commerce. Terry Cleland stood to one side as Ian walked up to the podium. The various business men , producers, farmers and shareholders sat back after taking a brief break from the proceedings." I know it is with a certain trepidation that many see the future of farming in this country . The European Union has always supported the market abroad and many of you have felt ham strung sometimes to some extent about the trading conditions. You've felt if we could trade abroad we could get a better price for our product.

I know others of you have felt anxious because you have fruit and produce from market gardens . For years you have had access to cheap labour and now all that is going to change. This means more automation more machines.

However this is the market of the future. We are all going to have to change as our markets get bigger in order to embrace a changing world. The face of farming is going to change beyond recognition in the coming decade. We will be using carbon neutral options . Having to deal with increased demands for grain such as Soya, and vegetarian products. My colleagues and I at Corporate Food Industries have a part in that future as I'm sure you know. It is with pride that I open this meeting of the European Alliance in Commerce , probably it's last meeting on British soil. Thank you."

As he stepped down from the Podium and the next speaker came up Terry came up beside him. "I think you could have underplayed the present Brexit situation. There are many here slightly nervous right now."

"To what end Terry? You and I both know where we stand. In the international markets we'll be dealing with international competition. If we're not ready we're dead."

"We'll find some new goal posts that's for sure. I'm just thinking about the shareholders."

That thought Beasley was typical of Cleland, careful, pedantic and sometimes unhelpfully pessimistic. Not a fault he shared . Thinking about the future he mapped out his progress in the next couple of days. Slowly the meeting hosted speaker after speaker. Each considering the course of action as they contemplated new markets . That evening Beasley made his way out of Brighton back to Branbourne farm.

Beresford stood in the corner of Folkestone General Hospital. Woods came up to him ."What's the prognosis Sir?"

"Well on the whole better than expected. The impact of the crash of course left its mark , a shattered arm. They've pinned it together, it should be okay with physio. She's in an artificial coma but they think she'll recover in a week or two. Apparently the car burst into flames only seconds from when you pulled her from the wreckage, you saved her life. "

Beresford thought for a moment. It seemed miraculous somehow that Anne Cameron should have survived the crash . It took weeks of making enquiries starting at Hastings and then to Folkestone and then to Thanet and they got lucky. The dash from the farm in Thanet was frantic . Davinia Peters was sticking to her story. Beresford knew there was more to it than she was letting on.

He came into the ward where Cameron lay in the bed. She seemed frail as she lay there. This was the second accident in two days. The body could only take so much. He was surprised at her resilience. "Hello, I'm Doctor Kelly. Are you the arresting officer?"

"I'm DI Beresford can you tell me something about the patient?"

"Yes, she's in an artificial coma. The body has gone through some punishment. The right arm is in traction . There is a slight fracture on the right hip. She's suffering from concussion. Apart from that she doesn't seem too bad. Her heart is giving some concern hence the artificial coma. Though I think she'll be okay."

"When do you think she'll be up to seeing anyone?"

"Two or three weeks."

"I'll keep someone here during that time. She is a suspect in a murder investigation."

"As you wish Inspector."

It was a late Tuesday afternoon the reception in Folkestone Hospital was experiencing a lax period. The messenger came in to the hospital wearing a helmet and went up to the reception. "I've got a package for Doctor Grange . I believe he's on the second floor. "

The receptionist looked up. "If you take a lift to the second floor you'll find his office at the end of the corridor. You can't miss it. "

The messenger took his helmet off and proceeded to the lift. However instead of taking the lift to the second floor he went to the third. He went along to the intensive care unit. Carefully he looked around to see if he could see anyone standing guard on the patient. He could see a uniformed Police man talking to a nurse and having a cup of tea. He carefully went in to a door nearby and found it was a locker room. He put on a white coat and walked past the Police man to the door adjacent to where he was standing. The Policeman seeing him wearing a white coat took absolutely no notice.

As he entered the room , he slowed down , he felt his heart beat quicken as he saw the patient lying in the bed. He looked carefully at the Plasma drip and the arrayed medication and the heart monitor. He took out a hypodermic needle and a vial of Morphine and filled the syringe. He took the needle with the syringe and pierced the line feeding the plasma to the patient . He began to depress the plunger when a hand gripped him very firmly by the wrist.

"I'm sorry Sir you'll have to come with us. " He turned and saw two Police Officers and the familiar faces of DI Beresford and DC Woods .

"You don't know what you're doing I'm a Doctor."

"No Mr Coombes . Last time we met you were a student studying archaeology at the Green Weald Site in Kessington Valley. I'm afraid you have to help us with our enquiries ." Beresford said.

Without fuss Coombes relented as he let himself be led

away from the Hospital bed where Anne Cameron lay. It was four hours later in an interrogation room in Thirton CID that Coombes sat facing Beresford and DC Woods and DC Hussein.

"It was quite logical really. Anne Cameron had a long time wish for revenge. Somehow Ian Beasley got to hear of it . I believe his wife Angela told him about it. He went to see Ann. Basically he wanted to buy out Gordon Williams who was very unwilling to sell. It happened that Ann knew that Andrew Williams was coming back to live in London. She saw this as an opportunity to make her   first strike. Well Davinia and Ann got Gordon to stop his truck by the South end of the Farm. Davinia fed him the poison cakes. He slumped forward so I whacked him for good measure . His hand caught hold of a lever then the hoist came down and hit him again.

They hit a snag because Davinia was having an affair with Jean Simmons. Ann fed her some tranquiliser mixed with orange juice . I strangled her because I thought it wouldn't have any effect. "

"What about Martin Grimshaw?"

"Well you'd be surprised. Davinia called upon him one night and spiked his drink. Ann and I came in later . Ann took his pulse , he was well and truly dead. Then Davinia split open his chest with a hydraulic jack. I was impressed. I took out the lungs and made it look messy. "

"What about Stanley Williams?"

"No, that was completely Ann Cameron that time."

"If you say Ian Beasley was behind all this , are you prepared to stand up in court and say so?"

"Yes."

"Have you got proof?"

"I've got at least a hundred thousand in my bank account that stands as proof."

"You do understand Mr Coombes you've committed a very serious offence. You will receive a lighter sentence for your co-operation, but the law takes a very serious view of this."

"I do."

"Very well. Interview ended. Thursday the twenty eighth of October."Beresford watched as Coombes was taken down to the cells.

Ian Beasley sat back in the dining room it had been a busy week. Setting up the new company . With his large holdings he spent more time in the office than on the farm. One of the penalties of success he supposed. Chloe and Adele had spent the evening finishing off their work for the University course. It had gone well so far.

Angela came in somewhat aghast at his lack of preparedness for the function they were to attend. As usual it was a fuss over nothing . He came to tire at the endless round of dinner dates of lunches representing this or that section representing this or that section of the farming community, or even worse supermarkets and wholesalers.

"You'll be late . You know Cranford doesn't like to be kept waiting." She opined.

Steven Cranford was head of Witham Consortium , an amalgamation of farmers he had come to grips with over the years. "I'll let Steven know we'll be late . He'll be fine."

"He won't . I'm tired of you letting me down like this." He knew that the reason Angela wanted to be on time was to chat to Veronica , Cranford's wife.

They both had a childhood in common growing up in Hastings . It gave them a certain view of life. A view he was aware of even if he didn't share it. Well it was going to be difficult meeting with Steven then so be it.

It was a quarter of an hour later that Steven and his

wife turned up at the hotel in Tunbridge Wells. Angela looked serene and magnificent in a blue sequin dress. Looking every inch the country lady, he knew veronica would be wearing something equally glamorous. As they entered the restaurant he could see Steven over the other side of the room, he could see Veronica was wearing a very flattering green dress and matching jewellery. Angela went over to Veronica and began to catch up on missed gossip. Steven on the other hand was wearing a very serious look. "Well Steven you were supposed to have the contract ready by now what went wrong?"

"They won't accept my price. I'll have to bring it down. It takes time."

"How much time do you think we have for God's sake?" He said drawing on a vapour stick and blowing out clouds of cherry flavoured blossom.

"It's simple Steven , I need time. I need other farmers to come up with the right price. We're on the cusp right now, all I have to do is give a little push and we'll be there."

"Well decision day is looming Ian. Soon you'll miss the boat and you know what that means. It's goodbye to the farm, it's goodbye to the company and your wife will be suing you for divorce and packing off to sunny Spain like the clappers."

"Yes, I'm aware of the situation Steven thank you. I have it under control. All I need is a bit more time."

"Just keep it in mind then." Cranford said as they turned to face their wives in a pretence of companionship.

Ian Beasley stood on the edge of the outbuilding that served as a barn. It looked out on the southernmost extremity of the farm. He took out his mobile and phoned Steven Cranford . "Steve I've got some news. It looks like I may get some closure today. I've had an offer from a farm nearby. I might make plans for expansion pretty soon. "

"That's good news Ian. I'll expect to be hearing from

you later on today."

"Of course." He packed up his mobile and went back to his Land rover. It was most unexpected , Iris Williams had phoned and told him she reconsidered his offer of three million pounds for the farm. She said her solicitor and accountants would be at the meeting. She told him she'd be at the meeting to be at Thirton Conference Rooms just outside Thirton on the road to London. He knew the place it was well situated for that sort of thing.

With a feeling of optimism he'd already contacted his solicitor to come and look at the contract he'd put forward , who had already given the go ahead. Angela and the girls were already busy planning their next skirmish into the retail section of Thirton High street. So he didn't have any distractions .

When he arrived at Thirton Conference rooms he found his solicitor and accountant waiting for him. Iris Williams was already waiting in the conference room and her brother Andrew was there also. He went up to Peter Aberford his solicitor and asked. "Well Peter how is it going?"

"I've inspected the contracts. It's quite a generous offer she should be quite pleased."

"Good then I won't anticipate any trouble . How about Massinger?"

"Colin's fine, the banks are okay. We're all set Mr Beasley."

" Good ." Feeling ebullient he went into the conference room where Iris sat. She was wearing pastel colours , somewhat pale looking after her bereavement. Andrew sat next to her looking slightly bored by the proceedings.

"Good morning Mrs Williams and Andrew of course. Good to see you both together . I take it you've read the contract and are familiar with its terms? "

"Yes we are Mr Beasley. It's a pleasure to meet under such circumstances. " answered Iris.

Beasley sat down taking in the relaxed air for a minute. "So what next?"

"Well before I sign there are just a few questions I'd like to answer if I may."

"Well of course what would that be?"

"Well Mr Beasley something very curious happened yesterday. A man answering to the description of Mr Simon Coombes entered Folkestone Hospital and tried to murder Ann Cameron. Fortunately the Police were able to stop him in his tracks and in so doing implicated you in a conspiracy to kill my husband and my son. Not only that but he has large amounts of cash in his account traceable to your firm in so doing. Do you think you can explain any of this?"

A look of consternation spread over Beasley's face. "I don't understand there must be some misunderstanding. Of course Mr Coombes has done work for me in the past. I never dreamt for a moment he would do this."

"Oh you mean the two hundred thousand pounds Mr Beasley?" She pointed to the door he just came in. "If you notice Detective Inspector Beresford and his officers are all waiting for your answer . Naturally I think you'll find have to finish your conversation down at Thirton Police station. Good day Mr Beasley . Keep your solicitor Mr Beasley you're going to need him. "

Beasley felt the ground give beneath him slightly. "But I'm a business man. This is preposterous."

"It's alright Mr Beasley you can come with us now." Beresford said as DC Woods slipped the cuffs on the farmer and led him away to the Police Car. Peter Aberford his counsel followed in tow.

Ann Cameron sat back in the hospital bed as she saw the light dim slightly outside. Beresford spoke first "The Doctor told us that you have more or less recovered and are up to giving us a statement Miss Cameron. Do you feel you could do that?"

Ann looked at them , seeing them and yet not seeing them. Her mind was far way. "Yes I suppose so. What can you possibly want to know?"

"I want to know how you came to pursue the course of events that we are now pursuing. It seems strange to me that an educated woman such as yourself should lower herself to such acts."

" From an early age I was subjected to abuse by my father and my mother did little to help. I've read the textbooks , I know Klein would say that because of maternal deprivation I became a psychopath. The truth was because my father and mother thought so little of me I thought very little of other people. There are many psychopaths in society , they are business men and managers.In a way Society is a managed itinerary of psychopathology . Psychopaths managerially trained to run administration because people can't run them."

"So you don't see yourself as anything unusual?"

"No , not really."

"But what about this long running feud with Gordon Williams and his family? Surely you can see that Gordon and Iris have done an enormous amount of good work for the third world."

"All I could see really was a career minded upwardly mobile legal expert getting another feather in his cap. I felt he was a vulture just like all the rest."

"That may be so but the planning , the hunting down, the sleight of hand. Didn't you ever feel you were doing something wrong?"

"I had what you might call an ontological faith that I was doing the right thing. People like Gordon, Andrew, and Martin Grimshaw accepted the World at face value. In helping the third world they only wanted to render

those countries into a more malleable from so they could be exploited by Capitalism."

"I've had a word with your friend Professor Thomas. He told me you advocate fascism. "

"That is correct."

"Surely that's the worst type of psychopathology you could imagine?"

"Not if it's managed according to Gentile's principles. Furthermore unfriendly fascist third world countries would be better at resisting the blandishments of the West."

Beresford could feel Woods staring over at him in wonder. "Alright Miss Cameron that will be all for now. There will be further questions later on. I hope you get well soon."

Ann smiled "Thank you officer."

Beresford walked out of the ward followed by DC Woods. Woods was going to say something but the look on Beresford's face told him to keep quiet.

Burnham sat back as the afternoon sun shined in his office. "I was talking to Gregory Mathews. He was a friend I made when I came to Thirton. He told me about Jeannie Smith and Martha his sister. I went to Jeannie's mother in Kessington. She's about eighty now. She told me that Jeannie was her father's favourite. Though he'd left home. Jeannie was always the strange one. It seems piecing it together that this accident that occurred in 1968 was always something of an enigma. Jeannie Smith and Martha his sister were standing in the courtyard of Kessington farm. Justin was driving the tractor when it backfired. Justin leapt off the tractor and hid behind some bales. For some reason Martha was strangled. They were aware that Justin had shell shock and felt that in his confusion he may have strangled Martha. He was committed to an institution and died in 1987. Going by what we now know Jeannie already traumatised by her father's abuse at home killed Martha. The psychologist states that Ann as she calls herself is highly intelligent. Though her character is a deeply unstable one. She befriended Davinia and induced her to follow in this revenge phantasy as a form of folie a deux. This of course followed after the incident in Bihac.

Of course Ian Beasley with his ear to the ground picked this up from Simon Coombes who was working on the dig in the Great Weald Site. All of this lay static like a bomb waiting to go off . It would have come to nothing if Andrew Williams hadn't made plans to come home. "

"Coombes got to know Beasley doing an archaeological dig in Sevenoaks. They found some sites near Knole Park . Of course Beasley knew his target. Coombes was heavily into betting and owed the bookies in Sevenoaks before he came to the Great Weald Site. Ann had seen him at the séance they held at the Great Weald Site and knew he was highly strung.

I do feel sorry for poor old Roy Cummings. He was taken in by Beasley too. Giving Davinia that warning before the attack on Andrew . However I hear that Stephen Cranford is looking for partner to amalgamate his company. Angela and the girls are going to sell up. Beasley looks set for a long stretch in jail. "

"I was doing further research on Ann Cameron. Her father left home when she was eight. He changed his name to James Holroyd. He led a battered sort of existence in Southampton. Ann studied history in Sussex University. There is evidence to suggest that she met her father. She met Martin Grimshaw there as well. Holroyd died from an overdose, I suppose we can read between the lines there."

"It's Stanley Williams I feel sorry for a young boy cut down in his prime. " Beresford said.

"You missed one. We all do. The slices of death as Poe said."

"I beg your pardon?"

"Poe said it. Sleep . I hate those slices of death."

"How apt. Though I hear the Yoghurt brand Amanda Mathews and Iris Williams have started have left Bowlson's sponsorship and started up on their own. "

"It won't make up for everything. Once the adrenalin has faded away she'll have her memories. Ann Cameron, Davinia Peters, Simon Coombes Ian Beasley

will pay a price. I suspect that Iris is in there in her own prison of memories. I can't let this distract me though. Chief Constable Ralston is going to give me a roasting for dragging Mr Beasley through the mud. That reminds me you have a disciplinary hearing to attend. Mr Beamish is accusing you of hampering his investigation. "

"Yes it is complicated. Apparently Jud Fareham and Patrick Stern had an arrangement with Charles Stangrove of the Ambrose Benton trust to set up a competition to commemorate the birth of Cezanne. This involved painting reproductions of paintings by modern painters. This meant Stuart Lynley had to buy materials that would enable him to reproduce the painting of the Judgement of Paris. Steinauer an art expert also used the same materials bought on the same receipt for another painter James Molyneux. He also was in St Ives at the time. It was James Molyneux who was actually painting the work that would replace the one in the gallery at Nice. It seemed that Jud and Stern were laying a false trail.

Neither Fareham or Stern are here. It seems that Beamish has got nothing to show for it. He's accusing you of stymieing his investigation. I've had preliminary interview with internal affairs. They seems to think it will all blow over."

"I feel sorry for Beamish . It's horrible when an investigation comes to a full stop. I expect they'll drop it soon."

Iris sat back in the porch over-looking the garden . Down

below Judith was sitting comfortably playing with dolls . Today was the one day of the week the Yoghurt production was closed. As she read the Sunday journals she heard a sound in the kitchen. As she waited Beatrice came out. She was holding a cup of tea and sat down opposite.

"How was Uni? You only just got back. I haven't had a chance to ask you."

"Oh fine. The finals are coming up soon. I should be okay. Lambert tells me the Yoghurt's doing fine. You managed to set up your own brand despite his best advice. I must say adversity suits you."

"Oh it was nothing . Bowlson's wasn't giving us a good deal. I decided we could do better. It was only paper work. Amanda has the knowhow. Her mother Mary isn't bad either. We're a great team."

Beatrice drew a sigh not of relief but of resignation. "I feel guilty about getting over Stanley. It'll get better I expect. It seems so futile . My exams study that's all I have."

"The future is all you and I have. It's the only thing to look forward to. " Iris said.

"Did you go and see her?" She gave her mother a guarded look.

"Yes I did. I didn't honestly expect a civil reception. I found her quite lucid."

"In what way?"

"Ann Cameron has a long and complicated history. She grew up as Jeannie Smith . She was abused by her father and had developed unhealthy tendencies at an early age. She left home and found a physical awakening as Lesbian in Greenham Common. It was when she left there she met Davinia. Then Gordon suggested the trip to Bosnia . I mean we were both working for the UN. We never gave it a second thought. We were on a coach trip to Bihac. I never even knew Jeannie and Davinia were there. We were stopped and the Serbian militia took all the Croatian girls off the bus.

Of course Gordon and I were upset. It was one upset amongst many in our careers. I never really appreciated how it affected Jeannie and Davinia.

After the trip she studied and became an academic and later a teacher. All that time she was watching and waiting for the right moment to inflict as much pain on me and Gordon as possible.

Of course I asked her how could she justify any of this. She explained she was a Marxist , she believed the means of production controlled everything. In order to obtain material goods people will do anything. As the first World progressed the third world would be used as it's work house. People's lives would be ruined all for the sake of maintaining commerce. She believed that dialectical materialism wasn't enough. She believed the Dialectical materialism espoused by Gentile. That there is no such thing as the individual That there was the corporate will. Fascist countries in the third world would eventually overthrow the first world . Mean while she would see through justice the only way she knew. "

"By killing Dad and Stanley."

"Yes it's terrible isn't it?"

"I can understand the path of her reasoning . I can't understand her. If she felt like that why not join Isis or something?"

"If she gets out of prison I suppose she might. However I don't think her health will be that good if she ever gets out."

"What about Beasley? I mean he's part of the evil first World. "

"Ah yes but she says he was only a tool. She was going to kill him too. "

"It all sounds ghastly Mum. I expect you're going to see her again though."

"Er, yes. I can't help but feel sorry for her. We're both at the end of a long road with nothing but memories. I shouldn't really. But there you are."

They both looked on as Judith played with a teddy and two dolls. As they sat back the sun came out giving the sky a tint of Azure blue. Yes thought Iris and with no joy. No joy at all.

ACKNOWLEDGE-MENTS.

A Kempis Thomas. (1965) *"The Imitation of Christ"* Fontana Books. London.

Drake, D. Muncie, J. Westmarland, L. (2010) , *"Criminal Justice. Local and Global."*Milton Keynes, The Open university.

Frank , R. (1984) "Viking atrocity and. Skaldic Verse . The rite of the Blood

Eagle" in *"English Historical Review Journals . xxcix(cccxci) pp552-343.*Oxford.

Freeland P. Marsh L. Dalton. (2006) "Aelred of Rievaulx . The lives of the Northern Saints." *Cistercian Father Series iii.* Kalamazoo Publishers. Birmingham.

Geetz C. (1993) *"The Interpretation of Cultures"*London. Fontana Press.

Gregor ,James , A. (1963) "Giovanni Gentile and the philosophy of the young

Marx " in *"The Journal of the history of ideas." Vol 24 No 2. Pp 213-230 @*

*(Https/www.jstor/stable) 2707846seq=1*accessed (1/3/2021).

Gibran ,K.(2017)*"The Prophet"* Create Space Independent Publishing . South Carolina.

Hopkins, V.C. (1949) "The Iceman cometh seen through the lower depths." In

"College English." (v) pp.81-87.

Hutton r. (1991) *"The Pagan Religions of the Ancient British Isles. Their nature*

and Legacy." Oxford. Blackwell.

Jordan . (1987) *"The Evolution od Dialectical Materialism"* London. Macmillan.

Macfall, R. Du Gay, P. and Carter, S. (2004) *"Conduct. Sociology and Social Worlds."* Manchester University Press/ Milton Keynes. The Open University.

Mangiene, H. Butler. (1973) "An investigation of pigments and technique used by Cezanne in painting *Chestnut trees."* In *"Bulletin of American Institute for the conservation of Historic and Artistic worksVol 13(1973) pp 77-85).*

Press, J.(1994) "Poets of World War 2" in Scot Kilvert (Ed.) "British Writers 007" New York.

Ratcliffe, W. (1921) "Fishing from Earliest times." London.

Restell, M. Assellbergs ,F. (2007). *" Invading Guatemala, Spanish native*

and Maya accounts of the conquest Wars." University Park Pennsylvania,

Pennsylvania University State Press.

Walton. Izaak. *"The Compleat Angler."* London and NewYork. The Bodley Head.

Watson J. (2015)*"Yogurt manufacturing and production and Processing.@ Watson Dairy consultingHttps /dairyconsultant.co.uk/ yogurt-yogurtproductionphp.accessed 1/3/20210*

Wells,P.(2003) *"The Battle that stopped Rome."* Norton and Company .NewYork.

[mo1]

[mo2]

[mo3]

[mo4]

Made in the USA
Middletown, DE
09 October 2021

49657213R00209